The shining splendor of our Zebr
reflects the glittering excellence
Lovegram whenever you buy a hi
guarantees the very best in quality and reading entertainment.

"I . . . DON'T . . . REMEMBER!"

Actually, Liberty remembered quite well, but pleading amnesia seemed the perfect solution. Pretending a lapse of memory would prevent her from fielding questions she preferred not to answer.

"You . . . don't remember?" Dylon raised a brow. "Then perhaps I should refresh your memory, my dear," he murmured. Dylon unfolded himself from his chair and tugged Liberty into his arms. Without preamble, his mouth slanted across her heart-shaped lips, stealing the breath from her lungs. His arms encircled her waist, pulling her full length against him. He bestowed another steamy kiss on her, losing himself in the taste and feel of her body molded provocatively to his.

Liberty had been kissed before, but never had a man left her gasping for breath. "What was that all about?" she demanded when Dylon finally allowed her to come up for air.

"I thought a kiss would refresh your memory, my love. You cannot know how I lament that you have forgotten the magic between us."

Oh, he was a sly one, thought Liberty. Two could play his little game. Pressing her hands against his massive chest, she pushed him away . . . but only a little. "Whatever was between us has changed," she whispered. "Now we are like strangers . . . we have to become acquainted all over again."

"Let me tell you . . ." Dylon generously offered. "Or better yet, let me show you the way it used to be . . . "

LOVE'S SWEETEST SECRET

GINA ROBINS

ZEBRA BOOKS
KENSINGTON PUBLISHING CORP.

ZEBRA BOOKS

are published by

Kensington Publishing Corp.
475 Park Avenue South
New York, NY 10016

First printing: March, 1991

Printed in the United States of America

This book is dedicated to
my husband Ed
and to our children
Christie, Jill and Kurt . . .
with much love. . . .

And to John Michalicka.
A good friend is
one of life's greatest treasures.
Your friendship is priceless!

Chapter 1

Charles Town, South Carolina
1764

How could a reasonably intelligent woman of twenty manage to twist her life into such a tangled mess? That's what Liberty Jordon wanted to know! Until the previous two months, her life had been running smoothly. And then all of a sudden, poof! Her world had gone up in a puff of smoke. She was living a nightmare in which one disaster followed hot on the heels of another!

Glumly, Liberty glanced out the window of the enclosed phaeton in which she was riding. *Forced* to ride, she bitterly amended. Silently, she pondered her options of escaping impending catastrophe. Her tapered fingers clenched in the folds of her satin wedding gown, one that had been selected for her without her approval. But then, this upcoming marriage didn't meet with her approval either, nor did her betrothed for that matter. For crying out loud, she had barely known the man a week! In Liberty's estimation, a reluctant bride and a stranger of a groom did not a satisfactory marriage make!

Briefly, Liberty's violet eyes darted to her uncle—the traitor—who lounged on the tuft seat across from her. He reminded her of a bat with his black coat, breeches and fluttering cape. Liberty wondered how she had come to have such a despicable relative. Godamercy, sometimes heredity could play cruel tricks on a person. Liberty didn't know what Luther Norris had to gain from this marriage he had contracted against her wishes, but he looked a mite too satisfied with himself not to have profited from these arrangements.

Although Liberty pretended she had finally accepted her fate, she had done nothing of the kind. She wanted Luther to think he had subdued her. She wanted him to let his guard down. There were only a few precious minutes left to make her third escape attempt. Just a precious few minutes. . . .

The carriage rolled to a halt in front of the quaint stone church on the outskirts of town. Every nerve and muscle in Liberty's body came to life. Adrenaline pumped through her veins, causing her heart to thump wildly. When Luther stepped from the coach and pivoted to assist her down, Liberty came uncoiled like a human spring.

A shocked squawk erupted from Luther's lips when Liberty launched herself at him like a pouncing cougar. Her forward momentum caused Luther to stumble backward. He landed flat on his back on the cobblestone walkway. Another pained grunt was forced from his lips when Liberty employed his sprawled body as her springboard. Leaving footprints on Luther's sunken chest, Liberty darted around the corner of the church and out of sight.

Simon Gridley dashed from the chapel when he heard Luther's howl of surprise. A muffled curse rolled off Simon's tongue when he spied Luther crawling onto all fours. Simon's intended bride was nowhere to be seen and that made him positively furious!

"You fool! I knew we should have posted guards at the church." Simon breathed fire on the pinch-faced little man who was massaging his skinned elbow.

"I thought Liberty had accepted her destiny," Luther

muttered, glaring in the direction his pesky niece had taken.

"You *thought!*" Simon growled. He spun himself around, sprinted around the corner and raced down the alley to give chase.

Luther scuttled along behind the powerfully built man who was in fast pursuit of his runaway bride. Damn, he should have known that feisty hellion had only pretended to be subdued. Since her arrival in the colonies two weeks ago, Liberty had shown herself to be outrageously independent and headstrong. That father of hers had allowed her to run wild the past fifteen years since her mother's death in the smallpox plague of '49.

After the loss of his wife, Benjamin Jordon had pulled up stakes in the colonies and set sail for "the islands," as Liberty insisted on calling her home in the West Indies. Because of Benjamin's indulgence, Liberty had never learned her place in this world. She was a firebrand from the top of her golden-blond head to the soles of her feet! And when Luther got his hands on that sassy, wild-hearted niece of his, he was going to bind, gag and drag her to her wedding. From this day forward, Liberty would become Simon's problem. Simon was young enough and physically strong enough to handle her.

Luther stared at Simon's broad back as he whizzed through the alley after the hellion in white satin. These two individuals deserved each other, Luther assured himself. They would make each other miserable and that would make Luther tremendously happy!

Liberty spared a hasty glance over her shoulder and then hiked up the hem of her skirt to burst into her swiftest pace. Luckily, her years of uninhibited excursions in the islands had prepared her for this race of endurance. Liberty could run like a gazelle and, if ever there was a need for winged feet, now was the time.

Although she didn't have the slightest idea *where* she was going, she knew for certain whom she was running *from!* Luther and Simon had plotted to use her as a pawn in some secretive scheme, she'd bet her life on it.

A muted curse bubbled from Liberty's lips when her foot struck one of the wooden crates that formed a maze in the alleyway. Liberty caught her balance the split-second before she fell prostrate in the dirt. Unfortunately for Liberty, the time it took to upright herself and clutch her hindering skirts allowed Simon and Luther to catch up with her.

Just as Liberty thrust herself forward, Simon's fist dug into the nape of her gown, yanking her backward. She tripped on the hem of her gown and slammed against Simon. The movement set off a chain reaction. Simon collided with the stack of crates that blocked the path. Luther, who was directly behind Simon, floundered to keep his balance. Amid growls, screeches and squawks, the threesome became entangled with each other. The stack of crates wobbled precariously. As bodies tumbled upon each other, the crates toppled.

Liberty couldn't tell what she had landed on and she didn't much care. With her teeth clenched in fierce determination, she slithered out from under the crates, letting them fall where they would.

While Simon and Luther untangled themselves from the fallen crates, and from each other, Liberty zigzagged back and forth between the brick and timber buildings that lined the alleyway. In the distance she could hear Simon and Luther ordering her to cease this ridiculous mischief. But Liberty didn't slow her pace; she accelerated.

Her frantic gaze lifted to the steep incline that led to one of the city's main thoroughfares. Uplifting her hindering skirts, she scaled the slope. To her dismay, Simon caught up with her halfway up the hill. When his fist twisted in the hem of her gown to drag her backward once again, Liberty pivoted on one foot and stuffed the other foot in his heaving chest. Employing the side of her hand like a hatchet, she chopped Simon loose from the hem of her dress. And then, with a forceful shove of her foot, she sent him staggering backward.

In wicked satisfaction, she watched her scowling groom teeter back against Luther who was huffing and puffing from overexertion. Thrown completely off balance, both men rolled down the hill like two balls of twine.

Liberty lunged up the slope, putting more distance between herself and her pursuers. Glancing in every direction at once, Liberty frantically sought a safe place to hide. When she spied the elegant black coach on the opposite side of the street, parked regally in front of a stately town house, she made a quick decision.

Like a lightning bolt, she streaked across the street and bounded into the luggage compartment that was attached to the back of the phaeton. Gasping for breath, Liberty tucked herself into the leather-covered cubicle and dragged her full skirts out of view. And there she lay, coiled in a tight ball like a mouse tucked in its tiny niche. Safe at last, thank the Lord!

"Damnit, where did that woman go?" Simon growled at the world at large.

His dark, beady eyes swept the peaceful street, searching for some clue as to Liberty's whereabouts. If he didn't know better, he would have sworn that troublesome witch had vaporized into a cloud of smoke. Muttering several disrespectful epithets to Liberty's name, Simon stalked toward the vacated carriage and peeked inside.

"She can't have gone far," Luther wheezed.

"Nay?" Simon scoffed caustically. "She managed to get this far, didn't she?"

"She's probably hiding in one of the gardens behind the town houses," Luther speculated as he cupped his hand over his eyes and squinted into the bright afternoon sunlight.

Firing orders like bullets, Simon sent Luther skulking around the stately homes to the west while he scouted the houses to the east.

When the footsteps had died into silence, Liberty poked her head from the compartment to determine if the coast was clear. A muffled curse tripped from her lips when the murmur of voices and a woman's shrill-pitched giggle shattered the afternoon air. When three sets of footsteps clicked along the brick path that led from the spacious town house, Liberty folded herself back into her niche and waited the opportune moment to make her escape.

To her chagrin, the voices and footsteps approached the carriage in which she was hiding. And to her discomfort, one of the men tossed a wooden trunk and several satchels of luggage into the compartment. Liberty bit back a pained groan when the trunk slammed against her head. In a matter of a few more seconds, Liberty found herself wedged farther into the corner, buried beneath the pile of luggage.

Well, at least my former-future husband and that weasel of an uncle of mine won't find me, she consoled herself. She had artfully dodged an unwanted wedding to a man she barely knew and was certain she didn't like. And before she set sail to the islands where she should have stayed in the first place, she was going to discover why her uncle was in such an all-fired rush to sell her into wedlock. Luther had known perfectly well that she had a fiancé awaiting her return to the islands. She'd told Luther that the instant he sprang this contracted marriage to Simon Gridley on her. Not that it did one whit of good, Liberty recalled. Luther had dismissed her previous engagement with an impatient flick of his wrist.

Liberty heaved a constricted sigh and massaged her cramping legs. She had sailed away from her persistent fiancé in the islands, but the voyage to Charles Town hadn't been her salvation. It had been another calamity waiting to happen. She had only traded one persistent fiancé for another.

Men! Liberty silently fumed. They were all so certain of their superiority over women. The males of the species, except for her dear departed father (God rest his soul) thought they could make women's decisions for them and the fairer sex would complacently settle into the roles men created for them without voicing protests. Maybe there were *some* females who docilely accepted their fate but Liberty Jordon was definitely not one of them! She was her own person. Her father had taught her to think for herself, to explore the world around her without being confined to the rigid social structure that England and the colonies had designed for women.

Liberty had always refused to be shuffled into her "place," just because she was a female. Benjamin Jordon had indulged his vivacious daughter to the extreme, it was true. All too often, he had allowed her to manage financial and business affairs that were usually left to men. His only failing grace was that he had singled out his young protégé, Phillipe LaGere, as a suitable mate for his only daughter. The gallant Frenchman was a likable sort, and an asset to the Jordons since he knew as much about the shipping business as Liberty did. But devoted though Phillipe was, Liberty had never fallen in love with him during the fourteen months that he had been courting her. And Benjamin hadn't pressured her into a marriage. That wasn't his way. It had simply been understood that when she was ready to settle down she would marry Phillipe.

In all fairness, Liberty had to admit she had employed

her engagement to Phillipe as a tactic to elude the endless rabble of suitors who landed on her doorstep without invitation. But Phillipe was only that—an evasive tactic to discourage eager beaus. Her affection toward Phillipe was more the brotherly type and she could nurture no romantic notions for the tall, lithe gentleman who had a comical flair for the dramatic.

Phillipe was amusing in his own way, but usually at his own expense. And maybe one day Liberty would be ready to marry Phillipe and take full command of the shipping business in the West Indies. In fact, she much preferred Phillipe to that domineering brute her uncle had selected for her!

A heavy-hearted sigh escaped Liberty's lips while she lay pinned beneath the luggage. Ah, how she missed her beloved father and the protection his presence provided. She felt so alone, so trapped, so desperate. The violent tropical storm that had ravaged the West Indies and claimed Benjamin's life had turned her world upside down. Benjamin had been struck and killed by falling debris and Liberty had been devastated by the loss.

It had been during that dismal period of mourning that Phillipe had become insistent on marriage. Then, Uncle Luther's letter arrived, expressing his grief and inviting Liberty to sail to Charles Town to take inventory of her inherited holdings in South Carolina. The invitation had seemed a perfect excuse to leave Phillipe's persistent pleas and the unpleasant memories behind.

And so, two months later, having narrowly escaped a second attempt to drag her into wedlock, Liberty lay scrunched in the baggage compartment of a carriage . . . Destination unknown. . . .

All Liberty could say about her life was that it had never been monotonous and it didn't look as if it would be getting dull anytime soon. She could only hope the worst was over. But she had the inescapable feeling that the solution to one problem would only create another.

Liberty prayed that whatever trouble lay ahead of her would be mere child's play in comparison to her frustrating ordeals with Simon Gridley and Luther Norris. She would prefer to lie here until she rotted rather than confront those two scheming scoundrels again. Damn them both! And damn all men everywhere while she was at it! The male of the species could make a woman's existence a veritable hell and Liberty was living proof of that.

Chapter 2

Employing her drumroll walk, Nora Flannery sauntered out the door of Dylon Lockhart's town house. Still chattering like a magpie and giggling in that shrill, nasal voice of hers, Nora plunked onto the carriage seat and settled her full skirts around her.

Percival T. Pearson rolled his eyes and shook his head at his prissy passenger. Nora's bright blue silk gown and contrasting scarves which were draped around her ivory neck left him comparing her to a maypole. Attempting to conceal his distaste for this particular female, Percy strapped the luggage in place and strode stoically around in front of the horses to join his master.

An amused smile quirked Dylon Lockhart's lips when he noticed his valet's reaction to the gushing female who had nestled back against the cushioned seat. "Is something troubling you, Percy?" he questioned, knowing full well there was.

"If you ask me, you could have found a better pigeon for your ploy. I thought it was your intent to pacify your grandfather, not annoy him . . . sir," Percival remarked with exaggerated politeness.

"I thought I'd strive for a bit of both." Another mischievous grin spread across Dylon's handsome bronzed features.

Percy straightened his cuff, flicked an imaginary piece of lint from his topcoat and spared his master a fleeting glance. "I think, sir, that you will be tipping the scales heavily toward *annoyance* when you arrive with this chattering bit of fluff in tow."

Dylon shrugged a broad shoulder. "Nora is the best I could do on short notice."

"Short notice?" Percy sniffed in contradiction. "Begging your pardon, sir . . ."

Mister Formality, thought Dylon, stifling a grin. After all the years Dylon and his valet had spent together Percy was still proper and dignified to a fault.

"You have known about this upcoming holiday for quite some time now, sir," Percy went on to say. "After all, your grandfather organizes these lively celebrations twice a year. I don't see how you can claim that it sneaked up on you."

Dylon chuckled good-naturedly at his valet and/or the personification of his conscience. Percival T. (the T. stood for Theodore) Pearson was devoted and as straitlaced as they came. But he did not consider it disrespectful to reprimand his master if the situation demanded. Percy dealt in dry sarcasm and he wanted it known that he did not approve of this little charade that would be played for Brewster Lockhart's benefit . . . again.

"Oh, lovey . . ." Nora cooed from inside the carriage.

Percy's somber features puckered momentarily before he managed to contain his mounting irritation. "Do climb in, Master Dylon," he insisted. "Your lady is obviously distressed by your lack of attention. I will see to checking the harnesses myself."

Snickering at Percy's caustic remark, Dylon pivoted to fold his tall, muscular frame into his coach. He had barely sat down before the buxom brunette attached herself to him like a leech and began smearing slobbery kisses on his neck.

"Oh, lovey, I'm deliriously happy," Nora gushed, pressing her ample bosom against Dylon's arm. "This is going to be a splendid holiday—the two of us together—making plans for our future."

In the luggage compartment that was built behind the carriage seat, Liberty Jordon muffled a giggle. The female (whoever she was) was making an outrageous play for her beau. The sticky sweet soliloquy caused Liberty to prick her ears. She couldn't help but wonder if the lady's suitor would pledge undying love after being openly invited to profess his affection and his intentions toward her.

Dylon pried Nora's arms off his shoulders and clutched her wandering hands in his own. He didn't like the way Nora had phrased her comments, not one whit. She sounded as if she were leading up to something and he had the uneasy feeling he knew what that *something* was!

"I'm sure you will find my grandfather's estate magnificent, Nora dear," Dylon replied casually, avoiding the subject Nora tried to broach. "Knowing Brewster, there will be entertainment galore and activities aplenty. No one organizes parties better than Brewster. He pays strict attention to every detail."

Nora tittered in that nasal voice of hers and sidled closer to Dylon. Behind the seat, Liberty fought to prevent gagging. That giggle of Nora's was sickening! She found no fault with the man's rich, mellow baritone voice. It was pleasing to the ear. 'Twas a shame she couldn't say the same for Nora's. It reminded Liberty of a clanging gong that dripped molasses.

My, but this chit's suitor must have been an exceptionally good sport to court her, Liberty decided. How could he tolerate that senseless giggle and those sugar-coated words? Frankly, Liberty found the female nauseating.

As the carriage rumbled down the street, Nora wormed her hands free to limn the rugged features of Dylon's face and comb her fingers through his thick raven hair. Unlike most men of the time, Dylon refused to wear a powdered wig. And why should he? Nora asked herself as she toyed with the wavy midnight strands. Dylon Lockhart was far more appealing without a wig and absolutely devastating when he wasn't wearing the fancy trappings of a gentleman. Just thinking about his virile, masculine physique made her tingle all over. He would make a fine catch, the best to be found in the colony, in fact.

Nora expelled a contented sigh and melted against Dylon's broad shoulder. "Oh, lovey, I cannot wait to announce our plans to all the world. . . ."

"*Our plans?*" he repeated cautiously, regarding her with a wary frown.

Nora erupted in another eardrum-splitting giggle. "Dylon, *dahling* . . . don't tease me so. After what we shared last night, you know perfectly well what I'm suggesting."

Dylon squirmed uneasily in his skin. "Nora dear, I don't think we should rush into anything. What we should do is enjoy Brewster's holiday in the Up Country and let nature take its own course."

It sounded to Liberty as if nature had already taken its own course. Unless Liberty missed her guess (and she doubted that she had) "Dylon dahling" had tripped the light fantastic with "Nora dear." Now Dylon was trying to weasel out of his obligations after he deflowered the wench. A confirmed bachelor, Liberty deduced. She could almost picture the rake squirming in his clothes while Nora was trying to stake her claim—permanently.

Liberty made no judgment in this affair because she had enough difficulties of her own with which to contend. Indeed, she didn't give a tinker's damn about "Dylon dahling" and "Nora dear." They were providing her with a mode of escape from her second unwanted fiancé and her conniving uncle. That's all that mattered.

Displeased with Dylon's diplomatic attempt to shrug off his obligations, Nora's lips puckered in an exaggerated pout. "You compromised my virtues last night," she reminded him waspishly. "I gave in to you because I love you and I presumed you loved me. But, being a man, I know you are not so free with those three little words."

Good God! How stupid does this chit think I am? Dylon asked himself crossly. If last night was the first night Nora Flannery had compromised herself in the heat of passion, he'd eat his hat, brim and all! And if there had been any "giving in" he was the one who'd done it to appease a craving that was second nature to him. Nora had secluded him, not the other way around. And Nora had been a mite too good at what she was doing to claim it was her first time. Nora was no blushing virgin, that was for damned sure! If he'd thought for one minute that she was, he wouldn't have gone near her. Dylon still had a few scruples left, even if Percy didn't think so!

And love? Dylon would have burst out laughing at her devious ploy if he didn't risk putting this scheming chit in a snit. Dylon had need of an escort to pacify his grandfather. This jaunt to the Up Country had nothing to do with love and marriage, even if Nora hinted at it. Dylon was merely tolerating her presence and that was the beginning and end of it. Last night had been mildly pleasurable. But Dylon was not going to spend the rest of his life listening to this wench giggle and whine in that irritating voice of hers.

While Nora glared at him, Dylon cleared his throat and carefully chose his words. "My dear Nora, you know that I am a man who enjoys life to its fullest. I never try to take myself too seriously. But it seems you are taking both of us extremely seriously . . ."

The remark served to detach Nora from him at long last. She puffed up with so much indignation that her bosom very nearly burst from the plunging neckline of her blue silk gown. "You expect me to take last night lightly?" she gasped. "How dare you even think I would bend to a man's will unless marriage was in our future! You led me to believe we . . ."

"I led you to believe nothing." Dylon's deep voice was firmer now. His gaze was direct. "I don't think it wise for a woman and man to allow one reckless night to dictate their future."

"Well, of all the nerve!" Nora's shrill voice hit such an unpleasantly high pitch that it almost shattered Liberty's eardrums. "If you think I intend to accompany you to your grandfather's estate without a proposal of marriage, you are sorely mistaken!"

"I didn't say I hadn't considered proposing," Dylon hedged, trying to calm the hysterical chit down. "I only suggested that we postpone a decision until we return from Brewster's estate."

Nora glared poison arrows at the handsome rake. She had known from the beginning that Dylon wasn't the kind of man a woman could catch and hold. But she had been so certain she could manipulate him when all other females had failed. Dylon and his younger brother were two of the most sought-after bachelors in the area. But it seemed Dylon was a masterful escape artist who could untangle himself from any matrimonial knot.

Folding her arms beneath her silk-clad bosom, Nora flung her pug nose in the air. "Take me back to my house this instant!" she demanded. She worked up a few crocodile tears for the occasion and let them spill down her inflamed cheeks. "We shall just see what my father has to say about your refusal to make a respectable woman of me!"

"'Tis a mite too late for your father to make you respectable. Even though Edgar is a famed surgeon and assemblyman, I seriously doubt that he can find a way to replace the virginity you lost long before you met me."

Dylon knew the instant the ridiculing remark was out of his mouth that he should have been more diplomatic. But damnit, good-natured as he was, there was a limit to how much he'd tolerate before he lost *his* temper. Unfortunately, Nora had pushed him to the end of his long fuse with her bald-faced lies.

Liberty broke into an amused grin when she overheard "Dylon dahling's" caustic rejoinder, one which was immediately followed by the crack of flesh meeting flesh. *His* face and *her* hand, Liberty speculated. "Nora dear" had retaliated to salvage her wounded dignity (what little she apparently had, if she truly was as promiscuous as "Dylon dahling" claimed she was).

"We shall see how seriously you take life when my father gets through with you," Nora sputtered furiously. "And if there is surgery to be performed hereabout, it will be your castration, Dylon Lockhart! You will marry me. My father will see to that or you will find yourself of no further use to any woman!"

Having spouted her threat, Nora thrust her head out the window, demanding that Percival reverse direction and take her home. That done, Nora flounced on the seat and scooted as far away as the coach would allow. To dramatize her frustration, Nora burst into great gulping tears, playing the role of the woman scorned to the hilt. She sat there sobbing noisily, the bottom half of her face masked behind her lacy handkerchief.

Dylon, however, was unaffected by her tearful display. Women had employed similar tactics on him before when they wanted their way. While Nora mopped her face with her handkerchief, Dylon stared thoughtfully out the window. Doctor Edgar Flannery was not only Dylon's associate in the Lower House of the South Carolina Assembly, but he was also an influential man. In Dylon's desperation to latch onto an escort for the holiday celebration, he had happened onto a deceitful female whose intent it was to drag him to the altar.

Well, it wasn't going to happen and this wasn't the first time some wench had sought to entrap him either. Because of his wealth and his position he was a target for many a husband-hunter. But for years Dylon had been chased without getting caught. He had taken a risk when he courted Nora. But he needed her to serve his purpose.

Dylon had his reasons for selecting this particular type of female to accompany him to his grandfather's estate. Brewster detested Nora's kind. That was why Dylon had sought her out. As long as Dylon and his brother kept bringing the unacceptable brand of women to meet Brewster, the patriarch wouldn't force his grandsons into marriage. And if Dylon arrived at the estate without a female escort he could expect . . .

"You'll be eternally sorry for this," Nora blustered, jolting Dylon from his pensive reverie. In stiff, angry jerks she snatched up a second handkerchief. (The first one was completely soaked by this time, though she had gotten considerable mileage out of it.) "I will not be used and recklessly discarded! I am a lady!"

That was debatable, thought Dylon, but he didn't fling the sarcastic remark at the blubbering brunette. That would have set her off again. "We will talk this situation over when I return to Charles Town next month." His voice reflected as much indifference as was humanly possible and that infuriated Nora to the extreme.

"There will be no more discussion," she blared in that shrill voice that grated on a man's nerves. "You will marry me and that is that! For once you are going to accept your responsibility toward a woman, you philistine! I shall see to that!"

When Percy reined the team of horses to a halt, Nora clambered from the carriage of her own accord. "Gather my luggage, Percival," she ordered brusquely.

Percy climbed down from his perch, strode around the phaeton and pulled Nora's trunk and satchel from the baggage compartment. Liberty scrunched deeper into the corner to avoid being spotted. When the leather flap was replaced, she breathed a relieved sigh, thankful that she was granted more space. Although there was still a mound of luggage stacked around her, she could now stretch out one arm and leg.

After Percy had carried the lady's belongings to the front door of one of Charles Town's most elegant town houses, he returned to the coach. His silver-gray eyes focused on the broad muscular man who had stepped from the carriage to mutter at the unexpected turn of events.

"Now that you have ruffled that hen's fine feathers, what do you intend to do, sir?" Percy inquired.

"I haven't puzzled that out yet," Dylon replied with a noncommittal shrug.

"Well, you shall have several hours to contemplate your next move," Percy reminded him. "We won't reach your plantation until morning, even if we drive all night. Surely by then you will have devised an alternative plan of action."

A teasing smile quirked Dylon's lips as he surveyed his valet. "If worse comes to worst, we could dress you in a woman's garb and I could escort you to the party."

Percy didn't bother to dignify the outrageous suggestion with a sarcastic rejoinder. He simply pulled himself onto his perch and waited for Dylon to join him as he usually did when the two of them were traveling together.

"I hope your brother has fared better in locating a female escort than you have," Percy commented as Dylon took up the reins and popped them over the team of horses.

Dylon sighed audibly. He could expect his brother to harass him unmercifully when he returned to the plantation empty-handed. No doubt Griffin Lockhart had found himself a suitable female to accompany him to their grandfather's estate in the Up Country.

"Griffin has never arrived home alone before," Dylon murmured.

"Neither have you," Percy inserted. ". . . Until now."

"Ah, well," Dylon replied with a lackadaisical shrug. "Perhaps I'll think of something to save me from Brewster's marriage trap."

Percy almost broke into a smile. Almost. "I'm not certain whose trap would be worse, Nora's or Brewster's."

Dylon inwardly cringed at both prospects. Why was it

that everyone else in the world was in such a rush to see a man married? It was Dylon's life, after all. "I intend to avoid all traps," he vowed determinedly. "The very last thing I need is a wife. I have yet to run across a woman who can be trusted. There are too many Nora Flannerys in this world."

Percy lapsed into silence. He knew why Dylon was resentful of women, but this was not the time to trample across the unpleasant memories in Dylon's past. His present plans had been spoiled by a shrewd female who had pretended to be something she wasn't. Once Nora had drawn Dylon in, she had sprung her trap. But Dylon was not to be intimidated by threats. Wild horses couldn't drag Dylon Lockhart to the altar. He was a confirmed bachelor who had only one use for women.

While Percy was mulling over that thought, Liberty lay curled in the back of the coach, thinking the very same thing. She had heard Dylon declare in no uncertain terms that he intended to avoid marriage at all possible costs. "Dylon dahling" was obviously a rake and a rounder who employed women for his physical satisfaction. Thank goodness Liberty wouldn't have to deal with that philanderer. As soon as this carriage rolled to a halt she would make her escape and scamper to the wharf to purchase a one-way ticket to the West Indies. *If* this confounded coach ever comes to a halt, she grumbled as she bounced over the bumps. She was beginning to wonder if it ever would! And by the time it did, she was certain she would be a mass of purple bruises.

An infuriated growl flew from Simon Gridley's curled lips. He and Luther had searched high and low and still they had no clue as to Liberty's whereabouts. That minx! She had thoroughly complicated his plans and he was positively livid.

"This is all your fault." Simon turned on the blanched-faced Luther Norris. "After that chit tried to escape us twice last night, you should have been more cautious in transporting her to the church."

"She assured me she had accepted our arrangements," Luther defended when Simon breathed fire at him. "I never expected her to . . ."

"I should think by now that you would have learned to expect the unexpected from that free-spirited niece of yours," Simon flared.

Luther expelled an exasperated sigh. "Perhaps she managed to run to the wharf to locate a ship to take her back to her precious islands," he speculated. "I'm sure if we check the West Indian-bound schooners we will find her. She has to be here somewhere."

Simon hated to admit that this imbecile might be right, so he didn't. Wheeling about, he stormed down the street.

Simon had gone out of his way to be polite and charming to Liberty in his effort to win her favor. But Liberty had remained courteously distant during his courting ritual. He'd never met another female who aroused him as quickly as Liberty Jordon. Since the instant he laid eyes on her, he'd been obsessed with her exotic beauty. Not only could she provide him with abundant wealth and connections, but he had been eager to get her into his bed.

And I will have her in my bed sooner or later, Simon assured himself confidently. Luther Norris would ensure the arrangements were made according to Simon's specifications. Simon had Luther exactly where he wanted him. And before long Simon would have that wild-hearted Liberty Jordon where he wanted her too!

Determined of purpose, Simon strode off to fetch his carriage. He was confident that a thorough search of the docks would turn up that curvaceous blonde. And before the day was out, Liberty would be his bride. Simon hadn't gotten where he was in this world by sitting back and watching life and opportunity breeze by. He was forceful and aggressive and he knew how to throw his weight around. And he couldn't wait to throw his weight on that sassy blond hellion. Taming Liberty Jordon was going to be a most satisfying diversion!

A muffled groan tumbled from Liberty's lips when she roused from sleep to find her right arm and leg numb. She had been coiled up in the luggage compartment of Dylon's coach for hours on end. Well, this was still far better than the wedding night she had been dreading. Sharing her bed with a man she wasn't sure she liked and knew for certain she couldn't trust would have been positively worse! If Simon Gridley was a friend or associate of her treacherous uncle, Liberty wanted nothing to do with him. And once she returned to the islands, she would find a way to exact her revenge on that scheming rodent-of-an-uncle of hers.

Luther Norris may have been her mother's stepbrother and Liberty's only living relative, but he was a worthless excuse of a man. He was one of those individuals who never asserted himself and who depended on the generosity of others to get him through life. Because Luther had never been successful in his own endeavors, Benjamin Jordon had allowed Luther to manage their plantation of Triple Oak in the South Carolina colony. But Benjamin had the foresight to hire a very competent overseer who kept the operation running smoothly. It was not because of Luther Norris that the plantation prospered. The man was nothing but an expense that Benjamin had felt obligated to assume because of his departed wife. Now, it seemed Liberty had inherited Luther's dead weight. But was he grateful? Hardly! The scoundrel had tried to marry her off. Damn, Liberty was itching to discover what motivated Luther . . .

A pained grimace tightened Liberty's elegant features when the carriage wheel dropped into a pothole in the road. Luggage toppled, slamming against her head and shoulders. Godamercy, where was "Dylon dahling" going? And how much longer was she to be wedged in this compartment like a sack of dirty laundry?

Several hours later, Liberty posed the same exasperating question. How much longer would she have to tolerate these uncomfortable accommodations? But still the carriage bumped and bounced down the road, even as sunlight filtered around the edges of the leather cover, signaling the dawn of another day.

Chapter 3

Wearily, Dylon climbed down from his perch atop the phaeton. He and Percy hadn't bothered to pause to eat, only to see to their needs. He had been anxious to return to Lockhart Hall after his extended sojourn in Charles Town.

Dylon glanced around the immaculate plantation that had been built on a hill overlooking the Ashley River. He had been away for three weeks, attending the Assembly meetings in Charles Town, enjoying the social season and searching for just the right escort to accompany him to his grandfather's estate near Camden. He and the other assemblymen had voiced their complaints about Parliament's new restrictive legislation and they had sent lobbyists to plead the colony's cause in England. But considering all the things he'd done *right* the past few weeks, he'd royally botched up his affairs when he tangled with Nora Flannery. He had wanted to locate a woman who would suit the role of a smitten maid. Nora had behaved as if she adored Dylon, but she had tried to rush him into a proposal he had no intention of offering . . . ever! He had courted Nora briefly but he had no plans of giving that female barracuda his name.

In Dylon's opinion, there wasn't a woman on the planet who could satisfy him for more than a week at a time. He'd had mistresses aplenty and scads of proper escorts, but none of them had ever fascinated him to distraction. Except one . . . he resentfully amended. And that particular woman was someone Dylon preferred not to remember.

The women of aristocracy were like China dolls who had been taught just the right words to say at the proper time. They were too frail and delicate and too shallow for Dylon's tastes. The wenches who catered to a man's physical needs weren't his cup of tea either. Although they were more rambunctious and uninhibited, they were far too earthy to make suitable wives for the gentry.

Dylon didn't consider himself a snob, but he did have certain expectations as to what a wife should be, even if he had no intention of marrying. Long ago, he had faced the realization that marriage simply wouldn't suit him, even if Brewster Lockhart thought it should! Brewster was determined to see both his grandsons wed to propagate the family name. But Brewster wanted Dylon and Griffin married to women who fit his expectations—well-bred, personable and intelligent. Dylon wasn't even sure such a creature existed! And so, Dylon and Griffin mischievously latched onto women who were well-bred but frightfully dull. Dylon always singled out females to introduce to Brewster who possessed some annoying quirk of personality that would wear on his grandfather's nerves—such as Nora's shrill giggle and hysterical tears. Unfortunately, Nora had been too pushy. God, Dylon hoped that spiteful chit didn't tattle to her father as she threatened to do. She could make his life miserable if she pressed the issue.

Lost in thought, Dylon strode to the back of the phaeton to retrieve his luggage. He couldn't wait to shed his gentlemanly garments, shrug on casual apparel and devour a three-course meal. Lord, he was tired and starved!

"If you want to catch a nap, Percy, I'll have Verna . . ."

"I am in splendid shape," Percy insisted as he clutched

his satchel and scurried to catch up with Dylon's long, graceful strides. "After all, 'tis my duty to see to your needs before my own, sir."

"Percy, I have told you countless times that you take your station in life entirely too seriously," Dylon chuckled.

"And if I may be so bold to say so, sir, you don't take your life seriously enough," Percy parried without exchanging expression.

Percy rarely changed expression. He strived to be the epitome of self-control. He was always straitlaced, conscientious and properly attired. There was never a hair out of place on the powdered Bag wig he wore, not even in a stiff breeze. Percy was the shining example of devotion, propriety and self-discipline. He never laughed out loud or cursed. He was self-contained and utterly sincere about his position as Dylon's valet, groom or whatever else the situation demanded. Nothing shattered Percy's composure. He was an incredible monument to restraint.

Before Percy immersed himself in a polite, respectful lecture on Dylon's lack of seriousness in any given predicament, the master of the house sailed in the front door. His gaze drifted up the wide, imposing staircase that sat at the end of the entryway and he admired the cypress-paneled hall and adjoining rooms. He couldn't imagine how Brewster could have left this elegant mansion behind to migrate to his new estate in the Up Country. This spacious home was a part of Dylon. He wouldn't want to live anywhere else. Oh, certainly, he employed the town house while in Charles Town, but this was where Dylon's heart was. . . .

His nostalgic thoughts trailed off when the housekeeper Verna Ross and several servants spilled down the steps and around the corner to greet him. Upon hearing Dylon had neglected to pause at the "ordinary" to rest and appease his appetite, Verna rushed to the kitchen to remedy the problem. The other servants plucked up

Dylon's satchels and scampered upstairs to ready his room.

"If you have no need of rest, come join me, Percy," Dylon invited as he ambled down the corridor. "We can discuss the arrangements for my departure to Grandfather's estate over a cup of tea."

"Thank you, sir, I would enjoy that very much."

Dylon didn't think Percy looked as if he was delighted with the prospect. But one could never be certain about Percy since he was so sober-faced and his voice was carefully devoid of emotion. Just once, Dylon would like to see his devoted valet step from behind that wall of self-imposed reserve. Just once Dylon would like to voice a witty remark that provoked Percy to display a broad smile. And yet, he wondered if Percy's face would crack if he actually did grin.

Ah, well, Percy had been an employee at Lockhart Hall for twelve years and he hadn't burst into a grin yet. There seemed nothing hereabout that surprised, amused or startled the courtly servant. Poor Percy was destined to go through life wearing a mask of indifference. Sometimes Dylon wondered if he did the things he did, just to get a rise out of Percy. Hell, he knew he did. Dylon would have been thrilled to get that stolid servant worked up about something. Just to get Percy to raise his voice would be quite a remarkable accomplishment!

Like a gun-shy rabbit, Liberty peeked out of the luggage compartment to survey her surroundings. The circle drive that graced the front of the monstrous brick mansion stretched almost a half mile to the gate of entry. The path was lined with color-splashed gardens and stately cypress, white gum and cedar trees. Godamercy, where the blazes was she anyway?

Liberty was able to inch from her niche without being noticed. Although her legs had been curled into a tight ball for endless hours and complained when she moved,

Liberty managed to wobble past the coach and dart toward the corner of the elegant mansion. She was anxious to shed her wedding gown and locate more comfortable clothing. And if she could borrow a horse from the stable, she might be able to sneak back to her own plantation at Triple Oak to confer with her maid.

Stella Talbot—the stout, robust woman who had seen to Liberty's raising after her mother's death—had accompanied her to the colonies. But Luther had refused to permit Stella to attend the wedding in Charles Town for fear she would try to aid in Liberty's escape. Stella had been confined to Triple Oak until Liberty returned as Simon's bride. The devoted maid was the only person Liberty could count on to help her elude Luther and Simon. Together they would sail to the Indies and put this unfortunate incident behind them forever.

If her luck held, Liberty could make her way to Triple Oak before Luther and Simon returned from Charles Town. She doubted the twosome had set records in returning to the country, as "Dylon dahling" had. The man had only slowed his pace to rest his team of horses thrice and that was only for a scant few minutes at a time. Simon and Luther would never inconvenience themselves in the least. They were too self-centered to make even one personal sacrifice.

Anxious to change into suitable garments and be on her way, Liberty scampered around the sprawling brick home. Her gaze flitted across the plush gardens that were teeming with an array of exotic flowers. Behind the great house stood a kitchen, smokehouse, stables, coach houses and servants' cabins. Below the rise of ground that was broken by a "ha-ha" wall, which prevented a flock of sheep from grazing too near the house, was a wharf that stretched out over the bay—the loading dock where farm produce was stacked and shipped to Charles Town. The plantation reeked wealth, thought Liberty. It was a splendid place that dwarfed her family's estate and made it look shabby in comparison, especially since

Luther had been left in charge.

Her violet eyes lifted to the gallery that encircled the back of the mansion. Liberty frowned thoughtfully. Somewhere in those upstairs rooms was a set of clothes that would serve her purpose. Male or female, master or servant's garb, Liberty didn't care. All she wanted was *out* of this hampering wedding dress!

Her keen gaze settled on the outstretched limbs of the magnolia tree that reached toward the surrounding piazza. Here was her makeshift ladder. If she could scale the tree and walk across the limbs she could gain entrance to the mansion and no one would be the wiser.

After yanking the lacy veil from her head, Liberty tied it around her waist-length blond hair. She tugged up her wedding gown until she could tie the yards of satin into a knot on her left hip, allowing herself freedom of movement. Leaving her slippers at the base of the tree, Liberty pulled herself onto a low-hanging branch. With graceful ease, she moved along the limb until she could grasp another sturdy branch. Although the tree was a thick mass of sprigs that sought to snare her, she made her way upward. Within a few minutes she climbed high in the tree toward a towering limb which would permit her to grasp the wrought-iron railing that surrounded the balcony.

Liberty smiled triumphantly. She had successfully managed to escape Luther and Simon. And very soon she would be on her way to Triple Oak to retrieve her maid. Ah, things were going splendidly!

Dylon collapsed in the chair in his study and stared thoughtfully at the impressive collection of books that filled the shelves to capacity. During his high-speed journey back to Lockhart Hall he had conjured up and discarded several inspirations to counter his grandfather's monotonous pleas to settle down with a wife and family. Dylon had no doubt that, if he arrived at

Brewster's estate without an escort in tow, his grandfather would have several females on the premises who bore the patriarch's stamp of approval.

Brewster Lockhart was a most persistent man. But then, so were his grandsons, Dylon mused with a wry smile. Brewster could no longer threaten to disinherit his grandsons because they had amassed fortunes all their own. Now Brewster simply badgered Dylon and Griffin, demanding they produce heirs to carry on the family tradition. Dylon had no qualms about fathering children, if only he didn't have to bother about having a wife. . . .

"Well, sir, have you decided on your strategy to counter Brewster?" Percy questioned as he grasped a cup to pour out the steaming tea.

Dylon had just opened his mouth to report that nothing ingenious had come to mind when a most extraordinary incident occurred. Percy had absently glanced out the window while he poured the tea. For the first time in the twelve years that Percival T. Pearson had been an employee, his well-disciplined mask cracked and a loud squawk of surprise erupted from his lips. The cup Percy held in his left hand clanked against the silver tray and he yelped as the scalding liquid dripped over his hand.

Never had Dylon seen Percy look so stunned. And never had he heard his devoted valet raise his voice in pain, surprise or despair. But Percy had done all three in the span of a few seconds. His gray eyes bulged from their sockets. (Dylon didn't even know his valet's eyes were capable of opening to such a wide angle!)

"Hell's fire!" Percy gasped, dropping the teapot as if he were handling live coals. His goggle-eyed gaze was riveted on the window. His jaw sagged on its hinges as if he were staring at a grotesque prehistoric monster that had slithered out of the swamp.

Dylon gaped in stupefied disbelief. Percy had uttered his first curse aloud! His mouth was hanging open wide enough for a pigeon to roost and his eyes were still popping.

"What the devil is the matter?" Dylon demanded to know when Percy continued to stand there in paralyzed shock.

Valiantly, Percy tried to gather his shattered composure. But it was impossible. He stared at the oversized bird in white satin who had hooked her bare leg over a tree limb and was in the process of hoisting herself onto a higher branch.

Percival T. Pearson, who had learned to take Dylon and Griffin's outrageous antics in stride, was aghast at what he saw. The female, garbed in a wedding gown (of all things) was swinging around the tree with devil-may-care panache. And what really shocked the starch out of Percy's collar was the young hoyden's agility and adeptness. Her outrageous mischief indicated she was accustomed to performing such daring aerial maneuvers. There was nothing clumsy about her movements, nothing to suggest the woman was ashamed of what she was doing either. The blond-haired sprite seemed perfectly at home in the towering tree and yet, it was the very last place Percy imagined seeing a bride!

Dylon darted to the window that held Percy's fanatical fascination. He was intent on discovering what had startled the valet to the point that he had spilled tea, broken a china cup, cursed out loud and stood frozen to the spot as if he'd been planted there.

"Good God!" Dylon croaked when his gaze landed on the bewitching creature high atop the tree. Tanned legs (very shapely ones) protruded from the yards of white satin that had been carelessly tied into a knot on Liberty's thigh. The daring neckline of her wedding gown exposed the creamy swells of her breasts. She was a veritable goddess with all the curves and swells in just the right places. Her long hair was a mass of gold that was highlighted by sunbleached strands that sparkled in the light.

Dylon felt his stalled heart slam against his ribs when the daring minx loosened her grasp on the limb to which she had been holding and launched herself through the air to latch onto a higher branch. While she momentarily hung upside down, the veil she had tied around her hair dangled beneath her and the hiked hem of her wedding dress slid farther up her thigh, exposing a most indecent but tantalizing amount of bare leg.

"Would you say, sir, that the young lady is trying to commit suicide in your magnolia tree? Or do you think she is actually enjoying herself?" Percy chirped, his voice two octaves higher than normal.

Dylon didn't spare the time to speculate on what the luscious beauty was doing in his tree. Like streak lightning he bolted out the door and down the hall to retrieve the daring maid before she broke her lovely neck.

Percy wheeled around to follow his master, leaving the broken cup and teapot behind. That was also unlike him. The particular valet had never left the scene of an accident without cleaning the mess up first. But then, Percy had just endured the most shocking jolt of his life and he'd completely forgotten himself.

A startled gasp erupted from Dylon's chest when the acrobat in her wedding gown dived between the branches to grasp another distant limb. "What in the sweet loving hell do you think you're doing?" he yelled at her before she killed herself and her appearance at his plantation remained a mystery that could never be satisfactorily explained.

Liberty glanced down while she hung by her hands. Her eyes widened in dismay when she spied the two men beneath her, both of whom were undoubtedly getting an eyeful, considering their position and her hiked hem . . .

The crack of timber distracted Liberty. She had dared to latch onto a limb that wasn't very sturdy. The fact that she hung there like a slug, staring down at the unexpected arrivals, put too much strain on the branch.

Before she could steady herself the limb snapped.

With a terrified shriek, Liberty found herself swooping downward, still clutching the broken limb. The branch crashed against a lower limb, catapulting her through space. Liberty heard the shouts of alarm beneath her, but no one was more aware of her precarious predicament than she, to be sure!

In midair, Liberty attempted a half twist to determine where she was about to land. Not that it mattered, she supposed. The fall was sure to kill her, whether she landed on her belly or her back.

Although Dylon and Percy rushed forward to break Liberty's fall, she swan-dived into the ferns and shrubs, leaving her imprint on the bushes, and they on her. With a thud and a whoosh of breath, Liberty fell with a clatter into the circular row of daffodils, jessamine and azaleas that surrounded the base of the tree.

The last thing Liberty recalled was the incredible speed at which the ground had flown up to hit her in the face. As the splash of colorful flowers gave way to silent darkness, the sweet scent of blossoms infiltrated her senses. And then there was a vast expanse of nothingness that was devoid of sound and color and fragrance. . . .

Chapter 4

"Is she dead? Of course she's dead! She has to be dead. Damnation, she's killed herself!" Percy babbled nonstop.

Dylon knelt beside the crumpled beauty and then glanced over his shoulder at his valet. Percival T. Pearson's composure had cracked wide open. And with good reason! Dylon had nearly suffered heart seizure himself while he watched this daring imp rocket through space to make a crash landing in the bushes.

His attention refocused on the young woman who had stupefied him with her appearance and her wild acrobatic maneuvers atop his tree. This mysterious sprite in no way resembled the genteel ladies he'd met in Charles Town, or even during his studies at Oxford in England. This pixie was in a league all by herself, Dylon instantly decided. Her skin was bathed with a warm coat of sunshine. Her long curly hair wasn't blond or brown, but rather pure gold, mingled with glimmering streaks of silver. Her long, thick lashes lay against her delicately structured cheeks in a motionless caress. Her heart-shaped lips—soft inviting lips that drew a man's undivided attention—curved up at the corners, even when she was dead or unconscious, whichever the case may be. Dylon wasn't certain.

Impulsively, Dylon bent to brush his lips over this sleeping beauty's sweet mouth. Why? Dylon didn't know. But as he anticipated, she tasted as good as she looked—absolutely delicious.

"Sir, this is not some silly fairy tale in which a prince can rouse a princess with a life-giving kiss," Percy admonished after he regained control of his shattered composure. "What do you suppose this woman is doing here? And in a wedding gown, for heaven sake! Where could she have possibly come from?"

Dylon withdrew and shrugged a broad shoulder. Bedazzled, he reached down to monitor the faint pulsations on her throat. He marveled at the soft satiny texture of her skin. Mmm . . . this delectable goddess also felt as good as she looked and he was ever so glad she was still alive.

His eyes wandered off on a journey of discovery. They lingered overly long on the full swells of her breasts that were exposed by the swooping neckline of her gown. Pensively, Dylon calculated the tiny indentation of her waist before his gaze roamed over the finely tuned and yet utterly feminine curve of her thighs.

Dylon had seen some breathtaking women in his time, but this nymph possessed unrivaled beauty. She had it all—the refined bone structure, silky flesh, exquisite features and a lovely head of hair. She had the face and body of an angel who visited every man's dreams. The total combination of her alluring assets was staggering. Even Percy, who rarely displayed any type of emotion, seemed enraptured by the vision that lay before him.

Good God, words seemed inadequate in describing how magnificently lovely this woman was. Just staring at her sent Dylon's mind wandering off in the most arousing direction imaginable. It also caused his male body to tingle with lusty appreciation.

"Do you think we should dare try to move her?" Percy questioned. "Or perhaps not. She may have broken her neck. A shame, that," he added with a noticeable sigh of regret. "She truly is a lovely creature, is she not, sir?"

Again, Dylon glanced back at Percy. His valet had

never been one for idle chatter or glowing compliments. But suddenly he was blathering, posing questions and then answering them before Dylon could squeeze a word in edgewise.

"Perhaps you should fetch some smelling salts and a damp cloth," Dylon advised. "She's still alive, but it will be impossible to determine what condition she is in unless she rouses to tell us where she hurts the worst."

"Aye, a very good idea, sir. I will see to it immediately." His old self again, Percy snapped to attention. Pivoting on his heels, he moved swiftly but regally toward the back door of the house.

A contemplative frown furrowed Dylon's brow as he reached down to straighten Liberty's leg, one that was bent sideways at a most awkward angle. The gesture was meant to make the unconscious sprite more comfortable and inspect her for broken bones. But merely touching her caused his heart to slam against his rib cage and race off like a galloping Thoroughbred.

Dylon blinked in astonishment. He, who had enjoyed the charms of more than his fair share of females the past decade, was behaving like a teenager on the threshold of manhood!

In truth, he had become bored with feminine conquests, having discovered that all women everywhere were pretty much the same. But this enchanting creature intrigued him to the extreme. She aroused him without even trying. . . . She is unconscious, for God's sake! Dylon reminded himself gruffly.

Her outrageous antics in the tree mystified him. The fact that she was garbed in a wedding gown piqued his curiosity. The revealing garment that had been carelessly knotted on her left hip, exposing a scintillating amount of leg, stirred him to the most astonishing state of arousal.

Where had this mysterious woman come from? Obviously, she was running away from her wedding, or from her newly acquired husband. But how had she gotten here? They were miles away from Charles Town and the other small settlements that dotted the countryside. Why had she selected *his* magnolia tree in which to frolic like a chimpanzee . . . ?

"Here, sir." Percy's voice interrupted Dylon's contemplations.

Giving himself a mental shake, Dylon clasped the bottle of smelling salts and waved them under Liberty's dainty, upturned nose. Her body involuntarily flinched and then slumped into lifelessness. Dylon retrieved the cold cloth and gently drew it across her ashen cheeks, down the swanlike column of her neck to the delicious cleavage of her breasts. . . .

Percy cleared his throat to gain Dylon's attention, one that was glued to the luscious swells that lay against the delicate lace on the gown's revealing neckline. "Begging your pardon, sir, but I think the cold cloth would be more effective if it were applied to the young lady's forehead."

Dylon's lighthearted chuckle clamored in the still air. "You, my friend, are no fun whatsoever," he teased playfully.

"So you have told me on numerous occasions," Percy replied in his stiff, straitlaced manner. "And you, sir, are taking unfair advantage of a damsel in distress. Chivalry is still an honorable trait in mankind . . . and particularly those in your station in life."

Dylon sighed as he draped the cloth over Liberty's forehead. "Percy, don't you ever grow tired of portraying my conscience?"

"Don't you grow tired of not having one of your own, sir?" Percy countered in a politely righteous tone. "'Tis enough that you and Griffin insist on deceiving your grandfather into thinking you are honestly attempting to find yourselves suitable brides to carry on the family tradition. Each time Brewster plans a holiday and invites half the population of South Carolina, you show up on his doorstep with a female who is nowhere near your match. You know perfectly well that Brewster won't impulsively announce an engagement when you drag women he can barely tolerate to his semiannual festivities."

Dylon shrugged off Percy's tactful attempt to chastise him for rebelling against his grandfather's fondest wish. "I'll not be shoved into a marriage I don't want," he said with firm conviction.

"Just as you refuse to don a wig because you claim it to be uncomfortable and inconvenient," Percy countered. "If I may be so bold to say . . ."

"Aren't you always?" Dylon smirked.

Percy was undaunted by the mocking rejoinder. "The rebellious side of your nature is leaking out," he pointed out philosophically. "You rebel against Brewster's wishes by ignoring his pleas to take a proper wife. You refuse to wear your wig because that is also customary and expected. And you trifle with this young woman who is a virtual stranger. Have you no respect for tradition or fair play?"

"I march to the beat of a different drum and I see no harm in playing by my own rules, 'tis all," Dylon defended.

"You, sir, make up the rules as you go along," Percy clarified.

Thankfully, Percy clamped his mouth shut when Dylon stuffed the smelling salts against Liberty's nostrils. Again she instinctively jerked away. He repeated the procedure relentlessly until he had drawn Liberty from the depths of silent darkness.

A muffled moan tripped from Liberty's lips when the beat of her own heart pounded against her skull like a sledgehammer. Pinpoints of pain in various regions of her body throbbed in rhythm with her thudding heart. The black veil that shaded her vision became fuzzy gray. Without daring to open her eyes for fear she was dead and hadn't yet been informed of her condition, Liberty tried to move her leg. When she raised her knee, it collided with an unidentified object and a discomforted groan rippled down the dark corridors that separated her from reality.

Dylon grimaced when Liberty's knee accidentally struck him in the private part of his anatomy. He had been straddling the sleeping beauty, crouched over her on his hands and knees. The unexpected blow caused him to *kerplop* on top of her.

Liberty's breath came out in a rush and another pained groan tumbled from her lips. The feel of heavy weight crushing her triggered something akin to a nightmare—the grim realization of what would have happened if she had not escaped Simon Gridley. Her arms flailed wildly about her, battling the intimate intentions of the man who had almost become her husband. Her head rolled from side to side and her voice broke in terrified protest.

"Sweet merciful heavens, she's having a seizure!" Percy croaked as he watched Dylon dodge the flying fists that had already hammered against the sides of his head twice.

Percy decided it was a good thing Dylon objected to wearing a powdered wig. It would have been knocked off by the repeated blows to his skull.

There were some men who would have been incensed and offended by the young woman's unwarranted attack, no matter what the situation. But Dylon wasn't. He didn't strike back. He agilely and quickly removed himself from harm's way, chuckling at the fact that he had roused a sleeping tigress.

Dylon sank down on his haunches beside the bewitching imp, still smiling in curious amusement. He was accustomed to taking life lightly and he found no complaint with Liberty's defensive tactics. Her attempt to defend herself in her dazed state lent testimony to her unusual abilities. He could only chuckle as she lay there swinging at the air like an overturned beetle attempting to upright itself.

The bright ringing laughter stilled Liberty's movements. Assured that she was not going to be molested, she pried open one eye. When her tangled lashes fluttered up she found herself staring at the most magnificent specimen of masculinity this side of heaven. Her gaze locked with dazzling pools of blue—like chips of azure sky. A thick fringe of black velvet lashes surrounded those gleaming eyes that were embedded in a ruggedly handsome face. Full, sensuous lips curved upward at the corners and dimples creased the man's bronzed cheeks.

There before her was a face that God had labored over with tender loving care. His features weren't haphazardly plastered on his face; they were carved and etched by the Master Sculptor. The word *handsome* seemed sadly lacking in description. His face wasn't boyishly smooth or refined like Phillipe LaGere's. It was craggy, utterly masculine and positively fascinating.

Stunned by her fierce attraction, Liberty dragged her eyes from his tanned face. Her inquisitive gaze wandered at will, admiring the broad expanse of the man's chest, the sensuous way his linen shirt strained across his ribs and lean belly. She could detect the powerful muscles of his thighs in the way his long legs were folded beneath him. He was like a sleek, graceful jungle cat in repose.

Distracted by her assessment of the man who crouched beside her, Liberty was unaware of her own indecent exposure. One leg was still drawn up to her chest, as if she intended to ward off an attack by kicking at her assailant. It wasn't until she noticed where the man's attention had strayed that she reached down to tug self-consciously at the hem of her skirt.

When her lashes swept up, she caught a glimpse of the older man who had repositioned himself behind her head. Liberty studied the powdered Bag wig that surrounded the man's somber face. Two tight white curls sat above his ears and a fall of straight hair tumbled over his left shoulder, held in place by a thin black ribbon. The man looked to be fortyish or thereabout. He was dressed like a servant and his very stance and expression suggested that he took his position quite seriously. He was tall and thin and he was staring at her with an indecipherable expression stamped on his plain features.

Her gaze shifted back to the younger man who looked to be in his early thirties and who was still sporting an amused grin that suggested he was harboring a secret joke he refused to share. Liberty idly wondered if this handsome rake also smiled in his sleep. The reckless expression seemed to suit him, just as sobriety suited his dignified servant.

Dylon may have looked nonchalant, but he was very perceptive and observant of all that transpired around him. His attention shifted from Liberty's shapely tanned legs to the most fascinating pair of violet eyes ever to be implanted in a feminine face. Even though the lovely elf appeared a trifle bit disoriented and dazed, there was still a spark of living fire in her eyes—eyes that completed the picture of absolute perfection.

Although Dylon had intended to allow this gorgeous chit ample time to get her bearings, Percy circled to stand at her feet. "Who are you and what are you doing here?" he inquired, cutting right to the heart of the matter.

Something flashed in those luminous lavender eyes and Dylon studied her ponderously while she licked her bone-dry lips and glanced apprehensively around her.

"I . . . don't . . . remember," Liberty squeaked. Actually, she remembered quite well, but pleading amnesia seemed the perfect solution. Pretending a lapse of memory would prevent her from fielding questions she preferred not to answer.

"You don't remember?" Percy raised a brow. He regarded her for another pensive moment, his countenance wavering between his obvious concern for her condition and a conscious attempt to hold his emotions in check.

"Nay, I can't say that I do," Liberty said with an air of deceptive innocence.

When she had levered up on her elbows, her gaze swung to the man who was still crouched beside her. He was peering at her with that engaging smile that could make the most wary woman put her guard down. His stare penetrated flesh and bone to probe out the secrets within, patiently waiting for her to admit that she had voiced a bald-faced lie. Unable to meet that twinkling gaze a second longer, Liberty glanced at the valet.

"Where am I?" she asked, struggling to conjure up a convincing expression of blank curiosity.

"You are at Lockhart Hall," Percy informed her in his customary stoical manner. He gestured toward his master who was still grinning in amusement. "This is Dylon Lockhart, esquire, and I am Percival T. (the T. stands for Theodore) Pearson." He folded at the waist and dropped into a courteous bow. "We are at your service, my lady."

When Percy's attention shifted to her crumpled wedding gown, Liberty followed his gaze to note that her dress was still knotted on her hip.

"Godamercy! Am I married?" she questioned with feigned surprise.

If this little imp's mind was racing, Dylon's was buzzing twice as fast. He didn't believe this daring young woman's plea of amnesia for a minute. The sparkle in her eyes was too lively and intelligent to pretend loss of memory. Oh, to be sure, she had attempted to portray a distressed female who had sustained a blow that shattered her memory. But judging from her antics in the tree and the way her alert gaze kept bouncing back and forth between him and Percy, Dylon doubted her story. She was definitely a woman with secrets in her eyes. She knew perfectly well who she was and what she was doing. He'd bet his entire fortune on that. But for some reason this hoyden refused to divulge her past or her intentions.

"You truly don't remember who you are or what you're doing here?" Dylon baited, studying her with a sly smile.

Liberty compressed her lips. She didn't like the way "Dylon dahling" was staring at her. He was smiling the kind of smile that nothing in their conversation could account for and he hadn't stopped smiling since the instant she'd opened her eyes. He looked as if he were having a silent laugh at her expense. What was that rake up to?

"Nay, I don't have the foggiest notion what I'm doing here, dressed like this," she said with pretended conviction. "I remember nothing at all."

"Then perhaps I should refresh your memory, my dear," Dylon offered with another disarming grin. "We were going to be married this afternoon at the quaint chapel in the village . . ."

He was interrupted by Percival's shocked gasp. The valet gaped at his master as if he had sprouted horns. "Sir, I . . ."

Dylon raised his hand to silence his servant, but he never took his eyes off the curvaceous blonde. "You were ambling around the gardens when you tripped over the stones and fell."

"Sir, I . . ." Percy tried to express his disapproval of Dylon's outrageous prank, but the master of the house was not to be put off.

Dylon sighed melodramatically as he reached out to comb a renegade strand of gold away from Liberty's enchanting face. "But considering the unfortunate spill you've taken, I think it best if we postpone the ceremony until you have recovered your memory."

While Liberty regarded the ornery rogue with wary trepidation, Percy lost his grasp on his composure for the third time in less than an hour. Muffled hisses and curses tumbled from his lips in indecipherable phrases.

"Percy, if you would be so kind as to send a message to the church, informing our guests and the clergyman of our change of plans, I'll take my fiancée back inside to recuperate from her fall."

"The church?" Percy chirped, valiantly battling for self-control and failing miserably. "The guests?"

Dylon's broad chest reverberated with a hearty chuckle. "Good God, man, one would think *you* were the one who was stricken with amnesia rather than my lovely bride-to-be."

Percy knew full well that Dylon intended to utilize this situation to his advantage, just as he always did. Dylon was a master at it, with much practice and success to his credit. He was in dire need of an escort to accompany him to Brewster's semiannual celebrations and this beguiling nymph had fallen out of his magnolia tree, right into his hands. But if Dylon thought Brewster could find fault with this angelic creature he was a fool. This scheme would backfire in Dylon's face, just see if it didn't!

"Sir, I feel compelled to warn you that if you're thinking what I *think* you're thinking, you might find yourself . . ."

"*Now*, will be soon enough to attend your task, Percival," Dylon demanded before his valet's runaway tongue revealed more information than necessary. "*The church*, Percival. Kindly contact the clergyman and our guests and inform them of the change in plans."

"But, sir . . ." he tried to object again.

Dylon half turned from his hunkered position beside Liberty to glare directly at his servant. "I have always been most indulgent and tolerant of you, as you well know," he reminded Percy with a meaningful stare. "But there are times, my friend, when I wish you would do as you're told without trying to counsel me!"

Percy was taken aback when Dylon's voice grew louder by the syllable. Master Dylon rarely raised his voice, rarely wavered from his façade of nonchalance. It wasn't difficult to tell when Dylon was on the verge of losing his temper, even if it didn't happen very often. *Now* Dylon was annoyed and hell-bent on having his way.

"Forgive me, sir." Percy apologized in a courtly tone. He straightened his jacket and adjusted his Bag wig. "You are right, of course. I have forgotten myself." His look indicated he didn't think he was the only one!

After flinging Dylon another disconcerted glance Percy executed an about-face that would have done the militia proud. He strode toward the house to send a message to the church where Dylon had not intended to go in the first place, and not one guest waited in the second place! He paused at the door and pivoted to stare at Dylon, hoping his master would come to his senses and reconsider. Dylon had no intention of aborting his scheme. With a heavy sigh of disapproval and a disappointed shake of his head Percy disappeared into the house.

When they were alone, Dylon focused his attention and his irresistible smile on the young woman who was still staring at him with wary consternation. "Do you think you broke any bones when you fell, my love?" he cooed at her.

Liberty wanted to curse and slap away the hand that moved familiarly over her exposed leg. But she had backed herself into a corner and allowed this rake to manipulate her. "Nay, I think not. Just kindly help me up."

When Dylon's hands clamped around her waist and he had set her to her feet, her leg buckled without warning. Liberty would have collapsed in an untidy heap if Dylon hadn't snaked his arm around her to lend additional support.

"Perhaps not broken, but most certainly twisted," he diagnosed as he scooped her up in his arms and carried her toward the house.

The feel of his muscular body brushing against hers, the feel of his sinewy arms wrapped around her bare legs sent unexpected shock waves undulating through every fiber of her being. Liberty flinched at her instantaneous reaction to this scoundrel. She didn't know why he had concocted that story about her (perfect stranger that she was) being his fiancée (which, by the way, was the last thing she needed since she had two fiancés already!). But in all fairness, Liberty did admit that she probably deserved this most recent tangle she'd got herself into. After all, she had lied through her teeth about her lapse of memory and she had tried to prey on Dylon's sympathy and hospitality. If "Dylon dahling" wanted to substitute her for "Nora dear," who had stamped off in a huff, that was understandable. As long as this handsome rake didn't get any ideas about how friendly Liberty would be in his company, she would play along . . . for a time.

Liberty was in dire need of sanctuary from her scheming uncle and from Simon Gridley. Apparently Dylon needed a female escort to replace the one who'd abandoned him when he refused to propose marriage. Of course, Dylon had no intention of marrying her, nor she him. She supposed he had only clutched at that tall tale of an upcoming marriage because she was garbed in a wedding gown. In order to spare herself a confrontation with Simon and Luther, Liberty would employ this situation to *her* advantage.

What could it hurt? she asked herself. This philanderer didn't really want a wife any more than she wanted a husband. Fate had simply offered both of them a solution to their individual problems. Why should she look a gift horse in the mouth?

Settling into her role as the woman without a past, Liberty allowed Dylon to carry her into the resplendent study that was situated on the west wing of the mansion. And whether Dylon believed her or not, which he obviously didn't, she was going to project the image of an amnesic. Sooner or later he would believe her. And later she would slip silently into the shadows, fetch her maid and sail back to the islands she never should have left to begin with!

Chapter 5

Leaving Liberty to her own devices, Dylon strode through the hall that attached his office to the main house. After briefing the servants on the arrival of his mysterious guest, Dylon cautioned the staff about asking prying questions or doing anything that would distress the young lady who had conveniently lost her memory.

With a heaping tray of food in hand, Dylon retraced his steps, only to find his staunchly proper valet blocking his path like a boulder.

"I sent a courier to the church with your message," Percy mocked in a tone that could not be labeled as offensive, only blatantly disapproving. "Now, kindly tell me what you are planning so that I may know how to proceed from here."

It was glaringly apparent that Percy did not condone Dylon's scheme of providing himself with an escort to Brewster's estate.

"I would appreciate it if you would simply follow my lead," Dylon requested. "We will see how the rest of the day unfolds."

Percy's thick brows formed a single line over his silver-gray eyes. "If this sly scheme of yours blows up in your face, I trust you will be gracious enough to allow me to say I told you so."

Dylon balanced the tray in one hand and patted Percy

on the shoulder with the other. "My good friend, when have you ever refrained from expressing your opinions in that critical but oh-so-polite way of yours?" he teased.

"I only speak out for your own good, sir," Percy contended. "'Tis my duty, my obligation in life."

Dylon peered down at the older man who stood five inches shorter than himself, marveling at Percy's unyielding sense of propriety. "Do you dislike the idea of utilizing opportunity when it practically lands in my lap?" A wry smile quirked his lips. "Has it not occurred to you that perhaps that vivacious young lady might be using *me* as well?"

Percy blinked like an awakened owl.

Dylon chuckled at the startled expression that was plastered on his valet's features. When it came to that mysterious minx in white satin, Percy seemed to have lost his grip on his composure and had suddenly become quite gullible. "Unless I miss my guess, and I doubt I have, the lady would prefer to forget that she is married or that she was about to be. I imagine it suited her purpose to pretend amnesia. I intend to see how far she has to be pushed before she confesses the truth."

"Surely she wouldn't lie about a loss of memory," Percy protested.

"Nay?" One black brow arched in contradiction. "Desperation and necessity are oftentimes the parents of invention. I know perfectly well that a woman is capable of lying when it suits her. Nora Flannery is a shining example and Patricia . . ." His voice trailed off, his face clouded and a scowl passed his lips.

Percy struck a stolid pose. His gaze flooded over Dylon with scornful mockery. "It also seems that desperation has led *you* to take the young lady as your betrothed, even when you know nothing about her."

Dylon shrugged with characteristic nonchalance. "I know that she is quick-witted and exceptionally lovely. I'm sure she will prove herself to be an amusing distraction."

"You amuse yourself too much," Percy had the

audacity to say.

"And you, not enough," Dylon countered with a good-natured grin. "Now, my friend, will you be joining my fiancée and me for our meal?"

Percy dusted his hands and brushed away the powder that had trickled onto his shoulder from his Bag wig. "Thank you, sir, but nay, I will not," he declined with elaborate politeness. "I find I have no appetite left, nor the stomach for your little games."

Having spoken his mind, the valet proudly drew himself up, wheeled like a soldier on parade and marched down the hall in swift precise strides.

Snickering, Dylon continued on his way. When he ambled into the study he found the pert blonde inspecting the numerous books that graced the shelves.

Upon hearing the whine of the door, Liberty spun herself around. The aroma of meat and fresh bread filled her senses. She stared at the tray like a famished creature. And indeed she was! After her first two unsuccessful escape attempts on the eve of her wedding, Simon had tried to starve her into submission. She had been served no evening meal and no breakfast. She had also been deprived of nourishment while she was coiled in the luggage department of Dylon's carriage.

When Dylon set the tray on the desk Liberty attacked it as if she had been on prison rations until this moment. Grinning in amusement, Dylon watched the mysterious nymph devour her meal like a python. He studied her bewitching appearance, the graceful way she moved, the fascinating way she perched on the edge of his desk, letting her bare leg dangle while she consumed the food with both hands.

Liberty was so engrossed in appeasing her ravenous appetite that she was oblivious to the unladylike fashion in which she sat, the indecent amount of flesh she displayed. Although she was distracted by the food, Dylon was distracted by the tantalizing picture she presented.

What was there about this rambunctious female that

fascinated him so? Aye, she was gorgeous by anyone's standards. And aye, she had a body that would stop a stampede of wild horses. But there was something else that captivated him, something in those lavender eyes that bespoke vitality, hinted at an incredible zest for living.

Portraying the role he had designed for himself—the love-smitten beau—Dylon unfolded himself from his chair and tugged Liberty into his arms. Without preamble, his mouth slanted across her heart-shaped lips, stealing the breath from her lungs.

Liberty had just recently worked the kinks from her strained knee, but it threatened to fold up again. When she wilted, Dylon's arms encircled her waist, pulling her full length against him. He bestowed another steamy kiss on her, losing himself in the erotic taste and feel of her body molded provocatively to his.

The warm threat of his powerful body assaulted her. Unexpected tingles of pleasure rippled through her, causing a fleet of goose bumps to cruise across her skin. My, but this rake oozed with earthy sensuality! And he seemed quite experienced in kissing a woman senseless. Liberty had been kissed before, but never had a man left her gasping for breath. She had considered herself immune to lusty libertines, but then, she had to admit she had never encountered a man who was as suave and skillful as Dylon Lockhart!

"What was that all about?" Liberty demanded to know when Dylon finally allowed her to come up for air.

His quiet laughter sensitized the small space between them. "I thought perhaps a kiss would refresh your memory, my love. You cannot know how I lament that you have forgotten the magic between us."

Oh, he was a sly one, thought Liberty. She had already concluded that Dylon had no principles where women were concerned. This rascal intended to take full advantage of the situation. But two could play this little game of his and she considered herself worthy competition.

Pressing her hands against his massive chest, she pushed him a respectable distance away and hobbled around the desk on her bum leg. "Whatever was between us has changed," she informed him, cursing the fact that he constantly smiled that devilishly attractive smile. Lord, the man would probably smile all the way to the gallows! Nothing seemed to faze him or crack his air of casual nonchalance. "Now we are like strangers who have to become reacquainted all over again."

Two thick brows elevated in mock surprise. "You expect me to forget how much we mean to each other? Forget how I have held you in my arms, touching and caressing your lovely body, memorizing each luscious curve and swell . . . ?"

"You most certainly have not!" Liberty burst out without thinking. Quickly, she slammed her mouth shut and presented her back. "That is to say . . . I have no recollection of those things. 'Tis as if they never happened."

An ornery grin pursed his lips as he swaggered toward the charading imp. Gently, he slid his hand around her waist and turned her to face him. "Let me tell you the way it was between us. Or better yet, let me show you. . . ."

"I'd rather you wouldn't," Liberty bleated, cursing herself for responding to this rake's touch, to the fragrant magic of his cologne which completely fogged her senses.

Tenderly, he reached up to trace her elegant features. "Even Romeo and Juliet did not share as great a love as we found with each other."

His hand slid along her partially bare shoulder and trailed down the daring cut of her gown. Liberty flinched at the arousing feel of his fingertips on her bare flesh. She wasn't dealing with the village idiot, that was for sure! Dylon was an incorrigible flirt and he was as quick-witted and wily as Liberty was. Godamercy, what had she gotten herself into this time?

"From the moment we met, we both knew we were

destined to be together. . . ." He breathed against the sensitive point on her neck.

"Were we?" Liberty gulped down her heart when it climbed the ladder of her ribs to constrict her throat.

"Mmm . . . most definitely." His voice dropped to a most seductive purr and his wayward hand continued to incite tingles which skittered down her spine. "And it was you who first kissed me, offering pleasures of the intimacies to come. You wound your arms around my neck like this . . ." He drew her hands over the broad expanse of his chest and settled them on his shoulders. "And you pressed ever closer, tempting me with promises in your eyes . . ."

His head came deliberately toward hers. His lips courted hers like a bee courting nectar. His questing tongue traced her soft mouth before gliding into the dark recesses. His arms enfolded her, molding her supple curves into his masculine contours.

Although Dylon's initial intent was to shock this lying little minx into a confession, his motive changed drastically when he lost himself to the delicious taste of her lips. He suddenly forgot everything except the burning need that uncoiled inside him. He could see the sparks, feel the fire. Desire raised its unruly head, straining against its chains of confinement.

Before Dylon realized it he was pulling Liberty closer. His hands wandered of their own accord, discovering the titillating curves and swells that were so enticingly displayed by her gown.

"Enough!" Liberty lurched around to flee from the sizzling sensations that swept over her like a forest fire, leaving her burning in places she didn't even know she had. Her foot caught on the leg of the tuft chair and she plunked down into it before she fell into an unceremonious heap on the floor.

With breasts heaving from the aftereffects of his arousing kisses, Liberty peered goggle-eyed at the six-foot-two-inch, two-hundred-pound mass of masculinity who loomed over her. Before she could compose herself, Dylon bent over her. His lips whispered over her bare shoulder and drifted down the soft swells of her breasts. Sparks leaped from him to her and back again, leaving Liberty doubting her ability to handle this skillfully seductive rake.

Sporting a flirtatious grin, one he wore too damned well to suit Liberty's tastes, Dylon brushed his index finger over the fabric which covered the taut tip of her breast. "Even if you don't remember the feelings, your body does. They're still there, aren't they, my love? Simmering just beneath the surface. . . ."

"I think I should lie down," Liberty squeaked. "My head is spinning again."

"And I will join you," Dylon murmured seductively. "Where you go, I go also. 'Tis how a love like ours is meant to be."

"Nay, 'tis not!" Liberty yelped. "I mean . . . I need to rest . . . alone. . . ."

"But of course." Dylon gathered his feet beneath him and drew Liberty up beside him. "Perhaps after you've slept, you will begin to remember what you *seem* to have forgotten. And if sleep does not remedy the situation, I will do my best to strike another chord of memory. . . ."

The look he gave her was a silent challenge, daring her to continue this charade and see exactly where it got her—in his bed, no doubt.

Liberty tilted a proud chin, infuriated that she had been outmaneuvered by this ornery rascal with laughing blue eyes. So he intended to provoke her and rattle her until she broke down and confessed the truth, did he? Well, she wouldn't do it! If he could be impossibly mischievous, she could be incredibly stubborn. That was, after all, one of her most noticeable faults.

Liberty sorted through her repertoire of impish smiles and offered him one of highest quality. "Perhaps I will remember what I have forgotten, Dylon *dahling*," she purred. "And perhaps by then, *you* will also have come to *your* senses. . . ."

With a graceful pirouette that was marred only by a slight limp, Liberty sashayed toward the door. Bug-eyed, Dylon stared after her. "Dylon dahling"? That sounded just like Nora.

"Why did you call me that?" he wanted to know that very second.

Wearing an impudent smile that rivaled Dylon's ornery grins, Liberty darted a glance over her shoulder. "That's another thing I can't seem to remember," she taunted him.

"How very convenient for you," Dylon grumbled.

"Isn't it though?" she said all too sweetly.

When Liberty ambled away, Dylon's dark brows puckered in a perplexed frown. How could this minx have known what Nora called him? Dylon drew a blank. Good God, who was this woman and where had she come from? Had Nora put her up to torment him for refusing to propose? Surely not, but how the devil did . . . ?

"Sir, the lady requests a room in which to lie down." Percival's bland voice jolted Dylon back to the present.

"Show her into the room beside mine," Dylon instructed, still frowning ponderously. "And Percy?"

The valet pivoted and raised an inquisitive brow. "Aye, sir?"

"Keep an eye on that sprite," Dylon requested. "Judging from her past track record, she might decide to leap off the balcony into the tree again."

Percy looked down his nose at Dylon. "And I wouldn't blame her one whit if she did," he replied stiffly before he turned around and walked off.

When the door clanked shut, Dylon ambled over to munch on his meal. Even after that saucy minx had left, her vision still lingered in the room, teasing him, tempting him, frustrating him. Who the blazes was that woman? Who was she hiding from? And where the sweet loving hell had she come from, that's what he'd like to know!

Very soon I'll find out, Dylon assured himself confidently. He would see how far that imp intended to carry her scheme to protect the secrets of her past. A tremor of anticipation riveted through him, visualizing tantalizing methods of prying information out of her. Damn, he could almost taste her petal-soft lips beneath his, almost feel her delectable body meshed against his, see her fluttering atop the tree like a carefree bird. . . .

Dylon suddenly thought about Percy and his grim predictions. Aye, Percy might very well be right. Before this little charade was over, Dylon might be wishing he *hadn't* taken life quite so lightly. For once, he may have found amusement at *his* own expense. He hated to admit it, but that shapely blonde in white satin mystified him, temporarily at least. But by the time they returned from the holiday in the Up Country, the lure would be gone, Dylon assured himself. By then, he would have tired of this particular female. He always had and he always would. Since Patricia had taught him the meaning of betrayal, Dylon had never allowed himself to become emotionally involved with a woman. He trifled with them until he lost interest and then sought out another conquest. This blond-haired sprite would be no different, Dylon mused as he sipped his Madeira wine. No different at all.

Now wasn't that a shining example of famous last words. . . .

Dylon broke into a smile when his younger brother sauntered through the front door with a pretty redhead on his arm. Lovely though the young lass was, she appeared painfully shy and reserved. Her velvet gown was modest in appearance with its lace tippet that covered her bosom and the empire-style waist concealed her shapely figure.

When Griffin made the formal introductions, the young woman smiled demurely and stared at the carpet as if something there fascinated her. She spoke only when Dylon directed a question at her and she knew just the right thing to say at just the right moment. Her prim little smile constantly remained intact, as if it had been glued on her lips.

When Cayla Styles requested a room to freshen up from her trip, Griffin called to the housekeeper to show his guest upstairs. After Cayla had taken her leave, Griffin, who was the spitting image of his older brother and two years Dylon's junior, raised an inquisitive brow.

"So . . . where is your escort, brother?" he wanted to know. "Is she as suitable as mine?" Griff chuckled lightly. "I'm sure Brewster will be disappointed to find my companion is as quiet as a church mouse and as obedient as a puppy."

Dylon eased back on the couch and nursed the brandy he'd been sipping before his brother sailed in like a flying carpet. "I expected you earlier this afternoon," he commented evasively.

Griffin eyed his older brother with blatant curiosity. "Don't tell me you returned from Charles Town without a female in tow?" He snickered. "You know perfectly well that Brewster will line you up with every available female in the area if you arrive alone."

"Your dear brother won't be alone," Percy declared as he marched stoically into the room, carrying Griffin's brandy. "In fact, we all have reason to celebrate. Dylon not only has an escort but also a fiancée." He flung Dylon a stony-faced glance before returning his attention to Griffin who seemed to have been frozen to his spot. "But alas, I had to cancel this afternoon's wedding because the young lady took a nasty spill from yonder magnolia tree and she cannot seem to remember who she is."

Having dropped the bomb in Dylon's lap and leaving Griffin thunderstruck, Percy spitefully took his leave.

Jaw sagging, Griffin gaped at his brother. "What on earth . . . ?" He tapped the side of his head. "I could have sworn I heard Percy say you almost got married this afternoon. Lord, I must have been imagining all this."

As was his custom, Dylon chuckled nonchalantly. "'Tis a long, complicated story."

"Condense it," Griffin insisted before gulping down his drink.

"Very well, I'll be brief. My original date, Miss Nora Flannery, refused to accompany me home without a marriage proposal so I left her pouting on her doorstep," Dylon reported. "When Percy and I returned, we discovered a young lady swinging in the magnolia tree in her wedding gown." Although Griff emitted shocked gasps and strangled on his swig of brandy, Dylon continued after whacking his brother between the shoulder blades. "She fell, of course, and knocked herself out. When she roused she declared she had no recollection of her past. And I, in need of an escort, insisted that she was my fiancée."

"That's crazy!" Griffin hooted in disbelief. "Who is this woman?"

Dylon casually sipped his brandy and shrugged. "I don't have the faintest idea who she is. But I . . ." His voice trailed off when lo and behold, the aforementioned young lady appeared in the doorway.

Liberty screeched to a halt when she spied the man who was obviously Dylon's brother, judging from the striking family resemblance. The younger Lockhart stared wide-eyed at her.

Liberty had doffed her wedding gown after Verna Ross, the housekeeper, had gathered more comfortable clothes to replace the dress the house guest had arrived in. The garments were not befitting a lady of quality, but rather a servant. But there was little else to be had. The gauze blouse lay across Liberty's shoulders, baring her tanned shoulders. The peasant-type skirt fit snugly at the hips and flared at the hem, presenting Liberty's feminine assets in a most intriguing manner.

Griffin strangled on his drink a second time as he ran an appraising eye over the luscious vision before him. It only took a second to realize this curvaceous elf wore nothing beneath the flimsy blouse. That in itself was enough to tantalize and distract, but the exotic beauty of her features and the glorious mane of unbound hair dramatized her sexual appeal.

In truth, Liberty had been delighted with the garments which resembled the style of clothes she had worn on the islands. Verna had apologized all over herself for being unable to present the young lady with proper attire. But Liberty had no complaints . . . until Griffin and Dylon's roving eyes made a feast of her. She didn't realize the sunlight was spraying through the thin fabric of her blouse, exposing the curve of her breasts and tapered waist. But Griffin and Dylon had definitely noticed and it was having an arousing effect on their male anatomies.

Like a stirring lion, Dylon rose to swagger across the room. He took Liberty's hand in his to guide her forward. "Griffin, you of course, remember my fiancée, even if she has no memory of either of us."

"Of course," Griffin breathed raggedly. "Who could forget such beauty." He pressed a kiss to her wrist and inhaled the scintillating scent that clung to her satiny skin. Lord, what a vision of loveliness! This delicious morsel of femininity looked good enough to eat. "How nice to see you again, my lady. As always, you are breathtaking."

Liberty spared Dylon a quick glance. So he had informed his brother of this little charade, she guessed. The entire household had obviously been advised to play along. Dylon Lockhart was very thorough, she'd give him that. He had explained her sudden appearance with skillful ease. She wondered how this suave rake would explain her abrupt *dis*appearance. But as smooth as he was, she imagined he had an explanation for everything.

"Dylon was just telling me why you had to cancel the wedding," Griffin commented with a smile. "I hope you are feeling better by now."

The only thing that would make Liberty feel better

would be to snatch up the expensive figurine that graced the tea table and club both these ornery galoots over the head with it.

"I have at least remembered my name," Liberty baited with a disarming smile. "'Tis a start. But sadly, I must report that I can recall very little else."

She could see both men straining at the leash, wondering how they were going to worm that precious tidbit of information out of her without appearing obvious. She intended to tell them, only to simplify matters . . . after she kept these two blue-eyed rakes in suspense awhile, that is. But the information would do them no good whatosever. She had been living in the islands for fifteen years and she doubted anyone in the area was familiar with the name. Her family's plantation was known as Triple Oak and since Luther Norris had been in charge, chances were no one would make the connection.

"Well, that is a relief," Dylon declared, unsure quite how to proceed. He could tell by that lively sparkle in her violet eyes that she was delighting in this mischievous prank of hers. But there were ways to wrest the information out of her—delightful, pleasurable ways. . . .

"If only you could remember the way we were . . ." Dylon said with a whimsical sigh. Despite his brother's presence, he molded Liberty's luscious body to his and threatened to kiss her blind.

"Liberty . . . Liberty Jordon," she announced, dodging his oncoming kiss. "There. You see? I did remember who I am."

Liberty . . . Dylon silently repeated the name that seemed to suit this spirited beauty perfectly. She was like a wild untamed bird who strained against any type of captivity. *Jordon* . . . Dylon frowned, certain he'd heard that name before. But he couldn't recall where. There was no one in the area by that name and he wasn't sure he'd heard it in Charles Town either. But, of course, this sly sprite wouldn't have divulged her name at all if she thought there was even a remote possibility of being recognized. And it could have been an assumed name, Dylon reminded himself. But at least it was a start. And little by little, he would draw vital information from her. (*Kiss* it out of her, he amended with wicked glee.)

When Cayla Styles swept gracefully into the room, Griffin performed the formal introductions. The fact that Liberty was garbed in a most unusual manner for a bona fide lady caused Cayla to fumble. She had been taught to compliment the attire of her female peers and now she was at a loss. For a moment, Liberty thought Cayla meant to break the mold and speak her own mind. Unfortunately, Cayla nibbled on her bottom lip, stared at the floor and sank primly into a chair.

Liberty tried very hard to communicate with the pretty redhead. Since her arrival in the colonies Luther had kept her in isolation and refused to allow her to form any friendships. And now that Liberty had the opportunity to associate with her own kind, Cayla had nothing to say except conditioned responses to anticipated questions. Twice Liberty thought she had succeeded in drawing Cayla out, but the redhead always seemed to catch herself before she broke some hard and fast rule that had been drilled into her head. She closed up like a clam, pasted a pleasant smile on her lips and sat docilely in her chair.

When Percy announced the evening meal was to be served, Liberty abandoned her attempt to converse with Cayla. It quickly became apparent that the redhead was a credit to her table manners and very little else. If Cayla possessed any intelligence she was doing a superb job of hiding it. It was also painfully obvious to Liberty that she would never fit in with the gentry of the colonies. She had grown up in the islands where social structure wasn't so vividly defined and her father had indulged her most every whim. Liberty was a misfit who had not a place in colonial society.

Ah well, Liberty mused as she gobbled her meal of

crabs, oysters, hot bread and a list of succulent vegetables that was too long to mention. She didn't plan to remain in the colonies long enough to fret about fitting in. As soon as opportunity presented itself she would flee from her pretended fiancé. "Dylon dahling" could find himself another pigeon. And there wasn't going to be any more kissing either, Liberty promised herself fiercely. Every time that raven-haired rake came near her she truly did forget who and where she was! He also knew his way around a female's body better than a practicing physician! The man made her extremely nervous, made her tingle with sensations that were wild and yet frightening . . . in an arousing sort of way.

Biding her time, Liberty listened to Dylon and Griffin discuss the workings of the plantation. But suddenly she found her curiosity getting the best of her. Whether they considered it a woman's place to be interested in business, Liberty leaped into the conversation with both feet. She was not about to sit through the meal, munching politely on little nibbles of food and minding her manners. If that was Cayla's goal in life, that was her business. But Liberty did not have to sit there like a bump on a log and so she didn't.

Naturally, that didn't surprise Dylon one iota. In fact, he wondered how this vivacious virago had managed to hold her tongue as long as she had.

Chapter 6

"How long have you been raising indigo?" Liberty inquired, plunging into the conversation. "I'm not familiar with . . ." She caught herself, realizing she was giving away information about her background with the careless comment.

And sure enough, Dylon peered ponderously at her, knowing this saucy blonde was not a resident of the area. He had suspected as much, judging by her slight accent and the golden tan that caressed her enchanting features. Ah, what an enigma this sprite was. He found himself more intrigued with each passing second. There were so many questions he wanted answered but Liberty stubbornly refused to supply them.

"What I meant to say was that I don't *recall* much of anything except my name," she continued with a smile that left Griffin and Dylon swearing the sun had just risen in the confines of the dining room to blind them.

Hypnotized by the radiance of the bedazzling smile, Dylon found himself telling her everything she wanted to know. "Indigo has become a substantial crop in South Carolina. The swamp country is ideal because of its fertile soil and the availability of fresh water," he informed her between bites. "And it will probably please you to know that it was actually a young woman by the name of Eliza Lucas Pinckney who first experimented with the flowering plants."

"I'm not the least bit surprised," Liberty insisted with another elfin grin. "Contrary to popular belief—ones held by those of the male persuasion—women are quite capable of filling successful and prominent positions in society."

Griffin glanced at the delectable blonde before his eyes settled on his older brother. Already Griffin was becoming envious. He had saddled himself with a taciturn female companion, but Dylon had stumbled onto a lively, spirited young woman who had already proven herself to be stimulating company—in more ways than one!

"Tell me more about Eliza," Liberty enthused. "I think I would very much like to make her acquaintance."

Griffin couldn't help himself. He dived into the conversation, preferring it to exchanging meaningless pleasantries with Cayla. "Eliza began her experiments in 1740 on Wappo Plantation, which is located six miles from Charles Town on the Ashley River. After three or four years of trial and error, Eliza managed to process the plants into blocks of blue dyestuff that London merchants claimed to be of excellent quality."

"Eliza was only sixteen at the time," Dylon inserted, amused by his brother's eagerness to converse with Liberty rather than his own date. Not that Dylon blamed Griffin one whit. Liberty was by far the most inquisitive and fascinating female he'd ever encountered. "Since indigo can be grown on uplands fields, out of danger from floods which plague our rice crops, it has proved to be an excellent crop. The plant is about the same size as a thin cotton stalk."

"Aye, I am familiar with the production of cotton, sugar, coffee and . . ." Liberty gnashed her teeth and silently cursed her runaway tongue. If she didn't think before she spoke she'd give herself away completely!

Dylon digested the information, growing more suspicious and curious by the second. Who was this woman?

She wasn't from Charles Town. But how had she known about his brief, unfortunate affair with Nora Flannery? And how had she become an authority on crops that were grown to the south of this colony? Damnit, where'd she come from!

Shoving his wandering thoughts aside, Dylon concentrated on the topic at hand. "Indigo has to be cut when mature and separated by soaking in vats that are diluted with lime. The process is laborious, messy and stinks to high heaven. But the price of indigo has skyrocketed. Since England has always detested paying France for their source of the blue dye, Parliament granted sixpence a pound to American producers. For years it has galled Englishmen to buy products from their natural-born enemy—the French. They encourage colonial production to avoid any more contact with France than necessary."

"And since England has been buying £200,000 worth of indigo cakes per year, the crop has become as profitable as rice," Griffin interjected.

"And all because of an assertive young woman," Liberty teased mischievously. "Where would this colony be without her?"

Dylon chuckled at the pert imp. "And where, my love, would I be without you?" he countered with a cunning smile and a seductive glance that put Liberty right back on defense.

Liberty squirmed uneasily in her chair. Dylon, lusty rakehell that he was, had reverted to contemplating her as if *she* were the meal he wanted to devour. Godamercy! How could he look at her in that provocative way of his, causing tingles to trickle down her spine, making her heart lurch with forbidden pleasure? Blast it, it wasn't fair. No man deserved to be as handsome and devastating as Dylon Lockhart. He was a definite threat to the female population and he didn't need to be running around loose, breaking hearts by the dozens.

What annoyed Liberty to no end was that she found it

impossible not to like Dylon. He was dynamic, personable, incredibly attractive and she expected that he was the life of every party he'd ever attended. He was that impressive and commanding. Liberty was confident of her ability to compete with him on an intellectual level. Her father had imported the most knowledgeable tutors available to instruct her the past ten years. But Dylon was far more worldly than she and she wasn't sure she could trust herself alone with him. Honestly and truly, when he captured her in those brawny arms and plied her with fiery kisses, she swore he had transformed her into a quivering jellyfish. How'd he do that to her? And how was she supposed to stop him from doing that to her? Was there no antidote for this charismatic rake? Liberty was beginning to think there wasn't. And if there wasn't, she was treading on thin ice. The sooner she made her escape from Lockhart Hall the better off she'd be! She found herself becoming more and more intrigued by that blue-eyed rogue with the captivating smile. And *that* was dangerous!

When the dishes had been cleared from the table, Griffin courteously asked Cayla if she would like to take a stroll through the gardens. With her polite smile intact, Cayla replied with, "If it pleases you, Griffin, it pleases me."

Liberty was absolutely certain she would never fit in here. She'd never be caught dead making such submissive comments to a man! Poor Cayla. She was a puppet who had been groomed to fulfill the position of an obedient daughter and dutiful wife. What a dull existence the poor girl led.

When Griffin excused himself and reluctantly ambled off with Cayla draped on his arm, Dylon eased back in his chair and stared thoughtfully at Liberty. "And what, my sweet Liberty, would please *you* this evening?" he mocked playfully. "Pleasuring you would pleasure me. . . ."

Liberty ignored the suggestive remark. She was not

about to fall into any sort of trap, other than the one she already found herself in. And if Dylon thought for one minute that she would ever aspire to be as subservient as that shrinking Southern violet, he'd damned well better think again!

"You can be sure, Dylon *dahling*, that pleasing you in any fashion whatsoever is the least of my concerns," she told him in no uncertain terms. "I'm nothing like Cayla and I shall never aspire to be."

Dylon threw back his head and laughed heartily. Liberty was such a drastic change from the women he'd courted in the past. She had the curiosity of a cat, the daring of a tigress and the tongue of a cobra. She constantly challenged and amused him . . . fascinated him. . . .

"Then what would you like to do to while away the hours, my love?" he asked generously. "You have only to voice your whims and I shall see them done."

"Cards perhaps? Or archery? Or maybe even target practice?" she suggested, attempting to shock that infuriating smile off his sensuous lips.

Just plain lips, Liberty hastily corrected herself. She was not going to notice what a luscious mouth he had, how his baby blue eyes twinkled at her, the way his garments hugged his powerful physique like a second set of skin. She was *not* attracted to this rake. He was just another of the many men she'd met the past twenty years.

"Cards, archery and riflery are men's pastimes," Dylon reminded her with a teasing smile.

"Are they?" she replied in a sugary tone. "I guess I must have forgotten."

Dylon wagered she had forgotten nothing. And he would also have bet hard-earned money that this free-spirited misfit was adept at every hobby she'd mentioned. And on what planet had she been living that permitted a female to dabble in activities that were considered masculine pastimes? Damn, he'd give his eyeteeth for the answer to that question. It was for certain this rambunctious nymph had not spent her formative years in the family parlor, perfecting stitchery! As vibrant and active as she was, she wouldn't have been able to sit still long enough to wield knitting needles.

"Perhaps we can amuse ourselves with a little of everything this evening," Dylon murmured, his seductive tone suggesting he had far more arousing activities in mind than handling weapons and shuffling cards.

"I have every intention of amusing myself . . . within reason," Liberty declared, casting him a warning glance. "Even *I* have my limitations as to what I will consent to do."

"Do you now?" One black brow arched in taunt. "After watching you swing through the magnolia tree like a chimpanzee, I wouldn't have thought so." For an instant his smile vanished, replaced by an inquisitive frown. "What the devil were you doing in that tree anyway?"

Liberty blessed him with an impish smile. "I'm so sorry to report that is another thing I cannot seem to remember."

"Nay, of course not. How silly of me to bother asking," Dylon grunted as he unfolded himself from the chair.

In long lithe strides, he circled the table to assist Liberty from her chair and into his arms. All the recently discovered sensations of desire hit Liberty full force when she found herself engulfed in Dylon's strong arms. His masterful kiss turned her legs to rubber, her brain to mush. It baffled her that this particular rake continued to have such an arousing effect on her. She had met his kind before and she could see no reason why this blue-eyed, midnight-haired rogue should affect her so. She knew he was only toying with her because she was convenient, because sex was second nature to him. That in itself should have repulsed her, but curse it, it didn't!

When he raised his raven head, Liberty peered up at him, struggling to maintain control of her chaotic emotions. "Why must you persist in doing that? I will tell you when I wish to be kissed!" she snapped, annoyed with him for kissing her senseless and herself for enjoying it!

Dylon grinned into her animated features. "You need to be kissed and kissed often," he assured her with great conviction.

Liberty gave him what *he* needed, a sound whack across his dimpled cheeks. "And you, Dylon *dahling*, need to be reminded that I am not a toy that can be snatched up and played with each time it meets your whim!"

He chortled at her explosive temper. "Come along, vixen. We'll set up a target and you can take out your frustrations with a bow and arrow."

Liberty glared at his broad back as he sauntered away. She visualized a bull's-eye pinned to his linen shirt and her arrow quivering right smack dab in the middle of it. "I've already found my target," she sniped. "I only hope he'll stand still when I draw down on my bow."

Dylon lurched around. His dark brows jackknifed at the spitefulness in her voice. "You would shoot me, the light and love of your life? The man who got down on his knees and pledged his undying love to you forevermore?" he questioned in mock horror.

Liberty sashayed past him, pausing to pat his clean-shaven cheek. "In a minute, Dylon *dahling* . . . in a minute. . . ."

While Percy was gathering the weapons and setting up the target as Dylon requested, Simon was cursing the air blue. He and Luther had wasted an entire day, searching every nook and cranny on the two West Indian-bound schooners in Charles Town bay. They had turned up nothing in their exhausting efforts. Simon still didn't have a clue what had become of his runaway bride.

Annoyed beyond words, Simon barked the order for his three henchmen to gather his luggage and follow him into the "ordinary" that was located between Charles Town and his plantation upriver. Along the way, Simon and Luther had questioned every traveler they'd happened upon. But no one recalled seeing a fetching blonde in a wedding gown. Damn, it was as if that witch truly had vanished into thin air!

Simon paused at the door of the tavern, searching the faces of the other guests, hoping to catch a glimpse of his elusive bride. But Liberty was nowhere to be seen.

"Where in the hell could she be?" Simon grumbled as he stamped toward the clerk's desk to demand a room for the night.

Luther wisely kept silent. Each time he dared to open his mouth, Simon chewed him up one side and down the other for permitting Liberty to flee before the wedding ceremony. Since Liberty had not scurried onto a schooner to sail to the Indies, Luther predicted his pesky niece had found some means of returning to Triple Oak to retrieve her maid. Attempting to outguess Liberty, Luther had sent a courier thundering to the plantation to alert his servants in hopes of apprehending her. He could only hope he would return to Triple Oak to find both Stella Talbot and Liberty confined to the house.

Chomping on that positive thought, Luther trudged up the steps to his rented room. Liberty had damned well better be locked in the house, guarded by his trusted servants! That would probably be all that saved him from Simon's wrath. And considering the hold Simon had over him, Luther could expect to endure nine kinds of hell if Liberty did manage to slip away scot-free.

A snake of apprehension slid down Luther's spine. If Liberty didn't turn up soon, Luther's life wouldn't be worth a shilling! Blast it, where was that sassy niece of his? She'd better be at Triple Oak, enduring the same confinement as that outspoken, disrespectful maid of hers!

* * *

While Percy was tacking up a target on one of the trees that graced the back of Lockhart Hall and Luther and Simon were lounging in their rented rooms, Stella Talbot was creeping through the corridors of Triple Oak. Earlier that afternoon she had overheard the conversations of two couriers who'd arrived within an hour of each other. Stella had heard one of the men announce that he was to deliver a message to Liberty Jordon. Since Liberty had been packed off to Charles Town to marry Simon, the message lay atop the stack of letters on Luther's desk. Stella had every intention of retrieving it, to ensure that it was placed in the hands of its rightful owner.

Casting a cautious glance over her shoulder, Stella inched from her chair in the dining room the instant her posted sentinel had wandered to the kitchen to fetch himself a drink. Her destination was Luther's study. *Liberty's study*, Stella bitterly amended. Just because Luther had made himself at home on the Jordon family plantation and surrounded himself with an army of devoted servants didn't mean this estate belonged to him.

That contemptible, miserable cad! Stella silently fumed. Luther had lured Liberty into a trap with his letter of invitation and he had bustled her into a marriage she didn't want or need. . . .

When Stella heard footsteps echoing in the far end of the foyer, she darted around the corner into the study. With her heart thudding beneath her breasts, praying that she hadn't been missed, Stella waited until the footsteps died into silence. Breathing a sigh of relief, Stella scurried toward the desk to retrieve the message meant for Liberty. After tucking the note in her pocket, Stella stepped back into the hall.

To her dismay, a stampede of servants materialized out of nowhere like hounds chasing down a runaway fox. She found herself surrounded and punished by condescending glares.

"Take your hands off me, swine!" Stella hissed, wrenching her arm away from the male servant who had latched onto her.

"You know the rules," the wiry little man snapped at her. "Mister Luther said you was to stay in yer room, 'cept when you was takin' yer meal."

"Which I just consumed," Stella snapped right back at him, refusing to be intimidated. "And I daresay those distasteful rations were barely fit for human consumption."

"Well, 'tis all yer gettin', like it or not," the little man sneered at her. "And since you've finished yer meal, you've no need to be wanderin' around downstairs. The master sent a message to say he would be returnin' tomorrow night." He failed to mention that Luther ordered all the servants to be on the lookout for Simon's missing bride. That was something Stella did not need to know! "When the master returns, *then* you can have free run of the house and not an instant before."

Gritting her teeth to prevent bursting into the unladylike curses that flocked to the tip of her tongue, Stella stamped toward the steps. She abhorred being confined in the very house where she had nursed Liberty's dying mother and tended the blond-haired, violet-eyed little girl who had grown up to be dragged off into a contracted marriage. And most of all, Stella detested the fact that she had been unable to come to poor Liberty's rescue. . . .

Poor Liberty, Stella moaned as she stepped into her room, only to hear the lock click behind her. By now Liberty would be Simon Gridley's bride. Stella's nose wrinkled at the disgusting thought.

And poor Phillipe. He would be devastated when he heard the news that his fiancée had been married off to another man while she was taking inventory of her property in the colony!

Stella's square shoulders slumped dispiritedly. She had promised Liberty's mother that she would keep a watchful eye on that high-strung sprite. And the one time Liberty had truly needed her, Stella was being held prisoner in a home that was guarded by Luther's dragons. Damn that conniving man!

After plunking down on her bed, Stella fished into her pocket to retrieve the envelope. Unfolding the letter, she read the note and then heaved another heavy-hearted sigh.

"And what good is this going to do Liberty now?" she questioned the room at large since there was no one around to talk to her—at least no one who was concerned about her or Liberty's plight.

"I told her to stay put in the islands," Stella muttered as she tucked the letter back in her pocket. "Didn't I tell her to marry Phillipe and get on with the rest of her life? But did she listen? Does she ever listen to the good advice I offer?"

Stella grumbled in answer to her own question. "Nay, she does not!" The maid shook her dark head in dismay. "Simon Gridley's bride? God have mercy on that poor child's tortured soul!"

Chapter 7

Disbelief settled on Percy and Dylon's faces when Liberty glided her bow into position with masterful ease and stared down the shaft of the arrow. With only a scant movement of her fingertips she sent the arrow zooming through the air, stabbing dead center in the target Percy had tacked to the tree.

"Beginner's luck," Percy murmured confidentially.

"I rather doubt it," Dylon grunted before he plucked an arrow out of the quiver and drew his own bow. He took careful aim at the arrow that Liberty had notched in the target.

Dylon enjoyed challenging competition, but he'd never before found himself matching his talents against a woman. The fact that he was competing against this particular she-male shook his confidence a trifle. It seemed Liberty was determined to prove herself his equal in any arena.

And why shouldn't she? he asked himself bitterly. Liberty had nothing to lose. If she won she would be hailed as an accomplished archer. But if she lost, the curious servants, as well as Cayla and Griffin who had gathered around them, would simply say she had challenged a man and she wasn't expected to win.

It was Dylon who faced an embarrassing predicament and that ornery imp damned well knew it! If he lost to this capable hoyden, word would spread like wildfire and he would become the brunt of many jokes. And if he won, well that was to be expected. Liberty had cleverly maneuvered him into a situation in which he couldn't possibly hope to enjoy a victory over her, one way or the other.

Oh, how Dylon longed to return this mischievous gesture, leaving *her* to feel the pinch of pressure. He was damned sure feeling it as he focused on his challenger's arrow and the target.

Taking aim, Dylon plucked the string and the arrow hissed toward its intended mark. To his relief, the projectile quivered beside Liberty's.

"It appears you are extremely skillful with a bow," she begrudgingly complimented before positioning herself in front of the target.

"Dylon is a war hero," Percy interjected. "He fought the Cherokees and returned with enough medals pinned to his chest to weigh him down."

Liberty eyed Dylon with newfound respect and a great awareness of just how masterful he was with weapons. "I only hope I can continue to provide ample competition."

Ample? Dylon gnashed his teeth as the curious crowd multiplied like a nest of rabbits. Liberty was as worthy an opponent as he'd ever encountered. Holding his breath, he watched Liberty make a second strike in the bull's-eye.

A murmur of voices whispered through the air, followed by applause from the ever-growing semicircle of onlookers. When Liberty stepped aside, smiling triumphantly, Dylon glided his arrow over the string and uplifted the bow. Just as he drew back, Liberty erupted in artificial coughs and sneezes that were designed to shatter his concentration.

"I'm terribly sorry," she insisted, her tone nowhere near sympathetic. "I hope I didn't disturb your aim, my *dahling*. . . ."

Dylon couldn't help but be amused at her mischievous prank. It had become increasingly apparent that this imp was every bit as ornery as he was, perhaps more so. This was her spiteful way of countering his amorous embraces that she had been most reluctant to accept.

When the arrow whistled through the air and shuddered into the tree, Liberty's smug expression slid off her enchanting features. Damnation, did nothing distract this rake? She had broken his concentration but that hadn't affected his aim one tittle.

As Liberty uprighted her bow, she fully expected Dylon to reciprocate in like manner by choking and coughing. It was her *anticipation* of his outburst that must have affected her aim. The arrow went astray, lodging to the right of center. Now, if Dylon found the bull's-eye with his third attempt he would be declared the winner. Damn!

"What a pity," Dylon murmured in mock sympathy. "You were doing so well."

Liberty bit at her bottom lip, anxiously awaiting the outcome. Silence fell over the crowd and even Percy, who detested displaying any emotion, looked tense.

As the arrow sailed through the air to quiver in the tree, Liberty gaped at the tall muscular man beside her. Dylon's arrow had split the shaft of her arrow that had gone astray on her third attempt.

Lowering the bow, Dylon expelled a sigh. "It looks as if we have played to a draw, love," he observed. "Shall we try our hand at pistols?"

Liberty stared into those sparkling blue eyes and frowned pensively. "You did that on purpose," she realized and said so. "Why?"

Gently, he curled his finger beneath her chin, holding her inquisitive gaze. "You are an extremely clever and astute young lady. Puzzle that out for yourself," he whispered as his sensuous lips grazed hers in the slightest breath of a kiss.

Uncertainty flickered in her amethyst eyes as she watched Dylon withdraw. "Were you trying to make me look good?"

A wry smile quirked his lips as he stared down at five-feet-one-inch and one-hundred-five pounds of perfectly formed feminine deviltry. "Were you trying to make me look *bad?*" he questioned her question.

Liberty lurched around to avoid his probing gaze. Aye, she had tried to make Dylon look the fool and now she was too ashamed to admit it. Quickly, she snatched up two flintlocks from their velvet-lined cases and turned to present one to Dylon.

"No pranks this time," she promised. "Winner takes all."

Dylon chuckled at her challenge. "All of what, my love? What are we betting?"

Liberty practiced taking aim with the weapon in preparation of firing. "You may set the stakes. It doesn't matter what the bet, for I intend to win—fair and square. You can wager whatever you please and I shall match it."

In her eagerness to get on with the challenge Liberty didn't realize how dangerous her generosity had become. But Dylon pounced on opportunity.

A roguish smile pursed his lips as he regarded the saucy nymph. "*Anything*, my sweet? You will meet *any* wager that meets my whim?"

Liberty gulped hard when she read that suggestive twinkle in his eyes, but stubbornness refused to permit her to retract the bet. "That was my proposition," she assured him aloofly.

He dropped an unexpected kiss to her heart-shaped lips. "And you know what I want if I win, don't you?"

She knew all right. It was written on his bronzed features in bold letters. But Benjamin Jordon had made certain that his daughter was a crackshot and Dylon Lockhart would *not* get what he wanted, at least not from her!

"Let the challenge begin," Liberty announced.

Dylon dropped into an exaggerated bow. "Ladies first."

"And men second," Liberty countered with a goading

smile. "That is the natural order of things in life and in competition."

Dylon muffled another snicker as Liberty sighted down her raised arm. The pistol's blast split the air. And sure as hell, the bullet found its mark—dead center. Another round of applause erupted from the crowd.

While Liberty reloaded her own flintlock, Dylon moved into position and took aim. He matched her impressive accuracy and his shot embedded itself only a hairbreadth away from hers.

Liberty cursed her impatience when her second attempt was low and to the left. Damnation, she had been in too great a hurry to pressure Dylon into a mistake. She should have known better than to employ any sort of strategy on him. Dylon Lockhart made very few mistakes . . . in anything!

With deliberate aim, Dylon cocked the trigger. The bullet zinged into the bull's-eye, causing Liberty to sag in disappointment. She expected him to taunt her unmercifully before she took her last shot, but Dylon did nothing of the kind. He conducted himself like a gentleman while she positioned herself in front of the target for the third and final time.

Returning the courtesy of holding her tongue while Dylon aimed and fired, Liberty stood aside, waiting with bated breath. In the manner of an experienced marksman, Dylon stared pensively at his target and then peered down the sight of his flintlock. The weapon barked in the cool evening air and a cloud of smoke curled upward.

Liberty slumped in defeat. Dylon had scored a bull's-eye.

Setting the pistol aside, Dylon stared down at the disgruntled blonde. A multitude of emotions chased each other across her bewitching features. Although Dylon felt like grinning in wicked glee, he restrained himself from goading her. Now he had this delightfully intriguing minx right where he wanted her. He wasn't about to antagonize her and incite her volatile temper. Gloating would accomplish nothing.

Liberty stared into those baby-blue eyes that were surrounded with a fan of black lashes and she felt a wave of respect flood over her. Dylon was aware of her sensitivity and her smarting pride, even when she had displayed little respect for his pride and reputation as lord and master of this plantation. She had purposely tried to embarrass him in front of his family and servants, but he hadn't retaliated when she'd given him every right to retaliate.

While she stared up at the six-feet-two-inch mass of masculinity an elfin smile spread across her lips. "Double or nothing on the game of piquet?" she questioned hopefully.

A deep skirl of laughter clamored through his chest as he laid his hand on the small of Liberty's back to guide her across the lawn that was now deepening with evening shadows.

"You are a most competitive young lady," he murmured, unable to resist the urge of dropping another kiss to her petal-soft lips, even though God and everyone else stood as witness.

"Does that offend you?" Liberty paused to stare him squarely in the eye. "Most men would be put off by a woman who dares to burrow her way into a man's world and challenge him at his own games."

Bedeviled, Dylon traced the tempting curve of her mouth with his forefinger. "Nothing you do offends me or puts me off, Liberty," he assured her honestly. "I am hopelessly fascinated with you."

And you probably say the exact-same thing to every female who catches your eye, thought Liberty, but she kept the speculation to herself. Trouble was, with each passing moment, she was actually beginning to like this handsome rake, despite better judgment. Liberty wasn't certain why she felt this compelling need to impress him with her unconventional talents, but she did. For some reason, it was important to her that he realized she wasn't like the other women he'd known, ones who catered to him in hopes of savoring the scraps of affection he tossed to them. She wanted to be different, to matter. . . .

You're being utterly ridiculous, Liberty scolded herself as she allowed Dylon to propel her toward the house. You won't be around here very long. If you lose your heart to this dedicated bachelor, you will be eternally sorry!

Dylon only amused himself with women. Liberty knew that as well as she knew her own name. Women were one of his hobbies, his pastime. And unless she wanted to become just another feminine conquest on his chain of broken hearts, she'd damned well better start sharpening her skills at cards! If she didn't keep her wits about her, she would spirit away from Lockhart Hall without her pride, dignity and unblemished virtues intact!

"I think you've carried this game of yours far enough," Percy declared as he fell into step beside Dylon. "I overheard the wager and I know perfectly well what you're planning." He peered disdainfully at Dylon. "Has it occurred to you that Liberty might truly be married to another man? How would you feel if some rakehell took unfair advantage of your new bride?"

The thought spoiled Dylon's lighthearted mood. He had preferred to think Liberty had escaped before her wedding, not after it. And damnit, who had she been running away from? Why had she refused to tell him?

"Why don't you fetch us some beverages," Dylon suggested, purposely ignoring his valet's unsettling remark. "Griffin and Cayla will be joining us in the parlor."

Percy's mouth narrowed into a thin slit. "Aye, sir, right away. And shall I also try to locate the good sense you were born with while I'm at it? You seem to have misplaced it since the young lady arrived."

Dylon slanted his valet a condescending glare. "I am perfectly capable of handling my own affairs without your assistance and your glib comments."

Percy adjusted his powdered wig, straightened the cuff of his jacket and spun on his heels. "That, sir, remains to be seen," he dared to say before he strode down the hall.

Although Dylon had not intended for Liberty to overhear the last part of the conversation, she did. The instant he veered around the corner, she focused her perceptive violet eyes on him.

"It appears that Percival T. Pearson is hopelessly devoted to you, despite all the faults he sees in you," she observed.

Dylon ambled over to retrieve the playing cards and frowned thoughtfully. Flashbacks of the meetings at Assembly raced across his mind. The assemblymen had complained about the ridiculous tax George Grenville and Parliament were proposing to attach to legal documents, cards and newspapers. Cards, for God's sake! Why, before the colonists knew it, Parliament would be levying taxes on life itself!

Shaking his wandering thoughts aside, he responded belatedly to Liberty's observation. "Aye, Percy does get a mite carried away at times. He takes me and himself much too seriously. In fact he has become so involved in my life that he has forgotten he has one of his own."

With masculine grace, he eased into a chair at the drop-leaf table which sat beside the bay window. "In my opinion, there are three kinds of people in this world. There are those who live to love."

"Like Cayla Styles, for instance," Liberty inserted as she sank down across from Dylon. "She has been groomed to serve her father and her future husband. She has been taught to put the needs of all others above her own."

"Exactly," Dylon chuckled as he shuffled the cards. "Then there are those who love to live, those who reap all the pleasure of each day, as if each one were a precious commodity."

"Like yourself," Liberty mused aloud.

"And very much like you, I believe," Dylon declared,

studying the curvaceous blonde with a contemplative smile.

The man could smile through every human emotion imaginable, Liberty decided. The dynamic Dylon Lockhart could laugh, even when he was angry or bored to tears. Liberty wished she wasn't quite so transparent. Then perhaps Dylon would have believed her tale of amnesia instead of taunting her with it.

"And the third category?" she questioned, distracting Dylon before he wound up posing prying questions about her past that she would refuse to answer.

"That category belongs to the Percy Pearsons of the world," Dylon responded philosophically. "He doesn't live at all; he exists. He has let himself become a fussy busybody who involves himself in the lives of his friends instead of living up to his full potential."

"In essence, your valet lives through you—the man who is all those things Percy isn't sure he could be, even though he secretly wishes he could be. He stays safely tucked in his place, watching you play out the role he would prefer for himself, though I doubt his deeply embedded convictions would permit it," Liberty finished for him.

Dylon froze in midshuffle, amazed at this young woman's depth of perception. "Good God, you have just summed up what I had never been able to put my finger on," he declared with admiration.

Liberty retrieved the cards from his hands and shuffled them with experienced ease. "I'm sure you would have figured it out if you had the time." She peeked impishly up at him from beneath a fringe of long curly lashes. "But in your pursuit of loving to live, I suspect you have been much to busy ensuring that all your female conquests have satisfied their need to live for *love.*"

Dylon snickered at her diplomatic rebuke of his previous encounters with women. "A man has his needs, Liberty," he defended himself.

"Are you suggesting that a woman does not?" Her brow elevated to a challenging angle.

Ever so slowly, his measuring gaze slid over the scooped neckline of her peasant blouse, scrutinizing her alluring assets (of which there were many). "And what are your needs, my love?"

Liberty was hoping he'd ask. Most men wouldn't have bothered to inquire and couldn't care less. In the past, only her beloved father had shown genuine concern for her. Her good looks and staggering wealth had been a plague and a curse. Liberty had never been certain if men were attracted to her or to the luxuries an heiress could provide.

"I need to be accepted for what I am," she proclaimed. "I need to be respected for who I am, not because I happen to be a woman and men arrogantly believe they know best when it comes to making a woman's life complete. I need my own space, freedom to grow, the chance to follow my own rainbows and . . ."

"Deal the cards, Liberty," Dylon requested with an amused grin. "I fear that if you get wound up your list of demands could go on all night."

His grin was contagious and Liberty smiled in spite of herself. "You are right, of course. Getting carried away is one of my worst faults."

"Besides your volatile temper, that is," he added playfully.

"Aye, beside that and among many others," she admitted.

When Griffin ambled into the room with Cayla on his arm, Dylon knew his brother regretted being left on the sidelines to watch the game of piquet. While Griffin hovered behind Dylon and then behind Liberty, studying both hands of cards, Cayla retrieved her crochet needles to impress her escort with her talents at stitchery. Unfortunately, Griffin was too engrossed in the game to remember the redhead was alive. He was having a grand time peering over Liberty's shoulder, enjoying the unobstructed view of cleavage that the neckline of her blouse provided.

And don't think Dylon hadn't noticed. He most certainly had! Amazed at the bite of jealousy and protectiveness that nipped at him, Dylon tried to concentrate on his cards, but without much success. Finally, he tossed in his cards and heaved an annoyed sigh.

"Griff, I'd much rather deal you into a game than have you hovering over Liberty like a hummingbird," he grumbled.

"I thought Percy said this was some sort of grudge match that had to do with some mysterious bet the two of you made on the rifle range," Griffin countered with a wide grin. "And I'm dying to know exactly what the stakes are."

Liberty conveniently glanced down at the strewn cards. Dylon glared at his ornery brother and cursed Percy's loose tongue.

"Sit down, Griff. You can die of curiosity just as easily in your chair as on your feet."

"What happens if I beat both of you?" Griff wanted to know.

"You won't," Liberty and Dylon chorused.

"My, aren't we bursting at the seams with overconfidence," Griffin scoffed sarcastically. "And how is it that Liberty cannot recall her past but hasn't forgotten how to wield a bow and pistol or turn a card?"

Dylon shoved the cards at his brother and stared him down. "Are you going to play or ask stupid questions?"

"I'm very versatile," Griffin boasted. "I can do both at once."

"I'd rather you wouldn't." The tight smile that stretched across Dylon's lips indicated the time had come for Griff to clamp his mouth shut. Wisely, Griffin did just that.

While the threesome played out their hands and tallied their scores, Cayla crocheted on her doily and Percy arrived with the refreshments. Under the pretense of rearranging the costly keepsakes that graced the mantel, Percy kept a watchful eye on the game in progress. He couldn't bear the idea of Dylon taking advantage of the pert beauty. He sympathized with any woman who dared to pit herself against a man as resourceful and capable as Dylon Lockhart.

Percy had scarcely been able to take his eyes off the striking blonde since the moment he saw her swinging through the magnolia tree. She was so lovely and vivacious that she drew a man's eyes like a magnet. And if she had knocked Percival T. Pearson completely off balance, he was positively certain she would have an even stronger effect on the Lockhart brothers.

That worried Percy to no end. As devoted as he was to the Lockharts and Dylon in particular, he felt the compelling need to protect this gorgeous creature from harm, even if she seemed quite capable of taking care of herself in most situations. She simply brought out the protective instinct in a man and made him want to do battle for her, whether she needed assistance or not.

Each time Liberty lost a hand of cards, Percy cringed. He found himself silently rooting for the unconventional sprite who was as adept with cards as she was with pistols and bows. Even Percy, who had made it a point to curb his curiosity, found himself speculating on the woman's background. She had the poise and grace of a well-bred aristocrat, to be sure. But she also possessed unique skills and abilities that very few women had mastered. Who had taught her to play cards? Who had seen to it that she developed skills with a various sundry of weapons? And what about that telltale accent? Percy mused as his assessing gaze drifted over her well-sculptured figure. He had the feeling she wasn't from the nearby colonies.

"Well, stab my vitals!" Griff grumbled in defeat. He had come in dead last.

Liberty sat quietly calculating her score. She was disappointed that Dylon had tallied enough points to claim victory. Discreetly, she shot forth a glance to determine if he intended to add insult to injury by bursting into a triumphant grin. If she had won, she probably would have. But Dylon didn't humiliate her or infuriate her by beaming in satisfaction. Gracious winner that he was, he simply gathered the cards and replaced them in the bureau.

Cayla made a big production of yawning and glanced placatingly toward her escort who had shamelessly ignored her for more than two hours. "If you don't mind, Griffin, I should like to retire for the night. The day's journey was most exhausting."

Liberty couldn't imagine how Cayla could claim exhaustion. The fragile little flower of a female hadn't exerted herself one whit since she'd arrived. And she'd taken two naps before supper. How much sleep did one woman require to endure a day?

Reluctantly, Griffin gathered his feet beneath him to accompany Cayla to her room. He would have much preferred to exchange places with Dylon. It was clearly implied in the lingering glance he cast Liberty before he exited.

Dylon had to stare Percy down to get the valet to leave the room. But finally Percy took his cue and marched off. But not without flashing his master a glance that was worth a thousand words—none of which Dylon dared to have translated.

When they were alone, Dylon stared at Liberty for a long moment. She squirmed awkwardly beneath his unblinking gaze—like an apprehensive rabbit who expected to be attacked from all directions at once.

"If I call in your debt, will you wail and cry that I took unfair advantage?" Dylon asked quietly.

Her head jerked up to meet those sparkling pools of blue. The silence that stretched between them fairly crackled with electricity. Liberty knew what he wanted—for her to come willingly to him. And fool that she was, she had wagered her virginity on her skills on the target range and at the gaming table.

You were a bit too confident, Liberty, she chastised herself. Her lips trembled when Dylon stared deliberately at her mouth and then let his gaze wander over her torso like a languid caress.

"Could we possibly wager all my losses on a horse race?" she squeaked in desperation.

"At night?" Dylon chuckled. Lord, this high-spirited sprite never gave in or up. "One of us might break our neck."

A pert smile twitched her lips. "And then the other of us wouldn't have to pay the debt."

This time Dylon didn't smile the way he usually did. He was dead serious. "Would you go to such drastic extremes to avoid my bed, Liberty?" he questioned point-blank. "Do I frighten you so much that you fear my touch?"

What she feared most was that she would grow to like his caresses too much! Although he was tall and broad and powerfully built, he had a gentle, compelling touch. And when he kissed her, her betraying body blazed with forbidden flames. Liberty was afraid of her own responses, afraid to retest her previous and very explosive reaction to this charismatic rake for fear she would yield in wild abandon. . . .

"Liberty?"

She flinched when his rich baritone voice sliced through her troubled thoughts. Hesitantly, she raised her gaze to find him staring intently at her.

"Come here, Liberty . . ."

His quiet, commanding voice rolled toward her, intensifying until it boomed in her ears like resounding thunder. "Nay, I had better not," she choked out.

Dylon rose to full stature and immediately turned away. He didn't want to make her more apprehensive than she already was. His instant arousal would have been too obvious to this wary sprite. Already she stared at him as if she expected him to take a bite out of her. And damn, just thinking about having her in his bed sent a throb of desire pulsating through his loins. When he peered into her enchanting face he wanted her to obsession. When he visualized how her tantalizing body would look without those concealing garments he went hot all over. Dylon didn't dare look at her for fear he would burn himself into a pile of smoldering coals.

"You are the one who offered the bet," he reminded her, staring at the wall which was superimposed with her beguiling features. "I have given you every opportunity to recover your losses. You know what I want from you and I will expect you in my room at your earliest convenience."

Dylon hated himself for pressuring her, but damnit, he wanted her and he was unaccustomed to denying himself when it came to women. And why shouldn't he call in the debt? he asked himself crossly. He was entitled, wasn't he? A deal was a deal!

When Dylon walked out the door without a backward glance, Liberty gulped down her stampeding heart. Hell and damnation! She and her big mouth! She and her cocky arrogance! She hadn't been dealing with an incompetent dandy and she'd known it. But she had considered herself Dylon's equal and he had proved time and time again that she wasn't.

On wobbly legs, Liberty staggered out the door. Her mind spun like a top, struggling to devise a solution to her dilemma. She couldn't afford to be generous and noble about losing when she had gambled her virginity! Besides, she had far more to lose than Dylon did. In fact, she doubted if that lusty rake even remembered when and where he'd lost *his* virginity. He would definitely be her first experiment with passion, but there was no telling how far down she would be on his list of sexual conquests. Godamercy, she shuddered to think of it. It crushed her pride to realize she would be just another of the many women he'd known intimately. And she wouldn't be the last either, not with his voracious appetite for females.

Liberty made a snap decision while she climbed the spiral staircase. She had intended to remain within the confines of Lockhart Hall for a few more days. But now seemed the time to take her leave, via the balcony and magnolia tree.

Simon Gridley might not be so anxious to have her as his wife if she were a tainted woman, but Liberty wasn't going to risk that possibility. Considering the drastic measures her uncle had taken to see her wed to a total stranger, Liberty doubted it would matter to either Luther or Simon that she had bedded another man. Her only recourse was to make her escape while Dylon was lying abed, awaiting her arrival. She'd be long gone before he came looking for her and he wouldn't have the slightest idea where to find her. Aye, this was the only solution, she told herself sensibly.

Determined of purpose, Liberty marched up the last flight of steps to her elaborately decorated room. She didn't have to bother collecting her belongings because she had arrived with nothing. But she would leave with even less if she didn't make her escape posthaste! And damnation, why had her life suddenly become one hasty escape after another? It seemed that since her father's death she had been running from one dilemma into another.

Ponderously, Liberty stared at the terrace door which would be her salvation. Well, there was at least one woman on the planet who would escape Dylon Lockhart's masculine charms, she consoled herself as she peered into the darkness. She rather thought she deserved a medal for resisting that raven-haired rake with eyes as warm and inviting as the morning sky. He was, after all, the devil's own temptation, even if it galled her to have to admit it. But Dylon only wanted to appease his physical needs with her feminine body. He cared nothing about the troubles and personality attached to it. Unfortunately Liberty came as a set and she couldn't separate herself from her personality and beliefs to surrender her betraying body to any man, even the one who had the uncanny knack of kissing her blind and senseless.

Compressing her lips in fierce determination, Liberty tiptoed toward the door. Dylon Lockhart was a threat to all women everywhere. She had enough difficulties without burdening herself with a broken heart! Her feminine curiosity was trying to get the better of her, but she didn't need to know what it would be like to share Dylon's bed. Leaving was the wisest choice she could make.

Besides, she reminded herself with a faint smile, she had made a career as an escape artist. Lately, that was what she did best. And considering her inexperience with men, she would probably disappoint Dylon and her own wanton expectations of what love should be. Better never to have loved at all, Liberty consoled herself as she eased open the door. This way, she would never know what she was missing. . . .

Chapter 8

Knowing Dylon occupied the room next to hers made Liberty extraordinarily cautious. She had left the whale oil lamp burning in her room, hoping not to arouse suspicion when she made her discreet exit. Quietly, she inched along the balcony toward the nearest limb of the magnolia tree.

Liberty swung her leg over the railing, prepared to spring onto the branch. A startled gasp erupted from her lips when an unseen hand snaked around her arm, yanking her off the railing. Liberty found herself captured in Dylon's powerful arms and listened to him scowl in annoyance.

Liberty was one of those individuals who detested having her private space encroached upon and she despised being restrained in any manner. It brought her self-preservation instincts and her temper to life in one second flat. Having Dylon clamp hold of her reminded her of her unpleasant ordeal with Simon's henchman the first time she tried to escape. Like a wild thing, Liberty bucked and wriggled to free herself from Dylon's chaining arms. Liberty had made up her mind to go and by damned she was going!

Clinging to that determined thought, Liberty kicked Dylon's shins to splinters. He momentarily lost his grasp on her when he doubled over to protect himself from the blow she had directed toward the private parts of his anatomy. Like a cannonball, Liberty shot across the balcony and then circled back to the outreaching limb. Again she swung her leg over the rail and again, Dylon jerked her backward.

"Let me go," Liberty hissed furiously.

"Not on your life, little wildcat," Dylon growled back at her.

Cursing like a trooper, Dylon carried Liberty back to her room and dumped her in the middle of her canopied bed. It annoyed him to the extreme that he had found himself in a full-fledged battle . . . with a woman, for God's sake!

Wide violet eyes peered up at the towering mass of masculinity who loomed over her. The linen shirt Dylon wore hung open, exposing the thick matting of dark hair that carpeted his chest and trailed down his lean belly to disappear into the band of his breeches. The smile that usually tugged at his handsome features had vanished, replaced by a thunderous glower.

Liberty's father had always insisted that the best strategy for defense was a strong offense. Employing that theory, she tilted a proud chin and crossed her arms beneath her breasts. "Well what did you expect? That you had charmed me with your suave smiles and gallant manners and that I would scamper to your room like a little mouse, pleading for the scant scraps of affection you might offer for this one night?" she sniffed caustically.

Dylon, peeved though he most certainly was with this sassy vixen, was hard-pressed not to break into a smile. Liberty sat abed, wielding her rapier tongue, attempting to cut him down to her size. That wasn't going to happen!

"What I did *not* expect, little imp," Dylon parried with an intimidating smirk, "was for you to take the cowardly way out without bothering to say good-bye. I thought you had more gumption than that."

Her chin tilted another notch higher. "I hardly think 'tis cowardly to walk the balcony railing and launch oneself into a tree!" she snapped defensively.

"You refused to come to my room to announce your departure," he reminded her. "*That* makes you a coward. Even in the midst of battle a coward will dodge bullets in his attempt to turn tail and run." He stalked closer, looming over her with ridiculing effectiveness. "You, my dear lady, are a lily-livered coward!"

"I am not!" she protested hotly. "I am not afraid of you!"

A taunting smile slid across his lips and Liberty itched to smear that irritating expression all over his face. "Then prove it," he challenged.

"I will do nothing of the kind," she bit off.

Damnation, thought Dylon. He had dealt with scores of women but he had never stumbled onto a female he wasn't sure how to handle . . . until this feisty harridan came along. He wasn't certain how to proceed with her. Most women ran toward him, but Liberty always seemed to be running away, refusing to let him close, selfishly harboring the mysterious secrets of her past.

When Dylon bent over her, bracing his hands on either side of her shoulders, Liberty involuntarily shrank back against the pillow. Her heart flip-flopped in her chest when she felt his warm breath against her flushed cheek.

"Then, by all means, allow *me* to prove what a coward you really are," he murmured as he sank down on top of her.

Liberty thrashed like a wild creature rebelling against captivity. When she tried to shove Dylon away, he grabbed her wrists, pinning her helplessly beneath him. His swarthy body settled suggestively over hers. His knee wedged between her thighs, making her vividly aware of the threat of his virile body and the intimate danger he presented.

And then, when Liberty swore he meant to ravish her with a kiss and physically force her into submission, Dylon simply stared down at her and smiled another infuriatingly nonchalant smile. When he made no other move to compromise her, Liberty stared bemusedly at him.

"Were you expecting me to rip off your clothes and attack?" he queried. "Is that what you think lovemaking is all about?"

"Aye," she answered honestly. Her heart screeched to a halt when she made the mistake of staring up into those spellbinding blue eyes—eyes the same fascinating shade of forget-me-nots waving in a gentle breeze, hypnotizing a woman against her will.

"Why? Because I'm a man and you believe a man wishes only to take what a woman has to offer?" he speculated.

"Aye. That's what men do best—take advantage of women every chance they get," she replied in a cynical tone. "I should know. I was very nearly forced into a wed—" Liberty closed her mouth so quickly that she very nearly bit off her tongue.

"So you are not yet married," he surmised.

With tigerish agility, Dylon pushed himself upright and eased down on the edge of the bed. "Who was this man you were to wed?" He flung her a stern glance. "And don't tell me you don't remember. I don't believe that nonsense about amnesia. It would have taken a mightier blow than the one you sustained to crack that chunk of bricks you call a skull."

"'Tis none of your business." Liberty punished him with a defiant glare. "I came to your plantation, hoping to retrieve another set of clothes before I went on my way. And I should do just that right now. . . ."

Dylon half turned to study her exquisite features in the flickering lamplight. The thought of allowing this fiery beauty to vanish into the night while he was still so fascinated with her was distasteful to him. He wanted answers and she stubbornly refused to supply them.

"I have a proposition for you, minx, one that can work to your advantage as well as mine," he announced out of the blue.

Liberty eyed him with leery consternation. "What sort of proposition, or dare I ask?"

Dylon unfolded himself and circumnavigated the room. "You are seeking asylum from an unwanted marriage. You refuse to explain more than I have been able to deduce all by myself. I am in need of an escort to accompany me to my grandfather's estate, day after tomorrow. It seems to me that we could both profit from a workable compromise that provides you with sanctuary and me with an escort."

He paused to glance at Liberty who had rolled to her side to brace her head on her hand. Unknowingly, she had struck a very seductive pose. This lovely creature was obviously an innocent who didn't realize what a temptation she presented to a man. But Dylon was definitely feeling the effects of frustrated desire. Damnit all, this tigress was such a distraction that he could scarcely keep his mind on conversation. But there were things that needed to be said and if he didn't get at it he *would* be tempted to ravish this gorgeous sprite, just as she feared he would!

"My grandfather has decided that Griff and I are long past the marrying age. He wants great-grandchildren to ensure his name will survive in generations to come. He harps on the subject constantly. Griff and I don't wish to be forced into matrimony simply because Brewster has decided now's the time. Obviously, you share the opinion that one should wed when one is damned good and ready or you wouldn't have fled your own marriage ceremony."

Phrased that way, Liberty began to understand Dylon's resistance to his grandfather's wishes. "I do sympathize with your problem," she murmured with genuine sincerity.

"Thank you," he said absently before he went back to his pacing. "Twice a year, Brewster organizes a holiday to celebrate his birthday and . . ."

Liberty blinked. "Twice a year? Most of us were born only once."

"My grandfather insists that if a man survives life's vicissitudes and reaches the age of seventy-three that he should be entitled to celebrate his birthday as many times a year as it meets his whim. Brewster celebrates in the spring and the fall."

"Just when is his birthday?" Liberty questioned curiously.

"In the summer but he detests summer," Dylon explained.

An amused chortle tripped from Liberty's lips. "Brewster sounds like a delightful character."

"Delightful?" Dylon smirked. "After spending considerable time with him, you might not think so. Sometimes he can be very persistent, plainspoken and annoying." He expelled a heavy sigh and continued. "Twice a year, my brother and I attend his holiday with female escorts, ones whom we permit Brewster to think might soon become our wives. That appeases Brewster and prevents us from enduring long-winded lectures on the benefits of marriage."

He pivoted to stare directly at Liberty, trying not to notice what an appetizing picture she presented with her golden hair spilling over her shoulder like a glorious waterfall. The lamplight filtered through her gauze blouse to mold itself to the tantalizing swells of her breasts. It wasn't easy to overlook this lovely sprite, believe you him!

"I will not call in your debt this evening if you will accompany me to Brewster's estate and portray my devoted escort for his benefit," he bargained.

"Devoted?" Her brow furrowed dubiously. "Just how

devoted do I have to be?"

Dylon let out his breath in a rush. "Is it asking so much for you to pretend you like me for three days?"

She *did* like him. That was the problem! "Nay, I suppose not," she replied, striving for a tone of indifference.

Liberty tried very hard to avoid staring at this masculine specimen of virility, but her betraying eyes had already wandered over the washboarded muscles of his belly. She found herself speculating on how his bronzed flesh would feel beneath her inquiring fingertips. Liberty had never been so curious about the male of the species before. But this lithe, muscular monument to masculinity kept drawing her eyes and inciting erotic thoughts that had no business darting through her mind.

Dylon ambled back to the bed. His hands clenched in the pockets of his breeches and he forced himself not to touch this luscious imp as he longed to do. "I will provide you with a refuge from your troubles if you will help me solve my problem with Brewster. I will pose no questions about your past if you will pretend to like me. Do we have a bargain?"

Liberty carefully reviewed her options. If she agreed to accompany Dylon, Luther and Simon wouldn't find her. And once they returned to the area, Liberty could venture back to Charles Town to book passage to the islands. It seemed the perfect solution . . . except for one minor detail that could evolve into a major complication—her growing attraction to this midnight-haired rake with entrancing blue eyes. Hadn't she already discovered that the solution to one problem was the springboard into another?

"I have one stipulation," Liberty declared, staring at his ruggedly handsome face instead of his broad expansive chest. "I wish to be allowed to fetch my own belongings tomorrow—no questions asked."

"Agreed," Dylon replied.

"Now that that's settled and out of the way, perhaps we should both get some sleep," she suggested.

"I couldn't agree more," Dylon remarked as he shrugged off his shirt and cast it aside with cavalier devilment.

Liberty tensed. Her violet eyes widened when Dylon sank down on the side of her bed as if he belonged there. "I didn't mean for you to sleep here!" she chirped like a sick cricket.

Dylon chuckled at the wild blush of color that stained her cheeks. Ah, what an innocent she was! Liberty needed to learn that men weren't creatures to be feared and fought tooth and nail. He'd only doffed his shirt, for crying out loud. He hadn't even touched her!

"The sight of my bare flesh shouldn't be offensive," he teased her. "And it cannot be my caress that upsets you because I haven't laid a hand on you."

"Your flesh isn't offensive. 'Tis arousing. . . ." Liberty turned blood red, humiliated by her blundering confession.

There wasn't an inch of flab on his virile body. He was masculine perfection in its purest most elegant form, except for the scar on his shoulder which suggested he had been hit by a Cherokee warrior's arrow during his battles on the frontier. Dylon Lockhart, Liberty begrudgingly noted, had the kind of earthy sexual appeal that wouldn't quit. One look at his well-sculptured physique sent her blood pressure right through the roof.

"Do I arouse you, Liberty?" he prodded. Dylon grinned rakishly as he watched her unguarded gaze sweep appreciatively down his torso.

She couldn't very well deny it now, even though she would have liked to. "Aye, but we hardly know each other and . . ."

Dylon's smile evaporated. "Perhaps not, but I feel as if I've known you forever."

Liberty gulped down her palpitating heart. The musky fragrance of his cologne was slowly but surely warping her senses, clouding her brain. Forbidden desire and stubborn denial warred inside her. But he was too close, too tempting and too . . . much a man for even the most capable woman to handle!

Carefully, Dylon lifted a bronzed hand to comb the recalcitrant strands of gold away from her creamy features. "You're the dream I've been having, little wildflower. You're the woman I've wanted but have only just found."

Another well-rehearsed line of flattery meant to strip me of my defenses, no doubt, Liberty cautioned herself shakily. Dylon was a skillful rogue who knew what to say to melt a woman into sentimental mush. It was on the tip of her tongue to mock his husky remark. But the moment his sensuous lips slanted over hers, the thought flitted off into oblivion. When his stray hand folded around hers, bringing it into titillating contact with the lean muscles that padded his chest, her pulse leaped like migrating frogs. Gently, taking great care not to alarm her, Dylon guided her fingertips on a sensuous tour of his hair-matted chest and the lean muscled flesh that curved around his ribs. Silently, he assured her that he was just a man, not a beast who sought to devour her in one gulp.

Tantalizing tremors undulated through Liberty. She never believed it possible to derive so much pleasure from merely touching a man. Dylon taught her how to caress him, allowed her to feel the accelerated beat of his heart, whispered his need to discover her feminine body by sight and touch.

Holding her unblinking gaze, Dylon drew her hand over his while his palm curled around her ribs and slid upward to cup her breast. When she gasped at his brazen caress, Dylon smiled knowingly. He had encroached upon unclaimed territory, touching her more familiarly than any man before him.

"You ignite the same forbidden flames in me that I arouse in you," he assured her as he moved closer to trace a scalding path of kisses along the rapid pulsations on her throat. "I have no wish to selfishly take, but rather to share the sweet pleasure until it unfurls into full blossom."

His mouth courted hers with unrivaled expertise while his hand continued its journey of intimate discovery. "You fear what you do not understand, but you will like what there is to learn about the delicious magic that transpires between a man and woman," he whispered in promise.

Liberty swore he had somehow managed to boil her body into the consistency of marmalade. Her movements had become sluggish. His slow explorations and erotic touch left her naive body burning inside and out. Wanton longings sprang from out of nowhere to sizzle through every nerve and muscle. Liberty felt as if she had plugged herself into a limitless supply of energy, one that sent sparks surging back and forth like an ever-constant current of living fire.

Godamercy, what had this seductive rake done to her? What sort of wizard was he that he could so easily and skillfully bend her will until it matched his own?

"I want to teach you the ways of love," Dylon rasped, battling the raging needs that roared at him like a captive lion.

Her fingertips had curled into the matting of hair on his chest and drifted across his male nipples. Only that, only the mere whisper of a touch, and he went hot all over! Good God, he never remembered feeling so completely out of control and yet so utterly aware of the innocence of the woman in his arms. But then, Dylon reminded himself, he'd never stooped to seducing a virgin before either. And he shouldn't be now. But damnit, he touched this delectable nymph and nothing else seemed to matter. She wasn't just another reckless conquest; she was a prize, a compelling need he had to fulfill.

As if he were unwrapping a priceless gift, Dylon drew the gauze blouse down her shoulders to expose the full swells of her breasts and the tapered contours of her waist. The lamplight curled around her satiny skin and a jolt of desire knocked Dylon sideways. Never had he seen such perfection. Never had he wanted a woman with the same wild intensity that he wanted this violet-eyed enchantress. He had but to gaze upon her luscious body and it put his hormones in a tailspin, his pulse on a drumroll.

When Liberty self-consciously reached up to cover herself, Dylon drew her hand away. His lips feathered over the throbbing peaks, fluttering from one rose-tipped crest to the other, causing fierce uncontrollable needs to uncoil inside her. His tongue flicked at each dusky bud before he gently drew it into his mouth to savor the succulent taste of her.

Liberty struggled to draw a breath, but she couldn't breathe without inhaling him, couldn't move without being vividly aware of his masculine body meshed against hers. Unprecedented sensations pelted her innocent body like bullets. She felt the fire spreading through every fiber of her being until fervent desire pounded in rhythm with her thundering heart. She was aching all over, shamelessly arching toward his moist lips and seeking hands, begging for more.

She surely must have been a trollop in another lifetime if she could surrender without putting up a fight. Why else would she have allowed this rogue to take such outrageous privileges with her body? Why else would these riveting feelings of pleasure lure her deeper into his sensuous web of seduction?

Another moan of sweet torment bubbled in her throat when his hands folded around her breasts—kneading, caressing, teasing her into total abandon. A feeble protest formed in her brain but the message became entangled with the wanton desires of the flesh. Her arms slid over his sinewy shoulders to hold him close instead of pushing him away as she should have done.

It was as if she had somehow become obsessed with the feel of his hands and lips cruising over her quivering flesh, as if she needed to feel his masculine body lying familiarly against hers. She inhaled his masculine fragrance again and her senses took flight. She returned his touch—caress for caress—and she was living only to appease the monstrous cravings that burgeoned inside her.

It must surely be true that forbidden desire knew no rhyme or reason, Liberty thought dizzily. She was no longer the mistress of her own soul, no longer able to contain the dozens of kinds of passion that raged inside her. Sensation upon fiery sensation rippled through her bloodstream and her body melted like candle wax. Suddenly she couldn't get enough of his overwhelming kisses and heart-stopping caresses. He was like the air she breathed—the vital necessity of life. . . .

When inhibition abandoned Liberty entirely her hands began to flood over the muscular planes of his body of their own free will.

Dylon swore he'd burn himself to a crisp long before he satisfied this white-hot ache of mindless passion. Her untutored hands drifted to and fro, memorizing each muscle, every contour of his flesh until she reduced him to a bubbling puddle of liquid desire. He was burning like the sun, flaming like a crown fire that was fueled by a fierce wind.

Dylon cautioned himself to be gentle and patient. He was painfully aware that this angel was unaccustomed to men. But it was difficult to restrain himself when he wanted her in the worst possible way. He had aroused her with wild, unfamiliar sensations but if he rushed her over the edge, he would spoil her initiation into womanhood.

He had to be sensitive to her needs and her innocence, even if it killed him. And it very well could, he realized bleakly. Already his heart was threatening to beat him to death and savage urgency was biting huge chunks out of his self-control.

Liberty strangled on a gasp when his migrating hands skied over her abdomen to explore the ultrasensitive flesh of her thighs. His fingertips delved and teased until the burning ache of pleasure engulfed her. His masterful kisses and caresses were no longer enough to satisfy the ravenous needs that multiplied with each passing second. He instilled colossal cravings inside her instead of appeasing the ones that already tormented her to no end. Liberty writhed beneath his intimate caresses, whispering a breathless plea to satisfy this pleasure beyond bearing.

When her naive body vibrated with tremors of unfulfilled desire, Dylon guided her thighs apart with his knees and settled himself exactly above her. The whisper of conscience scolded him for daring too much with this innocent beauty. But Dylon couldn't stop himself. The consequences be damned!

His hips moved toward hers, yearning to satisfy the hot aching pressure that left him swearing his capillaries were about to spring a leak. He craved this violet-eyed temptress as he'd craved nothing in all his life. Only when she was a beating breathing part of him would he be content, only then could he regain the self-control that he was beginning to wonder if he ever truly possessed. Lord, suddenly he couldn't even remember the meaning of the word!

Pain, like a sharp-edged sword, slashed through the fog of pleasure that clouded Liberty's brain. Involuntarily, she flinched and braced her hands against Dylon's chest. Her tangled lashes fluttered up to meet those shimmering pools of blue. There was something in the way that he was staring down at her that dissolved her fears. His tender smile held a promise and a silent apology as he bent to press his lips to hers in the most exquisite kiss imaginable. His tongue probed into her mouth, imitating the sensuous movements of his male body as he gently, caringly, took intimate possession. Ever so slowly, he set the cadence of passion, assuring her over and over that she had nothing more to fear.

"To compensate for your pain, I offer all I have to give. We will share ultimate pleasure and, very soon, you will know what you've been missing," he whispered as he folded her protectively in his arms.

Like a fog rolling in from the sea, erotic tides of pleasure drifted over her, pulsating in the gentle rhythm of his body gliding evocatively upon hers. Liberty slipped deeper into the unfamiliar dimension of time that sparkled with a kaleidoscope of rapturous feelings—ever-changing, ever-growing sensations that consumed her body, mind and soul.

Passion streamed through her like a river, sweeping her into a whirlpool of indescribable splendor. Hot, wild desperation claimed her. Her body moved of its own accord, meeting his demanding thrusts, craving an end to this wild burst of ecstasy that left her shuddering in spasmodic tremors.

Liberty held on for dear life when the world slid out from under her, leaving her plunging through a black abyss that crackled with profound sensations. She swore she was dying, swore that such sublime pleasure demanded the ultimate sacrifice of life itself.

Unexplained tears tumbled down her flushed cheeks as her body tumbled over cresting waves of ecstasy. And Dylon kissed the tears away before he too was consumed by pleasures that defied description.

Her energy spent, Liberty lapsed into sweet, tantalizing dreams that took up where reality had left off. The past two days had exhausted every emotion within the realm of human experience. Dylon's expert lovemaking had left her with a magical sense of contentment and security—something she hadn't enjoyed since her father had been unexpectedly taken from her life. Liberty slept, drifting in the peaceful tranquillity that only Dylon's mystical brand of passion had been able to provide. . . .

A tender smile pursed Dylon's lips as he peered at the exquisite angel in his arms. He marveled at the feelings of possessiveness that overcame him when he stared at Liberty. These unfamiliar sensations of protectiveness, however, were tempered with a sense of guilt. He had branded this wild, free creature. He hadn't tamed her; he had wooed her into submission with masterful skills of seduction that she had been too naive and inexperienced to counter.

It seemed a man obsessed would go to the farthest extremes to satisfy his cravings. And satisfy them this lovely creature had in the most remarkable ways! Dylon had enjoyed the quintessence of pleasure . . . but at the expense of the innocent maid who had not come willingly into his arms. . . .

The tormenting thought caused Dylon to flinch and ease away. Quietly, he donned his breeches and stood over the lovely nymph who had pleased and satisfied him in ways he never dreamed possible for one so innocent. He had wanted her beyond reason and he had taken her, even though he felt as if he had given a part of himself away in exchange for the delicious splendor they'd shared.

I hope you're proud of yourself, Dylon silently muttered as he drew the sheet over Liberty's well-sculptured form. In the past he'd taken pleasure where he'd found it and left without a regret or a backward glance. But making wild, sweet love to Liberty was another matter entirely. It was as if invisible chains tied him to her, refusing to allow him to forget what they had shared in a moment of reckless abandon.

Feeling more content than he had ever felt in his life

and ironically, more disturbed, Dylon snuffed the lamp and tiptoed out the terrace door. With catlike tread, he crept back to his own chambers.

The sight of Percy standing stiffly beside the door that opened into the hall caused Dylon to freeze in his tracks. Percy had flashed his master disdainful glances from time to time the past few years. But none of them matched the intensity or contempt that was stamped on his puckered features at that particularly awkward moment! God, Dylon wished the floor would open and he could drop out of sight.

"I hope you're proud of yourself." Percy's strained voice quivered with barely controlled anger—something he rarely displayed to anyone. But it was more than evident now!

"I hope you realize that whether I'm proud of myself or not (which he wasn't and he'd already been hounded by guilty thoughts) 'tis none of your concern," he finished abruptly.

Percy jerked up his head and hurled another daggerlike glare at his bare-chested, barefooted master. "I brought you a glass of brandy to help you sleep, *sir.*" He made a stabbing gesture toward the silver tray that sat on the nightstand. "Obviously *sleeping* has been the very least of your concerns this evening." There was a long, agonizing pause and the room became as silent as the grave. "She was a virgin, no doubt, and you, *sir* (he made the title of respect sound like a curse) are despicable!"

Dylon's tousled raven head snapped up to return the glower—dagger for dagger. "You may take your leave, Percival," he growled. "I have no more need of your services this evening."

"I'm sure that is true, *sir,*" he replied in a nasty parody of courtesy. "Had I known you would take such perverted pride in deflowering the innocents of this world who are already under duress for reasons we still do not know, I would not have devoted this past decade of my life to serving you, *sir.*"

"That is quite enough!" Dylon snapped, his tone carrying a clip of finality . . . which Percy flagrantly ignored.

Percy doubled over in a mocking bow. "If I thought *once* would be enough for you where the lady is concer—"

"Percy!" Dylon's voice cracked like a whip and he looked positively dangerous when he leveled a threatening scowl on his outspoken servant. "Get out!"

When Percy didn't stir a step, Dylon's jaw clenched and a menacing smile tightened his lips. "You can go on your own accord or I'll throw you out on the seat of your breeches. Take your pick."

Percy wisely chose the first option and wheeled around to take himself off. He didn't slam the door behind him, but he looked as if he would have liked to. The hour was late and most of the household was fast asleep. How he wished he could have said the same for that insensitive molester of women who went by the name of Dylon Lockhart!

When the door whined shut, Dylon cursed a blue streak. Wasn't it enough that he was battling this tormenting riptide of emotions where Liberty was concerned without the personification of his conscience materializing to nip at him like the hounds from hell?

Dylon felt like kicking himself for allowing his lusts to run rampant. He'd felt this obsessive attraction to Liberty the moment he'd laid eyes on her. He had wagered for her affection on the target range and at the card table. He had promised to disregard their scintillating bet and then he had, with premeditated forethought, set out to seduce her into submission.

His unforgivable behavior rubbed against the grain. And yet, he could muster no regret for making wild passionate love to that golden-haired hellion. She was like no other female he'd met in all his thirty-one years of existence!

Cursing under his breath, Dylon flounced on his bed. By dawn, he could expect guilt and humiliation to consume Liberty. And Percy would be a smoldering mass of resentful fury by then. Good God, how quickly he had turned his devoted valet against him. But what he dreaded most was facing Liberty's scorn. What she thought of him mattered—too much, all too quickly. . . .

"What spell have you cast on me, witch?" Dylon questioned the enticing vision that floated around his room like shadows on the wall. He had been bedeviled by that tangle of golden hair and those lively violet eyes that flickered with living fire. Even now, after the unrivaled pleasure he'd experienced in her silky arms, he still wasn't satisfied, just as Percy had predicted. Dylon still craved her . . . as if she were a mindless obsession. . . .

Dylon cringed at the thought of becoming so lost in a woman that she preoccupied his mind and colored every conversation. Liberty had her own mysterious problems and if he didn't watch his step he would stumble right into the middle of them! Hell, hadn't he already? She had wanted to leave as mysteriously as she had come and he wouldn't let her go. *Couldn't* let her go. . . .

A frustrated sigh tumbled from Dylon's lips. In the past he had carelessly shrugged away his concerns about women. But that lavender-eyed sprite who slept peacefully in the room next door could not be shrugged off. Already, she had burrowed into his heart and his fascination for her had increased rather than declined. That was the exact-opposite of what usually happened after his brief trysts.

Flopping onto his side, Dylon begged for sleep. But it was slow in coming. The splendor he'd discovered in Liberty's arms kept spilling through his mind, leaving him to wonder if Fate had finally rendered up to him the one woman who could make him forget the treachery and deceit of his first love in life. Liberty's memory filled the empty crevices of his heart, ones Patricia's betrayal and unrequited love had left behind. But being the untamed spirit Liberty was, Dylon wondered if she would walk out of his life, leaving his heart to bleed, just as Patricia had done. . . .

Well, that wasn't going to happen because he was older and wiser and he wasn't going to let himself care that much for a woman ever again! But he imagined Percy was silently wishing Dylon would wind up with a broken heart after what he'd done to Liberty.

Dylon could almost hear Percival T. Pearson spitefully declaring, "Justice, *sir*. True justice!"

Chapter 9

Just as Dylon predicted, Liberty awoke to tormented feelings of shame, regret and humiliation. Dylon had also speculated that she would prefer to awake alone, but the opposite was true. His absence from her room left her feeling as if she had been used and discarded. She was certain that once his masculine needs had been appeased he had swaggered back into his own chambers to carve another notch on his bedpost.

Liberty cursed herself a dozen times over as the events of the previous evening gelled in her mind. She realized that all Dylon's words and deeds had been nothing more than a clever ploy to get her into bed, no matter what their bargain. He was probably in his room at this very minute, gloating over the fact that he had stolen her innocence by making her want him.

Shame splashed across her cheeks in various shades of red. She had wanted him, curse her feminine desires! He had spun his web of black magic with hushed words and melting caresses. She had become bread dough in his hands—pliant flesh molded to fit his masculine contours.

Liberty muttered a string of colorful oaths and pummeled her pillow until feathers flew. How could she expect that unscrupulous rake to have any respect for her when she had not one smidgen of respect for herself?

She, like every other female on the planet, was susceptible to his magnetic charm. Dylon was an old hand at murmuring those oh-so-convincing and yet insincere whispers of affection.

The woman he'd dreamed of meeting all his life? Ha! Liberty swore in French, Spanish and English since she had command of all three languages. Dylon Lockhart dreamed of women, period! All women. Short ones, tall ones, blondes, brunettes and redheads—the more the better. Why, that scoundrel could probably populate South Carolina all by himself if he'd a mind to!

The fear of carrying Dylon's child paralyzed her momentarily. She could hear herself insisting that he should marry her to provide the baby with a name. And she could hear "Dylon dahling" hedging and procrastinating, just as he had done when Nora Flannery demanded a proposal after he'd seduced her. And there was no doubt in Liberty's mind that Dylon *had* seduced Nora. Liberty knew exactly how devastating that charismatic rake could be.

Godamercy, what a fool she had turned out to be. For the past few years, since men had begun to notice her, Liberty had artfully dodged amorous advances. And then along came that smooth-talking, suave rake who made mincemeat of her defenses. The walls had come tumbling down when Dylon set his practiced hands upon her and kissed her blind and stupid. . . .

Liberty grimaced when she glanced down to see the telltale signs of her lost virginity on the sheet. It made her fully aware that every form of refuge had its price. But she had paid a little too dearly in her crusade to avoid her uncle and Simon Gridley. Damn her foolishness! Double damn her feminine curiosity and wayward desire!! And triple damn Dylon Lockhart!!! He had taken what a woman could give only once in her life and should never give to anyone except her husband—which he most certainly wasn't and never intended to be!

No doubt, Dylon would expect her to behave like the pouting Nora Flannery who spouted terse demands and cried a bucket of tears to get her way. Well, Liberty Jordon wasn't about to let Dylon know that the previous night mattered one whit to her! Even if it killed her, she would pretend their tête-à-tête hadn't happened, that it was of no consequence whatsoever. The reckless affair would be another page from the past that she preferred to forget. She would not expect or demand a marriage proposal to save her reputation from ruin. She would return to the islands and carry the name of her secret lover to her grave. Her consolation would come in knowing she was probably the first female who hadn't groveled at Dylon's feet, begging for his love, his name and his devotion. At least she would be a first at something! And Dylon Lockhart didn't even know what love was anyway, curse him. But ah, wasn't he a connoisseur of lust!

After Liberty had fastened herself into her peasant-style clothes, she braced herself for the inevitable and ventured downstairs. Dylon, Griffin and Cayla awaited her arrival in the dining room. Pasting on a carefree smile, Liberty breezed inside as if nothing had happened because, after all, the previous night did *not* exist. She had erased it from the slate of memory.

While Cayla primly whittled at her slice of turkey, cutting it into tiny pieces and chewing daintily on each morsel at least twenty times, Liberty ate like a farmhand. And all the while Dylon watched her with a hawkish stare, trying to decipher her mood. She didn't ignore him as if she were furious with him. Neither did she shower him with overt attention. It was as if she accepted his presence without being influenced by it one way or another. In fact, she gave him the same polite consideration she gave her chair and her eating utensils.

Dylon had learned to deal with sullen, pouting females. But he was unprepared to cope with a woman who behaved as if their romantic encounter was of little concern. One would have thought Liberty had taken the incident in stride. That was supposed to be *his* role.

Although Dylon prided himself in possessing an easygoing, imperturbable disposition, Liberty's light-hearted attitude soured him. And it didn't help one whit when Percy puttered around the dining room, silently glaring at Dylon and mentally applauding Liberty for handling herself so superbly in what could have been a very uncomfortable encounter.

"More tea, my lady?" Percy inquired of Liberty.

"Aye, thank you." Her gaze lifted to bestow a grateful smile on the conscientious servant.

"I trust you slept well last night, my lady."

Percy had offered her the perfect opportunity to assure Dylon that he didn't affect her in the least, whether the valet knew it or not. Lord, she hoped he didn't know what had happened. Hiding her shame from Dylon was difficult enough and she had to rely heavily upon her theatrical ability.

"I enjoyed a splendid night's sleep," she assured the valet. "In fact, I am so well rested that I have been toying with the idea of a horseback ride to view the far-reaching perimeters of the plantation. There is nothing like an exhilarating ride after a good night's sleep to keep one in a cheerful frame of mine." Had she sounded convincing enough? Godamercy, she certainly hoped so!

"I would be happy to accompany you around the grounds," Griffin volunteered enthusiastically.

Dylon glared at his overeager brother. "We have a plantation to oversee after our absence and before our journey to Grandfather's estate," he reminded Griff tartly. "And I don't believe Cayla enjoys such rigorous outdoor activities. It would be most impolite for you to abandon your escort, dear brother."

Cayla looked as if she wanted to blurt out some mysterious remark. Then she reconsidered, stared at her plate and smiled a tremulous little smile. "Nay, I'm afraid I do not ride," she murmured. "But do go ahead, Griffin, if 'tis your want."

"He wouldn't think of leaving you to entertain yourself," Dylon insisted, even though no one looked more anxious to discard his escort and chase after Liberty than Griffin did.

Griffin slumped back in his chair, foiled again.

"I hope you don't mind riding alone, my dear Liberty." Dylon knew for a fact that she didn't since she had intentions of gathering her belongings from only God knew where.

"Nay, not at all," she answered cheerily.

"Would you prefer the grooms saddled a gentle mare or a spirited gelding for your riding pleasure?" As if he couldn't guess.

Liberty flashed him a saucy smile, even if it was forced and displayed none of her true emotions. She may have looked happy, but she was anything but! What she was, was humiliated, thoroughly ashamed and annoyed that Dylon didn't appear the least bit guilty about what he'd done. Damn his lusty hide!

While Dylon and Griffin discussed the order of chores that needed to be tended, Liberty polished off her meal. She had decided to let Dylon think she planned to return after she gathered her belongings. But he hadn't kept his end of the bargain and she wasn't going to either. He would never see her again, not in this lifetime leastways. He had already wounded her heart and she wasn't sticking around to let him bleed it dry! Why should she care about his ploy to hoodwink his grandfather by having her portray his adoring escort? She had her own problems—problems which he had complicated the previous night. This was good-bye and good riddance!

When Liberty excused herself and breezed out the door, Dylon rose from his chair and motioned for Percy to follow him into the entryway. Pensively, Dylon watched Liberty amble toward the stables to fetch a mount.

"Percy, I want you to follow her," Dylon requested.

Percy jerked up his head so quickly that his Bag wig slid back on his forehead. "Surely you jest!" he croaked in disbelief.

"Surely, I do not!" Dylon fixed his glittering blue eyes on his valet. "I don't think she plans to come back."

"I don't blame her." Percy sniffed, readjusting his cockeyed wig.

"I gave you an order and I expect you to obey," Dylon growled impatiently.

"I do not ride and you know it," Percy reminded him tartly.

"You can learn while you follow her."

Both men glared unblinkingly at each other. Finally, Dylon expelled a frustrated sigh and stared after the shapely blonde who had disappeared into the stable. "How do you expect me to compensate for what happened last night if I don't know where to find her?" he asked reasonably.

"Compensate? As in a proposal of marriage to meet your responsibility and obligation to one so young and so . . . innocent?" Percy prodded. "I suggest you be quick about proposing or you might find Doctor Flannery beating down your door, demanding that you marry *his* daughter instead. If I were in your ticklish situation, I know which woman I would prefer to take as my bride, whether we loved each other or not!"

Percy's explosive tone prompted Dylon to chuckle. He'd never seen his valet get so worked up. Percy was usually phlegmatic and impassive, displaying as little emotion as possible. But he always got himself into a royal stew when the subject of Liberty Jordon cropped up.

"My dear friend, has it occurred to you that *you* might have somehow fallen in love with that rambunctious sprite?"

"Has it occurred to you, sir, that *you* might have fallen in love with her as well?" Percy countered with a probing stare, one which Dylon refused to meet.

"A man can love his country and the land he works and owns. He can love his favorite steed for the purpose it serves. But to love a woman is to invite the kind of vulnerability that I detest."

"The kind you experienced with Patricia?" Percy dared to ask.

Dylon winced, feeling the sting of the well-aimed barb that stabbed at his male pride like a cactus needle.

"You would prefer to shrug off any affection you might feel for Liberty to satisfy your pride. But I cannot stand aside and allow you to toy with her as if she were your mistress. You would refuse to let her mean so much to you for fear she would take possession of your carefully guarded heart."

"Percy . . ." Dylon flung his valet a menacing glance. "Your tongue is greatly overworked. I suggest you give it the rest it so richly deserves."

Percy stared at Dylon for a long deliberate moment, uncaring that his next few comments would give him completely away and enrage the master of Lockhart Hall to the very limits of his temper. "And which of you, I wonder, truly is the bigger *coward.*"

When Dylon erupted in an explosive growl, Percy quickly scampered off the marbled steps and scuttled toward the stable before Dylon got good and mad. Percy preferred to climb atop a horse rather than stick around to watch Dylon come unglued. It didn't happen very often, but it wasn't a pretty sight when he did.

Now, Percy had a great respect and admiration for horses . . . while he stood on the ground. He did not, however, feel confident or at ease with those powerful, four-legged creatures beneath him. Although he would have preferred to take a buggy to keep a watchful eye on Liberty, as Dylon demanded, he would bob up and down in the saddle in order to put a safe distance between himself and his fuming master.

True, Percy had eavesdropped outside Liberty's door the previous night. He had grown more outraged with each passing second. Twice he had been tempted to burst inside, but he feared he would embarrass the innocent young lass to the extreme. Now that he had revealed the fact that he had been spying, Dylon was fuming. Percy expected to be severely punished when he returned.

A wry smile pursed Percy's lips as he strode into the stable to request a steed. Perhaps he would catch up with Liberty and announce his devotion to her. And if it was indeed her intent to make her escape, he would accompany her wherever she wanted to go and protect her from harm. Aye, that was exactly what he would do. And Dylon Lockhart would be eternally sorry that he had wronged that lovely sprite and driven off the most devoted servant he'd ever had!

An amused giggle bubbled in Liberty's throat as she paused in the skirting of moss-draped trees that lined the creek. She had expected Dylon to send his valet to keep surveillance on her. But it was glaringly apparent that Percival T. Pearson was not an accomplished equestrian. She watched him bobble in the saddle, valiantly trying to steer his mount—one that was unsure of his rider and what was expected of him.

Liberty had zigzagged through the trees to lose her most unlikely shadow. Twice, a tree limb had snagged Percy's garments and ripped his Bag wig from his head. Muttering, Percy had righted his wig and twisted his garments back into place before continuing on his way. Unfortunately, Percy was out of his element and he was getting more disoriented and confused by the minute. Liberty had him weaving through the vine-tangled woods until he completely lost all sense of direction.

Since Liberty had quizzed the grooms about the

location of Lockhart Hall in relation to other landmarks she recalled, she knew where she was going. Percy, unfortunately, did not. She had led him around in circles and was prepared to leave him to his own devices while she thundered toward Triple Oak.

Wheeling her steed about, Liberty took off like the wind, forcing Percy to battle his way through the jungle of underbrush and thick canopy of trees that followed the meandering creek. In less than an hour, Liberty reached the plantation that had been her home for the first five years of her life. Cautiously, she tethered her horse in the clump of trees and slipped through the surrounding gardens like a shadow. Employing the colonnades which formed an arcade along the back of the house, Liberty scuttled toward her upstairs room.

Stella Talbot gasped in astonishment when the wild-haired Liberty sailed through the balcony door. "Sweet mercy, child, what has happened to you? Where have you been and where is that horrible uncle of yours? Did he . . . ?"

Liberty pressed her index finger to Stella's lips to shush her before she roused the guards who had been posted in the hall. "I escaped from Luther and Simon before the ceremony and took refuge elsewhere. We have nothing to fear until Luther returns from Charles Town. Until then, we can stay here and . . ."

Stella gave her thick brown hair a negative shake. "The servants received a message last night that Luther will be returning this evening," she reported.

Liberty's shoulders slumped in disappointment. She had hoped to stay with Stella at least a day or two. Curse it, all the luck she seemed to be having of late was *bad*.

"There's more," Stella insisted, jostling Liberty from her troubled thoughts. "You also received a message yesterday, even though you weren't here to accept it."

She fished the envelope from her pocket and waved it in Liberty's face. "Phillippe decided to wrap up a few loose ends with your father's shipping business and he will arrive here at the end of this week."

Liberty groaned when Stella handed her the letter from her first fiancé who was supposed to be awaiting her return without chasing after her. According to the letter, Phillipe had left the shipping company in capable hands. He also declared that his place was beside his beloved fiancée and that he would keep her company in South Carolina until she was ready to sail back to the islands.

Collapsing on the end of the bed, Liberty muttered under her breath. She had hoped to cool Phillipe's pursuit by leaving the islands. Instead, he had decided to follow her. Now she had two fiancés trailing her and a reckless rake who wanted her to pretend to be his adoring escort to bamboozle Brewster.

Damnation, she'd had enough overeager fiancés and revolting dealings with various types of men to last her a lifetime! Was there no place on this continent where a woman could go to prevent being hounded by the male of the species? Apparently not!

"I cannot imagine why you are so chagrined to learn Phillipe is coming." Stella frowned bemusedly. "At least he can protect you from that treacherous uncle of yours and prevent your marriage to Simon. If you ask me, Phillipe's timing is perfect."

"Do you think, by wedding Phillipe, that I can foil whatever plans Luther had in mind when he contracted me in marriage to Simon Gridley?" Liberty sniffed distastefully. "I will only be trading one intolerable situation for another."

"Phillipe is hopelessly devoted to you," Stella declared with absolute certainty. "You could do worse, you know. In my estimation, marrying Simon would be far worse!"

"Phillipe is in love with the idea of love," Liberty

contended as she paced from wall to wall. "And I don't love him."

"But he's your father's protégé and he bears Benjamin's stamp of approval. He can help you run your business in the Indies and he will protect you from harm," Stella insisted. "In time you might come to love him."

"I've known Phillipe for three years and I haven't loved him yet," Liberty grumbled. "Phillipe is more like an overprotective brother. He sees in me only what he wants to see, not what I am. He makes a big production out of everything and he's an incurable romantic."

"He can't help being the way he is," Stella defended. "He's French, after all."

Liberty cast her maid a withering glance. "I do not wish to marry Phillipe or Simon and that is that."

"You have no wish to marry, period!" Stella clarified tartly. "Your father, God rest his soul, allowed you to run wild and free so long that now 'tis impossible for you to find a man who can match you stride for stride. You have become far too difficult to impress and you are too particular for your own good."

Liberty lurched around, aggravated that Stella had become so critical when she was already hounded by a myriad of frustrated emotions, most of which had Dylon Lockhart's name attached to them. "There is no hard and fast rule that proclaims a woman has to wed! I am managing just fine by myself!"

"Are you truly?" Stella sniffed caustically. "You have three men chasing after you at this very moment—two fiancés and a scheming uncle." (Actually, there were four men, but Stella didn't know about Percy who was lost somewhere between Lockhart Hall and Triple Oak.) "This wild romp that began in the islands and has continued throughout this colony with a raft of suitors hot on your heels, is not what I would call *managing* well, my lady!"

"Stella, 'tis not the time . . ." Liberty's voice trailed off when she heard her uncle shouting orders from the room below her.

Stella's hand flew to her mouth and she stared bug-eyed at Liberty. "Lord have mercy. He's back already!"

In a flash, Liberty dashed across the room to cram as many of her clothes into two satchels as she could manage in two minutes. "Stella, you must find a way to sneak back to Charles Town. Make arrangements for our return voyage to the islands," Liberty instructed as she tossed a purse of coins to her maid. "I will wait at Lockhart Hall to avoid Luther and Simon. I'll rejoin you in Charles Town next week and we will sail home where we belong."

"Lockhart Hall? Where in heaven's name is that?" Stella quizzed as she helped stuff Liberty's expensive gowns into her satchels as if they were a stack of dirty laundry.

"A few miles northeast of here on the Ashley River," she hurriedly informed her maid.

Stella threw up her arms in exasperation. "I don't see why you cannot turn to Phillipe for protection instead of scampering off into hiding again. He will be here soon."

Liberty paused from her task to stare into Stella's concerned expression. "Would you pit Phillipe against Luther and Simon? They held me hostage in the inn and posted those three big baboons who work for Simon outside my door. When I tried to escape the first time, Simon refused to allow me nourishment so I would be too weak to attempt another escape. His three rough-edged henchmen very nearly wrenched my arms from their sockets when they dragged me back to lock me in my room. I fear Simon and his three-man army were being lenient with me. I shudder to think what Simon and those wooly gorillas would do to Phillipe if he dared to cross that scoundrel."

Stella grimaced at the picture Liberty had painted of

her harrowing ordeal in Charles Town. She had no use for Luther or Simon or his three henchmen either. But she never expected any of them to treat a lady of quality so abominably. And Liberty was probably right. Phillipe would be a threat to Luther and Simon's scheme. He might turn up conveniently dead if he were to arrive to claim Liberty as his fiancée when Simon had other plans for her.

"I'm beginning to see your point," Stella replied with a defeated sigh. "I'll try to slip away tonight and make our travel arrangements."

"Find your way to the hotel where we stayed when we arrived from the islands," Liberty requested. "I'll meet you there as soon as I can."

The clomp of footsteps on the stairway put Liberty to immediate flight. She knew Stella would never divulge her destination to Luther and Simon, even under penalty of death. Stella was as devoted to her as Percy was to Dylon. In fact, the two of them were amazingly alike.

Liberty cast all her wandering thoughts aside and shinnied down the colonnade to dash into the garden. The last thing she needed was for Luther to catch sight of her and come charging after her. She was safe as long as Luther and Simon were unaware that she was in the area—an hour's ride away, in fact.

Like a discharging cannon, Liberty zoomed across the meadow, clutching her satchels in one hand and guiding her steed with the other. The thought of Phillipe's unexpected arrival put a frown on her elegant features. Although he was a dear man in his own peculiar way, Phillipe was bound to complicate the problem she already had with Luther and Simon. She hoped Phillipe didn't thrust himself into harm's way. Liberty wouldn't put anything past Luther, or Simon for that matter. And she wasn't certain how far those two conniving scoundrels would go to ensure that she became Mrs. Simon Gridley. . . .

Lord, that repulsive thought curdled her stomach. Liberty was positively certain she'd rather suffer a beating than be married to that man. There was something evil lurking beneath his pretentious smiles that worried her. Of one thing she was quite sure, Simon Gridley wasn't as pleasant as he wanted her to believe. She had seen another side of his personality when she attempted to escape on the eve of her wedding. Aye, Simon could be a menacing individual when he lost his temper. Liberty had no intention of being anywhere near Simon when he was prone to anger and violence. Next time, she doubted he would be lenient with her at all!

Chapter 10

A mirthful giggle erupted from Liberty's lips when she spied Percy in the distance. She had expected him to abort his attempt to track her after more than two hours of wandering around beside the swamp. But it seemed Percy was persistent and hopelessly devoted to his master.

Percy looked absolutely pathetic and Liberty could not squelch the laughter that flew from her lips when she rode up to view the servant at close range. The wig that Percy constantly fussed over had suffered considerable damage after being snagged by a score of twigs. White hair jutted from his head like corn shocks and powder lay on his shoulders like snow on a mountain. His face had been scratched and leaves, moss and broken vines dangled from his arms like straw protruding from a scarecrow. The cravat that was always neatly tied under his square chin dangled down his chest. Mud and slime from the swamp stained his stockings and breeches. Even his steed looked the worse for wear after tromping through the congested marsh. The animal was as scratched and mud-caked as his inexperienced rider.

"My lady!" Percy chirped. His face flushed with embarrassment before he managed to regain control of his voice and facial expression. He glanced awkwardly around the dense thicket and the dangling vines that hung behind him like the grotesque backdrop on a theater stage. "I was just taking a jaunt on horseback." He inhaled a breath, causing the leaves and twigs on his jacket to rustle before settling back into place. "I thought it was a perfect morning for riding too."

Liberty's lips twitched, valiantly trying to suppress another giggle. "Indeed, 'tis a fine morning for riding," she agreed and then coughed to camouflage a bubble of irrepressible laughter.

Percy shifted uncomfortably in the saddle. "I suppose you are wondering why I look so . . . so . . ."

"Bedraggled?" Liberty supplied since the valet suddenly seemed to have difficulty expressing himself. "Aye, I am."

Percy half twisted in the saddle and accusingly outthrust an arm toward the dense foliage and moss-draped thicket that clogged the creek. "My horse—the hideously *un*sure-footed creature that he is—stumbled in the marsh and catapulted me from his back."

That explained why the saddle had slid sideways, leaving Percy tilted at an amusing angle, Liberty reckoned.

"And then I got myself hopelessly lost in this tangle," Percy admitted sheepishly.

"It wasn't your fault," she insisted with a guilty smile. "I purposely led you in circles because I suspected Dylon had sent you to follow me. I didn't want you to know where I was going."

Her honest confession caused Percy to scowl under his breath—not at the fetching beauty, but at his master. "I wouldn't have blamed you one whit if you hadn't bothered to come back," he burst out. "Considering the situation, I don't think *I* would have. Indeed, I hoped to catch up with you and offer my services in whatever capacity I could assist you."

Liberty blinked and stared owl-eyed at Percy. "Situation?" she repeated warily.

Percy straightened himself as best he could in the lopsided saddle. "I am neither blind, deaf nor stupid, my lady," he announced with tremendous pride. "Although I have always been unfalteringly loyal to Dylon, I strongly disapprove of his treatment of you since the moment we found you unconscious beneath the magnolia tree."

Liberty reined her steed around to return to the path that meandered along the edge of the swamp. It was as she feared. Percy knew what had transpired the previous night.

"I appreciate your concern, Percy, but the truth is my association with Dylon is no less entangled than the rest of my life," she said deflatedly.

"Dylon should have offered a marriage proposal posthaste!" Percy erupted as he steered his steed along in Liberty's wake. "And if you will confide your misfortune in me I will do all within my power to assist you."

Liberty glanced over her shoulder at the bedraggled servant and flashed him an appreciative smile. "Dylon is lucky to have a man like you in his service. And I do thank you for your offer but . . ."

"Lucky?" Percy sniffed disgustedly. "He doesn't think so at the moment."

He cringed at the thought of confronting Dylon after their last encounter. Dylon had been positively livid. A rare occurrence, to be sure. But Percy dreaded facing the consequences of what he'd said and done to invite Dylon's wrath.

A frustrated sigh gushed from Percy's lips. "'Tis true that Dylon and his brother are most generous and tolerant masters of this plantation. They are kind and considerate of the slaves who work the indigo and rice fields and manage the other enterprises of this estate. Dylon is conscientious in all his business dealings with his associates and in the Assembly. In fact, he had every right to bring charges against the man who ran against him in the last election after the slanderous remarks made about him in the *South Carolina Gazette*. But I cannot condone Dylon's dealings with women. He never takes himself or females seriously in those instances."

Quietly, Liberty listened to Percy provide insight about the man who had preoccupied her thoughts far more than he should have.

"I'm sure Dylon would cheerfully strangle me if he knew I imparted this information. But to be forewarned is to be forearmed," he declared before he ducked beneath a low-hanging branch and very nearly slid off the saddle.

Uprighting himself, Percy continued, "Five years ago Dylon fancied himself in love with a merry young widow who was two years his junior. He had visions of settling down and making Patricia his wife. But a series of killings on the frontier instigated another conflict with the Cherokees who attacked Fort Prince George. The Indians were outraged because white traders were dousing their men with rum, violating their women and cheating them in the sale of furs and hides.

"When Dylon was again called upon to defend the outposts of the colony against the attacks of the Cherokees, Patricia Morgan turned her attention elsewhere during his absence. Before Dylon returned from the grisly battles in the wilderness, Patricia had latched onto a wealthy nobleman who was visiting the colony. It seemed the only things Patricia really loved was money and titles. So the duke was in and Dylon was out. Without so much as a letter of explanation or the slightest consideration for Dylon's feelings, Patricia sailed off with her duke. Dylon returned to Charles Town with the regiment of militia who escorted Chief Attakulla to surrender and sign the peace treaty. He turned the city upside down trying to find Patricia. When he finally learned she had callously discarded him for a titled lord he was devastated."

Percy glanced somberly at Liberty as they rode along the river. "Dylon swore, there and then, that he would never be a fool for love again. He is now of the opinion that if a man gives his heart to a woman she will return it in at least two pieces. Now he hides his bitterness behind a mask of nonchalance. And since that fateful day, he has never allowed any female close enough to reopen the wounds on his heart."

"Having never been in love, I cannot fully understand his torment," Liberty mused as her gaze stretched across the sun-splashed meadows. "But I'm sure the incident must have hurt him deeply and made him leery of lasting relationships."

"Leery?" Percy scoffed sarcastically. "You don't know the half of it! With Dylon's wealth, power and position, women trail after him like starved kittens after a bucket of fresh milk. But he refuses to take anyone seriously, refuses to become involved in anything except brief shallow affairs. He seems hell-bent on breaking hearts to compensate for his unpleasant experience with love. His motto has become love 'em and leave 'em and *love* is the only four-letter word that has been stricken from his vocabulary. His casual philosophy where women are concerned has even rubbed off on Griffin."

Percy reached out to draw Liberty's steed to a halt and stared her squarely in the eye. "Already I have become fond of you, my lady," he confessed with genuine sincerity. "I do not wish to see you hurt. Guard your step and your heart or you might find yourself experiencing the same devastating bout with love that soured Dylon. He hides behind that armor of imperturbable nonchalance, but he is deathly afraid of being hurt and abandoned and left to look the utter fool."

"And what do you suggest I do?" Liberty queried.

"Continue to behave just as you did this morning," Percy advised. "Dylon is a man of great pride. Nothing will get to him faster than thinking you are as casual and unconcerned about your relationship as he is."

Liberty stared soberly at the valet who had exposed Dylon's darkest secrets. "I have no wish to entrap him," she informed Percy. "I intend to go home where I belong as soon as arrangements can be made. Until then, we will both serve a purpose for one another."

"You don't want him?" Percy gaped incredulously at the bewitching blonde. "Whyever not?"

"I already have two unwanted fiancés to contend with," Liberty admitted, watching Percy's jaw fall off its hinges. "And forgive me for saying so, but love seems grossly overrated. Marriage, I imagine, is too. In fact, I'm beginning to think living alone is more practical than dealing with unscrupulous men. You, Percival T. Pearson, may be the exception of your species."

When Liberty nudged her steed forward, Percy sat there with his mouth hanging open. Sweet mercy, two cynics under the same roof? Percy slumped in the saddle. Perhaps he had worried about Liberty for naught. It seemed this feisty young she-male who'd caught Dylon's fancy was his equal match, as well as his worthy competition in any arena. It would be a challenge to see which one of them managed to break the other one's heart. They were both determined not to fall prey to Cupid's arrow. Unfortunately, Cupid was also an excellent archer. Liberty and Dylon might both wind up getting shot clean through.

A hint of a smile hovered on Percy's lips when Liberty halted her mount beside the pugmill where clay was being mixed with water to form a smooth consistency for bricks. One of the slaves who was referred to as the "mold man" stood waist deep in the pit beside the ox-powered mill. He glanced up from his task of rolling a lump of clay in sand and pressing it into wooden molds.

A greeting grin slid across the black man's lips when Liberty questioned him about the process. He quickly showed her how the brick molds were scraped clean and left to dry for a fortnight before the "green bricks" were stacked in the kiln and heated by oak wood fires for ten days.

While Liberty was making instant friends of the slaves by posing curious questions and complimenting them on their skills, Percy simply sat back and admired her astonishing rapport with slaves, servants and gentry alike. It was truly amazing the way people gravitated toward this vivacious beauty. She could draw warmth from the most reluctant of souls and bring sunshine into the gloomiest of days.

Maybe he was taking this matter between Liberty and Dylon a mite too seriously. Perhaps he should simply sit back and watch this high-spirited sprite counter Dylon's charm . . . and vice versa. Percy had the inescapable feeling that Dylon was about to get more than he'd bargained for when he pitted himself against Liberty Jordon. She could give as good as she got. And Dylon might find himself standing in line, vying for her attention if she already had two fiancés and who knew how many other eager suitors waiting to court her. Dylon delighted in competition, but he might not be so pleased when he found himself among the endless rabble of men who competed for Liberty's affection.

"Justice," Percy snickered spitefully (just as Dylon feared he would). "Now that would be true justice!"

When Liberty rode up to the throng of slaves who clustered around the Lockhart brothers, Dylon didn't notice her. He was busy firing orders to the work force that was in the process of transplanting rice seedlings from their nursery beds of small dirt hills in which the seeds had been broadcast a month earlier.

Since Dylon was preoccupied, Liberty quizzed Percy about the procedure, another with which she was unfamiliar since she had spent most of her life in the islands. Percy directed her attention to the water from a sluggish stream which was being flooded over the swampy banks to provide proper growing conditions for the crop. According to Percy, the rice plants only flourished when grown under a few inches of water. Dikes had been built by slave labor and the difficult task of clearing fields had been unnecessary in this particular area because nothing grew in these marshes except grass and rushes. The seedlings had only to be relocated in the sloppy muck and the only tools required to cultivate the crop was a strong back and a sharp hoe.

Delighted with the prospect of having an excuse to wade about in the muck instead of remaining on the perimeters like a dignified lady, Liberty doffed her slippers and slid from the saddle.

In amusement, Percy watched the rambunctious sprite draw the back hem of her skirt between her legs and tuck it in the front waistband, creating a pair of makeshift breeches that exposed the lower portion of her legs. In all his born days, he had never seen a lady of quality tromp out across the rice fields to inspect the goings-on. But Liberty cared nothing for social convention or proper limitation. If curiosity got the best of her, just as it had when she passed the pugmill, she appeased it there and then. It didn't matter one whit to her whether her behavior fell within the restrictions of acceptable aristocratic behavior or not! Liberty did exactly what she pleased, uncaring what others thought of her. External influences and conflicting opinions seemed to have no bearing on what she did or when she did it.

Liberty paused beside one of the slaves who had hunkered down on his haunches to drag mud around the clumped roots of the rice seedlings. Shocked though the man was to see her standing ankle-deep in slime, he fielded her curious questions. Liberty was intent on knowing when the water would be drained from the fields for harvest. The slave politely informed her that the area would be weeded and would stand in at least four inches of water until the grain ripened into a sea of gold—Carolina gold, as it had come to be called.

The slave flung the mud from his hand and gestured to the south. "The water will be drained through openin's in the dikes. When the grain is fully ripened and the heads curl over, sickles will be used to cut the stalks. Then the stalks will be tied in sheaves and toted from the field by mule-drawn carts."

"Surely, after standing in all this water, the stalks have to be left to dry," Liberty surmised.

"Aye, it does," the servant confirmed. "The crop is threshed with flails and winnowed by the wind. Tall platforms have been built to separate the grain from its straw before the final product is scooped up, loaded on ships and sent downriver to Charles Town."

"My, what a long, involved process," Liberty remarked as she shaded her eyes from the glittering sunlight that danced across the soupy field.

"Aye, m'lady," the slave assured her as he sloshed down the row to plant another bundle of seedlings. "But Master Lockhart's plantation boasts one of the finest rice crops in the area. While other men view the procedures from the distance, Master Lockhart involves himself in the plantin' and reapin' of his crops."

While Liberty was engrossed in conversation, Griffin glanced up from his task of digging seedlings from the nursery beds. A burst of laughter exploded from his lips when he spied Percy—wig atangle—sitting atop his mount. Griffin's expression changed to stupefied incredulousness when the sunlight glinted off Liberty's glorious mane of blond hair. She stood as casually in the muck as she had on the carpet in the parlor of the mansion. Her skirt was wrapped around her in a most unorthodox fashion and she was chatting with one of the slaves as if such unusual behavior was an everyday occurrence.

"Well, strike me blue!" Griffin croaked.

Upon hearing his brother's startled oath, Dylon wheeled around. His gaze followed Griffin's outstretched arm to see Liberty amid the glinting silver water of the field. "What in the hell does she think she's doing?" Dylon muttered to the world at large.

"Whatever she damned well pleases, when it pleases her, would be my guess," Griffin said, chuckling delightedly. His smile vanished, replaced by a wistful expression. "Dylon, I think you should know I'm falling in love with that unconventional, temporary fiancée of yours. . . ."

An annoyed scowl puckered Dylon's features. Muttering, he stuffed a clump of rice plants into his overseer's hand and stalked off. By the time Dylon had elbowed his way through the crowd of slaves who had gathered around him, Liberty had slopped down the row and leaped over the dirt dikes.

In the first place, Dylon hadn't expected this wild-hearted minx to return from her mysterious morning excursion. That was why he had sent Percy to determine her destination for future reference. And in the second place (although deep down inside Dylon was delighted that she had returned on her own accord) he did not appreciate seeing her tramp across the rice field like a servant. . . .

His breath stuck in his throat when the ripple of water behind Liberty caught his attention. The swamps were not only the location of rice seedlings, but also the stomping ground of cottonmouth water moccasins. Liberty had slogged through the muck, disturbing what looked to be at least three deadly vipers. Her thrashing about had startled the snakes and they were preparing to attack!

With his heart pounding like a sledgehammer, Dylon snatched the pistol from his belt and fired beside her feet. A shocked shriek exploded from Liberty's lips when buckshot danced in the water and splattered her skirt. Instinctively, she dived forward into the water, unsure which direction the shot had come from. Her first thought was that Luther had spotted her, followed her and was attempting to ambush her for eluding him again.

Her speculations scattered when the sound of slopping water filtered into her brain. Liberty glanced over her shoulder to see the serpents slithering toward her, despite Dylon's attempt to frighten them away. Feeling as if she were moving in slow motion, she tried to scramble back to her feet. Her clothes were saturated with mud and hampered her desperate attempt to leap over the dike to safety.

Another terrified squawk bubbled in her throat when the lead snake sprang at her. Its jaws opened wide, exposing the whiteness of its throat and the deadly fangs that were filled with venom. A second shot rang through the air and the snake dropped a few inches behind her ankle, writhing in spasms before it slumped lifelessly on the edge of the dike.

From her prone position in the mud, Liberty glanced up to see a pair of slimy boots, long powerful legs and a heaving chest. When her eyes elevated to Dylon's stony face, she gulped air. It was glaringly apparent that this rake could wear a mutinous frown as well as he wore a nonchalant smile. He looked like murdering fury at the moment—all of which was directed at the muddy bundle of femininity who'd come within a hairbreadth of suffering a poisonous snakebite.

With a growl that sounded inhuman, Dylon hurriedly reloaded his pistol and took aim at the other two water moccasins that had the good sense to retreat. After firing a quick shot to ensure the serpents took flight, Dylon reached down none too gently and jerked Liberty to her feet.

"You little idiot!" he growled into her mud-splotched face. "You have to watch where you're going out here! You can't gad about in these fields as if you were on a Sunday stroll in the park. Damnit, this is a snake-infested swamp!"

Before she could wipe away the mud and open her mouth to apologize, Dylon scooped her up in his arms, uncaring that he was as saturated with grime and slime as she was. Still muttering obscenities under his breath, Dylon slopped toward the edge of the field to find Percy still sitting atop his horse.

Dylon took one look at his bedraggled servant and his previous irritation with the valet was forgotten. Never in all his years of service had Percival T. Pearson looked so disheveled and unraveled! His Bag wig was a mass of leaves and mud. So were his clothes. The stricken look on Percy's face testified to the extent of his concern for the daring misfit who had wandered into the swamp to appease her insatiable curiosity.

"I don't know which one of you looks worse," Dylon scoffed as he plunked Liberty onto the saddle (where he wished she would have had the good sense to stay to begin with!) "Take her back to the house and get her cleaned up, if 'tis at all possible. . . ." His narrowed gaze flooded over the revealing gauze blouse and saturated skirt that looked as though they'd been painted on her flesh, revealing all Liberty's alluring assets. "And don't let her come out here again!"

"Aye, sir." Percy dusted the clinging powder from his shoulders and pushed into an erect position on his mount, trying very hard to look as stately and dignified as the situation permitted.

Although Dylon was still glaring at her for scaring the living daylights out of him, Liberty didn't look the least bit repentant. She still preferred to take her chances with snakes than to muck about the house like Cayla Styles, perfecting her talents with crochet needles. Liberty would always be a participant of life, never a bystander. Dylon could rake her over the coals for her reckless antics, but she had no intention of conforming. Why, the word wasn't even in her vocabulary!

"I rather think Dylon is now as irritated with you as he is with me," Percy speculated as he bobbled in the saddle.

"As for me, I don't particularly care what he thinks," Liberty declared haughtily.

A smile tugged at Percy's lips, just as it always did when he was with this feisty hellion. "I didn't think you did, my lady." His grin broadened to encompass every feature on his face. "When you return from Brewster's estate at the first of next week, perhaps you would like to inspect the indigo fields. That should put Master

Lockhart in another snit."

Liberty returned his mischievous grin. "An excellent suggestion, Percival. Are they also infested with poisonous snakes?"

"Nay, thankfully not. But judging from your track record, I'm sure you will manage to tangle yourself in some sort of mishap that will aggravate Dylon."

"You think I'm a jinx, Percy?" Liberty inquired, half jesting, half serious.

"Nay, my lady, only a bundle of inexhaustible energy and curiosity," Percy qualified. "Hopefully, you will always be adept at emerging from trouble as easily as you stumble into it."

Liberty fell silent, wondering if Percy hadn't summed up her life in one brief sentence. She did have a zest for living that always managed to land her in trouble. She had an uncle and one fiancé scouring the countryside to retrieve her and another fiancé sailing toward the colony to complicate an already unpleasant situation that had her scampering from one location to another like an escaped convict. And to make matters worse, she had stumbled onto a rogue with entrancing blue eyes who had seduced her for his own lusty pleasure. Godamercy, perhaps she *should* confine herself to the parlor and take up knitting. Chances were Cayla Styles wasn't facing such difficulties. The poor woman had only to decide when to replenish her energy with one of the many naps she took during the course of a day!

A wry grin tripped across Griffin's lips as he watched his brother tromp through the mud to return to his task. "I cannot wait to see what sort of catastrophe Liberty embroils herself into at Grandfather's holiday," he said, snickering. "If nothing else, that daring little imp will be the talk of the festivities."

"She might not live long enough to attend the celebration," Dylon scowled sourly. "By then, I may have choked the life out of her."

"My, aren't we in a huff all of a sudden," Griffin observed with wicked glee.

"Nay, we are not!" Dylon blared.

Playfully, Griffin shied away. "You needn't bite my head off. Just admit it, big brother. This time *you* bit off more than *you* can chew."

With an agitated sneer on his lips, Dylon slammed the rice stalks into his brother's hand and lurched around. "You oversee the planting. I'm going to read that minx the rules and regulations which she is to observe during her stay at this plantation!"

"A waste of time." Griffin chuckled at his brooding brother. "Liberty breaks more rules than she'll ever follow."

"She will abide by mine, by God!" Dylon roared as he stamped toward his horse.

Griffin didn't think so. Still chuckling, he ambled over to pass the rice seedlings to the overseer. "I'm leaving this to you, my friend. I have urgent business to attend."

Amos Potts frowned quizzically at his employer. "I thought rice planting was our foremost concern."

"It *was*," Griff corrected. "But I'm eager to watch that high-spirited hoyden defy my brother. She may need my assistance if Dylon doesn't regain his good disposition before he reaches the house."

Amos broke into a pensive smile. "Now that you mention it, I don't recall seeing Dylon quite so annoyed, especially with a woman."

"Delightful, isn't it?" Griffin tittered before he swaggered over to fetch his mount. "You keep me posted on the progress in the rice fields and I'll keep you abreast of this war of wills."

"We have a deal," Amos confirmed with a wide grin that displayed his lack of front teeth. "But be sure that you stay out of the crossfire. The battle might get a little rough."

Griffin didn't respond. His thoughts were on the

outrageous young imp who had turned Lockhart Hall upside down and his brother wrong side out. Griffin hadn't enjoyed himself so much in years. And he had never seen his brother growling like a wounded lion. So much for Dylon's carefree, nonchalant attitude, Griff mused spitefully. That violet-eyed spitfire had shot Dylon's unflappable disposition all to hell!

Chapter 11

Absently, Liberty followed Percy down the stone path that led through the gardens to a lattice pavilion. An appreciative sigh escaped her lips when she stepped inside the bathhouse that was lined with pots of orange trees, white star and Carolina jessamine. Sunlight splattered through the slats of wood that formed the ceiling and walls of the building. A spacious stone tub which had been built into the ground had been filled to capacity and heated by dropping glowing stones into the water.

"Had I known this place existed, I would have camped out here," Liberty enthused as she set aside her fresh set of clothes.

Percy frowned at Liberty's obvious fascination with bathing. "Lounging in a tub serves its purpose, to be sure. But one must be careful not to do enough bathing to endanger one's health," he advised. "I have even heard it said that overbathing can contribute to the painful condition of rheumatism. But I carry a potato in my pocket to protect myself from such afflictions."

Liberty burst out laughing at Percy's notion that potatoes in pockets could in any way ward off rheumatism or any other affliction. She quickly sobered when the valet fixed his stare on her. "I do have a penchant for bathing," she confessed, eyeing the sparkling water with eager anticipation. "But as of yet, I have suffered no ill effects from overextended periods of time in water."

Although there were some folks who believed bathing to be hazardous, Liberty did not share that opinion. She had always scoffed at the peculiar notion that baths were deterimental. Indeed, she never let a day go by without submerging in a full tub of water or in the ocean that surrounded the islands. In her estimation, swimming and bathing were two of the most pleasurable experiences in life and she had learned to swim like a fish. . . .

Percy clucked his tongue in disapproval of Liberty's comment. "It seems you and Dylon share a common perversion. He, like you, would soak in this tub for hours on end if I didn't insist that he climb out." He gestured toward the stack of towels, perfumed soap and sponges. "Enjoy yourself, my lady. But do not tarry too long. You will shrivel up like a prune and you will become susceptible to rheumatism, especially since you have not taken the precaution of arming yourself with a potato."

"Haven't you heard it said that cleanliness is next to godliness?" Liberty asked with a teasing smile.

"Aye," Percy replied. "But I do not honestly believe God is partial to clean people."

Deliberately, Percy fished his own potato from his pocket and set it atop her fresh stack of clothing, in hopes she would take preventive measures by tucking it in her pocket. With a polite bow, Percy took himself off, leaving Liberty to her much-welcomed bath.

"Potatoes indeed!" Liberty snickered as she shucked her mud-caked garb and leaped into the tub without the slightest feminine reserve. The tepid water swirled around her like a whispering caress, dissolving the mud and the remembered feel of Dylon's skillful hands upon her flesh.

Liberty submerged herself completely and swam around the perimeters of the large stone tub. Now this was heaven! Beneath the water, she was met with only the sounds that reminded her of the breakers rolling toward the shore of the islands. She could see only the stones and mortar through the wall of clear water that surrounded her.

Ah, to be a fish! The scaly creatures had only to contend with schools instead of fiancés who hounded a woman at every turn. This would be the life, Liberty decided. One would have thought the Lord would have seen His way clear to permit her to be a mermaid. In fact, Liberty rather thought she had missed her calling and her natural niche in life.

Bursting to the surface like a spouting whale, Liberty mopped her long hair from her face and grasped the bottle of fragrant bubbles. Amid a glimmering sea of pastel bubbles, she scrubbed herself to a shine. Next, she lathered her hair and massaged the caked mud from her scalp. When her eyes began to burn, Liberty groped along the stone tiles to locate the towel to wipe her eyes. Magically, the plush fabric floated over her arm. Clearing her vision, Liberty glanced up to see Griffin lounging in the chair only five feet away from her.

A startled gasp tripped from her lips when he grinned rakishly down at her. Liberty quickly plastered herself against the rim of the tub to prevent him from seeing more than he needed to see—besides her bare arms and shoulders, which was more than enough!

Her gaze drifted down Griffin's well-sculptured form and she chuckled in amusement. "It looks as if Percy has convinced you to carry a potato in your breeches pocket to ward off rheumatism."

The bulge in Griffin's breeches was definitely not a potato, even if the naive imp thought it was! Battling his profuse embarrassment, Griffin shifted his position in the chair to call less attention to his aroused state which had been caused by staring overly long at this enticing beauty.

"I came by to see if you had suffered any discomfort after your near brush with the water moccasin," he explained, purposely switching the topic of conversation.

"Didn't you just," Liberty sassed, flinging him a mocking glance. "You, sir, are just like your brother. Shame on you from peeking at a poor defenseless woman while she is enjoying the privacy of a bath."

Griffin smiled unrepentantly. His gaze flooded over Liberty's silky skin, wishing he could see more than he'd already seen while she was unaware. "I'm not exactly like my brother," he qualified. "And more's the pity that he's the one who found you first."

The unexpected compliment caused Liberty to blink like a disturbed owl. "Need I remind you that Cayla is in the house, crocheting her bridal trousseau, hoping you will approach with a proposal?"

Griffin smiled again, displaying that customary Lockhart charm. "If there is any proposing to be done hereabout, it will be *my* proposing to *you* after you and Dylon complete the charade for Brewster's benefit."

Whether he was joking or not, which Liberty was sure he was, the last thing Liberty needed was another fiancé! Already, she was rife with them. . . .

Her thoughts trailed off when she heard a low growl rolling toward her from the entrance of the pavilion. Lo and behold, Dylon appeared looking like black thunder. His countenance hadn't changed one iota since their last unpleasant encounter. His murderous scowl did his ruggedly handsome features no justice whatsoever. But this time, his snapping blue eyes were focused on Griffin who was sprawled leisurely in his chair, drinking in the tantalizing view of Liberty's bare arms and shoulders.

"What in the hell do you think you're doing in here?" Dylon snarled venomously.

Unabashed, Griffin grinned. "I was just proposing, if you must know," he informed his seething brother.

The light tone of Griff's voice discounted his comment, but Dylon knew his brother damned well meant what he said. Dylon very nearly ground the enamel off his teeth when he clenched them so tightly together to prevent yelling at Griffin.

"You, dear brother"—the endearment sounded suspiciously like a curse and that was exactly how Dylon meant it—"have overstepped yourself," he gritted out. "The lady has no need of another fiancé!"

He'd certainly got that right, thought Liberty.

"And to make matters worse, you are invading the lady's privacy," Dylon added with a glare that was as hot as the hinges on hell's door. "You seem to have forgotten that your escort is sitting in the parlor, waiting with bated breath for you to dazzle her with your wit . . . which, I might add . . . is only half of what it should be."

Griffin shrugged off the insult like a duck shedding water. "Liberty already reminded me that I intruded. But I'm waiting for her to accept my marriage proposal."

Dylon stalked forward like a fire-breathing dragon. Dried mud crumbled from his stained shirt when his chest swelled to phenomenal proportions. "I'm answering for her," Dylon all but shouted at his ornery brother. "The answer is NAY!"

Griffin would have had to be stone deaf not to have heard his raging brother. In fact, it was a wonder his booming voice, which echoed off the tile, didn't raise the dead *and* the roof!

Griffin threw back his raven head and laughed out loud. "For a man who has been so easily amused so often, you certainly have turned into a sourpuss in a great hurry," he observed between snickers. "Since when did you start taking yourself and life so seriously?"

His laughter died a quick death when Dylon pounced at him, snatching him out of his chair by the collar of his shirt. In four long strides, Dylon showed Griffin the door and shoved him through it.

"And stay out!" Dylon boomed. "I'll deal with you later."

When he wheeled back around, Liberty was peering up at him. Her chin rested on her folded arms that were braced on the rim of the sunken tub. Her amethyst eyes twinkled up at him like polished jewels.

"Did you also want something, *my lord?*" (Her very tone indicated she mocked the title and his position. Liberty was making it perfectly clear that he would never be *her* lord and master.)

Dylon gnashed his teeth. "I don't appreciate your tramping around my plantation without my permission. There are some places that ladies of quality do not go. A rice field is one of them. And I sorely dislike your working your wiles on my own brother. Because of you he has neglected his obligations to Cayla who has been rudely left alone because Griffin is hot on your heels."

The condemning accusation brought Liberty's temper to a rolling boil. "Work my wiles on him?" she parroted furiously. "I did no such thing! And even if I had, 'tis no business of yours. I agreed to pose as your enamored fiancée during your grandfather's festivities, but I'll make no other bargain with you, devil that you are. You played the first one to your advantage." Liberty inhaled an irritated breath and plunged on. "And I am not, nor will I ever be one of your slaves or servants whom you order about and expect them to respond out of fear of retribution. You can spout your commands until you are blue in the face, Dylon Lockhart, and I will defy them one and all!"

"You will do exactly what I tell you to do, when I tell you to do it!" Dylon bellowed as he stamped toward the edge of the sunken pool.

It annoyed him to the extreme that she had childishly submerged in the tub so she wouldn't have to listen to him rant and rave. Cursing fluently, Dylon snaked out a hand to clutch at her trailing hair and jerked her head from the water.

"And I will not have some precocious chit undermining the workings of this plantation and placing me in competition with my own brother! What happened between us last night allows me certain rights that . . . Argh!"

His high-handed remark infuriated Liberty beyond

words. With the quickness of a striking snake (and she knew firsthand how quickly a viper could strike, believe you her) she thrust out a hand to clutch at his boot. Dylon was thrown off balance while he bent over the tub, holding Liberty by the hair of her head and thrusting his snarling face into hers to read her the riot act. When she pulled his leg out from under him, Dylon was too top-heavy to upright himself. Although he flapped his arms like a windmill, gravity got the better of him. Like a giant tree falling beneath a lumberjack's ax, Dylon *kerplopped* facedown in the pool.

When he sputtered to the surface, choking for breath, Liberty slammed the saturated sponge in his face. "What happened last night makes no difference whatsoever," she fumed, forgetting modesty and all else except the need to voice her outrage. "You have no rights where I am concerned. You may have been the first man in my bed, but you will not be the last! If you think for one minute that I will drop at your feet and beg a proposal to salvage my reputation, you are sorely mistaken. Nora may whimper and beg to become your bride, but I will not! If it pleases me to gather a stable of studs to appease my feminine desires, then I will do just that! And if I wish to accept the eager attentions of your brother then I shall."

"You shall not!" Dylon blared as they stood eye-to-eye and toe-to-toe, yelling in each other's dripping faces. He yanked her to him, slamming her rigid body into his unyielding contours. His eyes flashed like blue blazes as he breathed down her neck. "You are mine by right of conquest . . ."

Another poorly phrased remark, Dylon realized too late. He'd made Liberty mad enough to spit nails. With a squeal of outrageous indignation, Liberty uplifted her knee, catching him squarely in the groin. A dull groan wobbled in Dylon's throat as he doubled over to protect himself against another devastating blow that was sure to cause his voice to rise two octaves from this day forward.

"Last night was a mistake that will never be repeated," Liberty hissed, pummeling his chest with her fists. "I wouldn't come to the likes of you for affection, even if I were starving for it! You are not God's gift to women and you are not the only man who can appease a woman. I . . ."

The words whipped off her curled lips and drowned in the pool when Dylon grabbed her to him and kissed her into silence. Rage prevented Liberty from succumbing to Dylon's overpowering assault. Liberty reached up to clutch his damp hair and yanked his head backward. Before he saw her fist coming, Liberty mashed his nose against the left side of his face. A pained grunt exploded from his lips. Good God, he'd roused a human wildcat who was as adept with her fists as she was with pistols and bows!

In a burst of fury, Liberty flung herself away. With no regard for modesty, she vaulted from the tub and wrapped the oversized towel around herself in angry jerks. "You, Dylon Lockhart, can go straight to hell and take the rest of your disgusting gender with you!"

"Where, my feisty witch, do you think I've been for the past half-hour?" Dylon growled nastily.

"Not as deep in hell as a crow can fly in a week," she blustered, eyes flashing like lavender flames. "And only when you are, will I be satisfied!"

Angrily, Liberty snatched up the potato that Percy had left for her. Taking aim, she hurled the missile at the source of her irritation. Although Dylon ducked, the projectile caught him on the side of the head instead of squarely between the eyes.

"And I hope you get rheumatism too!" she sneered spitefully.

In a full-blown huff, she scooped up her clothes and stormed out of the pavilion, garbed only in her towel. She didn't care if she shocked Percy and the rest of the servants all the way to their toes when she stomped through the house to her room in such an indecent manner. Dylon made her so furious that she could barely think straight.

When she stamped onto the first landing of the staircase she heard a bubble of laughter behind her. Lurching about, she glowered at Griffin who had negligently propped himself against the banister.

"My dear Liberty, you have the most extraordinary taste in wearing apparel," he teased. His appreciative gaze swept over the heaving swells of her bosom and the shapely curve of her bare legs, visualizing her without her towel. Gorgeous, he recalled with a mouthwatering smile.

"Go soak your head in a rice paddy," Liberty snapped. Thanks to Dylon she was in bad humor and in no mood to counter Griffin's playful taunts.

"And risk being attacked by poisonous vipers?" Griffin gasped in mock terror. "I'd rather not."

Muttering under her breath, Liberty stalked up the steps and slammed the door to her room.

The house shuddered and groaned.

Griffin was still lost to the appetizing vision of Liberty wrapped in her towel when Dylon sloshed through the foyer. His boots squeaked with each step he took and water oozed onto the floor as he tromped toward the staircase. His dripping wet clothes left puddles beside his soggy footsteps that would require a mop to dispose of the damage done to the waxed floor.

"Did you enjoy your bath?" Griffin snickered as his smoldering brother thrashed past him.

Dylon's mouth was set in such a taut line that Griff feared it would snap under the excessive pressure. Dylon looked like a bomb that was looking for a suitable place to explode. He uttered not one word for fear his temper would cause him to erupt into a raft of unspeakable curses that would cause a foul cloud to hover over the plantation for a full week.

While Dylon stormed toward his room, Griffin swore he saw steam rising from the collar of his brother's wet shirt. It was truly a wonder the fuming giant didn't evaporate into a puff of smoke.

When Dylon slammed the door to his room, the house shuddered and groaned a second time.

Griffin grinned wryly. It was glaringly apparent that Dylon and Liberty were on the worst of terms. That was fine and dandy with Griffin. It would give him the opportunity to charm that violet-eyed pixie who had begun to monopolize Griffin's thoughts and inspire the most erotic dreams!

"I told you that I have seen nothing of Liberty," Stella lied with commendable acting ability. A pained gasp erupted from Stella's lips when Simon backhanded her across the cheek, just hard enough to cause whiplash.

"You expect us to believe that my fiancée would make no attempt to contact you?" Simon scowled at the defiant maid.

Stella blinked back the tears and glowered at the tall, stout man who reminded her of an oversized rat with his pointed nose, close-set eyes and matching gray garments. In her past dealings with this ogre, Stella hadn't considered him particularly dangerous, only shrewd and sneaky. But the murderous glare Simon bestowed on her after he slapped her sent a snake of fear slithering down her spine. Simon Gridley, she decided, was like a chameleon who changed colors and moods to suit his whims. In the past he had pretended to be gentlemanly and polite, but he was anything but!

"If you think to protect your lady, you will live to regret it," Simon growled in a malevolent voice. "If Liberty tried to make contact with you, I demand to be told . . . immediately."

"She has yet to send word to me," Stella repeated, eyeing Simon with blatant hatred. "If she had returned, don't you think I would have raced off with her? After all, I am not residing here because 'tis my wont."

Simon slanted her a probing glance, trying to determine if she was lying. It was difficult to tell when her glare registered such a strong dislike—one which overshadowed all other emotions.

"You may return to your chambers," Simon said brusquely. "And do not forget what I said. It will not bode well for you if you defy us as Liberty did."

Stella surged out of her chair. With her back stiff as a ramrod, she marched out the door of the parlor. Curse that man. He spouted orders as if this were *his* home and she were *his* servant! Ah, but she would dearly love to know what kind of hold Simon had over Liberty's uncle. Those two scoundrels were up to no good and Liberty had become their pawn. Thank the Lord Liberty had escaped in the nick of time! Now, if only she could make *her* escape to Charles Town. . . .

Stella peered at the hugh black servant who propped himself against the wall beside her door. From the look of things, she would still be closely guarded, just as Liberty had been on the eve of her wedding.

Once inside her improvised prison, Stella peered at the terrace door. An apprehensive lump formed in her throat. There was only one way to escape, via the same route Liberty had taken—over the railing, across the arcade and down the colonnade. Stella was counting on the fact that Luther and Simon would not expect a maid who was pushing forty and slightly overweight to employ such a perilous route.

Although Stella detested looking down from great heights, she marshaled her courage and snatched up her belongings. Strapping the satchels over both shoulders and hips to cushion her in case she fell, Stella tiptoed onto the terrace.

As darkness settled over the obscure plantation like a black cloak, Stella eased over the railing and inched across the roof of the arcade. With extreme caution, she wrapped herself around the pillar and slid to the ground. She was intensely proud of her accomplishment, considering her apprehension of heights. But fortunately, climbing down at night wasn't as frightening because she hadn't been able to see how far she could fall if she lost her grasp.

Stella flitted through the gardens like a shadow and circled toward the stable. Her skills as a groom were sorely lacking, but she did manage to saddle and lead one of the steeds from the stable without being detected.

Flinging the satchels over the horse, Stella pulled herself into position and trotted toward the road that led to Charles Town. Lord, she couldn't wait to shake the dust of Triple Oak off her heels! Returning to the colony had brought nothing but trouble.

Despite what Liberty had said, Stella hoped to intercept Phillipe LaGere when he arrived at the docks. In Stella's estimation, Liberty needed assistance. Phillipe could very well be Liberty's only salvation. He could call for Liberty at Lockhart Hall and accompany them back to Charles Town without letting Simon and Luther know of his arrival and hasty departure.

Aye, that was the ticket, Stella thought with a decisive nod. She would camp out at the docks to meet Phillipe. She would explain the disastrous sequence of events without naming names so that Phillipe wouldn't plunge ahead to gallantly defend his fiancée's honor, or some such ridiculous pledge to right all wrongs. With Liberty in safe hands, the threesome could sail back to the islands and leave Luther Norris and Simon Gridley to mildew in this sticky South Carolina climate!

Feeling quite pleased with her successful escape and her sensible plans for Liberty, Stella rode through the night. In two weeks they would be safe within the confines of the Jordon estate in Barbados. They would be miles away from that diabolical duo. Then, and only then, could Liberty put this nightmare behind her and get on with the rest of her life.

And if Liberty had any sense at all, she would marry Phillipe the first chance she got. He might not be the love of her life but he was a damned sight better than that big rat Simon Gridley!

A muted scowl tumbled from Simon's pinched mouth as he paced the confines of the parlor. "Where could that sly little vixen be?" he asked himself for the umpteenth time.

Luther shrugged his thin-bladed shoulders while he paced two steps behind Simon. "Only God knows," he muttered bitterly. "We searched high and low in Charles Town. If she took refuge there, I cannot imagine where she could be hiding since she had no funds. She knows no one else in the area."

Simon wheeled to glare at the shorter, older man. "We alerted every ship's captain in port, but I won't be content to twiddle my thumbs until she turns up. And she damned well better turn up!" he threatened in a menacing tone. "Otherwise, you can expect to endure a very unpleasant future . . . and a *short*, unpleasant one at that!"

Luther gulped apprehensively. He knew exactly where he'd end up if he failed to produce Simon's third bride. Simon was not a patient man. Luther had learned that in his unfortunate dealings with his associate. But now he was in too deep to escape. He had to comply with Simon's demands or face the grim consequences.

"At first light, I want you to gather your most trustworthy servants," Simon ordered abruptly. "We'll scout the countryside from here to Charles Town to find that firebrand."

"I'll see to the matter," Luther promised faithfully.

"And while you're forming your search party, I will gather my three henchmen and servants to scour the area." In stiff strides, Simon crossed the room to fetch his hat. "I don't have two weeks to chase down my runaway fiancée. I also have a plantation to run and crops to plant, all of which I neglected in my attempt to claim the Assembly seat that Lockhart holds."

The reminder of losing the election to Dylon Lockhart put another disgusted scowl on Simon's face. He had fought with every means possible to rout that wealthy aristocrat from his political position but without success. Simon had held a grudge against Dylon since those days in the wilderness when Lockhart had been given command of the troops. It had galled Simon to no end to take orders from Lockhart. For the past five years he had envied the man and his position. But never once had Simon bested that raven-haired rake whose family owned enough property to form their own colony! And since the day Dylon had threatened to have Simon court-martialed after the battle near Fort Prince George, there had been bad blood between them. Simon was maneuvering to get himself into a powerful position which would allow him to ruin Dylon Lockhart, financially and socially. He hadn't forgotten his feud with Lockhart and the day would come when he could humiliate that bastard as severely as Simon had been humiliated in front of the British magistrate! Lockhart would pay dearly for that, Simon vowed. Some day, somehow, he would make Dylon realize he had stepped on the wrong toes. . . .

"I will find my niece," Luther declared, rousing Simon from his bitter thoughts. "And we will see that she speaks the vows posthaste."

Simon flashed Luther a disdainful glare. "Had I known how much trouble that woman was going to be, I might have made other arrangements. 'Tis fortunate for you that Liberty possesses exceptional beauty, the kind that bedevils a man. I assure you, 'tis not her damnable spirit that stirs my lust and desire for her. If I didn't want her in my bed, I would have hauled you off to prison and found some other wealthy heiress to wed."

With that, Simon stalked out.

Luther collapsed in his chair and shouted for his servants to fetch him a bottle of brandy. It was Luther's intention to get himself sauced. For a few uninterrupted hours, he wanted to forget this wild-goose chase that his high-spirited niece had sent him on.

Damnit, where was that wildcat? Luther wondered as he guzzled one drink after another. She was making his life miserable, even when she wasn't in his presence. Luther couldn't wait to hand that hellion over to Simon. He'd tame Liberty. She would no longer run wild and free after Simon taught her to remain in her proper place or face a thrashing for her defiance. Liberty would bend to Simon's wishes or she wouldn't last very long. Either way, Luther wouldn't have to deal with that saucy little snip again. She would be Simon's problem. And Simon deserved to have that five-foot-one-inch headache, Luther thought spitefully. Simon was a mean, sneaky, vengeful man who manipulated others to get what he wanted.

Luther threw down another drink and slouched in his chair. He wasn't going to fret over Simon or Liberty for the next few hours. He was simply going to sit here and drink until he couldn't think or feel or see . . . He stared at the amber liquid in his glass and sighed heavily. Ah, it had been ages since he'd been able to savor the taste of liquor. But tonight he would drink his fill and forget what was too unpleasant to remember. . . .

Chapter 12

The overland journey from Lockhart Hall to Brewster's estate in the Up Country progressed just as Dylon expected it would. Liberty had been giving him the silent treatment since their shouting match in the bath pavilion. And before they embarked on their journey, Liberty had insisted on riding horseback instead of being crammed into the coach beside Dylon. Rather than engaging in another battle of wills, Dylon had allowed her to mount the steed of her choice.

Although Griffin had graciously (and a little too enthusiastically to suit Dylon's tastes) offered to accompany Liberty on horseback, Dylon saddled his favorite mount. The procession had started off with Cayla and Griffin enclosed in the coach. Behind them rode Dylon and Liberty. And behind the twosome rode the head groomsman who led two of Dylon and Griffin's prize racers that were scheduled to run at the derby held at the country fair near Camden. Brewster always coordinated his holidays with the fairs so his guests would never be lacking for entertainment.

"I trust you are enjoying the scenery and the ride," Dylon commented to Liberty, for lack of anything else to say. They had been in the saddle for over two hours and she had ignored him as if he wasn't there (and she wished he hadn't been!).

"I always enjoy riding," Liberty replied breezily, "even if I don't particularly approve of the company I'm forced to keep." Her glance reduced him to the size of a pea.

Dylon sighed audibly. "I would like to call a truce before we arrive at the estate. My grandfather may be elderly, but he is still very alert and astute. He will detect your hostility toward me in a minute."

He peered solemnly at the curvaceous blonde who was decked out in an attractive green velvet riding habit. Her very posture shouted that she was as unapproachable as a rattlesnake. "I apologize for anything and everything I said and did to offend you."

Liberty smiled poisonously at the handsome rake who thought to pacify her with a blanket apology. "Your very existence offends me," she sniped. "I must've had rocks in my head when I agreed to this irksome bargain. Pretending to like you will be the most difficult role I've ever undertaken!"

Dylon couldn't suppress the grin that tugged at his lips. "You, my lady, are the ornieriest, most contrary and stubbornest female I've ever run across."

She batted her long eyelashes and smiled as if he had just paid her the highest compliment a man could pay a woman. "Why, thank you, kind sir," she purred with sticky sweetness. "And you are the most annoying and presumptuous man I've ever had the misfortune of meeting."

This conversation, Dylon realized, was on a collision course with another argument. Liberty was spoiling for a fight and purposely trying to annoy him. Dylon quickly changed the subject.

"There are a few things I think you should know about Brewster before you confront him," he began and then muttered when Griffin craned his neck out the window to offer to exchange places. Dylon responded with a curt, decisive "Nay!" and then continued where he left off. "My grandfather is a thirty-year-old man trapped in a seventy-three-year-old body. He is still aggressive and energetic and enjoys good health. Like many other aristocrats of the colony he migrates to Newport, Rhode Island, in the summer to avoid the heat and the mosquitoes. In fact, there are so many migrants from this colony who venture north for the summer that Rhode Islanders have come to call the community the 'Carolina hospital.'"

"I have developed the obsessive urge to escape this place myself," Liberty interjected. Her distasteful glance indicated that Dylon was the sole reason she was anxious to evacuate the colony.

Dylon caught himself the split-second before he flung a suitably nasty rejoinder. But he knew damned well he would never return to this sassy sprite's good graces if he antagonized her the same way she badgered him.

"Brewster left the fifty-thousand-acre plantation at Lockhart Hall to me and Griffin six years ago when our parents died of malaria. That was when he moved to the Up Country to construct his new estate near Camden, which sets in the High Hills of the Santee and Wateree rivers."

"A fifty-thousand-acre plantation?" Liberty croaked. Triple Oak wasn't a third that size. She knew Dylon was a man of property but she never dreamed he laid title to such vast holdings.

Dylon nodded affirmatively, amused by the thunderstruck expression on Liberty's animated features. "Brewster signed the land over to us and we agreed to present him with a yearly expense account from the profits so he can live out his life in the manner to which he has grown accustomed. My brother and I sold the interest in the shipping business that our father managed to invest in more property after we lost our parents."

"Why doesn't Brewster reside at Lockhart Hall with you?" Liberty couldn't help but ask. "Is it because of your domineering, high-handed manner and the constant flood of females who come and go from your and your brother's lives like ever-changing winds?"

Dylon ignored the insult, refusing to let this sassy imp get under his skin any farther than she already had. "Brewster insisted that Griff and I start our families and take complete charge of this plantation. He likes his privacy and he insists that we have every right to manage our lives without overseeing our every move. Brewster knows himself well enough to realize that he would be imposing his opinions on us daily if we all lived under one roof.

"And he definitely would," Dylon declared with absolute certainty. "Although I love my grandfather dearly, he spouts his opinions often enough during our visits."

"So that is where you inherited your overbearing attitude," Liberty concluded. "It seems you and your grandfather are too much alike to get along for extended periods of time."

Dylon presented Liberty with a tight smile, unable to resist the mocking rejoinder. "I only wish you could be as generous as I in revealing your past and your background. I would dearly like to know if you *inherited* your unreasonable, independent and infuriatingly precocious nature. Or has it become a force of *habit*, permitted by a lax guardian who let you grow up without insisting that you observe even the slightest restrictions?"

Her chin jutted out to that proud angle that Dylon had come to recognize at a single glance. "I am my own woman by habit and by nature," she declared tartly. "And that is all you need to know about me because I will be leaving the instant we return to Lockhart Hall."

"You are truly your own woman?" His dark brow elevated in mock surprise as he slid her a taunting smile. "Why, I hadn't noticed."

His tone was in direct contradiction to his words and Liberty had to restrain herself from unloading all the insults that were stacked on the tip of her tongue. "Shall we restrict our discussion to the topic of your grandfather before I have a change of heart and reverse direction? I should hate for you to have to face Brewster without an escort." She paused to fling him a goading smile. "Obviously, 'tis of utmost importance for you to hoodwink a poor, decrepit old man who only has your best interests at heart."

Again Dylon was stung by conflicting urges. Since their trenchant argument in the bathhouse he had found himself wavering back and forth between his desire to yank Liberty's luscious body to his and kiss her blind and the compelling need to snatch her up and shake the stuffing out of her for being so damned snide and sarcastic. If nothing else, this frustrating affair with this blond-haired terror had been a lesson in self-restraint. Valiantly, Dylon resisted both urges and concentrated on the subject of Brewster.

"My grandfather celebrates his birthdays in conjunction with the fairs because he devotes much time, money and effort to preserving the tradition. He is civic-minded and he strongly insists that we preserve the ways of our forefathers who sailed to this new continent to enjoy their freedom.

"When it comes to Griffin and me, Grandfather believes we should take wives and beget plenty of children to enrich our lives. Since we hadn't married by the age of twenty-five, he needles us every chance he gets. And until we wed, I doubt that he will grant us a shred of peace."

Liberty could fully understand Griff's and Dylon's refusal to be rushed into marriage by their demanding grandfather. Both rakes were too independent and set in their ways to comply with Brewster's wishes. Liberty had felt that same sort of pressure when her father began dropping subtle hints about her marrying Phillipe. But Benjamin Jordon had not been as persistent and forceful as Brewster obviously was. Liberty supposed she, too, would have devised some scheme to avoid marrying Phillipe if her father had pressed the issue the way

Brewster had. It seemed to be human nature to rebel when one found the opinions of others foisted off on oneself.

"And so, to keep the family peace, you and Griffin come dragging your female escorts to Brewster for inspection," Liberty speculated. "Brewster hopes the new lady on your arm will be one you decide to wed and he anxiously awaits news of an engagement."

"Exactly," Dylon replied as he shifted to a more comfortable position in the saddle. "As difficult as it will obviously be for you, I hope you will act as if you have fond feelings for me while you're in Grandfather's presence. Otherwise, he'll give me hell."

"I will have to polish up on my theatrical abilities," Liberty assured him. "But I did agree to this charade in exchange for asylum and I will keep my word."

"Thank the Lord for that," Dylon grunted.

"... Unless you don't keep your distance and persist in annoying me until my true feelings for you come pouring out," she tacked on as she flung him a warning glance.

Dylon snaked out a hand to grab her reins, forcing her to halt beside him. Soberly, he stared into the bright amethyst eyes that dominated her enchanting features. "Do you hold me in contempt because I find you wildly exciting and extraordinary, because I see you as a breathtakingly beautiful woman? And don't insult my intellect by proclaiming I'm the first man who has found you attractive and irresistible. Even my own brother has been bewitched by you. I have no doubt there is an endless rabble of men who envision claiming you as their own, as well as this mysterious fiancé who could not hold onto what he desired for all the obvious reasons."

Liberty pried Dylon's lean fingers from her reins and nudged her steed forward. "'Tis a source of irritation," she grumbled resentfully. "I do not wish to be desired because of my appearance. I had no control of that when I came into this world. Neither do I wish to be courted because of my position in society."

"What position in which society?" Dylon couldn't help but ask even though Liberty refused to answer.

"I want to be wanted for my intellect, for my own personality, such as it is. But men refuse to look deeper to see the woman beneath the flesh. 'Tis that shallow brand of affection to which I have and will always object!"

"I don't know who you are or from whence you came or if you are employing your own name," Dylon reminded her as he eased up beside her. "And even though you have been aloof and secretive I still like you for what you are."

Liberty scoffed at the suave, charismatic rogue. "Do you now? Then why did you rake me over the coals for tromping across your rice fields when I sought to appease my curiosity about the planting process? Satisfying my inquisitiveness is part of who I am."

"Damnit, I was concerned about your safety," Dylon exploded, despite his attempt to control his temper, the very one Liberty had been preying on since they began this conversation. "You are my responsibility and . . ."

"Your responsibility?" Liberty sniffed indignantly. "You are like every other man I've ever met! A woman is considered a man's possession, to be provided for and protected, like one of his prize steeds." She hitched her thumb over her shoulder to indicate the high-stepping horses who were being treated like part of the family. "I do not wish to hold the same position in a man's household as his damned horse!"

When Dylon chuckled at her comparison, Liberty glared poison arrows at him. "And you, Master Lockhart, remind me of a horse!"

"Oh, really?" he asked between snickers. "Which end, I wonder." As if he didn't know what this feisty misfit implied.

"'Tis clearly evident that you are not taking me seriously," Liberty fumed. "But then, you are not a man who takes much of anything seriously, are you?"

When Liberty slammed her mouth shut like a drawer and trotted off, Dylon continued to chuckle at her volatile temper. Then he thought of his alternatives—such as exchanging places with his poor brother who was closeted in the coach with the docile, submissive Cayla Styles. After meeting a woman like Liberty, Dylon wondered if he was ever going to be satisfied with the typical aristocratic female ever again. He had taken women for granted the past five years, patronizing them for his own amusement and carefully avoiding lasting entanglements. But then along came Liberty Jordon—the mysterious hoyden. She defied restrictions and rebelled against authority and limitation. She amused him, annoyed him and aroused him to the extreme, making it difficult to maintain his even disposition. Liberty was too explosive of temper and too unpredictable. But every time Dylon was hounded by tantalizing thoughts of the wild splendor they'd shared, he couldn't recall one of her faults. He just went hot all over, thinking about the feel of her satiny flesh beneath his fingertips, the feel of her ripe body moving in perfect rhythm with his. . . .

"Dylon, I insist that we exchange places," Griffin demanded as he stepped from the coach he'd ordered to halt. "I need some fresh air."

What Griffin needed, Dylon suspected, was a break in the monotony (who went by the name of Cayla Styles). Reluctantly, Dylon swung from the saddle. Perhaps he should spend some time with Cayla, to remind himself what most women of quality were like and the type of females he would again be forced to associate with when Liberty flitted out of his life. . . .

Dylon frowned ponderously as he folded himself onto the tuft seat across from Cayla. He couldn't help but wonder how long it would take to forget how he delighted in Liberty's unconventional antics, her unorthodox ways and her saucy disposition. She was like a breath of spring sunshine and ever-changing winds. Against his will, he found his eyes and thoughts straying to her, wondering what she would do next, wondering what was running through that complicated mind of hers.

Cayla Styles and her breed of women were shallow, transparent creatures. Liberty was anything but and she didn't cater to him the way most women did. In fact, she didn't seem to like him all that much. Dylon asked himself why it suddenly mattered what *any* woman thought of him. The fact that Liberty Jordon's opinion did matter to him was most unsettling. Why should he care what that feisty minx thought? She was nothing but trouble anyway. And since she'd dropped out of his magnolia tree, she'd become like an itch he couldn't quite reach to scratch. If he knew what was good for him he'd leave that itch alone before it festered into a rash that wouldn't ever go away. . . .

The sound of rustling bushes and the clatter of unidentified hooves caused Dylon to bolt straight up in his seat. A pistol exploded in the afternoon air and all Dylon's senses immediately came to life. With a scowl and curse, he thrust his head out the window of the coach to see four masked highwaymen plunging from the underbrush to attack.

Good God, a man couldn't even muddle through his thoughts without trouble erupting around him. And what scared Dylon half to death was the fact that he was confined to this coach while that blond-haired hellion was sitting atop her steed, prepared to do only heaven knew what!

The thought of Liberty getting caught in the crossfire turned Dylon's blood to ice. Curse that woman! Why couldn't she have been content to clamber into the coach like Cayla? But nay, not Liberty Jordon. She wouldn't want to deprive herself of all the action in case trouble broke out . . . which it had. And now she was right smack dab in the middle of it! And here he was, enclosed in a coach, watching bandits swarm out of the thicket like hornets. Damn . . . damn . . . damn!!!

When Dylon heard another round of exploding pistols, his gaze instinctively riveted on Liberty. He cursed her but good when she wheeled her steed and charged toward the lead rider who was trying to reload his pistol at full gallop. And to Dylon's further fury and disbelief, the blond-haired terror rammed her horse into the highwayman's mount. The steeds' shrill whinnies mingled with the whine of bullets. The bandit's horse faltered and fell while Liberty miraculously managed to remain in the saddle. Dylon decided, then and there, that her guardian angel was on call twenty-four hours a day to keep up with that bold minx who had more blind courage than common sense!

"My Lord!" Cayla erupted, her eyes wide as dinner plates. "Did you see what Liberty did?"

Hell's bells, of course Dylon had seen the whole damned thing and he could have cheerfully choked Liberty for thrusting herself in harm's way with such daring panache. Dylon wondered if Liberty Jordon ever considered herself out of her element. He swore that hoyden would take on the devil himself if he dared to cross her. That hellion was as bold as a badger and she could fight like a wolverine!

Unable to sit still a second longer, Dylon pushed Cayla to the floor to protect her from flying bullets and then flung open the door of the speeding coach. His loud bellow roared above the clatter of hooves, ordering Liberty to race toward the carriage.

When another pistol barked, Liberty flattened herself on the saddle and charged toward the wobbling coach, to which Dylon clung with one hand, leaving himself a perfect target for an oncoming bullet.

The instant Dylon leaped from the step of the carriage onto the back of her steed, Liberty let him have it with both barrels. "What were you trying to do? Invite a bullet?" she hissed at him.

Dylon yanked the reins from her grasp and took control of the steed. "I was trying to draw fire away from the idiotic female who runs *toward* trouble instead of *away* from it," he muttered furiously. "The next time you pull some damned-fool maneuver like that I'll shoot you myself!"

She was only trying to save the day and Dylon was yelling at her as if she had committed some unpardonable crime.

Still scowling, Dylon shoved Liberty against the steed's neck and collapsed on top of her when buckshot pelted his tricorn, causing the hat to topple from his head to the ground.

All the old familiar instincts of preservation sprang to life as Dylon aimed his pistol at the approaching highwaymen. He could almost smell the stench of death, hear the agonized cries that had haunted him during those days he'd spent battling the Cherokees in the wilderness. . . .

"You're hurting me!" Liberty yelped before Dylon succeeded in mashing her flat.

"Keep your head down," he snapped as he reared back to take aim at the desperado who trained his weapon on Griffin.

Griffin had the good sense to duck while he reloaded his pistol. The bullet with Griff's name on it sailed over his bowed head. But to the misfortune of the bandit who'd taken the shot, Dylon's aim was as good as his eyesight. Dylon's bullet caught the highwayman in his firing arm, causing it to sag against his side.

While the coach and the unarmed groomsman sped away from the battle, Dylon gouged his steed toward the canopy of trees that skirted the road. He had fought more battles than he cared to count in the underbrush, dodging Cherokee tomahawks and arrows. He'd mastered the technique of wilderness fighting and he fully intended to employ the same strategy on the two highwaymen who were still in the saddle.

After Griffin charged into the underbrush to follow his brother's lead, Dylon jerked him out of the saddle.

Swiftly, he hauled Liberty down between the two panting horses. Leaving the steeds as Liberty's shields of armor to protect her from an attack in any direction, Dylon motioned for his brother to bury himself in the bushes so they could both lie in wait.

The two highwaymen, seeing the horses standing in the sun-dappled shadows of the trees, plunged through the brush to locate their victims. Before they reached the riderless horses, two pistols screamed through the tangled vines.

Dylon's bullet found its mark. With a screech of pain one masked bandit pitched off his steed and landed facedown in front of Liberty's horse. Startled, the gelding reared up on his hind legs, exposing the young woman who was sandwiched between the two mounts.

A mutinous growl rolled off the lips of the remaining bandit. In desperation, he squirted between the two thrashing horses to grab hold of Liberty, employing *her* as *his* shield of protection.

"If you want this wench alive . . ."

The highwayman had no time to make any stipulations that would aid in his escape. Dylon had anticipated trouble when the wounded highwayman startled Liberty's steed. The instant the horse reared in fright, Dylon moved like streak lightning to circle behind the last remaining desperado. Before the bandit could complete his threat, Dylon surged out of the underbrush and made a spectacular leap through the air.

Liberty, Dylon and the highwayman tumbled off the skittish steed to land in a tangled heap on the ground. Instinctively, Liberty wriggled from the pile of twisted bodies and appendages. Unfortunately, her timing was terrible. Just as she rocked backward to pull the hampering hem of her skirt free, Dylon cocked his arm to level a devastating blow on the bandit's jaw. His elbow caught Liberty in the chin, sending her sprawling over the highwayman's legs.

Dylon had no time to apologize. His complete attention

was focused on the desperado who was fighting for his life. The power-packed punch to the thief's jaw dazed him momentarily, but he came up fighting. Dylon deflected the oncoming blow with his forearm and countered with a meaty "right cross" that jarred teeth and split flesh.

Meanwhile, Griffin scrambled from the brush to tie the wounded bandit's hands behind him with his own mask. When Griffin spied Liberty floundering to remove herself from the battle that was in progress he leaped to her assistance. Clutching her arm, Griff dragged her through the grass the instant before Dylon sent his victim skidding backward. If not for Griffin, Liberty would have found herself squashed into the ground with the burly bandit spread-eagle on top of her.

Liberty blinked bewilderedly when she saw Dylon come uncoiled like a raven-haired rattlesnake. For the most part, Dylon conducted himself like a well-mannered gentleman. But it was clearly evident that when he completely lost his temper, his veneer of sophistication cracked. He was suddenly fighting like one of the savages he'd battled in the wilderness!

Liberty had never seen a man pound another human being into putty as thoroughly or as efficiently as Dylon hammered away at the highwayman. She had the feeling that Dylon had only toyed with her in the past—the way a jungle cat toys with a defenseless mouse. Dylon had obviously tested his abilities to the very limits in the wilderness and incorporated the Cherokee's tactics of hand-to-hand combat into his own amazing battle techniques. There was an incredible explosive force in this man. His entire body had become a lethal weapon and the desperado was no match for such formidable competition.

Over and over again, Dylon leveled blows that mashed the bandit's belly into his backbone. It was no longer a battle between two equally matched opponents, but rather a dazed victim attempting to ward off the beefy blows of his astounding challenger.

"Dylon, for God's sake, that's enough," Griffin bellowed at his brother.

Dylon wheeled around, his arm still cocked and ready to strike. His massive chest reminded Liberty of an inflated bagpipe that swelled and expanded. A lock of midnight hair fell over his puckered brows and his sensuous mouth was curled in murdering fury. Liberty flinched when she saw the frightening glint in those slits of blue. But when his gaze locked with hers, the flames dwindled and died. In utter amazement, Liberty watched the awesome warrior disappear behind that well-controlled façade that concealed all emotion behind a lopsided smile.

"Some habits die hard," he murmured as he loosened his stranglehold on the unconscious desperado. The man dropped to the ground in an untidy heap.

Liberty sat there as if she had been rooted to the spot, stunned by the remarkable transformation that had taken place. Dylon was his old self again. He was enshrouded in an aura of reckless nonchalance. As leisurely as you please, he ambled over to scrunch down in front of Liberty. As vicious as he had been moments before, he was now as gentle as a lamb. Tenderly, he traced his forefinger over the red welt he had accidentally put on her chin.

"There have been times, sweet Liberty, when I would have dearly loved to punch you. But this wasn't one of those times. I'm sorry your face got in the way of my elbow," he murmured in apology. "Are you all right?"

Liberty was still too stunned to manage coherent speech. Watching Dylon split apart at the seams to reveal the deadly frontiersman who had battled the Cherokees in days gone by left her lightning struck. And watching Dylon mask his fury to project that image of good-naturedness left her thunderstruck. It was as if this magnificent body of his housed two drastically different men—the seasoned Indian fighter and the gallant gentleman. . . .

"Liberty? You are all right, aren't you?" Dylon frowned when she continued to gape at him as if he had sprouted another head, one equipped with devil's horns.

Liberty gave herself a mental shake and forced a reassuring smile. "Aye, I'm fine," she insisted.

"Good." Dylon's pleasant countenance changed to a threatening scowl. "Don't think for one minute that your beauty compensates for your idiocy!"

His harsh tone spurred her notorious temper. Her chin jerked up in a militant fashion and she snapped back at him before he could insult her again. "If this is going to turn into a lecture, I don't wish to hear it! I did what I thought needed to be done and that is that."

"Damnit, woman, you could have gotten yourself killed trying to take on those bandits single-handed!" He gave her a look that could have melted rock. "Just when I think you have reached ultimate heights of daring, you surpass yourself!" he blared at her as if she were deaf and dumb.

Stupid, he silently corrected himself. Any female who would take on four armed highwaymen without so much as a pea shooter had to be just plain stupid or too damned daring for her own good. For crying out loud, even David had armed himself with a slingshot when he went up against Goliath!

"Well, what did you expect me to do? Run the other way?" she flashed.

"I would have preferred it," Dylon muttered sourly.

"*You* didn't." She glared him down. "You plastered yourself to the side of the coach like a defenseless target. You could have stayed tucked inside with Cayla, you know."

"And leave you to battle those four bandits while my incompetent brother was doing only God knows what instead of protecting you?" Dylon hooted sarcastically.

"Now wait just a damned minute," Griffin scowled as he pushed his way between Liberty and Dylon who had both bounded to their feet to shout in each other's faces.

"I was dodging bullets and reloading my pistol. And if you ask me, you were both behaving like a couple of reckless children who were trying to upstage each other!"

A peal of laughter clamored through Dylon's chest as he glanced past Griffin's shoulder to stare into Liberty's animated features. "Griff is right, you know," he said in a calmer tone. "We both could have exercised a great deal more caution."

Liberty was reluctant to stay angry when Dylon bestowed such a disarming smile on her. "Aye, we both got a mite carried away and we did call a truce, did we not?"

"Indeed we did," Dylon confirmed with the utmost politeness. Agilely he stepped around his blockade of a brother to offer Liberty his arm. "I hope this incident was exciting enough for you, my dear. I know you live for thrills."

"Just as you do, Dylon *dahling*," she cooed sweetly before accepting his proffered arm. "I just don't know what this world is coming to. Why, the gentry of South Carolina cannot journey down the King's Highway these days without being set upon by vagabonds and thieves."

"'Tis absolutely dreadful," Dylon agreed. "I shall make a mental note to bring up the matter at the next Assembly meeting."

Griffin shook his head in astonishment as Dylon and Liberty ambled toward their horses, leaving him standing between their fallen foes. "What are we going to do about these scoundrels?" he called after his swaggering brother.

Dylon effortlessly lifted Liberty into the saddle and mounted his steed. "Tie them to a tree," he suggested. "We'll send the groom into the village and the constable can round up these ruffians."

Leaving Griffin with his assigned task, Dylon led Liberty through the brush and back to the road. Liberty chewed thoughtfully on her puffy lip as she regarded the capable and very resourceful man who rode beside her. When Dylon glanced in her direction he could see the questions in her violet eyes and he grimaced. He knew this curious she-cat was going to inquire about those unpleasant experiences from his past that molded him into being the brutal fighter he had learned to be when necessity demanded.

"Don't ask," Dylon blurted out before Liberty could pose her questions. "The scene you just witnessed was a flashback from another time, one I would prefer to forget. Like you, I have portions of my past that I don't wish to remember . . . ever again."

"But when duty calls or a crisis arises, you permit yourself to become the soldier you once were," she predicted.

Dylon expelled a sigh and nodded affirmatively. "Although I have seen enough war and killing to last me a lifetime, I would take arms to preserve our rights in these colonies and to protect you. . . ." To camouflage the reckless admission, Dylon presented her with a teasing smile. "After all, you are the light and love of my life, dear Liberty. I can't have thieves or anyone else threatening you or trying to steal you away from me before Brewster has the chance to meet you, now can I?"

It was obvious to Liberty that the subject of Dylon's battles in the wilderness was closed to discussion. He didn't want to dredge up old nightmares. Nor did he want to discuss his fisticuffs with the highwayman. He much preferred to put the incident behind him and taunt her in that lighthearted manner of his.

But Liberty had seen the dark, foreboding side of Dylon's personality—one born from a need to protect and survive. She had seen this powerful man in action. She knew he had suddenly found himself reliving those days on the outposts of civilization when it was kill or be killed. His fighting instinct hadn't died; it only lay dormant beneath that shell of lackadaisical nonchalance.

After watching Dylon beat the tar out of the bandit

who had tried to abduct her to save himself, Liberty knew for certain that she would prefer to be on Dylon's side if battle ever broke out again. He was a most intimidating foe when his murdering fury was aroused!

And Dylon was right, Liberty mused pensively. It was best not to excavate the memories of unpleasant ordeals. Both his past and hers were better left alone. Dylon had no desire to relive those dreadful nightmares of battle and Liberty had no wish to discuss Luther Norris and Simon Gridley. She was going to forget what she chose not to remember and enjoy the holiday at Brewster Lockhart's estate in the Up Country. Then she would sail back to her beloved islands to begin life again.

Liberty couldn't help but wonder if she could put this dynamic man out of her life as easily as she could forget Luther and Simon existed. She certainly hoped so! She was not going to let herself fall in love with this remarkable rake, even if it would have been the easiest thing she'd ever done. She and Dylon were only serving each other's purpose, that was all. She would continue to pester him to ensure they never ended up on as friendly terms as they had earlier in the week. In a week they would go their separate ways and Liberty vowed not to look back. She was going home where she belonged and that was that!

Chapter 13

Like a restless lion, Brewster Lockhart rapidly paced the veranda that shaded the front door of his brick mansion. He had seen his grandsons' carriage in the distance and he was practically hopping up and down in anticipation. Perhaps this would be the time those rogues arrived with a suitable young lady in tow. Perhaps this would be the time they happened onto a female who could match them stride for stride.

Dylon and Griffin hadn't pulled the wool over Brewster's eyes with their sly pranks. Brewster knew those ornery rakes constantly schemed to avoid the matrimonial noose (as they chose to think of wedlock). But Brewster was no man's fool. He knew what those rapscallions had been doing all along. Yet, he continued to badger his grandsons in hopes that they would accidentally stumble onto their perfect matches while they were trying to round up an escort who would *not* meet Brewster's expectations.

This time Brewster had personally selected two exceptional beauties, just in case Dylon and Griffin arrived with two more simpering twits who could not carry on an intelligent conversation to save their souls. The two young ladies Brewster had selected were well-bred, reasonably educated, and best of all, they showed signs of assertiveness and spirit.

Brewster's thoughts trailed off when he spied a mass of golden hair glowing in the dim rays of dusk. To his surprise, a shapely young woman in an emerald green riding habit sat atop her steed. She had been straddling the animal in an unladylike manner until she noticed Brewster perched on the stoop. With the most feminine grace imaginable, the young woman glided her right leg into proper position.

Who was this woman? Brewster wondered curiously. Surely she wasn't a servant or a lady's maid. And why was Dylon sitting atop his horse when he had a perfectly good coach at his disposal?

When the cavalcade came to a halt, Dylon swung to the ground and lifted his companion from the saddle. Simultaneously, Griffin stepped from the carriage to assist his redheaded escort down beside him. Brewster's shrewd, assessing gaze swept over both attractive women, but his eyes were helplessly drawn back to the striking blonde. It wasn't her obvious beauty that intrigued him so, even though she was the most dazzling female he'd seen in years. It was the living fire in those violet eyes which dominated her face that fascinated him. It was in her poised, graceful yet lively step. Lord, the young woman fairly radiated with spirit!

"Grandfather, I would like for you to meet Liberty Jordon," Dylon introduced as he slid his arm around her trim waist, even though he felt her flinch at his unwelcomed touch. "Liberty, this is Brewster Lockhart, one of the colony's founding fathers."

Instead of dropping into a demure curtsey, Liberty extended her hand and broke into an elfin smile. "'Tis a pleasure, sir. Dylon has told me a great deal about you."

Brewster's alert blue eyes twinkled behind his wire-rimmed glasses. "I was afraid of that," he snorted. "But you mustn't let that influence you, my dear. I would prefer that you wait until we are better acquainted so you can form your own opinion."

Liberty grinned mischievously. "I assure you that I

have no intention of allowing Dylon or anyone else do my thinking for me. Just because he said you were a horrible, pushy man with positively no sense of humor will have no bearing whatsoever on our relationship."

Dylon choked on his breath and Griffin burst out laughing at Liberty's teasing remark. But Griffin quickly sobered when Dylon glared him into silence.

A wry smile twitched Brewster's lips as he surveyed the pixielike grin that captured Liberty's exquisite features. This was definitely not the ordinary type of female whom Dylon usually dragged to the Up Country with him. Instead, Liberty playfully teased him, as well as Dylon who looked as if he had just swallowed a pumpkin after being put on the firing line.

When Griffin broke the silence to perform the other introductions, Brewster found himself facing a shy, retiring, shrinking violet. The redhead appeared so bashful and subservient that she did not meet Brewster's assessing gaze. Liberty, on the other hand, not only met Brewster's eyes, but she challenged him with her playful retort. Cayla Styles, unfortunately, was a tiresome repetition of the kind of women who usually appeared at the estate on Griffin and Dylon's arms. Quite frankly, Cayla was the sort who bored Brewster to tears.

Aye, Brewster decided. Cayla had been taught all the proper responses to comments. She had been ordered to remain quietly in her place without calling any unnecessary attention to herself. She could perform a graceful curtsey and bat her eyes just so. But the poor woman appeared as dull as a brick wall.

"If I may impose, sir," Cayla murmured with downcast eyes. "Our journey from Lockhart Hall was most exhausting and terrifying. I beg a few moments to refresh myself and to rest."

Godamercy, thought Liberty, not another nap!

"Terrifying?" Brewster glanced at Griffin for an explanation.

"We ran into a swarm of highwaymen en route,"

Griffin elaborated. His admiring gaze swung to Liberty, relieved that the welt on her chin had disappeared. "But Liberty and Dylon made short shrift of them."

Surprise registered on Brewster's wrinkled features. Although he was staring incredulously at the feisty blonde, he flicked his wrist to send Cayla on her way. "Take all the time you need to rest and recuperate, Miss Styles. Griffin will show you to your chamber." When the twosome ambled toward the house, Brewster grabbed Liberty's hand without preamble and laid it over his own. "Dylon will see to the luggage while Liberty offers the details of this attempted holdup. After her ordeal, she could use a tall glass of my special recipe."

"Liberty needs a nap as well," Dylon insisted. He didn't trust that minx and his grandfather alone together for even a second, especially after Liberty's teasing remarks. Lord, there was no telling what that female would say and do! Hadn't she proved her inability to remain within the confines of conventional behavior when she took on the four bandits without one bit of concern for her welfare?

"I am not the least bit sleepy," Liberty declared as Brewster ushered her up the steps.

Grumbling to himself, Dylon stomped off to collect their luggage from the compartment behind the carriage. Damn that woman. She was going to make this sojourn in the Up Country a living nightmare, he just knew it! Brewster and Liberty had instantly hit it off. They played upon each other's conversation like a team of comedians. Even as they trudged up the steps, Dylon could hear their playful banter, the teasing camaraderie. He felt like an outsider at his grandfather's estate! Curse that woman, did she have to bedevil men from eight to eighty with her charm, beauty and spunk? And why was he jealous of his own grandfather who was now the recipient of Liberty's sunny smiles?

* * *

While Cayla was having her nap, Dylon and Griffin were left to greet the other guests who arrived for the spring festivities. Brewster had locked himself and Liberty in his study and thrust his special recipe of rum into her hand.

"Jordon . . ." Brewster pondered aloud. "That name sounds familiar. Where have I heard it?"

"Perhaps you are confusing it with the river by the same name," Liberty teased before sipping the rum. Her breath lodged in her throat when fire scorched her vocal chords. She wheezed and sputtered until Brewster whacked her between the shoulder blades to revive her.

"My homemade brew takes some getting used to," Brewster informed her before he guzzled half a glass in one swallow. "But once you have developed a taste for it, even Madeira wine and brandy will seem a poor substitute."

"Approximately how long is it going to take to acquire a taste for it?" Liberty wheezed in question.

Brewster's clear blue eyes sparkled with mischief. "Two glasses should do it." He led Liberty to a wing-backed chair that sat across from his desk and gestured for her to plant herself in it. "May I be frank with you, Liberty?"

"I prefer that you were," she declared before taking another sip of liquid fire. "It will be a refreshing change from my usual dealings with men."

Brewster stared her squarely in the eye. "You are not at all what I expected," he told her candidly. "Usually Dylon arrives upon the scene with some fluffy puppet like Cayla Styles." His nose wrinkled distastefully. "What, may I ask, is that ornery grandson of mine up to this time?"

Liberty took another drink, allowing herself the opportunity to formulate her thoughts. "I think that question would be better answered by your grandson. He invited me here to enjoy the festivities of your birthday . . . and happy birthday, by the way."

"Thank you."

"You're welcome. I have come with no other intention than to enjoy myself and your generous hospitality," she finished before taking another sip of Brewster's special recipe.

"I've no doubt that you will enjoy yourself." Brewster chuckled. "You hardly seem the type to huddle in my parlor like Cayla. Don't tell me. Let me guess. The redhead has an avid fascination for embroidery. She cannot abide the offensive smell of a horse at close range and she wouldn't be caught dead atop one. She requires two naps a day to accommodate her delicate constitution."

Liberty chortled at the perceptive gray-haired man. She peered at Brewster and knew exactly what Dylon and Griffin would look like in their old age. The patriarch was still a fine figure of a man who carried himself with pride and grace. Except for the helmet of silver hair that capped his head and an excess of wrinkles, Brewster was exactly as Dylon said he was—a thirty-year-old man trapped in a seventy-three-year-old body.

"I'm sorry to say you are pretty near the mark in describing Cayla," Liberty replied, shrugging aside her pensive thoughts. "But Cayla leans more toward crocheting than embroidery and it takes *three* naps to get her through the day. But there have been a few times when I've wondered if Cayla resents the fact that she has not been allowed to live up to her potential. It seems to me that she has been terribly browbeaten. Why, with a little coaching, Cayla might emerge from that imposed shell of reserve."

Brewster grinned in amusement. "If your infectious zest for life rubs off on her, she could break the mold which has been cast for her," he contended. "But no matter how Cayla behaves, you will be allowed to have the run of my estate and behave in the manner to which you have grown accustomed." His smile grew melancholy as he nursed his drink. "You, my dear lady, remind me very much of my wife. She also detested the rigid confines of womanhood and defied them every chance she got."

Liberty studied the patriarch, noting how his voice rustled with sentiment when he spoke of his wife. He must have loved her deeply, Liberty speculated. She wondered how it would feel to be so devoted to love that even years later, thoughts of Brewster's beloved wife could put a mist in his eyes.

"You were not offended by your wife's refusal to obey the rules and meet the expectations that have been set down for women?" she asked with her customary brand of curiosity.

"Nay, why should I be?" Brewster chuckled as he tucked his forefinger behind his glasses to wipe away the cloud of nostalgia. "Lucinda shared my enthusiasm for life. She was far more than my wife. She was my partner, my companion and my friend. She worked beside me to build our struggling farm into a prosperous plantation. And if we would have had a daughter instead of a son, we would not have imposed strict regulations on her as Cayla's parents have obviously demanded of her. Lucinda wouldn't have stood for it."

Another faraway look glazed Brewster's eyes as he stared back through the window of time. "Lucinda and I did more living in our forty-three years of marriage than some folks can squeeze into an entire lifetime. 'Tis not quantity of time that married couples share, but rather quality," he emphasized. "And I wish for my grandsons to know and understand what Lucinda and I enjoyed."

Brewster inhaled another swallow of his rum. "Ah, she and I lived a year in a single month, a decade in the span of a year. Lucinda was no puppet of society. She was a full-fledged woman with her own hopes and dreams. I expect they would coincide closely with your own expectations of life."

"And because I share your wife's desire to be my own person, you won't mind that I do not waste my time with naps, that I detest stitchery and that I prefer the smell of a lathered horse to fragrant hankies?" Liberty inquired with an impish grin.

"Hardly!" Brewster chuckled delightedly. "What I *do* mind is that you are not married to one of my grandsons."

Liberty's gaze flitted away as she reached over to refill her glass from the stone jug which was on the edge of Brewster's expansive mahogany desk. "I would prefer to discuss something else, if you don't mind."

"I do mind because I prefer speaking of *nothing* else at the moment," Brewster declared with his customary candor. "If I thought you could be bought for a price, I would bribe you into wedlock with Dylon. You are, after all, exactly the kind of woman he needs." He stared unblinkingly at the pert beauty who was now eagerly consuming his special recipe of rum. "How much would it cost me . . . if you did have a price . . . and if I did agree to pay it . . . ? Hypothetically speaking, of course."

Liberty lounged negligently in her chair, amazed at the numbing effect the beverage had on her body. Her nose tingled and her appendages felt noticeably heavy. She was so relaxed that sitting upright seemed to require tremendous effort.

"Hypothet . . . ical*th*y . . . s*th*eaking . . . ?" she repeated and then frowned at her inability to form the proper pronunciation of the words over her thick tongue. Her syntax was out of whack and she had to concentrate to enunciate clearly. "Before I could ever discu*sh* the pri*th*e of a bribe, I would demand some drastic changes in your grandson's a*th*itudes." Another frown knitted her delicately arched brows. "I wonder if 'tis po*sh*ible for surgeons to perform per*sh*onality transplants . . ."

Brewster erupted in a horselaugh when he noticed the effect his special recipe was having on Liberty. Her words were growing more slurred by the minute and she seemed to have difficulty sticking to one topic of conversation. "Who needs a personality transplant?" he quizzed before taking another sip of rum.

"Dylon," Liberty said tipsily.

"The field of medicine has made tremendous strides the past few years," he contended. "But I doubt physicians have tackled such surgery, unless leeches can also suck out quirks of personality, along with bad blood."

Liberty sighed heavily. "I feared as much." Sluggishly, she helped herself to another glass of rum. Then she pushed forward to convey a confidential comment. "I'm sorry to report that your grandson has several very annoying foibles. Were he my husband, I'm afraid there would be plenty of times when I could cheerfully kill him."

Another amused burst of laughter erupted from Brewster's lips. "I have experienced the same urge myself each time he drags some simpering female to my stoop and tries to pass her off as his future fiancée."

Liberty slouched back and draped both legs over one arm of the chair. "I like you, Brewster. May I be so forward as to call you Brewster?"

"I would prefer it," he insisted before chugging another drink. "And thank you, Liberty. I'm quite taken with you too."

Her droopy violet eyes twinkled with irrespressible mischief. "Enough talk of Dylon. How do you feel about marrying a younger woman?" she tittered drunkenly.

Brewster snickered again. He hadn't laughed so much in years. "My dear Liberty, the soul is willing but the flesh is aged. If I thought I could keep up with you, stride for stride, I would ask for your hand myself."

"And I would accept," she replied, almost at once.

By this time, Brewster was matching Liberty drink for drink and it had a noticeable effect on him as well. "Then perhaps I should make you my bride. God knows, that may be the only way I can get another woman like Lucinda in this family."

"Is that a proposal, Brewster?" One delicate brow slid

to a quizzical angle, even though the excessive consumption of rum made it impossible for her facial muscles to hold an expression for too long at a time. "And God knows, this might be the first marriage invitation I've been inclined to accept."

"Then it's settled," Brewster slurred as he fumbled to retrieve the jug of homemade rum. "We'll get married and to hell with those pesky grandsons of mine." A silly smile dangled on the corner of his mouth. Without his usual amount of coordination, he grabbed Liberty's empty glass and refilled it, but not without sloshing his special recipe all over his desk. "Shall we drink to our wedding?"

Liberty clinked her glass against Brewster's and offered him an inebriated smile. "We'll drink to our wedding and then to our success in repelling those loathsome highwaymen who tried to accost us."

After gulping his rum, Brewster slumped back in his chair. "Tell me about the incident," he insisted slurrishly.

And Liberty did tell him that and many other things since her tongue had been loosened with Brewster's special recipe. As if they were old dear friends, Liberty and Brewster chatted over the jug of rum, giving not one thought to the guests who were piling up on the lawn and in the halls to help the patriarch celebrate his birthday.

Chapter 14

Dylon prowled the resplendent foyer like a caged cougar, pausing only at irregular intervals to glance at his timepiece. Carriage loads of guests had arrived and still Brewster and Liberty hadn't emerged from the office. The supper hour had come and gone and Cayla had taken two naps. Still no Brewster! What the devil was going on in there?

Behind the closed door, Dylon could hear Liberty's carefree laughter mingling with Brewster's baritone chuckles. He could detect the drone of quiet voices but he couldn't decipher the words. Having lost all his patience by this time, Dylon spun on his heels to locate a key to unlock the door. He had knocked twice already and he had been completely ignored. He doubted a third rap on the portal would make any difference. It seemed the only way to rout Liberty and Brewster was to spring the lock and pry them out of the office.

Within a few minutes, Dylon returned to cram the key into the lock. When he barged inside, he stopped dead in his tracks. His eyes popped from their sockets when he spied Brewster draped on the sofa, nursing his umpteenth glass of rum, puffing on his pipe. Seeing his grandfather completely sauced when he had a house full of guests to greet and entertain was unforgivable. But seeing Liberty lounging on the other red velvet sofa with her skirt hiked up and her bare legs dangling over the arm of the couch, nursing her glass of rum and puffing on one of his grandfather's pipes caused him to curse the air blue (what little air there was, that is, which wasn't fogged by clouds of smoke).

In swift, angry strides, Dylon stomped across the spacious study. Glaring holes in Liberty, he snatched the glass from her fingertips and jerked the pipe from her lips.

Like a gigantic overturned beetle, Brewster struggled to upright himself. But he was so far into his cups that it was difficult to determine which way *up* was. When Dylon hoisted Liberty off the sofa, causing her to buckle at the knees, Brewster wagged a limp finger in his grandson's puckered face.

"Take your hands off my fiancée," he demanded groggily. "We were having a marvelous time until you burst in without invitation."

Dylon gaped at Brewster as if he had grapevines sprouting from his ears. "*Your* fiancée? Good God, you're so intoxicated you don't even know who you are!"

"Of course he does," Liberty piped up. She concentrated on the blurred image of the older man. "He's Brewster Aloysious Lockhart, born the son of an English cabinetmaker in Coventry."

"Cambridge," Dylon corrected grouchily.

"Aye." Liberty nodded thoughtfully. "Coventry was Lady Godiva's stomping ground, wasn't it?" Her fuzzy gaze swung accusingly to Dylon who kept splitting in half and then merging before her very eyes. "No doubt you were there to spy on her, incorrigible rake that you are, Dylon *dahling* . . ."

Dylon rolled his eyes in disgust. Liberty was every bit as soused as Brewster was. She couldn't stand on her own two legs without support. Her eyes drooped as if they were about to slam shut and she kept tripping over her thick tongue.

While Dylon was muttering at the drunken duo, Brewster wobbled to his feet and then sat back down before he fell down. "Perhaps you should send Griff to assist me. My legs won't work." His glassy eyes swung to Liberty. "Perhaps we should postpone the wedding until the day after tomorrow," he suggested in a voice that sounded as if it had rusted.

"Wedding?" Dylon croaked, frog-eyed. "What the devil are you babbling about?"

"We're getting married." Liberty leaned back to peer up into Dylon's blurred face and her head very nearly rolled off her shoulders. A hiccup burst from her lips. "'Scuse me. You're welcome to come, if you wish."

Muttering a string of colorful profanities under his breath, Dylon steered Liberty toward the door. When she stumbled, he scooped her into his arms. "Both of you could do with some sleep," he advised. "You're both talking out of your heads."

While Dylon carried her out the door, Liberty cuddled up against him as if he were her pillow. A groggy sigh escaped her lips as she nuzzled against his muscled chest. Annoyed though Dylon was that Liberty had contributed to the delinquency of an elderly man, he couldn't contain the smile that tugged at his lips. He stared down at the intoxicated beauty and he forgot why he was irritated with her. For the first time ever, Brewster had been so distracted and inebriated that he was unable to greet his guests. This free-spirited sprite had managed to get both herself and Brewster drunk as skunks. Not only had Liberty turned Lockhart Hall upside down, but she had disrupted the normal routine at Brewster's estate. . . .

Dylon halted in midstride when Griffin appeared from his room to gape at the bundle in green velvet.

"What happened?" he questioned in concern.

"Liberty got Grandfather drunk," Dylon explained.

"I did not," she slurred out. "'Twas the other way 'round."

"Whatever," Dylon grumbled crankily. "Brewster is in the office. Go fetch him. He'll never reach his room under his own power. I don't want that silly old man to embarrass himself by falling flat on his face in front of his distinguished guests."

Muffling a snicker, Griffin shouldered past his brother to rescue his grandfather from further humiliation.

Maneuvering Liberty in his arms, Dylon unlatched the door to her chambers and carried her inside. When he lowered her to her feet, she folded up like a tent and Dylon was forced to lunge at her before she collapsed in an unladylike heap on the carpet.

The abrupt movement caused Liberty to blink bewilderedly. Her eyes had difficulty keeping up with the movement of her head. Her nose was so numb she had to pinch it twice to ensure it was still there.

The comical cross-eyed expression that claimed Liberty's features while she investigated her nose provoked Dylon to grin. "Aye, it's still there," he assured her as he propelled her toward her bed. "And, come dawn, your head will feel like it's about to launch itself into orbit."

When Dylon eased her down on the edge of the bed to remove her boots, Liberty frowned, perplexed. "Dylon, have you ever felt as if your eyes were windows and that you were being held prisoner inside somebody else's body?" she slurred out.

He glanced up, amused by her peculiar remark. And yet, after he had come to know this uninhibited minx (and he had come to know her amazingly well in a short span of time) he could imagine that was exactly how this rambunctious female felt. All that vital untamed spirit had been trapped in a woman's form. She had been imposed upon by rules and limitations and standards against which she constantly rebelled. No doubt, Liberty did feel as if she had been suppressed and held captive. She probably wished she had been born a man who was permitted considerably more freedom in chasing his own rainbows. But Dylon was ever so glad Liberty wasn't a man. He liked her just the way she was, despite the fact that she sometimes made him so irritated he wanted to shake her until her pearly white teeth rattled.

"Turn over so I can get you out of the contraption," Dylon instructed.

Liberty complied without protest. All modesty forgotten, she plunked down in the middle of the bed to stare at the far wall. The feel of Dylon's hands on her bare back triggered forbidden memories that no amount of rum could smother. Indeed, the liquor numbed some places and sensitized others. When Dylon touched her, no matter how harmlessly, those tantalizing feelings flooded out of her. Gone was inhibition and stubborn pride. Gone were the nagging whispers of her conscience.

When Dylon tugged her upright to draw the riding habit from her shoulders, Liberty peered into those hazy pools of baby blue. Blurred though her vision was, she could see Dylon as he had been that night when he had lain down beside her to introduce her to the mystical world of passion.

"You are far too pleasing to the eye," Liberty confessed, the rum working like a truth serum.

"Am I?" Dylon grinned at the inebriated imp.

Liberty nodded affirmatively, causing renegade strands of gold to tumble over her bare shoulder. "And you have the most kissable mouth ever to be carved on a male face," she admitted tipsily.

Slowly, Dylon peeled the velvet garment to her waist, exposing the lacy chemise beneath it. Suddenly, he lost all interest in conversation, even though it might be the only time in his life that he received compliments from this feisty pixie.

When Liberty impulsively looped her limp arms over his shoulders and raised tempting lips to his, Dylon forgot his original purpose for undressing her. He wanted to feel her petal-soft lips under his. He ached to rediscover every silky inch of her flesh. . . .

"Kiss me," Liberty requested in a throaty whisper. "I want to see if you still taste as good as you did the first time . . ."

That was all the invitation Dylon needed. In fact, even less would have been plenty. His lips rolled over hers, finding not one ounce of resistance. Liberty melted in his arms and instinctively arched toward him. A muffled groan rattled in his palpitating chest when leaping flames blazed through every nerve and muscle in his masculine body.

His reaction to this gorgeous nymph was just as it had been the first time—spontaneous and explosive. He wanted to savor and devour her all in the same moment. He couldn't get enough of her, couldn't get close enough to the fire that burned inside and out. . . .

"It's my turn," Liberty whispered and then giggled giddishly at whatever wicked thought sloshed through her pickled brain.

A bemused smile pursed Dylon's lips, wondering what she meant. But within a moment he understood. The first time, he had seduced her. Now, under the influence of Brewster's special recipe, Liberty wanted to explore his body as if he were the eighth wonder of the world. Although her numb fingertips fumbled with the buttons of his shirt, she divested him of the garment. In wonderment, she traced her hand over the padded muscles and dark matting of hair that carpeted his broad chest.

"Magnificent . . ." she breathed in compliment and then pressed her lips to his bronzed skin to taste what she had touched.

Dylon swore his lungs were filled with mortar, causing him to suffer severe oxygen deprivation. His heart was pounding against his clogged breathing apparatus, pelting the last ounce of air out of him. When her brazen caress coasted down his belly to loosen his breeches, Dylon completely forgot to breathe and why he even needed to. Liberty's adventurous touch suddenly became the nourishment he needed to exist. The feel of her moist lips skimming over his ribs put bonfires in his bloodstream. Inexperienced though Liberty was, she knew how to drive a man over the edge and send him tumbling pell-mell into the most sensual dimensions of desire.

The world turned black and Dylon's mind completely broke down. His body became putty in Liberty's questing hands. He lived only for her touch, her kiss, her scent. Never had he allowed a woman to take full initiative in lovemaking. He'd always been in command, bending a woman to his will. But he gave Liberty free license to appease her feminine curiosity about men, to discover the power she held over him when she was in his arms.

With each breathless second that ticked by, Liberty became bolder and even more inquisitive. She discovered all the ultrasensitive places he liked to be touched. She marveled at Dylon's reactions to her exploring caresses, reveled in the pleasure she received from memorizing the muscled planes and contours of his virile body. Feeling the potential power beneath her fingertips was far more addictive than Brewster's special recipe. She yearned for more, longed to return that same wild need she had experienced the first time this midnight-haired rogue sent her skyrocketing through the star-spangled universe.

Repeatedly, Liberty mapped the hard terrain of his hair-roughened flesh, teasing and tantalizing each sensitive point, seducing him with her hands, body and lips. Needs as ancient as time itself bombarded her as she caressed Dylon's rippling skin. Her hand folded around him, stroking him until he groaned in unholy torment. She invented ways to arouse him until her name burst from his lips, begging her to end the divine torment of having her so close and yet so intolerably far away.

Liberty glided over him, employing her own aching body in an erotic caress that drove Dylon over the brink into breathless abandon. She felt him tremble beneath her, felt the surge of ineffable pleasure in knowing she had made him want her as desperately and hungrily as she wanted him. . . .

Sweet secret desire . . . The thought flitted through her hazy mind like a skipping shadow. Aye, that was what this blue-eyed rake had become to her. She had hid behind her bruised pride, self-guilt and anger to shield herself against this handsome rake these past few days. But way down deep inside, Liberty knew she had been unwillingly and unreasonably attracted to this magnificent, dynamic man who oozed with charm and sensuality. If not for this hot, compelling need she would never have surrendered to him that first time, would not ache for him now. . . .

When Dylon twisted away to work his skillful magic on her, Liberty dripped into a puddle of bubbly desire. Her body seemed to beg for his bone-melting touch, for his soul-shattering kisses. He caressed her everywhere at once. It was as if he, like she, could not bear to enjoy this wild pleasure alone, as if sharing the ecstasy was all that could ensure sublime fulfillment.

His greedy kisses flooded over her. Flames leaped across every nerve ending until her entire body was on fire with wanting. His body half covered hers, crushing her into the mattress. His kisses were faintly forceful and the wayward passage of his hands caused another multitude of cravings to uncoil inside her.

And when he came to her, whispering his need for her, satisfying the monstrous hunger he had aroused in her, Liberty gave herself up to the powers of a passion that defied control. Sensation upon indescribable sensation swamped her, catapulting her into that far-distant realm of ecstasy that lay beyond the stars. Because of the hypnotic spell Dylon had cast upon her she could shrug off the hindering garments of the soul and soar like a wild free bird, orbiting in motionless flight. Only now had the walls of her prison come tumbling down. In this magical universe there were no rules or restrictions to limit her. In this world of splendorous sensations she was whole and alive and complete. . . .

Wild pulsations riveted her as she clung to Dylon in mindless ecstasy. Shudder after rapturous shudder pelted her, causing her nerves to hum like a musician plucking harp strings. Breathlessly, Liberty clutched Dylon to her, absorbing his strength, his very spirit. Sweet desire had blossomed out of nowhere to engulf her again . . . and again . . . and again. . . .

Liberty wasn't allowed to make a languid re-entry into reality after orbiting the universe of wild abandon. The potent rum she consumed left her drifting in erotic dreams. Their ardent lovemaking had siphoned her strength. The unparalleled sensations of splendor subsided, leaving her sinking into a deep, tranquil sleep. . . .

Passion-drugged, Dylon eased down beside Liberty. It was several minutes before he could breathe normally again. And it was another few minutes before he could gather enough energy to move, though he didn't go very far. He was compelled to remain by her side, watching the lantern light flitter over her bewitching features and delectable form like an invisible caress.

Dylon shook his head in utter astonishment. He felt as if *he* was the one who had partaken too much of Brewster's special recipe. Making love to Liberty produced the most intoxicating effects imaginable. How could one so young and inexperienced become such a skillful seductress so quickly? It baffled the mind!

The last thing Dylon had anticipated when he carried this sprite to bed was to be seduced. Not that he was complaining, mind you. But considering the way Liberty had been behaving the last few days, one would have thought she only tolerated his presence because of their bargain. But if either of them thought all that was going on between them was a pretense to satisfy their bargain, one of them was a fool! Passion such as the kind they ignited in each other didn't come along very often. Dylon had certainly been around enough to know that. Too bad Liberty didn't. She might not have made such a big production out of hating him.

Pensively, Dylon reached out to trace the heart-shaped curve of her lips, the delicate arch of her brows. He had thought their first ardent interlude with desire had shattered his self-control as if it never really existed. But this? This fervent eruption of emotion had left him trembling in the very quintessence of pleasure. How could a woman touch him so deeply, drawing out feelings that he vowed to keep dead and buried?

Dylon had felt this same sense of vulnerability when he fancied himself in love with Patricia Morgan. And yet, with Liberty it was vastly different. Good God, it was a zillion times worse! he realized with a start.

After drawing the sheet over himself and Liberty, Dylon cuddled her against him. He should return to his own room, he knew. But he couldn't leave her just yet. He wanted to go on holding her to him until this multitude of indefinable sensations faded, until he returned to his old self again. In a few hours, he would sneak back to his room and no one would be the wiser. Thank God, Percy wasn't here to spy and eavesdrop on him again!

Expelling a weary sigh, Dylon closed his eyes and nuzzled against Liberty's neck. The aroma of pipe tobacco clung to the silky strands of her golden hair and Dylon broke into a drowsy smile. He had been bedeviled and seduced by a rum-drinking, pipe-smoking temptress who instinctively knew how to satisfy even the most particular of men. Only this uninhibited imp would dare such things, he mused as he draped his arm over the shapely curve of her hip to bring their bodies into familiar contact. Only an unconventional nymph who had no regard whatsoever for social convention would accept the marriage proposal of a man who was more than thrice her age to avoid her mysterious fiancé. . . .

His head popped up and he blinked like an awakened owl. "Good God," Dylon chirped when the full effect of his grandfather's words soaked into his mushy brain.

Uncaring whether he roused Liberty or not (which of course he couldn't since she was four sheets to the wind) Dylon vaulted out of bed. Quick as a wink, he rammed his legs into his breeches and speared his arms through his shirtsleeves. Barefooted, he whizzed down the hall to interrogate his grandfather about his earlier remark.

When Dylon breezed into Brewster's room, Griffin was propped against the wall, sucking air and glaring at the snoring, gray-haired man who was sprawled spread-eagle on his bed. Brewster was still wearing the same clothes he had on a half-hour earlier, minus one silk stocking and one silver-buckled shoe.

"I don't recall ever seeing Brewster so damn drunk before," Griffin declared with a tired sigh. "I cannot tell you what an ordeal I underwent just getting this old billy goat up the stairs to bed. He collapsed twice on the steps. You probably heard the commotion . . ."

Griffin glanced at his barefooted brother, noting that his shirt was haphazardly buttoned and his hair lay across his forehead in reckless disarray. Griff's smile instantly vanished and a resentful glare puckered his handsome features. "On second thought, it seems unlikely that you heard the clatter on the steps or the thud on the floor when Brewster tripped over me and himself, knocking both of us to our knees. . . . Damn you, Dylon . . ."

Dylon chose to stare at his grandfather rather than his seething brother. "I predict Brewster and Liberty will both be plagued with horrendous hangovers," he said, purposely switching topics of conversation.

"Don't change the subject," Griffin growled in a furious tone. "How dare you take advantage of that innocent little sprite. She was too drunk to resist and you . . ."

Blast it, Griffin was turning out to be just like Percy. What was there about that she-devil that aroused every man's protective instincts?

"You've stooped pretty low once or twice, curse your miserable hide, but I never thought you would dare—"

"Enough," Dylon snapped. "What is between Liberty and me is our business and you will—"

"I told you I thought I was in love with her and you still trifled with her as if she were your private paramour," Griffin harshly accused. "But if you think this changes my feelings for her, you are mistaken." His voice had risen to a roar, one which Brewster never even heard in his drunken stupor. "It changes my feeling for *you*, but never her! I intend to get down on my knees and propose to Liberty the moment we return to Lockhart Hall."

"Griff, you—"

Dylon wasn't allowed to protest his brother's intentions. Griffin surged toward the door in angry strides. His boot heels pounded down the hall like a carpenter driving nails and echoed like thunder in the darkness. Dylon muttered a stream of curses and stamped back to his room.

Good God, how could one woman manage to entangle three men's lives in one week? Dylon asked himself incredulously. Brewster, under the influence of his own potent rum, had proposed to that vivacious elf. Now Griffin was making plans to propose the first chance he got. And Dylon was *supposed* to be her escort, her suitor and her prospective fiancé!

Dylon shuddered to speculate on how many other moonstruck men had fallen beneath Liberty's obvious charms. Lord, she'd probably received a marriage proposal from every man she'd ever met! She was just one of those women who would never be between men. They chased after her like hounds stampeding after a fox.

Still grumbling Dylon flounced on his bed. This wasn't going to be a carefree holiday; it was going to be a living nightmare. Griffin was disillusioned and resentful. Brewster had obviously lost his mind and proposed to a rambuctious hellion who was young enough to be his granddaughter. Now how in the hell did Brewster think he could keep up with a vivacious she-male like Liberty Jordon? Dylon wasn't sure it could be done, no matter what a man's age or state of health. And to complicate the situation more than it was, Dylon had buckled beneath his own uncontrollable desire for that gorgeous vixen and Griffin knew his brother had done far more than tuck Liberty into bed.

"Women!" Dylon growled at the ceiling. "*Woman*," he quickly corrected himself. One impossible, high-spirited, independent woman. Ah, how he longed to be the man he'd been before Liberty turned his world upside down. Things were much simpler then. He could walk away from his affairs without regret. But now?

Dylon's breath came out in a frustrated rush. He had offended Percy's sense of propriety because of this ungovernable desire for Liberty. He had alienated his own brother who had fallen hard and fast for that beguiling minx. Even his own grandfather had been bedeviled by that misfit. And Dylon was too intrigued by her to be sensible. He could feel himself getting in deeper and deeper with that violet-eyed spitfire. Good God, he'd need a ladder to climb out of the hole he'd dug for himself.

And yet . . . Smoldering fires radiated through Dylon's body when his thoughts circled back to those magical moments of splendor that he and Liberty had shared. His ardent desire for her had passed all rational bounds. He could grouse and moan about the tangle that golden-haired pixie had made of his life and his dealings with his own family, but he wouldn't have missed making wild sweet love to Liberty for all the jewels in the royal crown. There were just some things a man couldn't make himself regret, no matter how hard he tried. And Dylon did admit he wasn't trying hard enough. Sailing away on the most intimate of journeys with that delectable little temptress was something no man would ever want to miss in his lifetime.

As his eyes fluttered against his high cheekbones, Dylon found himself cruising off into erotic dreams. It was no wonder Griff was so furious with him, Dylon mused groggily. Griff would be in a bona fide snit if he knew exactly what he'd been missing. But he would never know, Dylon promised himself. Dylon was the one who had taught Liberty everything she knew about passion and no other man was going to discover that glorious world of splendor that unfolded when he was in the silky circle of her arms. Liberty was his possession, whether she chose to admit it or not. They set sparks in each other that burned hot against the night. And if Griffin thought for one minute that he would take Dylon's place . . .

Dylon jerked up his head and cursed the vivid picture of Griffin clutching Liberty in his arms and kissing the breath out of her. "Damn, sometimes I wish I were an only child," he muttered, annoyed with the unsettling picture that was framed in his mind. The thought of Liberty married to Griff, or even to his crazed grandfather, who was obviously undergoing his second childhood, spoiled Dylon's disposition. And that had been extremely difficult to do until Liberty came along, turning him wrong side out—him and half the colony's male population—Dylon mused bitterly.

He had the inescapable feeling that wherever that lavender-eyed hellion went there would always be trouble following in her shadow. She attracted men like moths to the proverbial flame. She's a forbidden flame all right, thought Dylon. She could turn a man into a human torch and leave him burning like a beacon in the night. All except me, Dylon told himself stubbornly. He wasn't going to become so smitten with that minx that he made an ass of himself! Dylon quickly checked to see if he'd already sprouted a tail and long ears and then cursed under his breath, thinking it was a little too late to wonder if he'd made an ass of himself where Liberty was concerned.

Curse it, he should have tucked her into bed and tiptoed out of the room. But nay, he, like the rest of his gender, didn't have enough willpower to resist that adorable little imp. She caused Dylon to misplace the good sense he'd been born with! *If* he had been born with any. Dylon honestly wondered if he had. . . .

Chapter 15

"You idiotic drunkard!" Simon roared in a whiplash voice. He backhanded Luther across the cheek. The chair in which Luther was sitting rocked on its back legs and crashed to the floor. "You let Stella sneak away while you were on your latest binge!"

Numb though Luther's facial features were after all the whiskey he'd consumed the past few days, nothing could take the sting out of Simon's devastating blow. Before Luther could roll off his upturned chair and stagger to his feet, Simon jerked him up by the lapels of his wrinkled jacket to breathe down his neck.

"I ought to have you strung up in the nearest tree," Simon raged savagely. "I've turned this countryside upside down in search of that sassy niece of yours and here you sit, drinking yourself blind and letting Liberty's maid skulk off to only God knows where!"

As if touching this man with the batlike features repulsed him, Simon flung him away. Luther slammed against the wall and slid to the floor. He didn't dare try to defend himself. His puffy lip and thick tongue prevented him from speaking at all. Not that it would have done one whit of good, Luther thought sickly. Simon was roaring like a fire-breathing dragon.

"If that elusive female doesn't turn up soon, the deal is off." Simon sneered at the lush who had locked himself in his office to indulge his drinking habit. "You'll find yourself in worse condition than you are now!"

Scowling, Simon lurched around to motion for his three burly henchmen to hoist Luther to his feet. "Get this drunkard cleaned up and sobered up," he demanded impatiently.

Luther, who was seeing double already, shrank back against the wall when Figgins, Gilbert and Donnely lumbered toward him. He was effortlessly jerked to his feet and propelled toward the steps. While Luther was being shoved into his tub and sobered up, Simon dropped into a chair and swore fluently. He had spent far too much time pursuing his would-be bride. And Luther, lush that he was, had been no help at all. Each time Simon left that miscreant alone, he wound up backstroking through a bottle of brandy.

An exasperated sigh gushed from Simon's lips when he glanced out the window, watching the evening shadows slither across the lawn at Triple Oak. Despite his fury with Luther, Simon was still compelled to seek out Liberty. Damn, what was there about that female that bewitched him so? In the short time he'd known her and despite his scheme to wed her for his own purpose, he had developed an insatiable craving for that golden-haired enchantress. He had never even touched her and yet he craved her like a starved man hungers for a feast. He had looked at that shapely beauty and fire sizzled through his bloodstream. And, by damned, I shall have her, Simon promised himself determinedly. Liberty Jordon would be more than his pawn. She would satisfy his lusts until he tired of her . . . if and when he caught up with her. . . .

Simon slammed the fist of his right hand into his left palm and let loose with another flood of profanity. If not for that bungling fop who went by the name of Luther Norris, Simon would have already had Liberty in his bed a dozen times. And when he finally did capture that spirited minx he would see to it that she compensated for all his frustration. He would bury himself in her exquisite body and reap all the lusty pleasures he should have been enjoying this past week while he searched high and low for his runaway bride.

Simon would have his revenge. . . . A wicked smile worked its way across his lips when he contemplated making up for lost time with his soon-to-be wife. She would pay penance ten times over for artfully eluding him. . . .

Dressed fit to kill, Phillipe LaGere swaggered across the gangplank as if he had springs in his shoes. With an air of confidence that nothing had ever been able to demolish, Phillipe hopped onto the wharf and strode toward the lights of Charles Town that twinkled in the night. He hadn't gone very far when Stella Talbot came racing toward him, inhaling air in surging gulps.

"I'm ever so glad you're here," Stella breathed in relief. She latched onto Phillipe's arm and hustled him down the dock. "I bear bad news. There is serious trouble brewing in Carolina."

Phillipe's refined features furrowed in a concerned frown. "What has happened?"

"What *hasn't* happened!" Stella burst out in frustration. "Liberty's scheming uncle has contracted her into a marriage with a horrible man. She has escaped him twice, but he is hell-bent on forcing her into wedlock."

"Where is she?" Phillipe clamped his hands on Stella's shoulders and stared down into her fretful expression. "Where is my beloved?" he demanded impatiently.

"At Lockhart Hall, upriver . . . on the Ashley . . ."

"I shall save my lovely Liberty from disaster!"

Before Stella could fill Phillipe in on all the details, he flipped his cloak over one shoulder and charged off like a misdirected bullet. Stella threw up her hands in exasperation and then let them drop limply by her hips. She hated to admit it, but Liberty was right about Phillipe. He did make a dramatic production out of every situation. And although Liberty was in a precarious predicament, Phillipe had bounded off like a rabbit without allowing Stella to elaborate.

No doubt, Phillipe had made a leap of certainty into the worst possible conclusion. Stella feared that Phillipe would vent his wrath on the first man he encountered at Lockhart Hall, even if it wasn't Simon Gridley! Lord have mercy, Phillipe had gone off half-cocked and he might wind up killing the wrong man . . . !

"Phillipe! Wait!" Stella called out.

But it was too late. The flamboyant Frenchman had disappeared like a shooting star fizzling out into the blackness of the night.

So this is what dying a slow, agonizing death feels like, Liberty thought sickly. Her stomach pitched and rolled like a storm-tossed ship on an angry sea. A pounding headache plowed through her skull to puncture her pickled brain. Her mouth was as dry as cotton and even her eyelashes ached!

The instant Liberty pried one eye open to greet the new day, she knew it was a mistake. Sunlight speared through the open window like stabbing needles. Lord, *dead* had to be better than this. In fact, Liberty swore she would prefer eternal sleep to this hellish hangover she was having.

For a few nauseating moments she lay with her head dangling over the edge of the bed, just in case . . . Gulping audibly, she crawled out of the bed and staggered toward the commode. She poured water into the basin, stared ponderously at it and then plunged her head downward to submerge it completely.

Ah, minimal relief! Liberty swore, there and then, that this was the first and last time she sampled Brewster's special recipe. She could barely function and she didn't feel anywhere near human, even after she soaked her head. . . .

A shocked gasp escaped her lips when she realized she was standing there stark naked. Godamercy, what else had she done besides get herself drunk as a skunk? Had she tromped through the mansion like Lady Godiva of Coventry . . . or was it Cambridge? Why did Cambridge stick in her mind like a porcupine quill?

Flashbacks from the previous evening whacked their way through the tangled jungle of her mind. On wobbly legs, Liberty retrieved her satchels to fish out a gown. And all the while, fragments of disjointed memories leaped at her, giving her a worse headache than she already had.

She and Brewster had sipped brew and conversed on a myriad of topics. She had been given a lengthy account of Brewster's life, as well as that of Dylon's. Although Dylon had refused to offer details about the bloody battles against the Cherokees, Brewster had spared no adjectives in describing Dylon's ride into hell.

Liberty had listened in horrified fascination while Brewster cited the atrocities of both the Indians and the whites which precipitated war. Dylon had been under Lyttleton's command when he led the expedition to Fort Prince George in '59. After a gory conflict (which Brewster described in a blow-by-blow account), the soldiers captured twenty-two hostages to hold until the Cherokees handed over the murderers of several white settlers and traders.

But the Cherokees hadn't surrendered. Instead they launched a vicious raid in the Carolinas, slaughtering whites in the settlements through which they passed. Despite Dylon's pleas to his superior officers, the twenty-two Indian hostages were massacred to retaliate the loss of one of their own men.

According to Brewster, Dylon had spent the next two years on the frontier amid a blaze of gunfire and hissing arrows, one of which had imbedded itself in his shoulder and others which had come perilously close to parting his hair and riddling his body as if it were a pincushion. His regiment had come upon the mutilated bodies of white men, women and children who were making their exodus from one of the ransacked settlements to the north. They had never reached their destination of Augusta, Georgia. One hundred Cherokee warriors had set upon them, leaving no survivors.

Outraged, the provincial government strengthened their forces with extra militia and ordered them to punish the Cherokees. The soldiers had burned Cherokee villages, chopped down crops and killed or captured as many Indians as possible. Dylon had protested the senseless murders and desolation of land, but his superiors in the regular army boasted that they would "chastise" the Indians for their butchery. The incident infuriated tribesmen, as Dylon predicted it would. The Cherokees came at the soldiers in ruthless fury—ambushing, killing and capturing as many prisoners as they could lead away from battle.

Again British and colonial soldiers retaliated. Lieutenant Colonel James Grant, with twelve hundred regulars, plus the four hundred militiamen in South Carolina, burned the Cherokee villages to the ground, completely destroyed their crops and drove the survivors into the mountains to starve. It was then that the Cherokees begged for humiliating peace and Dylon was allowed to put the bloody past behind him to resume his position as master of Lockhart Hall.

Having heard the dismal details, Liberty drank to forget what Dylon didn't want to remember. She wasn't sure, but she thought she had divulged part of her problems to Brewster in her drunken state. How much, Liberty couldn't remember. But she did recall Dylon barging into the room to carry her upstairs. . . .

Liberty gulped hard, searching her fuzzy memory for details. Ever so slowly, the hazy picture materialized. In her mind's eye, she could see a brazen young woman seducing Dylon, divesting him of his clothes, caressing him . . .

Her face flushed crimson red. Godamercy, that woman had been *her!* Liberty collapsed on the edge of her bed, holding her throbbing head in her hands. Lord, the things she'd done while she had been under the influence of Brewster's brew! Her complexion turned a deeper shade of red as the events of the night unfolded with painful clarity.

How could she face Dylon after she'd behaved so shamelessly? She had sworn she would never repeat that first careless night of passion. And hypocrite that she was, she had instigated it! She certainly couldn't accuse him of seducing her this time. God, how she wished she hadn't remembered any of it. But with each second that ticked by, the memories crystallized and lingering sensations pummeled her.

Inhaling a shuddering breath, Liberty pulled herself upright to arrange her damp hair in a neat chignon at the nape of her neck. After dressing in a fashionable pink gown, Liberty shuffled toward the door, mentally preparing herself to confront Dylon's mocking smile. She imagined he would never let her hear the end of this. She had made a liar of herself when she threw herself at Dylon like a common trollop. He would hold the embarrassing incident over her head for the rest of her life. Luckily, she wouldn't be around for him to harass indefinitely. She would sail off to the Indies and Dylon would be a page from her past.

Lady Luck was on Liberty's side as she trudged down the abandoned hall. There were no whispering voices to taunt her, no guests to speculate on why her bloodshot eyes looked like a road map. She had only to navigate down the flight of steps that led to the foyer. With great care, Liberty descended the steps, clamping her hand on the banister to ensure she didn't tumble her way to the ground floor and humiliate herself worse than she already had.

When Liberty staggered into the spacious dining hall, she spied Brewster slouched in his chair at the head of the table. He had wound a damp towel around his head like a turban and he sat sipping steaming tea. His wrinkled features were whitewashed and he looked every bit as bad as she felt.

Bracing one hand on the table, Liberty pulled out a chair. It screeched across the wooden floor and both she and Brewster howled in unison.

"Sorry," she apologized quietly before sinking into her seat.

Brewster stared at the far end of the table where Liberty sat. She looked like his own reflection—streaked eyes and a complexion that wavered between white and pea green.

"We missed the cudgeling bout and greased pig contest at the fair this morning," he squeaked. "The rest of my guests left hours ago."

"Thank God," Liberty breathed weakly. "If I would have had to muster greeting smiles for all your distinguished guests, my face would have cracked."

Brewster tried to grin in response to her remark, but even his wrinkles ached. He sat expressionless, listening to the drum that pounded against his soggy brain. When the servant appeared to set a tray before him, Brewster sent the man back to the kitchen to fetch food and tea for Liberty. Within a few minutes they were both nibbling on warm biscuits and hanging their pulsating heads over cups of steaming tea.

"You may be interested to know that Dylon waited for you to rouse," Brewster murmured. "But the young lady whom I invited, in case he arrived here alone, latched onto him. When I came downstairs, Olivia Thornton was draped on him like Spanish moss."

Jealousy stabbed at Liberty, but she stubbornly shoved it away. She had no right to be possessive of that handsome rake. He attracted females like flies and she had ignored him the better part of four days . . . until last night . . .

Liberty cringed at the mortifying thought. Damn, she

had turned out to be as much the rake as Dylon was! She had refused to have anything to do with him and then she turned right around and seduced him! She had accused Dylon of being insensitive to her feelings, for using her as the object of his lust. Then she had behaved exactly as he had . . .

"Are you all right, my dear?" Brewster questioned when he saw the color wane from her tanned cheeks.

"Nay, I'm not," Liberty groaned disparagingly. "I don't even know myself these days. First, I drank myself insane and then I . . ." The wild blush of color flooded back into her ashen cheeks. "Brewster, is there a nunnery hereabout? I think perhaps I should join one before I embarrass myself more than I already have."

Even though Brewster's face ached, he broke into a smile. Liberty hadn't explained what had happened after Dylon carried her to her room, but her reference to a nunnery suggested she felt the need to repent. Brewster could guess what happened in Liberty's vulnerable condition. A man and woman alone in a bedchamber . . .

While Liberty slumped dispiritedly in her chair, Brewster excused himself. Employing the wall to support him, he wobbled to his office to jot down a message. With the note signed and sealed, Brewster ordered it delivered posthaste. While the courier galloped toward his destination, Brewster trudged back into the dining hall.

"If you would like to bathe and rest before my guests return, I'll have the servants fetch water to your tub," he offered.

Liberty managed a grateful smile as she weaved toward the gray-haired man who had propped himself against the doorjamb. "Thank you, Brewster. Perhaps a cool bath will cure what ails me."

A cryptic smile quirked his lips. "I doubt it, my dear. But perhaps it will at least treat the symptoms."

Liberty was in no frame of mind to decipher Brewster's enigmatic smile and accompanying remark. All she wanted was to soak until the nausea and headache went away . . . which, judging by the way she felt, could take at least a century.

"I planned a fox hunt this afternoon, for those who wish to participate rather than view the craft booths at the fair," Brewster informed her as they tackled the mountains of steps, arm in arm. "If we feel up to it by then, perhaps you and I can manage to crawl atop our mounts."

"Fresh air and exercise will be just what I need," Liberty diagnosed and then groaned when her stomach flip-flopped. ". . . If I'm still alive this afternoon."

They parted company at the head of the steps, each one going his or her own way to recuperate from the devastating bout with Brewster's brew. And after the picnic-style lunch Brewster served on the front lawn, Liberty felt almost human again . . . Almost . . .

For the umpteenth time, Dylon pried the overzealous brunette away and retreated a step. "Let's concentrate on the participants of the greased pig contest, shall we, Olivia?" he managed to say without growling the words.

Olivia Thornton sidled closer to drape her arm over Dylon's wide shoulder. "Surely you know greased pigs are the farthest thing from my mind," she purred provocatively. Her free hand ventured up his arm like a crawling spider. "You know, I've admired you for years, Dylon. When your grandfather suggested that you and I become better acquainted at his birthday celebration, it was a dream come true for me."

A dream come true for her, perhaps, but a nightmare for Dylon. Since he had folded himself into the coach beside Olivia, she had been all over him like an eight-armed octopus. And he hadn't been able to take one step at the fair without Olivia's touching him somewhere or another. It was the *another* that had him shying away from her like a skittish colt!

Lord, what was the matter with him? There had been a

time when he was amused by fawning females. Now they put him off. He didn't want anything to do with Olivia or any other attractive wench at the fair. His thoughts constantly circled back to Liberty, wondering how she was faring with her hangover, wondering if she resented the night of ecstasy they had shared. . . .

Dylon leaped backward like a mountain goat when Olivia threw her arms around his neck and planted a passionate kiss to his lips. Rolling his eyes skyward to request divine patience, Dylon plucked her arms from his shoulders and shackled them in his own.

"In case you have forgotten, I have an escort waiting for me at Brewster's estate. In fact, we have contemplated announcing our engagement," Dylon lied for his own protection. Hell's fire, Brewster couldn't select suitable escorts any better than Dylon could!

It didn't faze Olivia-the-octopus one whit. She wriggled her hands free and let them wander over Dylon's muscular physique. Finally, Dylon had enough groping in public. He grabbed Olivia by the arm, towed her over to the craft booth where Griffin and Cayla were standing and left her in his brother's care. Mumbling a lame excuse about searching out an old friend, Dylon lost himself in the milling crowd.

What rankled Dylon most was the kiss Olivia had generously bestowed on him. From the instant her lips fastened on his, Dylon found himself making startling comparisons. Olivia Thornton appeared to have a tad bit more experience in kissing but she left him as cold as a block of ice. Not even once had he felt the spark of desire—that old familiar stirring he usually experienced when a woman was in his arms. What he had felt was . . . Dylon gulped at the bleak thought. So help him, he had felt *repulsed* by that woman's kiss. It had been Liberty's kiss he'd wanted. He had yearned to have Liberty's arms winding around his neck to draw him close!

"Damn that witch," Dylon mumbled as he paced the perimeters of the crowd.

He had been perfectly content with his life until Liberty fell out of his magnolia tree. He had enjoyed a wide variety in women. He had amused himself with females. And all of a sudden, that blond-haired, violet-eyed minx had begun to monopolize his thoughts. Well, he wouldn't have it! He was not going to get emotionally involved with Liberty.

Aye, they set fires in each other, but Dylon wasn't the marrying kind. He was a confirmed bachelor. He scoffed at love and devotion and commitment. In fact, if his brother still wanted to propose to Liberty (that was, if Brewster hadn't married her the minute he sobered up), Griff was welcome to her. Dylon cherished his freedom and he wasn't giving it up for Liberty. 'Twas only a fierce physical reaction, Dylon told himself rationally. It was normal and natural to be obsessed by a woman as vivacious and bewitching as Liberty Jordon. But his attraction was only skin-deep. There were no velvet chains to bind him to her. . . .

Dylon glanced up when he spied Olivia cutting her way through the crowd like a barracuda. If he had any sense he would let Olivia fawn over him and replace that high-spirited hellion who was recovering from her hangover.

So much for good sense, Dylon thought as he ducked down and skedaddled away before Olivia clamped onto him. The mortifying truth was he preferred to match wits and wills against the feisty Liberty Jordon rather than suffer Olivia Thornton's slobbery kisses. It seemed those things in life that came so easy to him were no longer worth having. Women like Olivia were simple conquests. Honest to God, on days like these, Dylon gave serious consideration to joining a monastery!

When a rake like Dylon Lockhart turned down an overzealous woman, whom he could have had for the taking, and longed for an independent, high-strung spitfire who spited him at every turn, it was time to evaluate his priorities. The only trouble was Dylon wasn't sure he could remain as celibate as a monk when, at this very moment, he was aching for the kiss and caress of the seductress who had taken him to heaven the previous night. Who would have thought that *hell* would be eluding an eager female who had made it clear that he could take anything he wanted without her putting up a fuss?

Godamercy, Dylon grumbled, unaware that he had stolen Liberty's favorite expression. That minx had turned his world inside out and upside down! He had never turned tail and run from a zealous female in all his life. And the most depressing part of all was that Dylon knew if it was Liberty who was giving chase he wouldn't have taken one step in the opposite direction. Damn that woman. Even when she wasn't underfoot, she was still giving him fits!

Chapter 16

Liberty was amazed at the number of fine horses that lined Brewster's stable, not to mention the pack of sleek dogs that had been bred to participate in the fox hunts. Brewster boasted of how he had patiently and carefully crossbred his foxhounds. According to the patriarch, the new type of hounds which replaced the staghounds were extremely fast, intelligent and very lively. They worked well in large packs and had been meticulously trained by the grooms.

"And of course"—Brewster went on to say as he led Liberty through the stable—"the choice of horses is extremely important for the hunt. I have bred these hunters to suit their specific purposes. I've crossed well-known breeds of horses to gain the needed characteristics." He gestured to a white gelding that stood calmly in his stall. "This is my best animal. He has tremendous endurance; he responds quickly to the rein and he is not easily frightened or alarmed."

"Pegasus is also capable of negotiating ditches and fences that lie in his path," Dylon added as he ambled up behind Liberty.

She swallowed hard, afraid to meet Dylon's gaze. She feared he would taunt her about her shameless behavior the previous night.

"Pegasus is also good-natured and docile," Dylon

declared. His lips twitched, amused by Liberty's superb job of ignoring him.

Brewster was quick to notice Liberty's reluctance to meet Dylon's grin. Dylon was as nonchalant as ever and Liberty appeared far more subdued than usual. Well, time would determine how unflappable Dylon's disposition was, Brewster mused scampishly. He had plans for this swaggering rake of a grandson of his!

"Have you ever ridden in a fox hunt, Liberty?" Dylon inquired, easing up beside her to prop his forearms against the top rail of Pegasus' stall.

"Nay, I haven't," she replied, staring at the muscular white gelding instead of Dylon.

"Then perhaps I should explain the procedure." Dylon gestured toward his grandfather who still looked a mite green around the gills after his bout with the brew. "Brewster is known as the Master of Foxhounds. He, of course, is responsible for organizing the hunt. His head groom is referred to as the huntsman and 'tis his task to lead the pack of hounds to the scent of the fox. The young grooms are called whippers-in and their duty is to ensure the pack remains together instead of scattering from here to kingdom come. The other grooms are in charge of keeping the stock in excellent condition for the grueling cross-country race."

"Master of Foxhounds, huntsman, whippers-in . . ." Liberty sighed, her face milk-white. "This is giving me another headache. I'm not sure I'm up to this after all."

"Nonsense," Dylon chuckled as he took her arm and led her past the well-groomed horses. "It was you who declared that riding was most exhilarating." He leaned close to whisper confidentially in her ear. "Not quite as exhilarating as last night, but . . ."

Liberty jerked her arm from his grasp and glared flaming arrows at the grinning rogue. "I wondered how long you could talk without bringing that up. Five minutes seems to be your limit."

"Is something amiss?" Brewster called when he saw

Liberty shake herself loose from Dylon's grasp.

Dylon pivoted to stare at his grandfather who had propped himself near the entrance of the stables. "Liberty is simply pouting because I told her it was improper to surge ahead of the Master of Foxhounds who leads the hunt," he explained with a wry smile. "You know how indignant this young lady becomes when rules are laid down for her to follow."

Brewster eyed his grandson skeptically. He doubted their private discussion had anything to do with the hunt—at least not the one comprised of foxes, hounds and horses. But he let the matter die a graceful death, wishing he could as well, considering how miserable he felt at the moment.

"I think perhaps I'll let Griffin lead the hunt today," Brewster announced with a fatigued sigh. "I'm not sure I'm up to the rigorous pace either. Dylon, I will leave Liberty to you. Since she is unfamiliar with the hunt, keep a watchful eye on her. I've become quite fond of this young lady."

When Brewster wobbled off to inform Griffin of the change in plans, Dylon peered down into Liberty's strained features. "Do you wish to discuss what happened last night, or do you remember well enough to discuss it?"

Liberty stared at the row of horses. "I'm sorry to say that I recall the incident to which you are referring, but I would prefer not to speak of it," she said stiffly.

A pleased smile tugged at Dylon's lips. Considering the condition Liberty was in the previous evening that was quite a compliment. He'd wondered if she would recall the splendor they had shared in each other's arms. She remembered, but judging from the pinched expression on her elegant features she was none too pleased about what had happened.

"*I* remember the night with vivid clarity," he murmured with caressing huskiness.

When he cupped her chin to lift her face to his, Liberty

slapped his fingers away as if he were a pesky mosquito and retreated a respectable distance. "If it was so memorable, how is it that you were lured away to the fair this morning by a certain young lady who obviously has set her cap for you . . . ?"

Liberty could have cut out her runaway tongue for spouting that jealous remark. Her face turned all the colors of the rainbow and she lurched around to make a hasty exit.

Dylon burst out laughing and lunged forward to clutch her arm before she shot out the stable door. "Could it be that you actually care what I do and with whom, little minx?" he teased unmercifully.

"I don't care one whit," she lied to save face. "Why should I? Brewster asked me to marry him and I am seriously considering it."

Dylon stared into those snapping violet eyes and felt a wave of jealousy flood over him, of all people! At least he supposed it was jealousy. He hadn't experienced the emotion in so long he very nearly forgot what it felt like. But one thing he did remember was the comparisons he had made between Olivia and Liberty earlier that morning. Olivia Thornton was no Liberty Jordon, believe you him! And against his will, Dylon had wished it had been this sassy sprite who had accompanied him to the fair.

Blast it, why was he so captivated by this high-spirited blonde? She would bring him nothing but trouble. Because of her, Percy was peeved and Griff was grumpy. And because of her, Brewster had gotten himself drunk enough to propose marriage and wound up with such a ferocious hangover that he couldn't assume his role as Master of Foxhounds in the day's hunt! And despite all the reasons why he should keep his distance from this habitual troublemaker, nothing ever seemed quite right unless she was underfoot. Good God, even the sun didn't seem to burn as bright when Liberty Jordon wasn't around. And how that could possibly be, Dylon would dearly love to know!

Shaking off his reflections, Dylon fished into his pocket to extract the gift he had impulsively purchased at the fair while he was dodging Olivia. Liberty peered curiously at the long gold chain that Dylon drew across the palm of his hand for her inspection. At one end was an engraved clip and on the other end was a decorative watch which could be fastened around the waist of the lady who wore it.

"For you," Dylon declared as he slipped his hands around her trim waist to fasten the watch in place.

Liberty peered up into those spellbinding blue eyes, wondering why Dylon was bestowing such an expensive gift on her. Was this costly trinket a payment for the night of passion he'd spent in her arms? Most likely, Liberty fumed.

Dylon was quick to decipher the resentment in her waxed features. "'Tis not what you think," he assured her with a soft laugh. He cupped the delicate watch in his hand and tapped his index finger on the glass casing. "You see, 'tis a few minutes fast."

Liberty frowned, befuddled. "Whyever would you purchase a watch that doesn't keep proper time?"

A teasing twinkle glinted in his eyes as he playfully flicked the tip of her upturned nose. "Because, my dear Liberty, the world ticks by on two time scales—yours and God's. 'Tis He who keeps the slower pace and you the faster one." He frowned in disapproval. "And because you travel at a swifter pace than most folks, it would be a mistake to marry my grandfather and you know it," Dylon declared with absolute certainty. "Brewster is very much a man in his own right. But he couldn't keep up with your pace. Nor could he give you what you need . . . And not nearly often enough to satisfy a woman like you. . . ."

When Dylon reached up to trace the delicate curve of her cheek, shock waves rippled through Liberty. She wanted to resist, she truly did. But forbidden flames flickered inside her, just as they always did when she dared to stand this close to this charismatic rake. She could feel her body burning in that familiar way, feel the titillating sensations that could so easily and so quickly consume her.

As his sensuous mouth slanted over hers, Liberty felt her traitorous body melting into his masculine contours. And before she knew it, her arms glided over his chest to link behind his neck. Liberty kissed him back. It was a wild explosive kiss that sent sparks leaping from her wanton body to his and back again . . .

"Dylon!" Griffin's strident voice chopped through the electrified silence like a hatchet. "'Tis time to bring out the horses."

The glare Griffin leveled on his brother was meant to maim, but unfortunately Dylon had the thick hide of an elephant. Wheeling about, Griffin stamped off to fetch the grooms, wishing that *he* had been an only child. Seeing Liberty in Dylon's arms turned Griffin's mood a darker shade of black.

A muddled frown knitted Liberty's brow as she stared at Griffin's departing back. "Whatever is the matter with him?"

Dylon laid his hand to the small of her back to propel her from the stables. "We had an argument last night and Griff is one of those individuals who believes in holding a grudge," he explained without complicating matters more than they already were.

Liberty chewed on her bottom lip, speculating on what the disagreement was about. Dylon hadn't elaborated and it didn't look as if he had any intention of doing so. Had she known what put them at odds she would have dug a hole and pulled it in after her.

And that was exactly why Dylon hadn't disclosed the nature of the argument. Liberty was still battling the aftereffects of her hangover. She didn't need to contend with the humiliation of knowing Griffin was aware of what had transpired between them. She was having enough difficulty coping with her own feminine desire as it was!

The instant Liberty emerged from the stable she found herself amid a milling mass of unfamiliar faces. Everyone seemed to know who she was, even though she had yet to be formally introduced to all of Brewster's guests.

Dylon left Liberty to the converging mass of men who took the liberty of making their own introductions while he made preparations to begin the hunt. Within a few minutes the horses had been led out and the hounds were yipping in eager anticipation—the four-legged ones, that is. The two-legged ones, who were drooling over the curvaceous blonde, seemed to have altogether forgotten they intended to participate in the fox hunt.

The drone of voices, whinnies and the incessant barking did Liberty's dull headache no good. She wondered if she shouldn't join Brewster for a sedate afternoon in the house. She wasn't sure she was up to a rigorous ride in her present condition, no matter how anxious she was to view a fox hunt firsthand.

"Your mount, my lady," Griffin declared as he dropped the reins in her hands. Then, with a flair of gallantry, he doubled over to drop a kiss to her wrist, much like Phillipe LaGere would have done if he were there. When Griff rose to full stature, he peered earnestly into Liberty's beguiling features.

"I think you should know that I love you," he said out of the blue.

Liberty half-collapsed when Griffin executed a stiff about-face and strode off to tend his duties as Master of Foxhounds.

Godamercy, what had brought that on? Liberty wondered curiously. She had done nothing to encourage Griffin. 'Twas true that she enjoyed his company, but he wasn't . . .

Her shoulders slumped as the rest of the thought and

its implication struck like an arrow through the heart. Griffin wasn't Dylon and that made all the difference. And the reason it made such a difference was because . . . Liberty gulped down her palpitating heart when the tormenting realization plowed through her mind. *Because I love Dylon,* Liberty mused disparagingly. Damnation, she had vowed not to fall in love with that dedicated bachelor. She had allowed her foolish heart to rule her head.

That was why that handsome rogue angered, annoyed and aroused her the way no other man could. That was also why she felt that illogical twinge of jealousy when another woman threw herself at Dylon. And that had to be why his mere touch sent her pulse leapfrogging through her bloodstream. Why else would she have succumbed to his persuasive charm and then seduced him? Love *had* made the difference, Liberty realized bleakly.

All these years, she had avoided intimate relationships, choosing to keep her freedom and individuality. And then along came that charismatic philistine who cherished his freedom as much as she treasured hers. Benjamin Jordon told her this might happen one day when she least expected it. He had prophesied that she would wake up and find herself in love. But, of course, Benjamin had expected his daughter to fall in love with his protégé, Phillipe LaGere.

But that would have been too simple, too preordained, Liberty thought glumly. She had sailed from the islands to avoid Phillipe. And that was when all the trouble started. Now she was hiding from her second fiancé, battling this newfound love for a man who didn't want a wife. Dylon didn't share the same depth of emotion for her that she felt for him and he never would. To complicate matters she was dodging the attentions of Griffin Lockhart, who had boldly and unashamedly confessed his intentions. Blast it, how could she keep getting herself into such tangles . . . ?

"Liberty?" Dylon's rich baritone voice slashed through her tormented thoughts. "I suggest you mount your steed unless you prefer to be trampled." He indicated the male guests who were already mounted, anxious to impress her with their equestrian skills.

"I think I would prefer it," Liberty muttered glumly.

Before Dylon could interrogate her about her sullen mood, a horn blasted the air. Guests jockeyed for position behind Griffin and horses collided broadside with one another. The huntsman trotted off with the pack of yelping hounds, much to Liberty's relief. Within a few minutes the hounds had found the scent and were bounding across the meadows in their swiftest pace. At Griffin's signal, the cavalcade of hunters thundered off, leaping fences and ditches and any other obstacle that stood in their path.

Liberty lost sight of Dylon. Although she had no aspirations to track the poor fox that probably felt as hounded as she did, Liberty intended to enjoy the fast-paced romp over hill and dale. She allowed the feel of the powerful steed beneath her to lift her sagging spirits and revive her energy.

When the steed sprang over a split rail fence and gobbled up the earth beneath him in long graceful strides, Liberty thrilled to the illusion of flight. For this space of time she would put her troubled thoughts aside and race against the wind.

The thunder of hooves around her matched the accelerated rhythm of her heart. Her unbound hair undulated behind her like a flag as she sailed across the fields of wild pea-vines and plunged into a thicket of oaks in hot pursuit of the hounds.

Liberty was just getting into the swing of things when her steed swerved around the cane brake that stood as an obstacle in their path. She had expected him to jump, but he didn't. The horse knew the area far better than she did and he seemed to prefer to save his energy to leap over the deep creek that lay beyond the patch of underbrush.

That was fine for the horse, but the unexpected lurch caused Liberty to slide sideways in the saddle.

A startled yelp burst from Liberty's lips when she felt herself jerked back in the opposite direction. Her head snapped backward when the galloping steed sprang over a fallen tree, bounded onto all fours and then vaulted over the creek. Having been flung sideways and then backward, Liberty was unable to maintain her grasp on the reins when the steed touched down. She had momentarily parted company with her saddle, but they met again with a jarring thud. Before Liberty could steady herself, the steed lunged up the steep creek bank and she was yanked loose from her perch.

The sun-splashed water came up at her with remarkable speed. With a gasp and a *kersplat*, Liberty completed only half of her unintentional back somersault to plop in the neck-deep rivulet. Luckily, the horse was well mannered and well trained enough to skid to a halt when he lost his rider and he didn't abandon her.

Liberty quickly removed her new watch and held it over her head before the delicate workings suffered irreparable damage. The dousing in the cool water was a welcomed treatment for her hangover and Liberty found herself in no hurry to remount.

Giggling at her unladylike tumble from the steed, Liberty clutched her soggy skirts and waded toward shallow water. Unceremoniously, she plunked down in the grass and set the watch aside. Drawing up her knees, she braced her elbows and rested her chin in her hands. She didn't care that the other riders had pelted off without her. She needed this time to sort out her emotions, to analyze them one by one and . . .

"Did I neglect to mention the object of the hunt?" Dylon snickered as he stared down at the soggy beauty.

He sat atop his horse, grinning at the mermaid who lounged beside the pool of rippling silver. Sunlight glinted through the canopy of trees to caress Liberty's exquisite features, as he longed to do, and kiss the tangle of gold hair that lay over her shoulders in disarray.

For once Liberty didn't rise to Dylon's taunt. She did, however, gather her feet beneath her to amble back into the stream. With her arms outflung and a devil-may-care smile twitching her lips, she toppled backward, sending ripples of silver undulating about her. Liberty peered up at the dashing rake in his indigo blue jacket and riding breeches and realized why it had been so easy for her and every other female on the planet to fall in love with him. He was so handsome it was sinful. Those baby-blue eyes lured a woman against her will. That engaging smile drew females like moths to flames, even if they did wind up getting their wings singed but good.

"To hell with the hunt," Liberty replied, shaking off her meandering thoughts. "I prefer to soak in the creek."

With masculine grace, Dylon swung from the saddle and ambled toward her. He clucked his tongue at the reckless naiad who frolicked in the brook. "'Tis a good thing Percy isn't here to see you," he said, chuckling. "He swears up and down that immersing one's body in water too frequently is a serious hazard to one's health."

"Percy is plagued by several peculiar philosophies and superstitions," Liberty countered. "The worst is carrying a potato in his pocket to ward off rheumatism."

Dylon sank down cross-legged on the creek bank. Leisurely, he plucked up a blade of grass and chewed upon it. Odd, how content he was all of a sudden, despite the unusual circumstances and the external influences that bombarded him. Watching Liberty had become his favorite pastime these days. It was as if he felt some unexplainable need to memorize her every expression, to study the melodic inflection in her voice, to observe her in every habitat.

"Don't think that because Brewster requested that you keep an eye on me that you must lose sight of the hounds," Liberty insisted as she trailed her hand through the water, watching the fan of diamond-studded ripples. "I can find my way back to the house. And if I can't my steed surely will. I have never met a mount yet who didn't know how to navigate his way back to the barn and his manger of hay."

Dylon's wide shoulders lifted and dropped in a careless shrug. "I've been on enough *fox* hunts." His eyes held hers prisoner for a long moment. "'Tis this unconventional *vixen* who intrigues me most."

Liberty chortled at the ridiculous compliment. "I look as appealing as a wet mop and you damned well know it," she admonished.

"Wet, aye," Dylon agreed in a voice that rumbled with unfulfilled desire. "But no less appealing, Liberty. I find you fascinating, no matter how you look."

Her head tilted sideways, spilling the damp strands over her left arm. She had to be very careful not to take this suave rogue's words to heart. Aye, she had fallen in love with him, but he was toying with her, just for his own amusement.

Mischievously, Liberty flicked water at him, expecting to irritate him and hurry him on his way. But the gesture had the reverse effect. Dylon didn't bat an eyelash at her prank. He continued to stare through her as if he were searching out the dark secrets of her soul.

"Go flatter someone else," Liberty insisted as she rose to wade back into deeper water. "I recognize a lie when I hear one."

Dylon unfolded himself and ambled into the water, uncaring that he soiled his fashionable garments. "Do you?" he parried softly, his eyes feasting on her intriguing curves and swells that were accented by her clinging clothes. "Or is it that you do not wish to accept the truth?"

When Liberty spun around, Dylon was towering over her, waist-deep in water. Curse it, she was too vulnerable where he was concerned. When he stared at her lips as if he longed to make a meal of them, her heart tumbled pell-mell in her chest. Desire tugged at her like a kite against the wind. Liberty didn't wait for him to make the first move. Her arms instinctively glided over his massive shoulders and she blessed him with a saucy smile.

"Do you want to kiss me, Dylon?" she inquired.

"You know I do, minx." He chuckled, delighted by her brazen mood. It amazed him that he had shied away from Olivia this very morning when she became as provocative as Liberty. But when this lavender-eyed temptress flashed him a come-hither glance, he couldn't get close enough, fast enough.

"Nobody's stopping you . . ." she murmured, shocked by her own brash invitation. She'd never said any such thing to any other man in all her life! But the words leaped to tongue and sprang from her lips before she could think to bite them back.

Dylon couldn't resist such temptation. The smile that alighted her elegant features lured him into that black magic spell. The feel of her luscious body meshed familiarly to his compelled him ever closer.

With a tormented groan, his lips descended on hers, savoring the honeyed taste of her. His tongue darted into the soft recesses of her mouth and she returned the intimate play without hesitation. When he clutched her to him, she instantly responded. And suddenly they were standing in a cloud of steam. White-hot fires sizzled like lightning bolts and the world faded into oblivion.

Dylon forgot all about the fox hunt, his brother, his grandfather and everything else that had any semblance to reality. This temptress was like a fire in his blood, a fever he couldn't cure. With a growl of hungry desire, Dylon lifted Liberty into his arms and wheeled toward the creek bank. He longed for nothing more than to shed these hindering garments and make wild passionate love to her in the thick carpet of grass.

So intent was he on his purpose that he tripped over a submerged log. With a startled squawk, Dylon stumbled forward and lost his balance. Still clutching Liberty in his arms, Dylon fell facedown, sending them both plunging beneath the surface without a breath of air to sustain them.

Ah, so much for the romantic mood and the moment, thought Dylon as he floundred to thrust his head above water. He was behaving like a clumsy fop. For a man who had made a career of seducing women he wasn't making much of an impression on the woman who had distracted him to the point that he couldn't even walk through water without baptizing them both!

A merry giggle erupted from Liberty's lips as she hooked her arm around Dylon's neck and wiped her face with her free hand. Still snickering, she reached out to remove the clump of moss that clung like a helmet to his head.

"I can tell you are duly impressed," Dylon grumbled as he plucked up the wad of waterlogged weeds that was draped over Liberty's shoulder. "I had planned to sweep you off your feet, not dunk you in the creek."

Playfully, Liberty tugged at his soggy jacket. When she had removed it, she carelessly flung it toward the creek bank. "What impresses me most is that you waded out here in the first place. Most proper gentlemen would loathe the idea of staining their expensive garments."

"And what impresses me most is that you wouldn't have given one whit if we made love in the grass rather than a conventional bed," Dylon murmured as he absently limned her enchanting features. "It wouldn't have mattered, would it, Liberty?"

Suddenly they were right back where they started—staring into each other's eyes, intrigued by the reflection of each other's uncontrollable desires.

"I wouldn't care if we made love in midstream," she whispered. "I want you, Dylon. God forgive me for saying so, but I do . . ."

His kiss was living fire. It scorched the body and inflamed the soul. The saturated garments melted away, leaving them flesh to flesh, aching for the fulfillment of this obsessive passion that knew no beginning or end. It was a wild coming together, like a turbulent thunderstorm billowing and churning. Liberty returned each scorching kiss, each urgent caress. When he guided her trembling body to his and wrapped her legs around his muscled hips, Liberty shuddered with shock waves of unrivaled pleasure. Only when this man was a living breathing flame within her did she feel whole and complete. Only when he sent her spiraling above the clouds did she feel deliriously content.

Dylon clutched Liberty to him as his body set its urgent cadence of love. He watched the rapturous sensations spill through her and echo back to him, watched the glow of passion become a flickering flame in her violet eyes. He felt her respond to each hard-driving thrust, felt her dig her nails into his back as the splendorous sensations engulfed her. And still, he couldn't get close enough to the tormenting fire that seared his flesh and emblazoned her name on his soul. He was truly obsessed, driven by such savage emotions that he had no control whatsoever.

Sensation after spine-tingling sensation bombarded him. Dylon felt himself soaring from one dizzying plateau to another, reaching upward to grasp that one elusive feeling that called to him.

And then the world avalanched upon him. His body shuddered in sweet satisfying release and he couldn't let go, couldn't ease his fierce grasp on the angel in his arms. For long breathless moments, Dylon struggled to inhale a normal breath. It took an incredible span of time to regain his composure and his strength.

Finally, he eased away to lift Liberty into his arms. Impulsively he bent to savor her kiss-swollen lips. And this time he took great care in feeling his way toward the bank without falling on his face.

In the aftermath of love, Dylon leisurely caressed Liberty while they lay side by side in the grass. Earlier, he had been too caught up in the heat of passion to worship and cherish the feel of her satiny flesh beneath his fingertips. Nuzzling against her shoulder, Dylon cuddled against her back to trace the curve of her derriere. His hand swam over the swell of her hip and then wandered to the taut peak of her breast. He felt her body quiver in response to his light touch and he smiled in male satisfaction.

"If you could be anywhere in the world, where would you be?" Liberty questioned, her voice still thick with the potent effects of passion.

His warm kisses drifted across her shoulder to the sensitive point beneath her ear. "Right here . . . with you," he replied huskily.

"Seriously," Liberty insisted, flinging him a reproachful glance.

His blue eyes twinkled and an easy smile cut dimples in his cheeks. "I think you should concern yourself with where we both should be as quickly as possible." He paused momentarily, allowing the distant sound of pounding hooves to reach Liberty's ears. "Unless I miss my guess, that sly fox has circled back to the timberland. If we don't get dressed, the hunters might find more than the *fox.*"

An impish giggle gurgled in her throat. "I can just imagine the look on the hunters' faces when . . ."

The yelp of the hounds grew louder with each passing second. Liberty and Dylon glanced at each other in alarm and then dived for their clothes. The thunder of hooves was beating a quick path toward the creek. If they didn't get moving and quickly, the fox, hounds and hunters were truly going to get an eyeful!

Chapter 17

In record time the twosome jumped into the garments and bounded into their saddles. Like fugitives, they blazed a new path through the timber and brush. Thundering at breakneck speed, they galloped back to the house. Liberty issued the challenge of a race and suddenly the hunters were far behind and completely forgotten.

Impishly, she swerved her steed in front of Dylon's, causing his horse to break stride so she could assume the lead. Dylon chuckled at her devious technique and nudged his mount into a dead run. But his challenger was skilled at racing on the straightaway. As they neared the stables, Dylon reached out a hand to snatch Liberty from the saddle before she could claim victory.

"Cheater," she scolded as she looped her arms around his neck and settled onto his lap.

"Me?" Dylon cocked an incredulous brow, but it slid back to its normal arch when she tilted his face to bless him with a heartwarming kiss. "Mmmm . . . I . . ."

His voice trailed off when he felt his steed come to a halt. Dylon glanced up to see that they had rounded the corner of the stable. "Damn, of all the rotten luck."

All the guests who had attended the afternoon festivities at the fair had returned. They were clambering from the coaches, blocking the path that led to the barn.

Liberty stared at the throng of people who stood between them and the front door. If they had trotted around the barn, they would have been left to explain why they were sharing the same horse and looking like drowned rats.

Bounding to the ground, Liberty motioned for Dylon to follow her. In amusement, Dylon watched Liberty hike up the hem of her wet riding habit and dart from one outbuilding to another like a fleeting shadow. When she sprinted to the back of the house and clutched the vine-choked lattice that reached toward the balcony, Dylon hesitated. But it seemed there was no other way to gain entrance to the house without being conspicuous. A steady stream of servants filed out the back door, scuttling to and from the kitchen and smokehouse. Dylon didn't particularly want to offer an explanation to the guests or the servants. He may as well invite gossip to spread like wildfire.

Following in her wake, Dylon clamped onto the lattice and inched upward. Playfully he patted Liberty's backside, urging her to set a swifter pace.

She paused to peer down at Dylon who was below her and who was making a comical display of trying to peek up her riding habit. (As if he hadn't seen enough of her already, the lusty rake!)

"Behave yourself or I'll tell Brewster . . ."

"Tell me what?"

Brewster's voice and his gray head materialized above the balcony railing. Through his wire-rimmed spectacles, he assessed Liberty and Dylon's outrageous appearance. Their damp clothes were covered with mud, moss and leaves—the same varieties that clung to Liberty's windblown hair.

Brewster could not recall seeing his grandson blush beneath his bronzed tan in the thirty-one years of his existence. But Dylon was definitely blushing now. And Brewster had the suspicious feeling that, judging by appearance, Dylon was also suffering a sunburn on certain portions of his body that were unaccustomed to outdoor exposure. Brewster bit back a knowing grin.

Liberty looked every bit as guilty and embarrassed at being caught in such an awkward predicament. There was nothing dignified about either Liberty or Dylon. They were certainly old enough to know better than to be doing what they ought not to be doing when the estate was jumping alive with guests.

"We do have doors, Dylon," Brewster chastised his grandson. "You could have employed either of them instead of utilizing the lattice as your ladder."

Dylon shook his ruffled raven head in contradiction and gestured toward the string of servants who resembled a colony of ants scurrying out of their den. "The servants are clogging the back entrance. Your guests have returned from the fair and they're blocking the front door. Perhaps you should go greet your guests while Liberty and I make ourselves presentable."

Brewster snorted explosively. "I don't dare ask what the two of you have been doing that would cause you to arrive here in such a bedraggled condition. I don't think I want to know!"

"I fell from my steed during the fox hunt," Liberty hurriedly explained. "Dylon waded into the creek to rescue me."

If ever there was a woman who was in less need of being rescued from any predicament, it was Liberty Jordon. In their brief but thorough acquaintance, Brewster had learned that much . . . even if she had been most reluctant in disclosing the full extent of her secretive past. Jordon . . . Damn, that name rang a bell but Brewster had yet to place it. It would come to him eventually, he was sure of it.

Grumbling at his failing memory, Brewster lurched around to stomp off. "I expect the two of you to be clean and properly attired for dinner and the evening ball. I have hired a local group of musicians to entertain us and I am anxious to see if the two of you misfits can dance as well as you can lollygag about under the pretense of hunting the fox!"

Although his tone was gruff, Brewster broke into a wry smile as he strode back to his bedchamber. It was purely delightful to see Liberty leading Dylon on a merry chase. Usually, where women and Dylon were concerned, it was the other way around. Ah, this time . . . this time, Dylon had met his match. Brewster hoped that very soon Dylon would realize he was every kind of fool if he let Liberty slip away. She belonged with Dylon. Together they made life an adventure, just the way he and Lucinda had in their heyday. And if Liberty didn't agree to become Dylon's bride, then by God, Brewster really would marry that misfit! One of the Lockharts should have enough sense not to let a treasure like Liberty Jordon escape his clutches!

While Liberty made herself presentable for dinner and her formal debut at Brewster's estate, she arrived at an important decision. There were only a scant few days left before she disappeared from Dylon's life. She would meet Stella in Charles Town and they would return to the islands from which they had come.

The hours Liberty had spent with Dylon, while she cast caution to the wind, would become cherished memories. She was in love for the first time in her life and she wanted to enjoy the wondrous experience, even if only for a few brief days.

Liberty had demanded no commitment from Dylon, as Nora Flannery had done. Nor would she. Nor had Dylon confessed any lasting affection for her. But she and Dylon had created their own special paradise for those few hours while they were in each other's arms. And until it was time for her to go, Liberty intended to make the most of each magical moment.

No longer would she pretend indifference or indignation. She had fallen in love with Dylon because he was the way he was. She had no intention of trying to change him. He had been consistent in his behavior since the moment they met. Liberty had been the one who had taken herself too seriously and had become infuriated when Dylon didn't take her seriously enough. But from this day forward, Liberty vowed to live each precious minute to its fullest, demanding and expecting no more than the moment could offer. If this was her one time in life to love, then she would enjoy it. She wouldn't suppress her feelings, only the words Dylon didn't want to hear.

Resolved to adapting Dylon's philosophy of taking life as it came and not quite so seriously, Liberty double-checked her appearance in the mirror. Satisfied with the reflection that stared back at her, Liberty breezed down the hall to find Brewster waiting at the head of the steps, sporting a fond smile.

"Gentlemen, did I not tell you it would be worth the wait?" Brewster declared to the crowd of men who hovered at the foot of the stairs. "Dear friends, may I present Miss Liberty Jordon."

When Brewster took Liberty's hand to accompany her down the steps, his brows narrowed on several young men who were drooling over this enthralling goddess in lavender silk and speculating about her with wolfish leers. No one of the male persuasion seemed the least bit concerned that Liberty had come as Dylon's guest. The instant she reached the bottom of the steps she was surrounded by an endless rabble of men who were anxious to enjoy her undivided attention.

While Liberty fielded scores of questions and accepted another score of requests as a dance partner, Dylon stood propped against the doorjamb, clutching a glass of his grandfather's special recipe in one hand. He was stung by jealousy and yet consumed by an indefinable sense of pride while he watched Liberty handle herself amid a cluster of male admirers. Her keen wit and sense of humor was evident; her stunning beauty was more than obvious in the form-fitting silk gown.

There was a natural lure about her that made men gravitate toward her. She reminded Dylon of a rare, exotic bird, a vision of absolute loveliness. And yet, he alone had discovered all her endearing charms. She was not only an angel, but a mischievous elf and a seductive enchantress. She was all things rolled into one complicated, intelligent woman who made a man ever so glad he was a man.

"It seems there will be plenty of competition for the lady's attention tonight," Griffin mocked as he came to stand beside his brother. "At least with this sizable congregation of men hovering around Liberty, you cannot take unfair advantage again."

Dylon flung Griff a withering glance. "How long do you intend to hold this grudge, little brother?"

"Until the sky turns green," Griffin growled resentfully.

"Green with envy?" Dylon questioned without glancing at his sulking brother. "For you, I think it already has."

Griffin scowled. "I think I'm in love with her and you toy with her. 'Tis not envy that turns me green and spoils my disposition. 'Tis outrage. And don't think I didn't notice that you and Liberty mysteriously disappeared halfway through the fox hunt. Why do you think I directed the entire brigade back to the timberland?"

Dylon shifted uncomfortably. "Why don't you go find Cayla and amuse her with your sparse wit rather than boring me with it," he suggested flippantly.

"Because I'm sick and tired of watching Cayla crochet doilies and take naps," Griffin grunted disgustedly. "'Tis time for me to take the initiative and claim what I really want." He thrust his glass of rum into Dylon's free hand. "And you, big brother, can take a flying leap for all I care."

"I already did, Griff. I already did," Dylon mused aloud as he watched his brother shoulder his way through the crowd to wedge himself beside Liberty.

When Liberty glanced in Dylon's direction to share a secretive smile, he raised his glass in silent toast. Liberty had taken the mansion by storm. But Dylon rather imagined that was customary procedure for this vivacious nymph. Her unrivaled beauty and undaunted spirit shone like a beacon in a blizzard. If Liberty walked into a room half full of women she would be the one the room half full of men noticed. She was that bewitching, that vibrant and exciting. Men naturally fantasized about her. Dylon could see them doing it at this very moment. Even as Griffin led Liberty into the dining hall, she received more than her fair share of speculative and appreciative glances. But Dylon took solace in the fact that he was the only man alive who knew how breathtaking Liberty Jordon truly was. And he was ever so glad that the rest of the world didn't know what they were missing. Liberty was, Dylon thought with a dreamy smile, far beyond a man's wildest expectations. He went hot all over just thinking about the things they'd done that afternoon. . . .

Liberty glanced around the spacious dining hall before her gaze came to rest on the dignified patriarch who stood at the head of the table. Brewster gestured for her to sit at his right hand and then privately scolded Griffin for abandoning his date who was still waiting for him in the vestibule. Brooding, Griffin gave Liberty up to his grandfather and surged off to locate Cayla.

Tray after tray of succulent meat, fruit and fresh bread was set upon the table. Liberty eagerly devoured the meal and participated in the numerous conversations that were in progress on each side of the table. After dessert had been served, the women excused themselves as they always did at these formal gatherings, leaving the men to discuss politics and business.

Feeling awkward and yet reluctant to go, Liberty rose from her chair. To her surprise, Brewster grasped her arm and drew her back to her seat.

"I prefer that you stay, my dear," he insisted. "After all, you own land hereabout and you have every right to voice your opinions on matters of state." He broke into a rueful smile as he leaned close to convey his confidential remark to Liberty. "Lucinda always did and she never vacated the room when it was time to discuss politics and business."

An amused grin quirked Dylon's lips as he gauged the other men's reactions to Brewster's unexpected request. He wondered how Brewster knew Liberty owned land in the area and if he had discovered *where.* No doubt, the rum Liberty had consumed the previous night had loosened her tongue. To what extent Dylon didn't know. Lord, he'd have loved to have crept unnoticed into the study to eavesdrop on that conversation between Liberty and Brewster. No doubt, it would have been entertaining and informative.

Hiram Cutberth cleared his throat and smiled tightly. "Brewster, you seem to have forgotten that these matters are better left to the superior minds of men. Although an individual has a right to vote on issues in this colony if he owns land, he must also be a *he.* I am not in the habit of discussing politics with women."

The remark got Liberty's hackles up in a hurry and she let Hiram know he had offended her. "You, sir, talk as if only the male of the species is capable of complex thought and intelligent conversation. I'll have you know that nothing could be further from the truth. Such narrow, inflexible attitudes are insulting and should be outlawed. Freedom of speech should be a privilege enjoyed by both men and women."

Hiram sank a little deeper in his chair and glared at the feisty chit who had dared to debate him.

Brewster silently applauded Liberty for voicing her thoughts to one of his least favorite associates and then he let Hiram have it with the other barrel. "I think the Assembly should rewrite the regulations and state that an *individual* who owns land must also possess a good deal of common sense and intellect, whether 'tis a he *or* she . . . Don't you, Hiram?" He didn't wait for the rotund gentleman who reminded him of an overstuffed robin to respond. "But of course, some of us might find ourselves without a vote, faced with such restrictions."

Having been properly put in his place a second time, Hiram scrunched down in his chair, stared at his glass of brandy and kept his mouth shut.

Brewster leaned over to Liberty and grinned. "I forgot to tell you to beware of Hiram." His voice dropped to a whisper. "He's the only man I know who can strut into a room and have everyone annoyed with him in less than five minutes."

The patriarch opened the discussion with his concern about Parliament's and George Grenville's outrageous intention of imposing taxes that would cripple the colonies' economy.

"As I see it, England has ultimate plans of limiting us to the coastal shores," Dylon remarked. "This year's Proclamation Act, which has been passed by Parliament, prohibits western expansion and trade beyond the Appalachians. It seems England wishes to keep us dependent on her indefinitely by restricting our trade to only the manufactured goods brought here from England. We have been refused the chance of making use of the vast resources which lie beyond the mountains. Many of the pioneers on the outposts are up in arms over the new law that restricts them from settling in the fertile valleys to the west."

"And many a seaman has been forced to put ashore because of the stiff enforcement of the Sugar Act," Liberty piped up. "As we all know, 'tis long been a policy of sea captains to trade their goods in the West Indies to the most profitable ports, whether they be English, Dutch, French or Spanish. 'Tis not within the letter of the law for colonial ships to trade with anyone except the English. But if colonists had complied with the Navigation Acts which were passed over one hundred years ago, it would have pinched pockets and prevented trade for much-needed goods which England cannot supply. This three-penny tax on each gallon of molasses, which has to be smuggled back to the colonies from the islands, is ridiculous."

"And I think we have forgotten that we are all subjects of the Crown," Hiram inserted, unable to keep his mouth shut for extended periods of time. "Parliament represents all English subjects, wherever they reside and whether they can vote. The theory of essential representation has long been the policy and we are virtually if not actually represented in Parliament."

A wry smile pursed Liberty's lips as she peered at Hiram's pinched face and puckered lips that reminded her of a small beak. "I hardly see how it can be considered fair for Grenville to assume what is right and necessary in the far-reaching corners of England's domain. 'Tis like trying to make comparisons between two entities which have very few similarities."

"But we are all still subjects of the Crown," Hiram reiterated firmly.

"If you believe that then you seem to have forgotten why our forefathers dared to colonize this continent to begin with," Dylon inserted. "This country has become accustomed to a government that leaves us alone and wields little authority in our daily lives. We are too far removed from England to consider ourselves English."

"And those who came to build this new nation were

self-reliant and independent-minded," Liberty declared proudly. "I consider it an injustice that those who assert themselves and toil from their labors are not allowed to profit from them. England dares too much when she taxes these colonies and outlaws the issue of paper money with the new Currency Act."

"It was for liberty itself that the pilgrims came." Dylon chuckled and then winked at the pert beauty. He glanced back at the sour-faced gentleman whose opinions were of the minority at this particular table. "Hiram, I think it ill-advised to debate the issue of rights and freedom with a young lady who bears the name of *Liberty*. It stands to reason that she will never agree with your opinions of bearing the burden of these taxes without actual representation in Parliament."

"And why do you think the Crown has found herself so far in debt?" Hiram dared to argue. "British troops arrived upon the scene to help us resolve the tedious French and Indian wars. After all, calling out the British regulars to fight our battles for us is a tremendous expense."

"But the British were not the only ones involved in the wars," Brewster pointed out. "There have been many American officers who fought and were driven away from their ranking positions in the army because of the overbearing commanders and arrogant regulars sent from England. Dylon fought alongside some of the most stubborn, arrogant men on the planet who did more to lengthen the war with the French and Indians than to terminate it. The British were not as efficient and successful as our own colonial militias. Braddock's crushing defeat is a prime example of English inability to handle affairs we should have assumed ourselves."

"The army of regulars did serve to alienate us from our English cousins. And I saw to it that one of the most bloodthirsty scoundrels in the regiment was dismissed from his position. But he wasn't the only one, I'm sorry to say," Dylon declared, forcing back the painful memories of the bloody past. "And to make matters worse, dishonest customs officials, who line their own pockets, and judges in the court of admiralty, who eagerly take bribes, have caused many more of us to lose faith in the English system and their inconsistent sense of justice. Like growing children, the colonies have been weaned from the Mother Country. We no longer face the same crises or share the same needs. Yet, England insists on treating us as if we were her dependent, misbehaving children. Our punishment comes in being forced to pay staggering taxes on everything that moves!"

"And this new Stamp Act which is to go into effect at the first of next year will only embitter more colonists," Liberty predicted. "Every lawyer will have to buy stamps for every legal document and transaction. Every newspaper will have to bear stamps, as well as playing cards, dice and other ridiculously insignificant articles. First England refused us our own money, then she taxes us to death, making an even worse financial burden for us to bear while she demands that we ship our produce to her. It seems England plans to do all the taking and make us do all the giving."

"Eight colonies have sent separate petitions to Parliament to protest these taxes without proper representation in Parliament," Dylon informed the group. "And if this problem is not resolved in a satisfactory manner, I fear England will find herself at war against her own colonists. As much as I detest war, I would take arms against my English cousins to preserve our rights to life, liberty and freedom."

"Perish the thought!" Hiram gasped. "'Tis heresy to speak of revolution." He puffed up with so much indignation that he very nearly popped the buttons of his ruffled shirt.

When Liberty opened her mouth to counter Hiram's remark, Brewster flung up his hand to forestall her. "'Tis my birthday celebration and I invited all of you here to enjoy the festivities. We will not immerse ourselves in a heated debate which puts us at odds. 'Tis Dylon's duty as an assemblyman to resolve the affairs of state."

Brewster pushed out his chair and assisted Liberty to her feet. "Come along, my dear. I hear the orchestra warming up in the ballroom. You and I shall have the first dance. We have all exercised our lips long enough. 'Tis time to give our feet those same *equal* and inalienable rights."

When Brewster and Liberty made their exit Hiram muttered under his breath. "I still say women should listen instead of speaking. 'Tis their place to obey without question, without spouting their views on subjects," he blurted out resentfully. "There is nothing worse than a stubborn, opinionated woman. I swear Liberty . . ." His voice trailed off when he realized Dylon was still at the table.

An amused chuckle tripped from Dylon's lips as he unfolded himself from his chair and watched Hiram turn a bright shade of red. "I believe God created stubborn, opinionated women to counteract narrow-minded men," he declared. "They neutralize each other, don't you think, Hiram?"

As Dylon swaggered out the door, Hiram clamped his lips together in an exaggerated pout. "Demagogues and radicals, that's what the Lockharts are. They will bring down the wrath of England on all of us. Rebel against the world's most formidable power? Why, that's suicide!"

Hiram shrank back in his chair when Griffin gathered his feet beneath him and glared at their outspoken guest. Hiram's face turned another shade of embarrassed red, having forgotten that the youngest Lockhart was at the far end of the table.

The look on Hiram's face sweetened Griffin's sour mood. With a mocking smile, Griffin swaggered toward the door. "'Tis quite all right, Hiram. I realize there are those who just cannot seem to voice a thought without sticking their feet in their mouths." He paused at the portal and grinned again. "*Now* you may talk behind our backs since there are none of us demagogues and radicals left in the room."

For once in his life, Hiram had the good sense to refrain from speaking his mind. He simply sat there and pouted for several minutes before skulking out the door.

Chapter 18

After Brewster had danced the first waltz with Liberty, Dylon watched a string of men form a line beside the refreshment table to wait their turns with the lively blonde. There wasn't a man with eyes in his head who didn't devour that delectable goddess on sight. Even a blind man could have felt the sensual vibrations in the air when Liberty walked by.

Dylon patiently bided his time for the first hour by making the rounds to chat with as many guests as possible. But finally he decided enough was enough. The line which trailed out behind Liberty grew longer instead of shorter and Dylon ached to have that feisty beauty back in his arms.

Since their romantic interlude that afternoon, a delightful change had overcome Liberty. She was no longer cautious and defensive. She had emerged from her protective cocoon and Dylon had become even more intrigued by this new facet of her personality. He began to see even more depth in her complexity. Her carefree recklessness and flirtatiousness utterly fascinated him.

Without even one glance toward Liberty's lengthy line of suitors, Dylon approached. Taking her hand, he drew her luscious body into his arms. And suddenly the restlessness that had plagued him throughout the evening evaporated. Lord, what a potent spell this delightful witch had cast on him!

"Mmm . . . do you have any idea what you do to me?" Dylon growled against the swanlike column of her throat. "Have you any idea what I want to do to you . . . ?"

"Here? Now?" She raised her delicately arched brow in mock horror and leaned back in the possessive circle of Dylon's arms. "Don't you think Brewster's guests might object?"

A peal of laughter reverberated in Dylon's chest. "I suppose you are right. It would be too outrageous, even for you, little minx."

"I should like to dance with the lady," Griffin demanded, tapping his brother soundly on the shoulder. "'Twas my turn and you butted in."

"You have an escort," Dylon reminded him, refusing to take his eyes off the enchanting nymph in his arms.

"Cayla is taking another of her confounded naps," Griffin grumbled. "No doubt, she even crochets in her sleep."

"If anyone would know about that, you would," Dylon teased playfully.

Unfortunately, Griffin didn't find the remark the least bit amusing. He had been in a permanent snit since the previous night and his bottled-up emotions came pouring out. Griffin did something he hadn't done to his brother in years. He doubled his fist and implanted it in Dylon's smile.

A shocked gasp broke from Liberty's throat when she was flung sideways. In stupefied disbelief she watched Dylon spin like a top after the unexpected blow. And although Dylon had no intention of answering the punch in the jaw, Griffin had no intention of stopping what he was doing until he appeased all his frustrations. He pounced on his brother, knocking him against the wall.

So much for Dylon's well-disciplined self-control!

Liberty's jaw fell off its hinges when Dylon came up fighting. She knew he was skilled with pistols, bows, knives and fists, but she never expected him to clobber his own brother in a ballroom jam-packed with startled guests. Again, she found herself thanking her lucky stars that she was not on the receiving end of those powerful punches. When Dylon was thoroughly angered he was the most formidable fighter she'd ever laid eyes on! Although Griffin was of equal size and stature he was no match for his brother in hand-to-hand combat.

The blow Dylon delivered caused Griffin's head to snap backward and he plowed into an unidentified body, causing gasps and squawks to erupt from the wall of humanity which formed around him. Before he could regain his balance, Dylon sprang like a tiger. The oncoming punch smashed into Griffin's midsection and he instantly dropped to his knees to gasp for breath.

"Are you both crazed?" Brewster's voice boomed above the shocked murmurs that rippled through the crowd. His arms flapped in expansive gestures as he cleared a path to his grandsons who were behaving like idiotic fools. "Stop this nonsense at once!"

"That was just what one would expect from a couple of defiant rebels," Hiram smirked caustically.

Liberty wheeled on the pudgy gentleman. "And you are just what I expected from a loyal bigwig!" she insulted him.

Hiram's chest inflated like a balloon. "Of all the nerve! I'll have you know I'm a highly respected subject of the Crown!" he trumpeted.

Liberty didn't care what he was. As far as she was concerned, he was nothing but an obnoxious nuisance.

"And you, young woman, are in no position to . . ."

Liberty was in a perfect position actually. She and Hiram stood face to face and she found herself itching to slug this pompous stuffed shirt. Before she realized it the thought had transmitted itself into action. She doubled her fist and smashed her knuckles into Hiram's plump jaw.

Squealing like a stuck pig, Hiram staggered back. With eyes as round as saucers, he gaped aghast at the spitfire who had dared to strike him. "I'll have you strapped to the ducking stool and doused in a pond of mud for this!" he screeched furiously.

"You'll do no such thing," Brewster snapped as he turned from his subdued grandsons to his outraged guest. "Liberty only did what I would have liked to have done if I'd been a few years younger." His arm shot toward the door. "Take yourself out, Hiram. Both Liberty and I find your presence and your opinions offensive."

With a wordless scowl, Hiram lurched around and stalked out. And although Hiram wasn't popular in the area, the other guests politely refrained from applauding his departure. Hiram was indeed one of those loyal locals who had hurriedly applied for a position as tax collector the instant news of the Stamp Act reached colonial ears. Uncaring that his neighbors would feel the pinch of another tax, Hiram intended to profit from it. His new position in the community suited him perfectly. No one liked him much anyway and everyone despised tax collectors.

When Hiram had taken his leave, Brewster wheeled on his grandsons. "The two of you will apologize this instant," he demanded gruffly.

Dylon extended his hand to his brother, but Griff was reluctant to call a truce. After Brewster jabbed him in the ribs, Griff did shake hands.

"I'm sorry," Griff muttered, his voice nowhere near apologetic.

"So am I," Dylon replied in the same insincere tone.

Brewster sent one of his servants to fetch two glasses of his special recipe. When the errand boy returned, the patriarch thrust the drinks at his misbehaving grandsons. "This should cure what ails you. If it doesn't, at least it will make you forget what this fisticuffs was all about." He glared at Dylon and Griff. "Bottoms up."

With an expansive wave of his hand, Brewster instructed the orchestra to burst into song before his grandsons broke every stick of furniture in the house!

"I'm truly sorry," Liberty murmured as Brewster led her away.

Brewster shrugged lackadaisically and stifled a grin. "To be honest, I thought the party was getting dull anyway. It will give the citizens of Camden something to gossip about. Besides, it was only a matter of time before Hiram was served his just desserts. He is one of those loathsome individuals who claims loyalty to the Crown and sets out to cheat his own neighbors every chance he gets. Hiram is loyal only to himself and we all know it. You did what many of us have pictured doing many a time."

The gray-haired patriarch frowned disconcertedly as he glanced over his shoulder at Dylon and Griffin. "As far as those two rapscallions are concerned, they will have to resolve their own problems." A cryptic smile pursed his lips. "And very soon Griffin will have to accept what he cannot change. He'll come around, given time."

Liberty chewed on her bottom lip, wondering whether to voice her thoughts. Expelling a long sigh, she made her decision. "I fear I am to blame for Griffin's outburst. He professed to love me, though I doubt he truly does. Since I am Dylon's guest it has put a strain on their relationship."

"Griffin told you that?" Brewster chirped incredulously.

Reluctantly, Liberty nodded in confirmation.

"But you don't love him," Brewster speculated. "And no doubt, he sees his own brother as a threat to what he wants. I'm sorry you got mixed up with those two. But, rest assured, I don't hold you responsible."

Liberty said nothing. Despite Brewster's attempt to console her, she knew she was causing turmoil and that had not been her wont. She longed to enjoy these last few days with Dylon before she sneaked back to Charles Town. But it seemed she needed to make her discreet exit earlier than she had planned.

After Brewster wandered off, Liberty inched toward the stairway and scurried to her room. She wanted to bid farewell to Brewster but she didn't dare alert him to her intentions. Being the gracious host, he would insist that she stay. But when he awoke in the morning she would be long gone and that would be the best for all concerned.

Resolved to that noble and sensible purpose, Liberty slipped into her room to change into her breeches and shirt. After she gathered her belongings, she tiptoed across the balcony and inched down the lattice that served as a ladder from the second story of the mansion to the ground floor.

Lord, it seemed that, of late, she had been running from everything! But she could think of not one reason to stay. She knew Dylon didn't love her, that she was living on false hopes if she expected them to enjoy a future together. Dylon was one of those dynamic men who would never settle down. When she walked out of his life, there would be another woman to catch his roving eye. She was just the time he was killing, a temporary and disposable amusement.

Loving Dylon changed nothing, Liberty assured herself dispiritedly. If she dared to think in terms of a future with that blue-eyed, midnight-haired rake, she would only find disappointment, just as Nora Flannery had. If Dylon honestly wanted to settle down, he would have done so long before now. But he didn't, not with her, not with any one woman. Dylon wanted to remain footloose and fancy-free because that was his way.

Chomping on that depressing thought, Liberty buried herself in the darkest recesses of the shadows. . . .

"I have this odd feeling of *deja vu.*" Dylon's rich baritone voice rumbled with amusement.

A startled squawk erupted from Liberty's lips when she heard the familiar sound below her. Liberty missed a step as she climbed down the vine-covered lattice. The fact that her arms were laden down with satchels made it difficult to reclaim her grasp on the lattice. A victim of gravity, she plummeted backward.

Dylon positioned himself beneath the shapely, airborne bundle. Liberty fell neatly into his arms rather than flat on her back.

"What are you doing out here?" she hissed as she squirmed for release.

"I could ask you the same thing," Dylon muttered at her.

"I'm leaving before I cause unnecessary trouble," Liberty insisted.

"If that is your motive, you should have left as soon as you arrived." Dylon snaked out a hand to latch onto her elbow, pulling her in the opposite direction that she intended to go.

"I tried," Liberty reminded him as she stubbornly set her feet. Dylon uprooted her from the spot. "That was when you and I made this ridiculous bargain, as I recall. And look where it got us . . . into more trouble."

Dylon didn't slow his swift pace or speak until he'd towed Liberty into the skirting of trees that encircled the back garden. When he got where he was going, he wheeled on Liberty. "These escape attempts of yours are growing tiresome. I think it's time you told me everything."

He'd have had to have a crowbar to pry that information out of her! Just because she had fallen in love with him and she had allowed him to use her body for his pleasure did not give him the right to probe into her past! One-sided love did have its limits. Liberty Jordon was now and would always be the mistress of her own fate. She had never thrown herself at a man's feet, begging for him to untangle her problems for her. And by damned, she wasn't about to start now!

"I haven't the faintest notion what you're talking about." Liberty put out a stubborn chin.

Dylon expelled an irritated growl. "I've had my fill of

this secretive nonsense of yours. I had hoped you would confide in me in your own good time. I have been patient, thinking you would freely divulge your past after we . . ."

Liberty glared furiously at him. "After we made love?" she finished for him. She could have clobbered him! "Were you trying to seduce the information out of me? And for what purpose? Was this another of your amusing pastimes, Dylon?"

Dylon couldn't fathom how he and this firebrand had gotten on such unfriendly terms so quickly. It was only a few hours ago that they had been as close and compatible as two people could get. And all of a sudden . . . *poof!* He and this blond-haired hellion were back to bows and arrows. How could she drag him into an argument before he even realized he was there?

"I have no intention of fighting with you," Dylon bit off, struggling to grasp the trailing reins of his temper.

"Thank goodness for that," Liberty sniffed sarcastically. "Beating your brother to a pulp should be enough for one night."

Clutching her satchels against her chest, she stared him squarely in the eye. "And now, if you will excuse me, I have a life of my own to lead. You can turn your pretended affection on that eager brunette who has been eyeing you as if she were the rat and you were the cheese. I'm sure you'll find her more than willing to appease your needs . . . if she hasn't already. She has 'ready and willing' stamped all over her."

Again Liberty wheeled away and again Dylon halted her retreat. But this time he employed a more devastating method to detain her. His mouth took possession of hers and he molded her into his masculine contours. His masterful hands flooded over her curvaceous body, rediscovering the location of each ultrasensitive spot, making her wanton flesh sing with sensuous pleasure.

Ah, what stupendous power love had over the body, mind and spirit, Liberty thought when she felt her defenses come crumbling down like a dam besieged by turbulent flood waters. This persuasive rake could charm the spots off a leopard. No woman could resist him when he enveloped her in his arms. He plied her with skillful caresses and her brain broke down. He kissed her and the world faded into nothingness. Sensation after delicious sensation swamped and buffeted her, leading her deeper into that rapturous dimension of time that caused her to lose all sense of objectivity.

Just this one last time, her feminine needs whispered to her. *Just once more before I go.* She longed to experience the sweet forbidden desire that had blossomed into love. This would be the one sublime memory that sustained her when she returned to her world and left Dylon in his.

As his nerve-shattering caresses migrated over her quaking flesh, Liberty felt the earth move beneath her feet. Suddenly they were lying in the dew-kissed grass, exchanging kiss for devouring kiss, caress for impatient caress. Lord, this man was a poison in her blood, a flame that never burned itself out! When he touched her so intimately her senses took flight. Nothing in this world seemed as important as loving him—body, heart and soul.

It was vain, she knew. But Liberty suddenly found herself wanting to leave her own special brand on this magnificent man. She longed to forge her memory on his mind—a memory that would burn throughout eternity. She could never claim this rambling rake as her own because he cherished his freedom even more than she did. But in the future, he would remember her, remember this night of wondrous lovemaking beneath the canopy of stars. She would be that secretive smile that hovered on his lips when no one else was around, the lingering memory that refused to die.

When Liberty set her hands and lips upon him to express the secret love she felt for him, Dylon resigned himself to death by splendorous torment. He could almost hear the harps playing in the distance. He was floating on a puffy white cloud, experiencing a multitude of fantastic sensations that made breathing virtually impossible.

There was something different in the way Liberty touched him tonight that boggled Dylon's mind. Her worshipping kisses and reverent caresses turned his bones to steam and his flesh to fire. He craved her; he survived only on the incredibly delicious sensations that channeled through every fiber of his being. He felt like putty in her hands, molded to fit her voluptuous body and to serve no other purpose in life except to pleasure her and himself. And all the while that she turned him into leaping flames, she drove every emotion from deep inside him, leaving no part of him untouched.

When Dylon twisted away to return the exquisite pleasure, Liberty surrendered completely to the splendor that tumbled through her. She cherished his hot, moist kisses, his wildly intimate caresses. He was the air she breathed, the song that strummed in her soul.

Adoringly, Dylon trailed his fingertips over the full swells of her breasts, awed by the way the moonbeams spotlighted her flawless curves and swells. His lips followed, suckling at the rose-tipped peaks, drowning in the taste and scent of this mysterious elf who had taken up permanent residence in his mind.

As his lithe body slid upon hers, Dylon felt passion rumbling inside him like a volcano that was about to erupt. Very soon he would lose the last remnant of self-control. Already he wanted this gorgeous sprite to maddening obsession. No other experience in life was as precious as sharing the sweet torment of desire, of being one with this spirited beauty. It was as if his very soul called out to hers. The thought of her leaving had struck him like a physical blow, just as it had the first time she tried to escape from his life. Then, as now, he had been compelled to hold onto her, to clutch her to him as if she were a vital part of himself . . .

When Liberty instinctively arched to meet his

demanding thrusts, Dylon forgot how to think. His body was ablaze with savage passion, the kind that consumed and devastated. He became a creature of needs that were as ancient as time itself. And yet those monstrous cravings had mushroomed until they engulfed his body, mind and soul. Wanting her had become far more than a physical thing. It was a deep-seeded emotional obsession that obliterated all rational thought.

As they moved in ageless rhythm, their hearts beat as one. Their bodies glided in the cadence of fierce uncontrollable passion. Pleasure built like a resounding crescendo until it burst inside them, shattering self-restraint as if it never existed.

Shudder after spontaneous shudder racked Dylon's body. He felt as if he were being swept away by tidal waves and plunged into the very depths of mindless desire. And even in the calm that followed passion's storm, Dylon still found himself clinging fiercely to the witch-angel in his arms, marveling at the incredible flood of emotion that poured out of him.

Liberty felt tears of pleasure, mingled with regret, trickle down her flushed cheeks. It seemed so unfair to find herself in love with a man she could never have. And even when she'd known she was leaving herself vulnerable to heartache, she still surrendered to these foolish whims of love. She had wanted to carry this treasured memory with her always, in remembrance of a love that could never be. And secretly she had hoped that Dylon would confess to love her in return. But the words never formed on his lips. He wanted her, desired her, yet lust was a world away from love.

There wasn't a woman on God's green earth who could tame Dylon Lockhart's restless heart, she realized dismally. The man was a hopeless cause. Far more experienced and worldly females than she had tried to win his heart and failed. Liberty may as well hitch a ride on a passing cloud. She would never earn Dylon's love and he wasn't about to risk it again. According to Percy,

Dylon had dared to love only once in life.

If only he could see that I am not like that heartless widow, that I . . .

"I lo—," Liberty clamped her mouth shut when her thoughts came dangerously close to finding their way to her tongue. She tore her eyes away from those entrancing pools of blue that twinkled in the moonlight. "I had better leave," she murmured raggedly.

"Wait a few more days. Give me a few more nights, even if 'tis all you can spare. . . ." he whispered.

Lord, why did the possibility of never seeing this lovely imp again tear his heart out by the taproot? He knew a woman like Liberty would never be content to remain in one place. She was always flitting off, destination unknown. She never stayed in one place long enough for any man to capture and hold her.

And damnit, why should he want her to? She had pitted him against his own brother without even trying. She had bedazzled everything in breeches at the ball with her beauty, charm, spirit, and wit. All except Hiram Cutberth, that is, Dylon quickly amended. In that instance, she had given that pompous ass exactly what he deserved.

When Liberty looked as if she were about to demur his request, Dylon pressed his forefinger to her lips to shush her. It didn't matter what was best for everyone involved. He couldn't bear the thought of watching her go. He had to have time to adjust to the fact that she wanted to walk out of his life, leaving a hole the size of South Carolina in his heart. Being the one left behind was an agonizing role for Dylon. He hadn't coped well when Patricia flitted off with her wealthy duke. Dylon detested the thought of losing Liberty even more.

"Tomorrow is the last day of Brewster's scheduled activities. He'll be bitterly disappointed if you abandon him without a word. He has grown very fond of you."

And what about you, Dylon? she wanted to ask but she didn't.

"You will place Brewster in an uncomfortable position if you spirit away and leave him to explain your disappearance."

"But . . ."

Again Dylon shushed her. A wry smile pursed his lips as he bent over her. "I'll even let you ride my swiftest Thoroughbred in tomorrow's race," he tempted her. "And if your skills exceed mine on the track, you can go without offering the explanations I keep demanding and you keep refusing to give."

"But what about Griffin?" Liberty questioned hesitantly. "If I had a brother, I don't think I would wish to be at odds with him. And I'm afraid I'm the reason . . ."

"Griffin's a grown man," Dylon argued. "And 'tis obvious that he is not the first man who's fancied himself in love with you. 'Tis hardly your fault you have such a profound effect on men."

When Liberty peered into those blue eyes that shimmered like moon-kissed forget-me-nots, she knew she'd lost the battle of mind over matters of the heart. What could a few more days hurt? she asked herself. When they returned to Lockhart Hall she would go her own way.

"Very well, a few more days," she finally agreed.

"And more importantly, the nights . . ." Dylon murmured before he dropped a steamy kiss to her petal-soft lips. "When you're in my arms, sweet Liberty, I love the nights best of all. . . ."

When Dylon proceeded to show her why he'd grown so fond of the night, Liberty forgot about tomorrow and everything else. This sensuous rake had a most remarkable way of making a woman forget there was a world beyond the magical circle of his sinewy arms. With a soft moan, Liberty surrendered to the potent magic of Dylon's incredible brand of passion. . . .

When harmonious giggles erupted in the still of the

night, Brewster levered up in his bed and strained to catch the sound which had awakened him. He had a pretty good idea what caused the noise. Brewster threw his legs over the edge of the bed to retrieve his robe. Quietly, he pushed open the terrace door to stare across the moon-splashed balcony. When a head—capped with golden hair—appeared above the railing, Brewster muffled a chuckle. Then a raven head rose like a jinni from a bottle. While Dylon and Liberty pulled themselves and her belongings over the railing, Brewster shoved his hands into his pockets of his robe and ambled forward.

"Had I known the two of you were going to make a habit of this, I would have nailed a ladder to the lattice," he declared, causing Liberty and Dylon to jump straight up in the air.

Dylon grumbled at the unexpected sight of his barefooted grandfather propped negligently against the wall. "Good God, don't you ever sleep?"

"Good God, don't *you?*" Brewster parried. "It seems to me, m'boy, that you keep forgetting *who* proposed to *whom.* The way you've been behaving of late, one would think *you* did, not I." That said, he pivoted and strode back to his room.

That old coot really can't be serious, Dylon assured himself as he propelled Liberty across the balcony. As intelligent as Brewster was, he had to know that he couldn't keep up with a wild-hearted hoyden like Liberty, even if he was enjoying his second childhood!

When Liberty and Dylon disappeared into the shadowed room, Brewster broke into a devilish grin. He wondered if Dylon even knew what had happened to him since Liberty came into his life. Whether Dylon did or didn't, Brewster recognized all the symptoms. A change had overcome Dylon of late. Those things which had brought him amusement and diversion the past few years were no longer enough now that Liberty monopolized his time and his thoughts. That feisty elf had bewitched

Dylon, as well as his younger brother. 'Twas a pity Dylon was too stubborn and set in his ways to realize that on his own accord, thought Brewster. That confirmed bachelor would have to have a fire lit under him before he could see the light.

Another wicked smile pursed the patriarch's lips as he plunked down in his bed. He couldn't wait to see the look on Dylon's face when he realized Brewster expected him to answer for these secluded trysts with that saucy sprite. Oh, Dylon would answer all right, Brewster mused confidently. He had decided on the exact time and place for Dylon to pay his comeuppance. And that rapscallion dare not protest. If he did, Brewster would remind him of this very afternoon and this night.

Let that ornery rake try to weasel his way out of his obligations to Liberty! Dylon could try, but this time he wouldn't succeed. Brewster would see to that. Brewster Lockhart was every bit as determined as Dylon. Where'd that young rakehell think he'd gotten all of his stubborn determination in the first place? Why, he had inherited it from his grandfather, of course!

Chapter 19

Liberty couldn't remember feeling quite so blithe and carefree! The day's activities at Brewster's estate had provided oodles of entertainment for all the guests. The incident at the ball had been forgotten and Griffin was on his best behavior (especially after his grandfather had drawn him aside to demand that he mind his manners. Brewster had threatened to let Dylon thrash him again if he caused one speck of trouble.)

As Dylon had promised, Liberty was allowed to ride his dappled gray stallion in the race on the track that had been staked out on the road to Camden. Citizens for miles around had arrived with their steeds, anxious to pit their Thoroughbreds against their neighbors'. A flurry of boasts and bets had preceded the race. And indeed, it had been fiercely competitive from start to finish.

Although Brewster had declared the race a tie when the two lead horses thundered across the finish line—nose to nose—Liberty wondered if Dylon had purposely held back. He, unlike so many men of the time, had no qualms about competing with a woman. And he was so confident of his own masculinity that he found no complaint in allowing Liberty to display her talents and enjoying her whims.

She rather thought Dylon could have inched into the lead had he whipped his steed with his quirt. But he didn't beat his horse as he raced toward the finish line alongside Liberty. Neither had she. And Dylon had cast off the teasing remarks hurled by his male acquaintances with an unconcerned shrug and a nonchalant smile. Lord, the man smiled constantly, through thick and thin.

She wondered if he would also be smiling when she walked out of his life. Honestly, she couldn't imagine him doing anything else since he took the world and all its pitfalls in stride.

After an afternoon picnic was held on the lawn, the other guests had gathered their belongings and expressed their sincere appreciation to Brewster. When the guests made their departure, the Lockharts and their two female companions spent a quiet evening in the mansion. Cayla, of course, spent the quietest evening of all, having ascended the steps to take another of her confounded naps.

Dylon was also true to his word when he promised the nights would be long and filled with ardent passion. He had come to Liberty's room, whispering his desire for her, assuring her that she fulfilled his every dream. It would have been so easy for Liberty to let herself believe all his quiet murmurs, to think that she truly mattered to him, even though he hadn't said those three little words.

But for her heart's sake, she told herself that this was a one-sided love, one that sadly reminded her of the short-lived beauty of a rose. Their passion was exquisite, with sensations that created their own sweet fragrance above a stem of thorns. And all too soon, the blossom would wither and Dylon would lose his fascination for her, just as he had with all other women. It seemed Patricia Morgan had stolen his heart years earlier and the pain from the invisible scars had never really healed. Liberty had forced herself to accept the limitations of this forbidden love, but it hurt no less when she kept wishing that it could endure forever. Love, it seemed, had its season, just like everything else. . . .

* * *

The journey back to Lockhart Hall was not as Liberty had anticipated. At the spur of the moment, Brewster had decided to accompany his grandsons back to the plantation while his servants put his estate back in proper working order. In less than an hour, Brewster had seen to it that his bags were packed and loaded in his own phaeton. The procession had rumbled off down the road with Liberty and Cayla confined to one carriage and the Lockhart men tucked in the other. Liberty had hoped to spend these last few days in Dylon's company, savoring every second. But Brewster had thrown a wrench into her plans.

And what she would never have expected in a million years came to pass during the third day of travel!

"I'm so envious of you that I could scream," Cayla Styles erupted, as if she'd held the words back so long that they simply exploded out of the blue.

Liberty gaped in stunned astonishment at the redhead. The quiet, self-contained Cayla Styles could actually speak in something other than the timid, monotone voice? Wonders never ceased!

When Cayla realized how shameless her outburst sounded, she blushed blood red and huddled in her corner to stare out the window.

Having recovered from her shock, Liberty burst out laughing. "Well, don't just sit there, tell me why you're so envious," she demanded. "I should like to know exactly what you think and feel and why."

Cayla's gaze dropped to her lap while she self-consciously fiddled with the folds of her gown. "I'm sorry. I should have held my tongue. If my father would have heard me, he would have thrashed me severely."

"Well, he didn't," Liberty reminded her saucily. "It seems to me that you spend too much of your time behaving as your father obviously thinks you should. But 'tis your life to live, not his."

Cayla sighed miserably. "I would be far more content if I could shed these strict limitations of womanhood and air my wings the way you do. You conform just so far before you tell conformity to take a hike." Her lashes fluttered up to meet Liberty's bright violet eyes. "I look at you and I see what I wish I could be. I watch you bedazzle men with your spirit and I die inside, bit by excruciating bit."

It was glaringly apparent that Cayla had been stifled and suppressed about as long as she could stand. There was another personality trapped beneath that shell of reserve. Propriety and the necessity of staying in one's place had been drummed into her head. Cayla had tried to live up to her father's expectations, but her desire for independence had come bursting loose after she had watched Liberty dare to do as she *pleased* instead of what she was *told*.

"Do you think I like to crochet these stupid doilies?" She held up the dainty object and then wadded it into her fist and hurled it against the wall. Unfortunately, it toppled onto Liberty's blond head. Cayla started to apologize as she should have done, stopped herself, and then giggled at the comical sight of Liberty draped in a doily.

"There, you see, doing what you feel rather than what you have been trained to do isn't so difficult." Liberty tugged the doily from her head and carelessly tossed it out the window. "What else do you dislike about this life you lead, Cayla?"

"It would be more expedient to list those things I *do* like about my life," Cayla muttered bitterly. "To tell the truth, I despise being ordered to stand erect and told never slump. Never ride because 'tis not ladylike. Never discuss politics and business with men. ''Tis unacceptable,'" she quoted her father. "And I detest slinking off to pretend to nap because Papa says all delicate ladies need their beauty sleep. Instead, I snatch up books from the library and read everything I can get my hands on."

Liberty blinked owlishly. "You approve of nothing you do?" she hooted.

"Would you?" Cayla questioned the question. "I happen to have opinions of my own and I have eavesdropped on many discussions at parties and gatherings such as the one you and the men held the other night. I have read every volume in my father's extensive library. I taught myself to ride when no one else was around and I even bribed one of the grooms to keep his mouth shut when he caught me racing across the meadow on my father's favorite mount."

Cayla inhaled a deep breath and plunged on, exposing the flare of temper she had carefully kept under wrap until this moment. "I hate mucking about like a spineless puppet! I detest listening to less educated men than I spout their opinions and whims while I am forced to smother my own as if they counted for nothing. And how I wish I could have punched Hiram Cutberth in his pudgy jowls! That lecherous old toad tried to pinch me on the derriere when I danced with him. And when it comes to courting men . . ." Cayla sighed heavily and stared at her knotted fists.

"Don't stop now," Liberty encouraged her. "What about courting men?"

"I loathe letting them think I am what they see," she finished and then slumped deflatedly. "There are scores of men like Griffin who don't even know I'm alive because my father demands that I be so submissive."

"Well, 'tis high time the men of this world sat up and took note of you," Liberty decided.

She reached over to remove the plumed hat that sat atop Cayla's strawberry red curls. After pulling the pins from her hair, Liberty sent the strands tumbling over Cayla's shoulders in reckless disarray.

"That's much better." In three quick jerks, Liberty plucked the childish bows from the neckline of Cayla's mint green gown. "Hand me your scissors," she demanded impatiently.

With shears in hand, Liberty cut away the lace and gauze tippet that modestly concealed the swells of Cayla's bosom, thereby displaying her womanly assets to their best advantage. No longer did Cayla look like a coy young girl, but rather a fully blossomed woman. There was even a new sparkle of spirit in Cayla's eyes to match the radiant smile on her pretty face.

"Now, look me straight in the eye instead of staring humbly at your lap. You are a man's equal and don't ever let anyone convince you otherwise," Liberty spouted.

Cayla's pale green eyes swept up to focus squarely on Liberty's face and she broke into a saucy smile that looked quite becoming on her.

"That's more like it," Liberty enthused. "Now, you have to forget everything you have been told about being a subservient woman and express your own thoughts and your own needs. If men don't notice the change in your appearance, they will definitely take note of the intelligent, strong-minded female who has declared her independence."

"And if men don't like what they see?" Cayla queried apprehensively.

Liberty shrugged her shoulder as nonchalantly as Dylon would have done, had he been there. "Then you can tell each and every one of them to go to the devil."

Cayla settled herself casually in the seat and smiled broadly. "I feel better already."

In the next few hours, Liberty found herself delighting in Cayla's company. Liberty took an immediate liking to the redhead who had shed the rigid shell her father had strapped to her. Cayla had read extensively—books, newspapers and pamphlets, anything she could get her hands on—and she kept abreast of the activities of the Assembly. Thanks to Cayla, Liberty was briefed on all the political and economic goings-on in South Carolina during their journey back to Lockhart Hall.

When the procession was a few hours away from the plantation, Liberty poked her head from the carriage to instruct the grooms to halt. Before she could clamber down, all three Lockharts had stepped from Brewster's coach to determine what had caused Liberty's distress.

"There is nothing wrong except that we are tired of being cooped up in the carriage. Cayla and I wish to ride horseback," Liberty announced.

"Cayla wishes to ride?" Griffin croaked in disbelief. "I thought . . ."

His voice trailed off when Cayla appeared on the step. Her unbound hair tumbled recklessly around her bare shoulders and the alterations in her gown displayed the creamy swells of her breasts to Griffin's astonished stare.

"Well, don't just stand there gaping as if you've never seen me before," Cayla admonished with a teasing smile.

Her firm, melodic voice and the drastic change in her personality and appearance caused all three men's jaws to drop off their hinges. When Griff finally came to his senses, he stepped forward to assist Cayla to the ground.

"I'm not helpless and I no longer wish to be treated as if I were," she declared as she bounded to the ground without his assistance.

When Cayla sauntered over to grasp the reins to one of the horses the head groom was holding, Brewster chuckled in delight. "I like the new Cayla Styles. I wonder what came over her?" he mused aloud.

"Liberty Jordon would be my guess," Dylon replied with a sly grin. "It appears Liberty's independent nature rubbed off on Cayla."

"Rubbed off?" Griffin frowned pensively. "I have the feeling Cayla has always been keen-witted and vivacious, but she has never allowed anyone to know it. There has been a time or two that I have detected hints of this alter-personality. But before I could lure her out, she withdrew behind that wall of strict propriety."

"And I apologize for the remark I made at the ball," Dylon murmured, watching Liberty and Cayla thunder down the road, leaving a cloud of dust behind them. "It was uncalled for and I deserved the punch in the jaw."

Griffin stared after the two women on horseback. As much as he delighted in Cayla's newfound independence, his eyes were still drawn to the stunning blonde. Despite Brewster's loud booming lecture on keeping his distance from Liberty when she wasn't his escort, Griffin was still green with envy. . . .

"We had better be on our way before the ladies leave us far behind," Brewster insisted, dragging Griffin from his ponderous musings.

Dylon eyed his grandfather warily when the elderly gentleman scurried back to his coach and instructed the groom to set a swift pace. "You seem to be in a great rush to catch up with the ladies and reach the plantation."

"Well, of course I am," Brewster snorted impatiently. "These brittle old bones can tolerate just so much of these washboarded roads." He gestured for his grandsons to take their seats. "Just get in here, will you. Time's a-wasting."

With masculine grace Dylon folded himself onto the seat beside Brewster and frowned dubiously. "If you were concerned about brittle bones, why didn't we pause at the inn to sleep last night as I had originally planned instead of pushing on through the darkness?" he interrogated the gray-haired man who was staring out the window to keep sight of Liberty and Cayla. "There's something you're not telling me."

"Quit being so suspicious and clam up," Brewster grumbled crankily. "I am in no mood to be given the third degree."

Dylon did as he was ordered, but he couldn't help but wonder why Brewster fidgeted all over the seat. The old man couldn't seem to reach the plantation soon enough to suit himself.

And sure enough, Brewster had his reasons. But the patriarch wasn't about to divulge his purpose to his grandsons. They would both find out soon enough.

Chapter 20

Dylon's eyes bulged from their sockets when the phaeton rolled over the circular drive that led to Lockhart Hall. Carriage after carriage lined the path, causing a traffic jam. Hordes of people milled around the lawn and spilled out the front door.

When all the occupants from the Lockhart coaches filed out, they were greeted with rounds of cheer and applause.

"What the sweet loving hell is going on?" Dylon croaked as Percy strode forward to formally greet them.

A yard full of guests was the very last thing Dylon wanted. Lord, there were acquaintances from Charles Town, the nearby village and several men with whom he'd fought in the Cherokee Wars. Good God! Almost everyone he knew was congregated around his home. Dylon had been entertaining visions of a quiet evening in his chambers with Liberty, hoping to persuade her to stay at least one more day. Damnit, he'd attended enough parties of late to last him a year!

"Everything has been arranged according to specification, sir," Percy announced in a courtly tone.

"According to *whose* specifications?" Dylon demanded in annoyance.

"Mine, of course," Brewster declared, smiling triumphantly. "And you have done a superb job of handling the arrangements, Percival. I knew you would."

"I hope these people aren't planning to stay long," Dylon grumbled crankily. "I have socialized quite enough already."

A devilish smile quirked Brewster's lips as he grasped Liberty's hand and drew her up beside him. "They will be here long enough to celebrate the announcement of Liberty's wedding," he informed the stunned group.

Having dropped the bomb, Brewster waited for Dylon to explode. Sure as hell, he did.

"You can't be serious!" Dylon howled, staring at his grandfather as if he'd sprouted another head. "You can't marry Liberty."

Liberty stood there speechless, blinking like an owl adjusting to glaring sunlight.

"Nay, it would never do for me to marry this rambunctious young lady," Brewster concurred. "But *you* can, Dylon, and you *will.*" His smile faded, replaced by a stern stare. "Did you honestly think I would stand aside and allow the two of you to carry on the way you did at my estate?" Brewster expelled a volcanic snort. "Dylon has an obligation and so do you, Liberty. There *will* be a wedding. I insist upon it. And after all these years of waiting, I will demand that the ceremony take place immediately. Percy has seen to all the details."

"But . . ." Liberty only managed one word before Brewster threw up a hand to silence her.

"'Tis done!" he proclaimed with absolute finality. "Now, we're going to mingle with the guests and if either of you tries to sneak away, I'll have Percy form a search party to drag you back."

Liberty's wide-eyed gaze swung to Dylon. His expression revealed nothing but stunned astonishment. She couldn't tell if he was pleased or furious with the unexpected turn of events. But one thing was certain. Neither she nor Dylon appreciated being maneuvered. She imagined this surprise wedding went against Dylon's grain. He had spent years practicing and perfecting his talents of avoiding the marriage noose. Now he had been roped, tied and would soon be dragged to the altar.

With a snap of his fingers, Percy summoned the servants who scurried through the crowd to offer glasses of spiked punch. When drinks were clasped in the hand of every guest and family member, Brewster raised his arm in toast.

"I hereby announce the marriage of my grandson Dylon Lockhart to Liberty Jordon. Friends, help me wish them years of health, happiness and good fortune."

Another round of cheers rippled through the crowd. Hesitantly, Dylon glanced at Liberty, wondering at her reaction to this startling development. She was staring into the distance. Her petal-soft lips were tightened in something akin to a grimace. The sunny blush that usually highlighted her cheeks had evaporated. In an instant Dylon concluded that Liberty was opposed to the marriage. She didn't look the least bit happy. No doubt, being bamboozled into matrimony stung her independent nature. She would flee, just as she had attempted to do twice before, he predicted.

Blast it, there were scores of women who would have killed to exchange places with her, Dylon thought indignantly. In years past women had tried to run him down to catch him. But Liberty didn't look the least bit excited about the prospect of marrying him. *Not that I'm crazy about the idea myself,* Dylon told himself. If Liberty didn't want to marry him then he didn't want to marry her either! He still had his pride after all and he was not going to endure the same torment Patricia had put him through when she had sailed off with her duke, crushing and humiliating Dylon.

Dylon had completely misread the tense expression on Liberty's features. In an instant, Dylon and the rest of the world faded into oblivion. Her worst nightmare had materialized before her. It wasn't Brewster's surprise announcement that upset her to the extreme. It was the unexpected sight of Luther Norris and Simon Gridley standing on the perimeters of the crowd that provoked her apprehensive stare. Both men were glaring mutinously at her and Liberty swallowed with a gulp.

The impulse to flee overwhelmed her. When she pivoted to yield to primal instinct, Dylon clamped down on her arm. "Damn you," he growled, even though he'd pasted on a cheerful smile for appearance' sake. "This unexpected wedding is bad enough without you making an ass of me by darting off to only God knows where."

The harshness of his voice did her frustrated emotions no good whatsoever. It was glaringly obvious to her that Dylon was disgusted with the idea of being dragged to his wedding by his scheming grandfather. Well, if he was irritated, then so was she! She wasn't about to marry a man who didn't want her, even if she did love him to distraction. She had her pride after all!

"Who would have thought male pride was such a fragile thing. Your irrational fear of facing the embarrassment of being left on the altar is exceeded only by your desire to avoid marriage at all cost," Liberty retaliated in a quiet hiss. "I could make this easy on both of us by beating a hasty retreat. After all, 'tis hardly the first time I successfully escaped an unwanted wedding."

Dylon gnashed his teeth until he very nearly ground off the enamel. So she really didn't want to marry him, damn her fickle hide! He thought as much and expected as much from the female of the species. Not that he had even asked her to be his bride, mind you, but his male pride *was* smarting because Liberty appeared more anxious to avoid marriage than *he* was.

"For appearance' sake, we will both behave as if we approve," he muttered through a pretentious smile. "Later we will decide how to avoid this high-pressure marriage."

It *was* true, Liberty realized bleakly. She truly had been nothing more than the time Dylon was killing. That was just what she thought. When faced with the possibility of spending the rest of his life with only one woman, Dylon balked like a stubborn mule. All those softly uttered words and well-rehearsed lines of flattery were only his customary technique of wooing a woman into his bed. She meant nothing special to him. If she married him, he would begrudge being tied to her as if she were his albatross.

The thought stung Liberty like a swarm of hornets. Damn that man! Ah, how aptly he had been named—*Lock*heart. How could she have fancied herself in love with such an impossible man? Aye, he was all smiles and compliments until he found himself tangled in a matrimonial knot. He had nothing against wedlock as long as he had no part in it. Suddenly, Dylon sounded just like he did that day she'd overheard him in the carriage with Nora Flannery. Dylon wanted out! That was as obvious as the wart on the end of one's nose.

And if this surprise wedding of Brewster's hadn't caused enough conflict between them, there was Simon and Luther standing on the sidelines, waiting to confront her! Liberty inwardly groaned. She was on a collision course with disaster. She could feel it in her bones . . . !

Liberty wasn't allowed to dwell on that dismal

thought. A wave of humanity surged toward her and her would-be husband. She was bombarded with enthusiastic congratulations while Dylon was being teased and taunted for taking that giant step into matrimony.

All the while that Liberty was fielding questions and accepting the good wishes of the guests, she monitored Luther and Simon's activities. Like circling vultures they seemed to be waiting for the right time to approach her. Godamercy, of all the citizens in Charles Town and the surrounding area, why did Luther and Simon have to wind up on the guest list? Damn, what lousy luck! Even if she did try to make an escape those two scoundrels and their henchmen would be waiting to capture her. Curse it, what were they planning?

The first stumbling block to appear belonged to Griffin rather than Liberty, thank the Lord. She hadn't expected to be so fortunate. Joseph Styles was aghast to see the transformation in Cayla's appearance and disposition. Naturally, he blamed Griffin, who had escorted his young daughter to the holiday in the Up Country.

"You had bloody well better explain yourself, young man," Joseph demanded huffily. "'Tis obvious to me that you have taken advantage of my daughter. You unscrupulous rake. How dare you trifle with her and leave her looking like a trollop!"

Griffin didn't have time to defend himself. Cayla thrust herself between Griffin and Joseph. Her chin tilted to a rebellious angle as she stared her indignant father down.

"Griffin has been nothing but a gentleman where I'm concerned," she told Joseph firmly, shocking him speechless. "I have grown sick of living according to the rules you laid down for me. I am neither your puppet nor Griffin's paramour, nor will

I ever be an obedient servant to any man again!"

A gust of wind would have knocked Joseph Styles flat on his back. "Good Lord, girl, what has gotten into you?" he bugled in astonishment. "I have taught you better than to spout your thoughts and opinions at others."

"And I have obeyed your wishes as long as I can stand," Cayla informed him. "From this day forward I intend to lead my life according to my expectations, not the maddening demands you have impressed on me."

"How dare you speak to your own father in such a sharp tone," Joseph gasped furiously. "I will disown you if you don't cease this belligerence and behave as you have been instructed to do."

"And I will find somewhere else to call home," Cayla countered. "I will no longer be dictated to, Papa."

When Joseph stamped off in a huff, Griffin laid Cayla's hand over his proffered arm. "If it pleases you, my lady, we will enjoy a few of the refreshments Percy has prepared for us."

"It doesn't please me," Cayla insisted with a confident toss of her strawberry curls and a sly wink at Liberty. "What I prefer is to try my hand with a bow and arrow, just like Liberty did. And when I master that skill, I should like to sharpen my talents with pistols."

Brewster blinked in disbelief. "Liberty is handy with bows and pistols?"

"Handy?" Dylon smirked, casting his intended bride an annoyed glance. "*That* is the understatement of the decade."

"I should like to see it for myself," Brewster chuckled delightedly.

"And so you shall," Liberty complied, returning Dylon's agitated glare. "I only wish I had a more interesting target than the one Percy nailed to the tree the last time I took target practice."

There was no question in Dylon's mind as to what Liberty would have preferred as her target—*his* head. Muttering at the entire state of affairs, Dylon stamped off to assist Percy in gathering the equipment and preparing the target range.

When the crowd dispersed, Liberty found herself bookended by Luther and Simon. She was forced to stride beside her two least favorite people in all the world—her uncle and her former-future husband.

"You devious little witch," Simon growled at her. "Don't think I intend to let this marriage take place. If you don't tell Lockhart about the contract Luther and I signed, then I most certainly will."

Luther tapped the legal document that he carried in his vest pocket. "You cannot break this contract to wed another man," he snapped. "I am your legal guardian until you reach your twenty-first birthday."

"I'll tell him when the opportunity arises," Liberty promised, even though she had no intention of doing any such thing.

"You had damned well better," Simon demanded, giving her arm a painful squeeze. "I have had my fill of turning this countryside upside down trying to find you. Imagine my surprise when I received an invitation to attend my own fiancée's wedding to a man I . . ." He broke into a gritted growl. "I will not be humiliated and if you dare try to escape me again I'll make you wish you hadn't. . . ."

"Liberty!" Brewster called impatiently. "Come here. I'm anxious to see how well you wield a bow."

Thankful for the excuse to remove herself from such unpleasant company, Liberty squirted from their grasps.

"I'm warning you," Simon hissed at her departing back. "Starving you the night you tried to escape will be mere child's play compared to what you can expect if you try to double-cross me again."

While Simon propped himself against the tree to keep close surveillance on his elusive fiancée, Liberty grabbed her bow. Impulsively, she wheeled toward her nemesis. A gasp broke from Simon's throat when he found the bow and arrow trained on him. Before he could think to move, Liberty had sent the arrow hissing through the air. The hat that sat atop Simon's Periwig slammed against the bark of the tree with an arrow through its crown.

While Brewster, Griffin, Percy and Cayla stood there with their tongues frozen to the roofs of their mouths, Dylon frowned disconcertedly. Here, on his back lawn, stood the one man who could turn Dylon's mood pitch-black in one second flat. Their long-standing feud had lain in his stomach like an indigestible meal. They had clashed many a time while they battled the Indians because they operated on two entirely different moral planes.

This was the arrogant, ruthless regular army officer who had soured Dylon against all English soldiers in general. The aim of the militia was to enforce fair dealings with the Cherokee and create a lasting peace, not exterminate the tribe from the face of the earth! But Simon derived far too much pleasure in slaughtering his foe, whether it be warrior, woman or child. When Simon came back to camp, flaunting the scalp of a squaw, Dylon had all he could stand. (And the Americans thought the Indians had invented scalping. Not hardly!) Because of Simon's ruthlessness on the battlefield, Dylon had brought charges against him and had seen to it that Simon was dishonorably discharged.

Simon had become a man of slender means after his discharge. Then Simon had married a wealthy young heiress who had mysteriously died less than a year after their wedding. Of course, Simon had gained control of his deceased wife's landholdings. And then only a few months later, Simon had married again, only to have his second young wife turn up dead in less than a year. Some folks said she had tripped down the steps of their plantation home. Others wondered if she hadn't been pushed. But whatever the case, Simon was left with his wealthy wife's estate, doubling his fortune.

Having acquired wealth by highly suspicious methods, Simon had set out to rout Dylon from his seat in the Assembly. He had spread vicious lies and rumors, seeking to undermine Dylon's respectability. No doubt, losing the election had given Simon one more cause to despise Dylon. They simply seemed to be natural-born enemies who clashed on every battlefield imaginable.

Having Simon here was bad enough, but watching Liberty pin his hat to the tree suggested she too had clashed with this scoundrel who could never do more than *pretend* to be a gentleman. Simon Gridley was anything but!

While Dylon was trying to puzzle out Liberty's connection with Simon a round of laughter erupted from the crowd of bystanders, infuriating Simon more than he already was. With a muttered curse, Simon yanked the arrow from his tricorn and Periwig, broke it in two and stomped on it. He and Liberty stood like two combatants, separated by a wall that rippled with tension. The way Simon kept glaring at Liberty made Dylon wonder . . .

Good God! Surely this wasn't the man Liberty had fled before she was coerced into marriage. *Surely it was*, the logical side of his brain yelled at him. Why else would Liberty target a man who should have been a perfect stranger to her? And what connection did Simon have with Luther Norris who was scuttling along behind the taller, broader man? And what possible association could Luther have with Liberty?

Dylon found himself plagued with far more questions than he could hope to answer. He suspected Liberty could supply those answers but she had remained as tight-lipped as a clam.

"Turn around here and quit scaring the daylights out of our guests," Brewster insisted of Liberty. "I admit I'm duly impressed with your talents and I have little use for the man you pinned to the tree, but let's restrict our targets to inanimate objects that are not sitting atop human heads, shall we?"

Liberty's and Simon's eyes met like clenched fists. Simon looked as though he were contemplating charging forward to reciprocate, but he dismissed the idea when Liberty plucked another arrow from her quiver. Only a fool would attack a well-armed woman who hungered for revenge.

When Simon and Luther stormed off to cool their tempers with spiked punch, Liberty pivoted to focus on her target. Teaching Cayla the skills of archery was a welcomed diversion. Liberty was determined to bide her time until dark. Then she would bound onto a horse and thunder off to Charles Town to rejoin Stella. It was for damned certain that she had excellent reason to flee from Lockhart Hall. Dylon didn't want her for his bride and Simon and Luther were breathing down her neck. Godamercy, did trouble always travel in pairs?

It certainly looked like it, Liberty mused as she turned her bow on the target and scored a bull's-eye. As she placed the bow in Cayla's hand, Liberty reminded herself that there was no such thing as a convenient catastrophe. Disasters fed on each other and multiplied. . . .

"*Now* I should like to have that drink," Cayla declared as she laid the bow aside. It was evident that even with Liberty's patient instruction Cayla needed to practice to perfect her skills. But for the moment she was content to spend time with Griffin and chat with the other guests.

While Griffin and Cayla ambled off and Dylon was immersed in conversation with several assemblymen from Charles Town, Brewster drew Liberty aside.

"I suppose you are annoyed with me for springing this surprise on you," he speculated.

"I have enjoyed better days," Liberty grumbled, keeping an ever-watchful eye on her uncle and Simon. "Surely you realize this isn't going to work."

"I happen to think it has worked out splendidly thus far," Brewster said with enthusiastic confidence.

"You have overlooked two major details," Liberty pointed out. "Dylon doesn't love me and he is fiercely opposed to marriage. I hardly need to remind you how many times in the past few years he has artfully dodged wedlock. You are the one who cited all those instances to me."

"That was all before you came along, my dear," Brewster responded, magically waving away her objections with a flick of his wrists.

"Nothing has changed," Liberty said with perfect assurance.

"On the contrary, everything has changed," Brewster parried with absolute certainty.

Liberty peered into his sparkling blue eyes and wrinkled features. "I only hope you won't be disappointed when things don't turn out as you have anticipated," she murmured before spinning around and ambling away.

"Ah, but they will," he called after her.

Liberty didn't think so. Brewster knew nothing of her ongoing conflict with Luther and Simon. . . .

Speak of the devils and they appeared, thought Liberty. She had only rounded the corner of the mansion to fetch a drink and there were her nemeses, glaring daggers at her.

"Have you told him yet?" Simon scowled in question.

Liberty kept walking toward the refreshment table. "Nay. We have not been granted a moment's privacy."

"You aren't trying very hard to get him alone," Luther

muttered in a sour tone.

"Shall I drag him away from his guests and arouse curiosity?" she countered sarcastically.

"Don't take that tone with me," Luther hissed at his sassy niece.

Liberty wheeled on her despicable uncle. "Just what sort of scheme did you and Simon devise? I'm not so foolish to think you have my best interest at heart," she snapped disrespectfully. "If you think to manipulate me out of my fortune, you will find yourself homeless and destitute."

Just what Luther needed—another threat. "How dare . . ."

Simon clutched Luther's arm before he blurted out their arrangements in a fit of temper. "Make no mistake, minx," he snarled at Liberty. "Our contract is within the letter of the law. 'Tis legal and binding. We hardly need your permission or consent." His dark brows formed a severe line over his narrowed brown eyes. "I will give you one hour to beg off this engagement and confess that you are pledged to me. One hour, woman. If you haven't disclosed our previous arrangements I will show Lockhart the contract and put an end to this waiting game. You and I will be married tomorrow and that is the beginning and end of it."

Liberty had tremendous difficulty controlling her anger and frustration. And every time Simon clamped onto her arm to cut off circulation, a snake of revulsion slithered across her flesh. When she tried to jerk her arm away, Simon practically pinched it in two. Liberty countered by uplifting her knee, gouging Simon in the groin. Although Simon doubled over to protect himself against another agonizing blow, he managed to shackle her arm a second time.

"Take your hands off my fiancée."

The gruff command caused Simon to loose his grasp. Unfolding himself, he met Dylon's venomous glare.

Simon had his fill of these cat-and-mouse games. He wasn't giving Liberty the hour he'd promised. If he dared to confront this she-cat again there was no telling what she would try to do to him. She had already attempted to turn him into a human pincushion and a punching bag.

"She is not your fiancée, Lockhart," Simon sneered spitefully. "She's mine." He outthrust a hand to fish the contract from Luther's vest pocket. "We were to be married two weeks ago but my contrary bride-to-be took flight."

A look of smug satisfaction spread over Simon's features when he met Dylon's icy glare, as well as the incredulous stares of Brewster, Percy, Griffin and Cayla.

"What?" Brewster hooted when his vocal apparatus began to function once again.

Simon tauntingly waved the contract under Dylon's nose. "'Tis all perfectly legal. Luther and I made the arrangements after Liberty arrived from the West Indies to take inventory of her inheritance."

"Jordon!" Brewster's eyes popped. "That's where I've heard that name before. Benjamin Jordon, the shipping entrepreneur who amassed a fortune in the Indies, is your father!"

Brewster recalled hearing stories about the titled lord who had migrated from England to South Carolina and then to the Indies. Benjamin was too active and energetic to settle for a sedate style of life. He thrived on challenges. Benjamin had gone from lord to planter to merchant and shipping agent. He had overseen the complicated shipping lanes between England, the Indies and the colonies.

When fish and lumber from New England, and flour from the Middle colonies, and rice, indigo and tobacco from the South were shipped to the Indies, Benjamin Jordon made certain the colonists weren't neglected or cheated. The sugar and molasses grown in the islands were to be shipped to London and Bristol, not to the colonies. Only manufactured goods from England were supposed to return to America. And although Benjamin did arrange for the shipments of colonial rice, pork, flour and indigo to be loaded onto English-bound schooners, he also arranged shipments of sugar and molasses to be sent directly to the colonies.

Even though the earlier Navigation Acts prohibited the colonists from trading with anyone except England, Benjamin had defiantly bent the rules, being partial to colonials since he had lived among them for a time. The islands in the West Indies which were owned by France, Spain and Holland provided good markets for colonial products and profitable exchanges. Benjamin put ship captains in contact with merchants in the islands to ensure colonial profit.

Benjamin had also worked to arrange marine insurance for the colonists. Before he organized the benefits, all damages from wind and inclement weather were borne by the shipowners. But thanks to his efforts, sailors were no longer devastated by natural disasters. . . .

"Benjamin Jordon was killed during a tropical storm almost four months ago," Luther declared, dragging Brewster from his pensive musings. "I was named Liberty's guardian and I have every right to contract her marriage to the man of my choice."

The confrontation had gathered an even larger crowd. Scowling in disgust, Dylon clutched Liberty's arm and propelled her toward the private side entrance which led to his office. "You should have told me you were mixed up with these scoundrels," he muttered at her.

"What do you care?" Liberty flashed, jerking her arm free. "All that ever concerned you was making another female conquest. Of course, you hadn't expected Brewster to catch you in his cunning trap. But now you needn't worry that you'll find yourself eternally bound to me."

"Me? Worry?" Dylon growled as he led the procession

toward his office. "*You* are the one who has made it clear that you have no wish to marry *me*."

Liberty would have objected to his erroneous assumption but Simon wedged his way between them the instant they stepped into the study.

"Now that the truth is out, I expect you to honor this contract and retract your marriage proposal, Lockhart," Simon demanded harshly.

"He will do no such thing," Brewster spouted off. When he stamped over to snatch up the contract and rip it to shreds, Simon jerked it from his reach.

Dylon glowered at the wiry little weasel of a man who claimed to be Liberty's uncle. He was a miserable excuse for an uncle and an even worse excuse for a man. Luther Norris had a reputation for squandering excessive amounts of money at the gaming tables and consuming tremendous amounts of liquor. Unless Dylon missed his guess (and he doubted he had) Simon Gridley had taken advantage of that irresponsible lush.

"Did Simon know you did not lay title to your own fortune, Luther?" Dylon questioned in a ridiculing tone. "Knowing your penchant for cards and whiskey, I rather imagine you wrote a promissory note on land and property that didn't belong to you." He regarded Luther with loathing disdain. "You may be Liberty's guardian but I rather suspect you are, in essence, a ward of *her* estate, an expense she had the misfortune of inheriting."

Luther's batlike features puckered in an indignant glare. "I do not have to stand here and listen to your insults!" he fluted.

"Would you prefer to take them sitting down?" Dylon smirked caustically. "Do take a load off your feet, Luther. I'm sure the burden of your outstanding debts must weigh heavily on your shoulders."

"Is that what all this is about?" Liberty interrupted with a furious hiss. "Did you gamble away property that wasn't yours to begin with? Did you bargain me away to

Simon to pay for what you had lost to him?"

"My previous arrangements with Luther have no bearing on this marriage contract," Simon declared with a haughty sneer. "No matter what methods Luther and I have devised to pay his debts, 'tis no one's concern but our own."

"They bear great concern to me," Dylon growled. The smile he usually managed to hold intact, despite the most frustrating situations, transformed into a thunderous frown. "Since your first two wives didn't live long, I would suspect Liberty's marriage to you would also affect *her* longevity . . . or lack of it."

Simon cursed the shadows of suspicion Dylon had flung on him and the look of wary trepidation Liberty cast him. "My former wives died of natural causes," he insisted.

"Didn't they just!" Griffin piped up.

"I have heard the whispered speculations myself," Cayla inserted, only to be drowned out by Simon's infuriated snarl.

"I will not have my good name and reputation bandied about!"

"What good name?" Dylon scoffed caustically. "You seem to forget that I knew when you first came to the colonies. As I recall, you had little or nothing until you acquired the property which belonged to your unfortunate wives." He stared ponderously at the contract and then glowered at the disgusting scoundrel with whom he had clashed several times in six years. Honest to God, Dylon didn't know why he had suffered this bastard to live so long. Simon certainly didn't deserve to.

"How much will it cost me to buy this contract and pay Luther's outstanding debts?"

"You will do no such thing!" Liberty erupted, her face flushing with frustrated fury.

"Then I shall do it," Brewster insisted.

"Nay, you will not!" Liberty almost yelled at him. "I

will not be bought and sold like livestock on the auction block."

"This contract is not for sale," Simon interjected, casting Liberty a gloating smile. "I not only hold this legal contract, but I also have a moral obligation to my fiancée. Although we have yet to speak the vows, we have already enjoyed our wedding night."

The erupting gasps of shock mingled with Liberty's outraged growl. Like a panther, she pounced on Simon, clawing the haughty smirk off his face, taking the top layer of skin with it.

"'Tis a vicious lie!" she screeched. "I would never have . . ."

Her voice trailed off into a pained groan when Simon backhanded her on the cheek. Liberty's senses reeled as she stumbled back against Dylon, making it impossible for him to do what he itched to do—smash his fist into Simon's face a couple of times. Instead, Dylon had to snake out a hand to catch Liberty before she fell into a crumpled heap on the floor.

Before Dylon could restrain her, she pushed away from him to launch her second attack on the vile vermin who had lied through his teeth! Curse him, she wouldn't have let him touch her whether they were married or not!

Her fists pelted Simon's face before he could uplift his arm to deflect the repetitive blows. With an enraged growl, he leaped sideways and struck out at the hissing tigress who had dared to attack him.

Dylon's protective instincts sprang to life. But before he could beat Simon to a pulp Griffin leaped on his brother from behind. He knew that Simon would make it even more impossible to free Liberty from the contract if Dylon did what he looked as if he were contemplating doing. After Dylon beat the tar out of Simon, the scoundrel would spitefully prevent Liberty from gaining her freedom, just to infuriate the Lockharts.

As Liberty tumbled to the floor, dazed by Simon's

blow, Brewster charged forward and uplifted his hands like a policeman halting traffic on the bustling streets of Charles Town. "Stop this at once!" he demanded.

And there Brewster stood, glowering at Simon for daring to strike a woman, refusing to let another fisticuffs break out when feelings and emotions were running so high. Brewster didn't know what to do next but it was for damned certain no one was going to throw another punch if he could help it!

Chapter 21

In swift lanky strides Phillipe LaGere propelled himself around the corner of the mansion to confront Percy who guarded the office door. Percy was so distracted with his eavesdropping and the startling revelations that were unfolding inside the office that he didn't realize the gallant Frenchman had arrived upon the scene until he felt the insistent tap on his shoulder.

"Monsieur, I have been told that you can direct me to the abominable cur who has attempted to steal my fiancée away from me," Phillipe declared with his usual flair for the dramatic. "Lead me to this vermin immediately. I shall right every wrong that has befallen my ladylove."

"Fiancée?" Percy choked, goggle-eyed. "What fiancée?"

"Why, Mademoiselle Liberty Jordon, of course." Phillipe stared at Percy as if he were addle-witted. Striking a dignified pose, Phillipe dropped into an exaggerated bow and attempted to explain to the startled valet. "*Pardonez-moi*, monsieur. Allow me to introduce myself. I am Phillipe LaGere. When I arrived in Charles Town, Liberty's maid explained that she had been contracted into a marriage she did not want and that she was at Lockhart Hall. I demand to see this lout who is trying to marry my fiancée!"

Phillipe spoke with a heavy French accent and waved his long spindly arms in expansive gestures. Once Percy had digested the information he rolled his eyes heavenward and groaned. No wonder Liberty had been running away and refused to disclose her past. The vivacious beauty had more men chasing after her than a fruit tree had peaches!

"I shall run this Lockhart scoundrel through! I shall have him shot and hanged," Phillipe declared with his customary theatrics. "Take me to him at once, *mon ami*. I shall slay this hideous dragon."

Percy wasn't quite sure who Phillipe LaGere was, but the man certainly didn't have his story straight! Somehow or another, he had come to the conclusion that Dylon was the scoundrel who had contracted Liberty into marriage. But that wasn't quite right either. It was Brewster who had schemed to marry Liberty and Dylon after she escaped from the contracted marriage to Simon Gridley. . . .

The clatter of tumbling furniture inside the office jerked Percy from his thoughts. Impulsively, he pushed open the door to determine what had caused the racket. Phillipe interpreted the gesture as his cue to plunge into the melee in the study. Phillipe hiked up one leg, jerked back his arms and thrust himself inside in time to see Liberty tumble across the floor.

"I have come, *ma chérie*, to save the day!" Phillipe bugled as he stamped up to Brewster who was trying to keep another fight from breaking out.

Dylon's gaze slid over the elaborately dressed coxcomb who had sailed into the room like a cyclone. "Who the hell is that?" he demanded to know as he shook loose from his brother's grasp and then hoisted Liberty off the floor. A muted growl tumbled from his lips when Liberty tried to lunge forward to tear Simon to pieces with her bare hands. Clamping his arm around the seething beauty, Dylon focused on the tall blond Frenchman who looked and sounded as if he would be much more at home on a stage.

"I am Liberty's fiancé," Phillipe declared before Percy could scuttle forward to respond to Dylon's question.

A look of disbelief settled on Dylon's rugged features as he glanced down at Liberty. "Good God, woman, just how many more fiancés do you have chasing after you?"

Liberty was too busy spitting curses at Simon to respond. She strained against Dylon's chaining arms, visualizing herself beating Simon into the floor. It wasn't a pretty picture, but it was immensely gratifying.

Phillipe was quick to notice that Dylon was holding the fuming blonde against her will and he stalked forward to glare at the raven-haired colonial. "Unhand my future bride, monsieur, or I will be forced to challenge you to a duel!"

Finally Liberty slumped, frustrated that she had been unable to get her hands on the contract or the disgusting varmint who held it. And if she didn't have enough trouble already, Phillipe LaGere darted in from out of nowhere. Accusingly, her eyes flew to her maid who had just breezed in the door, gasping for breath. Liberty quickly surmised that Stella had taken matters into her own hands and had managed to make them worse . . . if that were possible!

"Well, what did you expect me to do?" Stella grumbled defensively when Liberty flashed her a condescending glare. "Phillipe is your rightful fiancé and I tried to explain what had happened. But you know Phillipe, he didn't give me time to finish relating the incidents before he dashed off to rescue you."

Simon growled at the new arrivals. "This changes nothing. I was the first man in Liberty's bed and she belongs to me physically and legally."

When Simon dared to voice the same lie a second time,

Dylon had to tighten his grasp on Liberty to restrain her. She was still itching to beat Simon to a pulp for voicing that crude remark. And unfortunately Dylon was the only one in the room, other than Liberty, who knew for a fact that Simon was lying. But if Dylon dared to contradict Simon while Liberty was in her murderous frame of mind he feared she would scald him with her boiling temper. It would also serve to put Simon in a rage. And then where would they be? In a worse tangle than they were already in, he reckoned.

Good God, how'd things get into such a complicated mess? Only a few nights ago Dylon had held Liberty in his arms, enjoying life's simplest and most gratifying pleasures. And suddenly the world flipped upside down. Liberty had transformed Cayla Styles into an independent, strong-minded woman. Brewster had sprung an engagement party on him and he was trying to manipulate Liberty into a marriage she obviously didn't want or need. Hell, why should she? She had fiancés galore and they would have to be categorized in alphabetical order to keep up with all of them!

Now Simon (a man Dylon thoroughly detested) had lied to ensure he got what he wanted. Then, along came that overdramatic Frenchman who claimed his rights to Liberty. What else could possibly go wrong!

With a flourish, Phillipe stepped forward to confront Simon who was obviously causing Liberty the most distress at the moment. With stiff, exaggerated jerks, Phillipe tugged his white gloves from his hands. With so much pomp and circumstance that it was almost laughable, the Frenchman clutched his gloves and slapped Simon on both cheeks.

"I challenge you to a duel, monsieur. You have tainted my beloved fiancée's reputation with your vulgar remarks. I demand satisfaction!"

Simon growled at the chivalrous Frenchman. "I'll be happy to kill you any day of the week, Frenchy."

Phillipe yanked up his blond head and glared at his opponent. With another ridiculous flair for the dramátic, he slapped Simon again. "My name is Phillipe and you have dared to add insult to injury. I challenge you on behalf of Liberty and myself. Name your weapon and the time, monsieur."

"Nobody's going to kill anybody," Dylon said, scowling, still holding Liberty at bay.

"You stay out of this, monsieur," Phillipe insisted, fixating his disgusted glare on Dylon. "I intend to kill *you* after I finish with this scoundrel who claims to have molested my fiancée."

Phillipe refocused his glower on Simon. "Name your weapon. I will be most happy to run you through with my rapier, for I am a master swordsman. Or if you prefer to die with a bullet in your black heart, then I shall display my fine skills with a pistol. Or a dagger in your chest will please me just as well."

Simon looked the Frenchman up and down and grinned wickedly. "I choose bows and arrows."

The confident expression which was usually plastered on Phillipe's face slid off. "Very well, bows and arrows it is," he agreed with pretended bravado.

"Tomorrow at midday," Simon decided. "When I finish with you, Liberty and I will be wed."

"*Au contraire*, monsieur," Phillipe corrected. "By tomorrow, you will be dead and my beloved Liberty will be married to me!"

Dylon bit back a chuckle. Phillipe was so sincere and so dramatic he was comical. Dylon had never seen a man make quite such a production out of every situation he confronted!

"Phillipe, this is the most ridiculous . . ." Liberty broke off into an audible sigh when the gallant Frenchman flung up his hand to forestall her.

"I will not shirk my obligation to fight, and even to die if I must for your honor and for mine. This repulsive cretin has slandered both of us. Your father would have expected no less from me than to defend you to the death!"

"We will meet on the cliff above the river," Simon informed Phillipe. "And when you tumble with my arrow in your overinflated chest, Frenchy, the river can carry you back to the islands where you belong."

"Come along, Liberty," Simon demanded. "We have arrangements to make."

"She stays here," Dylon growled in a tone that brooked no argument.

"Then I shall also stay here," Phillipe declared as he stepped in front of Liberty like a human shield. "For wherever my love goest, I goest! No other man will touch my beloved Liberty again." He glared at Simon and then at Dylon. "I believe I told you to unhand my lady, monsieur. Do it at once or I shall have to run you through!"

Muttering, Dylon released Liberty. With a mutinous glare, he watched Simon swagger toward the door, waving the contract like a matador waving a red cape at a bull. Behind him, Luther Norris scuttled along, anxious to make his departure.

Before Simon and Luther could weave their way toward the door, Nora Flannery and her father came barging in.

"Now see here, Lockhart," Doctor Flannery sneered as he wagged a stubby finger at Dylon. "You are not marrying anyone except my daughter. She told me all about your little tryst, how you seduced her and then refused to marry her after you . . ." His voice trailed off when he glanced at the throng of individuals who were crowded in the study. "You are going to fulfill your *first* obligations *first!*"

This, Dylon decided, was the *what else* that could go wrong. It seemed he was doomed to encounter one dilemma and, before it was satisfactorily resolved, it was upstaged by another! Edgar Flannery hadn't the good sense or the decency to wait until the office had been cleared before he voiced his damaging remarks. One shocked gasp after another echoed around the room. All eyes swung accusingly to Dylon. He found himself itching to pound Edgar and Nora flat for bursting in uninvited, just as Liberty longed to beat Simon to a pulp for voicing his derogatory remarks.

"I will refuse to allow this ceremony to take place," Edgar raged on. The veins on his flushed face pulsated as he stalked toward Dylon. "I'm warning you, Lockhart. If you don't accept responsibility I will ruin you politically."

Nora discarded her air of regal poise and made a magnificent display of bursting into sobs and wailing about how the man she loved had betrayed her and used her. That made Edgar all the madder.

"Not only will I ruin you politically," Edgar seethed, still wagging his finger at Dylon. "But I will—"

"There is no need to threaten him," Phillipe interrupted as he swaggered forward. "If this philistine doesn't comply with your demands, I will kill him for you after I dispose of this scoundrel." He pointed an accusing finger at Simon who was gloating more than ever.

Not to be outdone by Phillipe's theatrical performance, Nora rushed forward to fling her arms around Dylon's neck. Through blubbering tears, she confessed her affection for him and pleaded with him to make a respectable woman out of her after what he'd done. The performance continued for several minutes in her attempt to soak up sympathy like a sponge and persuade Dylon to do the right thing by her.

There were a scant few times when Dylon had claimed to be positively furious. At this moment Dylon was seeing the world through a crimson red haze. His conflicting emotions were rumbling around inside him like butter in a churn. With a wordless scowl, he pried

Nora loose and stepped away, only to find Liberty glaring poison arrows at him. Nora's teary display had Liberty wondering if perhaps Dylon truly had taken unfair advantage.

"Get out of here, all of you!" Dylon roared. "I refuse to battle more than one crisis at a time!"

Chuckling triumphantly, Simon tucked the contract in his pocket and sashayed out the door with Luther following in his wake.

Still fuming, Edgar wrapped a supporting arm around his sobbing daughter and propelled her toward the portal. "This isn't the end of it, Dylon," Edgar promised in a gritted hiss. "You will do your duty where my daughter is concerned. I will see to it!"

Griffin filed out with Cayla Styles on his arm, even though he was dying to know how Dylon was going to worm out of the tangle he'd gotten himself into. Percy, clutching Stella Talbot's arm, fell into step behind the youngest Lockhart. Brewster, however, refused to budge from his spot. He merely propped himself against the wall and glanced speculatively between the outrageously flamboyant Frenchman and Dylon who looked like the makings of a thundercloud that could spawn tornadoes.

Liberty barely had time to gather her wits and her composure before Phillipe engulfed her in his arms and showered her cheeks and brows with loud, smacking kisses.

"*Ma chère amour*, I was beside myself with worry when Stella told me of the tragedy that had befallen you. And so soon after you lost your father, my poor darling! I am most thankful I decided to follow you to South Carolina."

Dylon wasn't!

"You must explain this disastrous turn of events in detail," Phillipe insisted. "But never fear. I will protect you and defend you and together we will sail away to our beloved islands to begin our new life."

Like hell they would! Dylon fumed.

Feeling self-conscious, Liberty pushed back as far as Phillipe's encircling arms would allow. "I will not have you dueling on my behalf. You have never drawn down on a bow in all your life!"

"But I will learn," Phillipe declared. "And I shall spear that vermin's hard heart!"

Not damned bloody likely, thought Dylon. Simon had learned to handle a bow after the massacres in the Cherokee villages. In fact, Simon was reasonably skilled with all weapons. Phillipe was living on false hopes if he thought he could match a man with Simon's military background.

Liberty clutched Phillipe's hand and pivoted to tow him out the door. "We are leaving for Charles Town tonight," she insisted. "All I want is to go home where I should have stayed in the first place."

Phillipe set his feet like a stubborn mule. "*Non, chérie,* I will not shirk my duties. I am honor bound to defend you. I promised Benjamin that I would love and protect you and I shall!"

"No one is going anywhere!" Dylon blared as he stamped over to shove the door shut before Liberty breezed out. With arms crossed over his broad chest and feet apart, Dylon blocked the path and glared into Liberty's agitated features.

"Let her go," Brewster demanded, biting back a wry grin. "It seems there are too many men pledged to Liberty already."

Traitor, Dylon thought mutinously. Brewster had schemed to get him married to this blond-haired hellion and now he was willing to give up without a fight. Well, Dylon wasn't! The thought of seeing Liberty married to this melodramatic Frenchman turned his disposition as sour as a lemon.

"Liberty, are you going to tell him or am I?" Dylon questioned, his voice rumbling with barely suppressed anger.

"Tell me what, monsieur?" Phillipe wanted to know

that very second.

"If you dare, I'll . . ." Liberty hissed, only to be cut off by Dylon's explosive snort.

"You'll what?" he mocked, managing an infuriating smile for her benefit. "Challenge me to a duel with your mighty bow?"

"Nay," she snapped. "I'll simply shoot you in the back and be done with it."

"My darling Liberty, I insist upon knowing what this molester of women is talking about," Phillipe ordered. "And it had better not be what I think he is insinuating!"

Both men glowered at each other for a long tense moment before Dylon lost the last shred of temper. Clutching Phillipe by the nape of his jacket and the seat of his breeches, Dylon escorted the lanky blond out the door and slammed it behind him. When he wheeled on his grandfather, the patriarch flung up a hand and smothered an amused grin.

"I shall leave on my own accord, thank you very much," Brewster announced before he strode out of the office.

When Liberty tried to buzz out the door, Dylon clutched her arm and swung her around to face him. "You aren't going anywhere until we get this straightened out."

"As far as I'm concerned, there is nothing to straighten out," Liberty bit off. "You have your problems and I have mine. We will solve them separately."

"We most certainly will not!" Dylon yelled into her defiant expression. "We are engaged. My grandfather's invitations and announcements have made it so!"

"I hardly see how you can marry me while Edgar Flannery is breathing down your neck, threatening to ruin your life and your reputation," Liberty countered sardonically.

"And no doubt it will be difficult for us to marry with

Simon waving his contract and that French baboon slobbering all over you every chance he gets," Dylon muttered. "But it can be done and it will be done!"

Liberty blinked in astonishment and then her expression transformed into wary disdain. "Ah, so that is the way of it," she smirked. "You plan to use our supposed wedding to weasel out of your obligations to 'Nora dear.'"

"I have no obligations to Nora," Dylon vehemently denied.

"Edgar and Nora seem to think you do," she sniffed distastefully. "It seems your promiscuity has finally caught up with you. But I shudder to think how many other innocent maids have fallen beneath your persuasive charms and were without powerful influential fathers to plead their causes for them."

"There was nothing innocent about Nora Flannery. She was no stranger to a man's bed," Dylon assured her frankly. "And I've certainly been around enough to know! If there was any seducing going on, *she* was doing it, not *I*."

Liberty didn't call him a lying philistine, but it was clearly implied in her countering glare and her sarcastic rejoinder. "I'm sure Nora wrestled you to the bed and forced her affection on you, Amazon that she is!"

"And I'm positively certain you have been stringing that Frenchman along, just like you do every other man who falls beneath your spell, witch," he hurled nastily.

"I did no such thing!" Liberty loudly protested. "But I would sooner marry Phillipe than that scoundrel my uncle selected for me."

"And what of me?" Dylon asked, carefully gauging her reaction to his question. "Would you find marriage to me intolerable?"

The arrogant cad! He wanted to hear her say she cared about him, even when he felt nothing but temporary lust for her. Well, hell would sooner be encased in a glacier!

"I would imagine that marriage to you would be an exercise in patience," Liberty replied flippantly. "A woman could tolerate only so much indiscretion on the part of her husband before she either shot him or left him."

Two black brows jackknifed. "You don't think I could be faithful to you?" he queried indignantly.

"Do mules fly, Dylon?" she smirked.

"And what of you?" Dylon parried, irked by her insult. "You bewitch men and leave them groveling at your feet for the mere sport of it."

"I do not!" Liberty defended herself. "I have no need for men in my life, but they come like a plague of locusts."

"I do not appreciate being referred to as a plague," Dylon growled.

The look she gave him indicated she didn't give a flying fig what he appreciated. "And I detest being one of the countless women you've had," she flashed resentfully. "A marriage between the two of us would prove disastrous."

"It would be better than winding up as Simon's wife," Dylon assured her in a gruff tone. "He has been married twice and his brides have lived just long enough to ensure that he gained control of their inheritance. No doubt, you would wind up a casualty of Simon's greed."

The comment took the wind out of Liberty's sails. Dylon had painted a grisly picture and she couldn't help but wonder why her own uncle, miserable excuse for a human being he was, would sell her to that scoundrel. If she were smart, she would grab her belongings and attempt to . . .

"Don't even think it," Dylon muttered, watching the emotions race across her animated features. "You're not deserting me to your pack of would-be husbands and my would-be bride."

"You got yourself into this tangle and . . ."

"I?" Dylon scoffed in contradiction. "'Tis because of you that I am in any sort of predicament at all!"

"I had nothing to do with your affair with Nora," Liberty reminded him hotly.

"But you are the one who brought this to a festering head, like a painful boil!"

Liberty had been called a lot of things in her life, but never a boil!

With lightning tongue and thundering voice, Dylon thrust his face into hers to chew her up one side and down the other. "If not for you, Brewster wouldn't have seen to it that the announcement of our sudden engagement spread from here to Charles Town and back again. That served to draw out every human who holds a grudge against us out of the woodwork. And all along you have refused to divulge your problems and now they have sneaked up on us all at once," Dylon harshly accused. "You dared to be stubborn and independent. You dared to work your wiles on my grandfather and now he . . ."

"I refuse to shoulder all the blame for simply being myself!" Liberty protested. "And I hope you wind up married to that teary-eyed twit. You would be getting exactly what you deserve after taking women for granted as if their feelings and pride counted for nothing." She inhaled a furious breath and plunged on. "As for me, I will stay long enough to rescue Phillipe from his own noble blunder. Since he refuses to back down from this ridiculous duel, I will ensure that he can hold his own against Simon. And day after tomorrow, we will sail to the islands. You, Romeo, will be left to resolve your conflict with Edgar and Nora the best way you can."

Having said her piece, Liberty lurched around and stormed out. She didn't have to look far to find Phillipe. He stood waiting for her like an obedient puppy. Tugging on his hand, Liberty led Phillipe to the target range. And lo and behold, Cayla Styles arrived to request further instruction in the art of archery as well.

While Griffin tended to the unsuspecting guests who wandered around the estate, Cayla and Phillipe perfected their skills under Liberty's patient instruction. She hoped to train Phillipe well enough to discourage Simon from pressing the issue of the contract. Perhaps then she could buy Simon off with cash and toss that despicable uncle of hers out on the streets with the rest of the rubbish. And then, if all went well, she could sail home and forget that blue-eyed, raven-haired rake who had burrowed into her heart and left it to bleed. With any luck at all, she wouldn't even remember his name in a few months. Liberty certainly hoped so. She didn't relish the idea of carrying a torch for that lusty libertine for the rest of her natural life!

A muted growl tumbled from Dylon's curled lips. He had been keeping constant surveillance at his office window, watching Liberty instruct Phillipe on the target range. Damn, that Frenchman relished all the attention Liberty was bestowing on him!

Unfamiliar possessiveness washed over Dylon for the umpteenth time in less than two hours. After cursing and pacing, he had begun to feel like his old self. But then he glanced outside to see Phillipe and Liberty together and it made him mad all over again.

If he had a lick of sense, he would tell Liberty good riddance and await with impatient anticipation until that troublesome misfit sailed out of his life forever. What did he care about her anyway? She had no true affection for him. He had only been her first experiment with passion and she had no wish to marry him or any other man who chased after her.

From the very beginning he and Liberty had been like a mathematical equation he couldn't figure out. The cynic in him shied away from commitment, for fear of being betrayed again. But the man in him longed to have that gorgeous violet-eyed sprite all to himself. She had tapped that deep well of emotion inside him that he had wanted to leave capped forevermore. But nothing had ever hit him so hard or lasted so long and . . .

"Well, you certainly have managed to get your life in a pickle," Brewster snickered as he eased the door shut behind him.

"I thought I asked to be left alone," Dylon grumbled, unable to take his eyes off the tormenting vision on the target range.

"Left alone?" Brewster burst out laughing. "I can't imagine how you'll find one moment of peace and quiet, considering the mess you've made of things. You are doomed to be hounded to death by a various sundry of external influences, my dear boy." He ambled over to see what had demanded Dylon's absolute attention. Silence stretched between them for a full minute before Brewster sighed audibly. "How much truth is there to Nora Flannery's claim that you are honor bound to become her husband?"

Dylon flinched at the direct question. "It would have been difficult for me to spoil the reputation of a woman whose virtues had been tainted before I met her," he muttered acrimoniously. "'Tis only Nora's devious way of latching onto a wealthy husband."

"Do you think Edgar is aware of his daughter's ploy and condones it?" Brewster inquired thoughtfully.

Dylon gave his ruffled raven head a negative shake. "Edgar obviously believes the lie. He is blind where his only daughter is concerned and he tends to accept anything she tells him. I could talk until I was blue in the face and I doubt I could ever convince Edgar that his precious daughter is trying to trap me."

"Then perhaps we should . . ."

"Damn that Frenchman, there he goes again," Dylon grumbled bitterly. "He uses every excuse in the book to get his hands on Liberty."

"Will you pay attention!" Brewster snapped. "If you don't, you'll wind up married to Nora and I will not raise a hand to prevent it. In fact, you probably deserve just that!"

"That's what Liberty said," Dylon said, scowling.

"As well she should have," Brewster parried unsympathetically. "If you would have found yourself a wife three years ago when I made the suggestion, you wouldn't be in this awkward predicament."

Finally, Dylon pried his eyes away from the window to focus on his grandfather. "And just what do you suggest? Shall I permit Phillipe to challenge me to a duel and let him win? I suppose I would be free of Edgar Flannery's demands if I were dead."

"Just once I wish you would be serious," Brewster muttered. "Do you love Liberty or don't you?"

"I do love my freedom," Dylon declared with a sly smile.

"That is not the kind of *liberty* I was referring to and you damned well know it," Brewster blustered.

Again, Dylon found his eyes swerving toward the window to monitor the activities of the shapely minx and her overzealous Frenchman. "What difference does it make how I feel?" Dylon countered evasively. "Liberty has her heart set on sailing home."

"Do you want her to go?" Brewster prodded.

"Nay . . . Aye . . ." Dylon threw up his hands in resignation and then braced his arms on the window sill. *You're letting that minx get to you, Lockhart,* Dylon scolded himself.

"How do I know what I want, what with this flock of men pursuing that golden-haired terror and Edgar spouting demands at me?" Dylon grumbled resentfully. "Honest to God, fighting the Cherokees wasn't any more difficult than the mental anguish I'm enduring at the moment. I wish I hadn't resigned my commission in the militia. I was better at giving commands than taking them. I never did like someone telling me what to do and when to do it."

"'Twas always one of your worst faults," Brewster heartily agreed.

"Obstinacy and determination runs in the family," Dylon shot back. His pointed glance indicated who was responsible for passing on those inbred Lockhart traits.

"But you are horribly stubborn, Dylon, and sometimes you can be blindly stupid as well," Brewster went so far as to say.

"Thank you so much for the insults," Dylon purred with sticky sarcasm.

"You're entirely welcome," Brewster said generously. "If you don't realize what a difference Liberty has made in your life then you *are* an idiot."

"Difference, aye," Dylon concurred and then muttered when he spied Phillipe giving Liberty another smothering hug. "But I cannot say the change is for the better. I never feel in complete control when I'm with that hellion. And I swear she purposely goes out of her way, looking for some kind of trouble in which to embroil herself, just for the challenge and sport of it."

Brewster chuckled. "Well, you must admit that life would never be dull and monotonous. If I were you, I would prefer adventure with Liberty to that blubbering brunette who has set her cap for you. But 'tis your life, Dylon, I should not have interfered by springing this engagement party on you. Then Simon and Luther wouldn't have known where to find Liberty. Consider yourself free of any pressure from me." He glanced out the window and smiled slyly. "Somewhere in this world there is a man who is *man* enough to handle a firebrand like Liberty Jordon." He shot Dylon a discreet glance, gauging his reaction to the remark. "I thought perhaps you were man enough, but perhaps I was wrong. I will leave matchmaking to the Lord above and leave you to your own worst enemy—yourself."

"You're a lot of help," Dylon grunted crankily.

Brewster's shoulders lifted in a careless shrug. "I'm no longer trying to be." A devilish grin crinkled his wrinkled features. "For once, I have decided not to take your life quite so seriously. After all, you never do."

While Brewster strutted off, leaving his grandson with plenty of food for thought, Dylon glared out the window, watching the evening shadows drift across the lawn. Despite his attempt to appear unconcerned and nonchalant, Dylon was on a slow burn. Every time he stared at that gallant Frenchman, he swore under his breath. And every time he thought of Liberty walking out of his life forever, he cursed the air blue. Blast it, he'd been content with the way of things until a few weeks ago. He'd pursued his whims, hobbies and his business ventures without complaint. After those tormenting years of battle in the wilderness, Dylon had vowed to enjoy every moment as if it were his last, taking all adversity in stride. He'd wanted to forget those bloody battles and brutal killings and Patricia's heartless betrayal. Those were nightmares of a previous life. Dylon had promised to put the past behind him and never take himself quite so seriously ever again.

Since his return to civilization, Dylon had flitted from one female to another, living every moment to its potential. He had increased the profits on the plantation and had become political-minded. He hadn't disregarded even one responsibility but he had enjoyed his life . . . Or at least he had until these uneasy feelings about Parliament and George Grenville's plans for restricting the colonies got under his skin. To compound those suppressed frustrations of upcoming conflicts with England, Dylon found himself dealing with a spitfire who dragged too many emotions out of him and left him to re-evaluate his goals in life. He had sworn off love after Patricia's betrayal and the last thing he needed was to fall in love again. . . .

Dylon squelched the taunting thought and scowled at the golden-haired pixie in the distance. This turmoil he was experiencing after years of peaceful existence was all Liberty's fault. She had dared to be different. She had upset his well-organized scheme of things, sending his cynical philosophies about women into orbit.

Hell and damnation. There were days when he wished he hadn't rushed to his magnolia tree to revive that reckless imp who had swung out on a thin limb. This was definitely one of those days when Dylon wished he'd never laid eyes on that wild-hearted hellion. He was forced to deal with a half-dozen crises simultaneously, and thoughts of that lively blond firebrand were driving him straight up the wall!

Chapter 22

By the time the duel between Phillipe and Simon rolled around, Dylon was in the worst of all possible moods. At the crack of dawn, Liberty and Cayla had escorted Phillipe to the target range for more practice. It wasn't that Phillipe didn't need extra practice, for he most certainly did. But damnit, it was making Dylon crazy. He stood at the window, watching the handsome Frenchman fawn over both females in a way Dylon had never catered to a woman since Patricia broke his heart. He could feel himself losing his grasp on Liberty, bit by exasperating bit. She didn't have time for him, what with all her last-minute instructions for Phillipe.

As hard as Dylon tried, he couldn't pry himself away from his terrace door. Unreasonable jealousy kept him glued to the spot to ensure Phillipe didn't drool and slobber all over Liberty. Phillipe did, of course, and he had since the moment he'd arrived. Dylon was sorely tempted to march himself down to the target range to break both of the Frenchman's arms and bust his lip!

Heaving a heavy sigh, Dylon reached over to grope for the biscuit which sat on his breakfast tray. Absently, he munched on his meal, tasting nothing, seeing only Phillipe and the two women who were fussing over him.

"Damned French Casanova," Dylon muttered when

he saw Phillipe give Liberty a hug that very nearly squeezed the stuffing out of her. "I swear the man never met a woman he didn't love at first sight and couldn't wait to seduce."

Percy strode over to the table to refill Dylon's tea cup. His eyes followed Dylon's gaze to the target range to observe its three occupants. A worrisome frown knitted his brow as he watched Phillipe unloose Liberty to draw his bow and miss the target by a mile.

"I doubt you will have cause to fret over the Frenchman much longer, sir," Percy speculated. "He cannot seem to hit where he aims, even with all of Liberty's dedicated instruction. Simon Gridley will make short shrift of Phillipe." His somber gaze swung to Dylon who'd worn a permanent frown for the past twelve hours. "Are you going to allow Phillipe to sacrifice his life for Liberty's honor?"

"I've already tried to dissuade that French Don Juan from this madness," Dylon grumbled. "But his flair for the dramatic is exceeded only by his idiocy. Phillipe perceives himself as Liberty's knight in shining armor. He is the epitome of chivalry." Dylon glanced briefly at Percy. "Remind me to have those very words etched on his tombstone when he gets himself killed because of his overactive sense of honor and duty."

"You could take his place," Percy quietly suggested. "You have the skills Phillipe will never possess."

Dylon broke into bitter laughter. "I made that very suggestion last night when I showed Phillipe to his room. He slapped my face with his gloves and declared that I had insulted him and that he still had every intention of dueling me after he'd disposed of Simon."

"He is exceptionally proud and bursting with nobility," Percy agreed. "We shall have that inscription chiseled on his headstone too."

Dylon watched Liberty set the arrows aside and make one last plea for Phillipe to withdraw his ridiculous challenge. Expelling a tormented sigh, he turned away from the window. "Fetch my coat, Percy. Even though that foolish Frenchman has forbidden me to interfere, I intend to watch this duel. No doubt, Simon will ignore the code of ethics. He never fought fairly in all his miserable life."

Relief washed over Percy's features. "I was hoping you would say that, sir. Although Phillipe is sincere to the point of comical, he seems to have a good heart. I should not like to see him killed because of Simon's treachery. I think Phillipe will make an honest attempt to see that Liberty is loved and protected in the years to come."

The comment did not set as well as it should have with Dylon. The thought of that high-spirited sprite living out her life with Phillipe turned Dylon's mood black as pitch. He could visualize Phillipe cuddling Liberty to him, showering her with affection. The picture had absolutely no appeal, even though it would allow Dylon to preserve his precious freedom.

Damnation, he should have married that minx the day she dropped out of his magnolia tree and landed in his garden. Simon's contract would have been worthless. Doctor Flannery's demands would have been futile and Phillipe wouldn't be facing a devious opponent on a dueling field. . . .

Marry Liberty? Good God, what was he thinking? He had religiously avoided matrimony and now he was wishing he'd wed that blond-haired wildcat? He must be mad . . . or hopelessly in love. . . .

"Sir, are you all right?" Percy inquired, watching the color seep from Dylon's bronzed features.

Dylon stabbed his arms through the sleeves of his jacket and then paused to glance at his concerned valet. "Nay, Percy, it has just occurred to me that I may have taken a nasty fall."

Confusion cut deep lines in Percy's plain features.

"I'm not sure I comprehend your meaning, sir."

"'Tis all right," Dylon consoled his valet with a pat on the shoulder. "I'm not exactly certain when I fell. But I'm just beginning to understand why I feel so bruised."

When Dylon ambled out the door, Percy peered bemusedly after him. Casting his confusion aside, Percy fell into step behind his master. Even if he had to straddle a horse, he intended to oversee the duel between Simon and Phillipe.

Percy shuddered to think of the flamboyant Frenchman lying dead on the dueling field, a victim of Simon Gridley's treachery. A man who would wed two women and conveniently dispose of them to acquire wealth, a man who had contracted a marriage to a third heiress, would not bat an eyelash at cheating on the dueling field, that was for sure! Phillipe was too naive to realize his opponent had no intention of playing by the rules. . . .

Percy broke stride when the light of understanding dawned on him halfway between the mansion and the stables. Dylon's cryptic remark had finally soaked in and Percy smiled knowingly. Now he knew what Dylon had meant about taking a fall and feeling so bruised. Dedicated bachelor though Dylon had become, he had finally fallen in love with that amethyst-eyed beauty!

"Justice," Percy snickered as he scurried toward the stable. "True justice. . . ."

Liberty peered beseechingly at Phillipe while they stood at the far end of the bluff that overlooked the river. A stiff breeze swept across the meadow, causing Phillipe's hair to tumble over his eyes.

"'Tis not too late to reconsider," Liberty reminded the Frenchman. Her wary gaze swung to Simon and Luther who lingered beside their carriage at the peak of the bluff. "I still think it wiser to simply pack up and leave posthaste."

"Reconsider? Never!" Phillipe scoffed in that overly dramatic way of his that was accompanied by wide expansive gestures of the arms. "I shall strike that evil vermin from the face of the earth and not one more crude lie will pass his poisonous lips. What I do, Liberty love, I do for you and for all mankind. Simon Gridley does not deserve to live after he scandalized your good name. And for that, the despicable scoundrel will pay the ultimate sacrifice!"

"Phillipe, do be careful," Cayla pleaded, clutching at Phillipe's waving arm. "I couldn't bear to see anything happen to such a fine, honorable man as yourself."

Phillipe dropped into an exaggerated bow and pressed a gallant kiss to Cayla's wrist. "Mademoiselle, your concern touches my heart. And ah, how I wish there were two of me so I could marry both you and my betrothed. I would take you away from here and show you the islands where life is not so . . ."

Phillipe grunted uncomfortably when Liberty gouged him in the ribs and gestured toward his impatient opponent. "Now's not the time for whims of the future." She met Simon's insolent smirk with a murderous glower and then glanced back at the Frenchman. "Now is the time to consider the problem at hand. I think a graceful withdrawal would be most appropriate."

"Never ever!" Phillipe unfolded himself and made a big production of placing both women behind him as if he were their shield of defense. "The villain comes. But never fear, *mes amies*, justice will prevail!"

"Just try to remember everything I taught you," Liberty advised as Phillipe whizzed off to confer with Luther and Simon. "And don't expect a fair fight. Simon doesn't know the meaning of the word."

Phillipe marched toward midmeadow and proudly drew himself up in front of Simon. "This field of honor will tell the tale, monsieur," he proclaimed as he clutched the bow and quiver of arrows to his chest. "I regret that I must kill you. But you, monsieur, have asked for it."

Simon scoffed at the ostentatious Frenchman. "I have no use for all your pageantry, Frenchy. Shall we get on with this? I have a wedding to attend after I finish with you."

When Liberty impulsively stepped forward to spout a few well-deserved insults at Luther and Simon, Phillipe held up his hand to halt her. "*S'il vous plaît*, Mademoiselle Styles, take Liberty to a safe place to await the outcome of this duel. It is for life and Liberty that I face this demon and send him back to hell from whence he came."

Simon growled at his challenger. "Enough talk. Let's be done with this. Since you did not choose a second to stand with you, Liberty's uncle will serve as my second and marshal of this duel." He glanced briefly at his companion. "Luther, explain the rules to my opponent."

For what possible purpose? Liberty asked herself resentfully. Simon had no intention of abiding by them! The sneaky lout! And damn Phillipe for being so blasted noble and honorable. He was going to get himself killed, sure as hell!

Luther stepped between the two men who were staring each other down. "As is the custom, you will stand back to back. After you walk twenty paces, you will turn and draw down on your bow. When I drop my handkerchief, you will aim and release."

While Phillipe and Simon pivoted to stand back to back, Liberty stared apprehensively at both men. Confound it, she had pleaded with Phillipe to let her stand as his second, but the chivalrous Frenchman would not hear of it. Phillipe was bound and determined to confront Simon alone. He was convinced that since he was in the right he would win, no matter what the odds. Phillipe, as always, was far too idealistic for his own good.

Liberty could hear her heart hammering as Luther

counted off the twenty paces. Her gaze bounced back and forth between both men, nervously awaiting the outcome of a duel she would have preferred to fight herself. Phillipe had yet to master the art of archery. He was still slow and methodic with his bow. Liberty wasn't sure how skillful Simon was, but chances were he could wield a bow with some degree of proficiency or he wouldn't have chosen that particular weapon.

"Fourteen, fifteen, sixteen," Luther counted while Liberty waited with bated breath. . . .

Liberty's violet eyes popped from their sockets when Simon pivoted three steps before he was supposed to. Her cry of alarm was drowned out by Dylon's booming voice. Dylon bounded out of the bushes like a mountain goat to charge at Simon.

Suddenly everything was happening at once and Liberty felt as if she were moving in slow motion. She lunged toward Simon, hoping to deflect his shot before he buried the arrow in Phillipe's back. Cayla was hot on her heels, screaming at the Frenchman to dive to the ground.

With a malicious curse, Simon swung about. His attention riveted on Dylon. Simon was furious that his archenemy had been spying on him.

The choked fingers of panic clamped around Liberty's throat when she realized Simon intended to shoot Dylon. She couldn't move quickly enough to stop him. As the arrow hissed through the balmy air, Liberty wheeled about. Her heart flip-flopped in her chest when the projectile shot toward Dylon's heart. If not for the gust of wind, Liberty swore Dylon would have died where he stood. But the arrow was blown off target by the breeze. Dylon dived sideways when he saw the arrow sailing toward him. But quick and agile as Dylon was, he wasn't quite swift enough to miss the missile entirely. The arrow stabbed him in the thigh and caused him to erupt in a hiss of pain.

Oblivious to the fact that Cayla had darted toward Phillipe who was still fumbling to draw his bow, Liberty dashed toward Dylon who had collapsed on the grass. All sorts of curses filled the air as bodies scattered for advantageous positions.

Liberty pulled up short when she heard the blast of Luther's pistol. Luther, fearing Phillipe still intended to draw on Simon, had shot at the Frenchman to keep him pinned to the ground where Cayla was sobbing hysterically at his side.

Before Liberty could reach Dylon, Simon leaped on her. Liberty choked on her breath when Simon flung his bow aside to fish out the flintlock he had stashed in his pocket. The weapon rammed into Liberty's throat, discouraging her from making an escape attempt.

While Percy scuttled from his hiding place to reach Dylon, Simon dragged Liberty toward his carriage. "No one will deny me my rights to my intended bride!" Simon roared triumphantly.

Despite Dylon's attempt to gain his feet and give chase, Percy plunked down on top of him. "If you take off running, you might bleed to death," Percy snapped.

"Damnit, get off me!" Dylon growled at his well-meaning valet.

"That arrow has to come out before infection sets in," Percy persisted, refusing to remove himself until Dylon realized the gravity of his condition. "You shouldn't move your leg until I fetch a surgeon."

All the while that Dylon was struggling to untangle himself from his valet, Simon was dragging Liberty toward the awaiting carriage. When Phillipe scrambled to his feet to give chase, Simon fired over his head and then shoved Liberty into the coach.

After the pistol had been discharged, Liberty clawed at Simon, determined to make her escape. She was going nowhere with this treacherous bastard!

A ferocious growl erupted from Simon's lips when

Liberty peeled the hide off his face. With a mutinous snarl, he flipped his pistol in his hand and clubbed her over the head the instant before she launched herself from his arms.

A dull groan tumbled from Liberty's throat as pain crashed through her skull. Her legs buckled beneath her. Cayla's distant scream and Dylon's furious bellow faded into silence. . . .

"Help me get her back in the coach," Simon snapped at Luther. He flung Dylon a quick glance before he wrestled Liberty's limp body onto the seat. With his intended bride sprawled beside him, Simon directed Luther to sit down across from him. A gloating smile slid across his lips as he motioned for the driver to zoom away. At last he had satisfied his thirst of revenge against Dylon and had succeeded in retrieving Liberty from his enemy's clutches!

Wearing that infuriating grin of satisfaction, Simon listened to Dylon spout every curse word in his vocabulary as the carriage whizzed down the path. Simon settled himself comfortably on the seat and gloated. He had what he wanted and very soon, Liberty would be his wife. There was nothing Dylon Lockhart or that flamboyant Frenchman could do to stop him!

A frustrated growl burst from Dylon's lips as he struggled to unseat his valet. But Percy was as determined to hold Dylon down as Dylon was determined to get up. The painful leg wound wasn't helping matters one whit. The arrow had lodged in the meaty flesh of Dylon's thigh, soaking his breeches with blood. Every movement was pure and simple agony.

While Dylon wrestled with Percy, Phillipe's blond head appeared above the floundering twosome. "Never fear, I shall save Liberty from that vile demon!"

Before Dylon could declare that Phillipe couldn't fight

his way out of a gunny sack, much less battle Simon Gridley, the Frenchman dashed toward the horses. Of course, by the time Phillipe gallantly assisted Cayla into her saddle, the carriage had sped down the hill and disappeared on the tree-choked path that ran parallel to the river.

"Get the hell off me!" Dylon roared like a wounded lion.

Percy flagrantly disregarded the loud command.

While Phillipe and Cayla thundered down the slope, another coach, carrying Brewster and Griffin, rolled to a halt. The instant Griffin spied the arrow protruding from Dylon's thigh, he bounded from the coach and knelt beside his brother. Although Dylon cursed a blue streak and demanded to give chase, Percy, Brewster and Griffin clamped hold of him and laid him on the floor of the carriage.

"Doctor Flannery will have you patched up in no time," Brewster assured his scowling grandson.

"Patch me up?" Dylon burst into sardonic laughter. "More than likely he'll amputate my leg because I refused to marry his daughter." Again Dylon tried to upright himself, but three pair of hands mashed him into the floor. "Griff, for God's sake, if you won't let me chase down Liberty at least go after her!"

Griff felt absolutely terrible about all the wicked thoughts he'd enviously directed toward his brother. He had wished he were an only child so he could have Liberty all to himself. But God, that didn't mean he wanted his brother dead! Griffin repented, there and then. He was thoroughly ashamed of himself for wishing ill of his brother.

"I thought Phillipe and Cayla were attending to Liberty's rescue," Griff noted. "I want to ensure you're all right before I chase down Simon."

"Phillipe will only get himself lost in the swamp," Dylon predicted gloomily. "He has more confidence than common sense. Go help him! He'll do Liberty no good whatsoever if he doesn't know where the hell he's going!"

With a nod of compliance, Griffin halted the coach and raced back to the bushes to fetch Dylon's horse. While the Lockhart carriage sailed back to the plantation, Griffin thundered off in the direction Phillipe and Cayla had taken.

A frustrated hiss tripped from Dylon's lips as he clutched his throbbing leg. He detested this feeling of helplessness. He was worried sick about Liberty. She was too daring for her own good and she very nearly got herself shot trying to escape Simon and Luther. Dylon had suffered nine kinds of hell when he saw that she-cat claw at Simon. And Dylon would have charged toward Simon, wounded leg and all, if Percy hadn't sprawled on top of him and held him down. Damn that well-meaning Percival T. Pearson!

Even now Dylon was itching to race off in hot pursuit. But Brewster and Percy would have none of that. Although Dylon was begrudgingly appreciative of their concern for his condition, he was scared as hell about Liberty. He could think of nothing worse than for her to be held captive by those two scoundrels. They had proved how ruthless they could be to ensure they got what they wanted. Lying on the floor of a speeding coach while Liberty was being whisked off to only God knew where was killing Dylon, bit by excruciating bit. . . .

"'Twas a most heroic and honorable deed you performed, sir," Percy complimented his wounded master. "You saved Phillipe from certain death."

"But who will save Liberty?" Dylon growled disgustedly.

"She has obviously escaped her uncle and Simon before," Brewster pointed out. "Do not sell the lady short. Liberty appears to be a very resourceful young woman."

"Aye," Dylon mumbled reluctantly. "But even she is no match for those two bastards. They won't be foolish enough to take her for granted after she escaped them the first time. On that you can depend."

Brewster clamped his mouth shut and willed the carriage to sprout wings and fly back to the plantation. He had tried to console his wounded grandson but he, too, was worried sick about Liberty's welfare. Yet, he couldn't send Dylon off with an arrow sticking out his thigh. Dylon would be of no use to Liberty if he bled to death. Griffin would come to Liberty's defense, Brewster assured himself. And in the meantime, Dylon was going to get patched up, whether he had the patience to wait that long or not!

Chapter 23

The murmur of voices gradually filtered into Liberty's dazed brain. When she felt the jostle of the coach bumping over the washboarded road, she forced herself to remain perfectly still. She had to think! She had to plan her escape! All she had to her advantage was the element of surprise.

Liberty lay there, pretending to be unconscious. Silently, she conjured up and discarded several inspirations. When a workable solution hatched in her mind, she awaited the right moment to spring into action.

When the coach slowed its furious pace to navigate the sharp bend in the road, Liberty burst to life. Although her head throbbed in rhythm with her thudding heart, she bolted toward the door latch and hurled herself out of the carriage before Simon and Luther could react.

Clutching the hem of her skirt, Liberty zigzagged through the grove of trees, wading calf-deep in the murky bog. Behind her she heard Simon's outraged growls and Luther's high-pitched shrieks. Liberty never looked back. She ran for her life.

"Damn that vixen," Simon snarled as he slopped through the murk and reeds. His narrowed gaze focused on the infuriating female who appeared and disappeared in the sun-dappled shadows of the trees and underbrush.

Luther scuttled along behind Simon, cursing his

annoying association with his pesky niece. That female had led him through a never-ending nightmare. Each time Luther thought Liberty was sufficiently trapped she found some ingenious method of escape. This was the second time she had leaped from the coach to elude them, but it would be the last! This time that hellion would not escape, Luther promised himself.

A frustrated hiss floated from Liberty's lips when her skirt became entangled with the gnarled roots of a tree. Frantically, she ripped the fabric loose, but she had been detained just long enough for Simon to catch up with her.

Wheeling about, Liberty doubled her fist and buried it in Simon's malicious smile. With a splat, Simon *kerplunked* in the swamp, swearing in unprintable expletives. When Liberty sloshed away, Simon coiled and sprang at her.

As if an anchor had been chained to her legs, Liberty felt the weight of Simon's body forcing her into the mucky water. Before she could worm free, Luther waded over to hook his arm around her waist. Futilely, Liberty attempted to wriggle free. She found herself chained in Simon's arms and dragged back to solid ground. When she tried to claw at him, Luther shackled her hands.

"Troublesome bitch," Luther growled. His eyes blazed fire and brimstone. "This is the very last time you'll escape us."

When Simon shoved her into the carriage, Luther scurried around to the front of the coach to order the driver to retrieve ropes—anything to ensure Liberty's captivity. Luther returned with heavy leather straps and bound her wrists and ankles.

Although Liberty continued to fight with every ounce of strength she could muster, she found herself in a prone position on the seat. Her arms were latched to one door and her legs were bound to the other.

The fact that Simon sat across from her, grinning

triumphantly, infuriated Liberty to no end. Never in all her twenty years had she been struck by such a fierce compelling urge to kill. She despised Simon and Luther so much that the very sight of them made her skin crawl with revulsion.

"No matter what you do, I'll never consent to become your wife," Liberty spluttered furiously.

"There are ways, little witch, to ensure that you do exactly as I wish you to do," Simon insisted with a diabolical sneer.

Liberty stared warily at Simon when he reached into his pocket and smiled a treacherous smile.

"I mixed up a potion for you." He held the vial up for Liberty's inspection. "After a dose of whiskey and gin, mixed with substantial quantities of laudanum, you will be too dazed to resist. You and I will be married, my dear Liberty. There is no question about that."

When Simon leaned forward to force the drugging potion down her throat, Liberty clamped her mouth shut. Even when Luther gouged her in the ribs, Liberty refused to open her lips to emit a painful whimper. But when Simon snarled impatiently and clenched his fist in her hair, yanking her head back to a vulnerable angle, her mouth involuntarily flew open to gasp in pain. And in that tortuous second, Liberty felt the potion filling her mouth. Before she could spit it in Simon's face, he clamped his hand over her nose and mouth, forcing her to swallow.

The whiskey and gin accelerated the time required for the laudanum to take effect. Although Liberty fought to keep her wits about her, she could feel her body slumping and her thoughts drifting aimlessly. The second time Simon forced her to drink the sleeping potion, her body refused to resist him.

The bouncing motion of the speeding carriage began to feel more like the gentle sway of a hammock. Liberty battled to keep her eyes from slamming shut on the blurred images that floated over her, but nothing helped.

She slid into the hazy gray abyss that lured her into thinking she didn't have a care in the world, when, in fact, things could hardly have been worse than they truly were!

"You expect me to tend his wound after what he did to my poor daughter?" Edgar Flannery scoffed as he stared at the protruding arrow and seeping wound on Dylon's left thigh.

Brewster stamped over beside the bed on which Dylon lay and glowered at the resentful physician. "If you do not tend my grandson you will never practice medicine again in these colonies," Brewster threatened. "On that, Doctor Flannery, *you* can depend! You took a noble oath to treat the sick, whether you liked them or not!"

While Edgar stood there debating whether Brewster Lockhart had the power to do as he promised, Dylon clutched the arrow to remove it himself. Quick as a wink, Edgar's hand folded over Dylon's.

"Oh, for heaven sake, I'll do it, but I want your word as a gentleman that you will marry my daughter."

"There will be a wedding," Brewster insisted before Dylon could refuse the bargain. "I'll make the arrangements myself. Just remove the arrow posthaste!"

When Edgar pivoted to fetch the laudanum to numb the pain, Dylon scowled impatiently. "Take it out and be quick about it. I have other errands to attend and I can't see to them if I'm groggy."

Edgar gaped at his patient. "This is going to hurt, no matter how gentle I try to be. And you will have to lie abed until the wound seals itself."

Dylon gestured for the surgeon to clutch the arrow while he clasped his hands around his thigh. "I took a Cherokee arrow in the shoulder during battle and there was no one there to make a fuss about lying abed, not with a score of whooping warriors itching to chop me to bits with tomahawks. Now get to it, Edgar!" he demanded gruffly.

Dylon sucked in his breath when the lodged arrow was extracted from his thigh. True, it hurt like hell and burned like fire, but Dylon had definitely endured worse during the Cherokee Wars. His concern for Liberty overshadowed the stinging pain. All he wanted was to be bandaged up so he could track down the two bastards who had stolen Liberty away from him.

Dylon fought down the lightheaded sensations that swirled around him when Edgar doused the wound with brandy to counter infection. Impatiently, he waited for the physician to pack salve on the wound and wrap the leg. When Edgar completed his ministrations, Dylon tried to swing off the bed. Unfortunately, Percy, Brewster and Edgar shoved him down before he could get up.

"At least wait a few hours before you go bounding off to attend this mysterious errand of yours," Edgar insisted. "And while you are recuperating, I'll inform Nora of her upcoming wedding." He stared meaningfully at Dylon. "And don't think you can worm out of our bargain. We made an agreement and I expect you to uphold your end of it."

"I already assured you that Dylon would speak the vows," Brewster muttered. "I give you my word that my grandson will wed."

"And he damned well better," Edgar grumbled before spinning toward the door.

When the surgeon took his leave, Dylon glared at his grandfather. "*Et tu, Brewster?*"

"What did you expect me to do?" Brewster snapped defensively. "Stand here and let you lose your leg because you were too stubborn to pacify Flannery? No matter what you think, marriage is still better than dying of gangrene!"

While Dylon was rolling his eyes heavenward, begging

for divine patience and muttering at his predicament, Griffin burst into the room looking like a slimy creature that had just emerged from the swamps. Behind him, leaving puddles on the carpet, stood Phillipe who held Cayla protectively in his arms. All three of the late arrivals were covered with grime and moss and were soaked to the bone.

Dylon scowled at the obvious implications of what had happened. No doubt Phillipe had taken a wrong turn. Dylon had expected as much.

"Phillipe and Cayla got lost," Griffin explained hurriedly. "By the time I rescued them from the bog, Cayla had suffered a bite from only the Lord knows what. Where's Doctor Flannery? Cayla needs immediate attention."

While Percy scurried down the hall to fetch Edgar, Griffin plunked down on the edge of the bed and heaved a frustrated sigh. "I never did catch sight of the carriage. I could hear Liberty screeching somewhere in the distance, but I already had one disaster on my hands," he elaborated. "I couldn't trust Phillipe to find his way back to the plantation without getting lost again. And Cayla was so nauseated from whatever bit her that she was on the verge of fainting."

Griffin inhaled a deep breath and slowly expelled it. "And Phillipe was hell-bent on saving Cayla because he holds himself personally responsible for her plight. And you know how seriously Phillipe takes his responsibilities," he finished with a snort.

Brewster unfolded himself from his chair and sighed heavily. "I had better check on Cayla and reassure Doctor Flannery. Griff, you see to it that your brother stays in bed while I'm gone. Anxious as he is to chase Liberty down, I can't trust him to stay put."

"I'll ensure that he doesn't get out of bed," Griff promised, staring after his grandfather.

When Griffin swiveled his head back around to speak to the imprisoned patient, an unexpected fist connected with his jaw. Like a wilted flower, Griffin collapsed on the bed in a limp heap.

Grimacing, Dylon inched off the bed and carefully pulled on a clean pair of breeches. Even though his grandfather and brother were concerned about his condition, Dylon had more important things to do besides nurse his wound. Injury wasn't going to slow him down more than a passel of fleas on a dog. He was going after Liberty and that was that! Dylon didn't trust Simon and Luther for even a second. There was no telling what they were planning. They had utilized the duel as an attempt to dispose of Phillipe and kidnap Liberty. Knowing those two conniving scoundrels (and Dylon knew Simon a helluva lot better than he would have liked to, believe you him!) they wouldn't delay one moment in putting their plans into motion.

He cringed internally at the thought of his grandfather declaring that Dylon would marry Nora Flannery. But he shuddered repulsively at the prospect of Liberty wed to Simon Gridley. He didn't expect Liberty to last a week in wedlock. Simon would force his intentions on that hellion and she would claw out his eyes. When Simon lost his temper (and he definitely had one) he would dispose of that firebrand. Dylon had to find Liberty before Simon coerced her into marriage or her life would be a nightmare that would end in catastrophe!

Darkness blanketed the countryside by the time Dylon reached Simon's upriver plantation. As he anticipated, henchmen guarded the door like dragons. After Dylon had tethered his horse in the brush, he limped toward the elaborate plantation home that Simon had inherited after the death of his first wife.

Quietly, Dylon reached down to retrieve the tree branch he had stepped on. In his haste to escape, via the magnolia tree, he had arrived at Simon's home without a weapon of defense.

Like a skipping shadow, Dylon circled toward the side of the house. When he raked the tree limb against the pillar, Figgins and Gilbert inched across the porch to investigate the sound. Dylon launched himself at both men as they rounded the corner of the veranda. Like a striking snake, he clubbed Figgins over the head with the branch. With a pained grunt, Figgins staggered backward, lost his balance and flipped over the railing into the shrubs. When Gilbert charged at him, Dylon kicked him in the groin. As the surly brute doubled over, Dylon clamped both hands on the tree limb and uplifted it. The makeshift weapon collided with Gilbert's chin. As Gilbert's head snapped back, Dylon doubled a fist and landed a blow that packed enough wallop to fell a grizzly bear. After Gilbert slammed against the wall and dropped to the porch, Dylon hobbled toward the door.

Although Dylon had made quick work of the burly guards who had been posted on the veranda, he found himself facing Simon's cocked pistol the instant he burst into the foyer. Simon sat on the second step of the spiral staircase, grinning maliciously at the intruder. To his left, also holding a loaded flintlock, stood Luther.

"It sounded as if you battled your way past my henchmen," Simon speculated, flinging Dylon another goading smile. "'Tis just like in days gone by, Lockhart. But this time you will receive no medals for valor as you did when I was dishonorably dismissed from my commission. In this instance, *I* have bested *you.*" He leaned negligently against the step to regard his wounded competitor with scornful mockery. "'Tis a pity that you arrived too late to witness my wedding to Liberty."

The words dropped like stones in the silence. The very thought of Liberty married to Simon hurt worse than a physical blow. Instant rage seeped through Dylon's veins. Oh, how he wished the Lord would call down His wrath on His most obvious sinner!

When Dylon took an impulsive step forward, his fingers curling in his eagerness to choke the life out of his archenemy, Simon threateningly raised the pistol. Holding Dylon at gunpoint, Simon fished into his vest pocket to extract the marriage bonds for Dylon's inspection.

"'Twas all perfectly legal, of course," Simon taunted mercilessly. "The clergyman officiated the ceremony and Luther gave the bride away. She is upstairs, anxiously waiting for me to come to her to consummate our vows."

The past few years, Dylon had managed to take all of life's pitfalls without breaking stride. But he did have a pressure point. Losing Liberty to this shrewd, ruthless bastard put his temper on a rolling boil. Dylon had refused to recognize his love for Liberty until it was too late. While he stubbornly clung to his desire to remain footloose and fancy-free, Fate had conspired against him. Dylon had lost Liberty before he fully understood how deeply he loved her. She had come along to interrupt his life and make mincemeat of his cynical theories about women, marriage and love. Of all the females he'd courted for his careless amusement, Liberty was the only one who mattered to him. Now she was legally tied to a man Dylon despised, one who wanted her only because of his animal lust and his insatiable greed for power and wealth.

"You miserable son of a bitch," Dylon growled through gritted teeth. "I'm not leaving until I see that Liberty is safe from harm."

"Surely you do not expect me to invite guests into my home on my wedding night," Simon scoffed sarcastically. "My bride and I will be enjoying all the intimacies which you have only dreamed about." Simon's tone changed to a harsh snarl. "You can't imagine the pleasure I derive from taking something you want away from you, Lockhart. For years I've watched you flit about with all your wealth, courting every female who caught your eye. I was left to struggle and overcome the black eye you gave me when you saw to it that I was discharged from my position. You had prosperity handed to you on a silver platter while I scratched and clawed to build an empire. But now I have the chance to pay you back for all the untold injuries. With Liberty's vast holdings in the Indies and her property in the colony I will be wealthier than the Lockharts ever thought about being."

Simon glared menacingly at Dylon. "And now, 'tis time for you to take your leave." He glanced over his shoulder and snapped his fingers. A huge woolly faced heathen appeared at the head of the staircase. "Donnely, come escort my guest outside."

On cue, the oversized brute thumped down the steps. Dylon didn't care if this giant of a man beat him blind. He itched to wipe that gloating smirk off Simon's lips. With a flick of his wrist, Dylon sent the tree limb sailing across the room to collide with Simon's pistol. When the weapon misfired, Dylon lunged at his foe. Before Simon or Luther could react, Dylon's beefy fist buried itself in Simon's midsection. Then he wheeled to give Luther the punch in the jaw he so richly deserved. But before Dylon could relieve his pent-up frustration on its true source, Donnely pounced on him and bellowed for Figgins and Gilbert to provide reinforcements.

To Dylon's dismay, the pelting blows he had delivered to the other two henchmen had only incapacitated them momentarily. Figgins and Gilbert stumbled into the room to shackle his wrists. While they held Dylon in place, Donnely reared back a muscled arm and leveled a blow that knocked the air out of Dylon's lungs. Employing Figgins and Gilbert as braces to support himself, Dylon lifted his good leg and kicked Donnely to splinters. The blows only infuriated the fire-breathing Goliath, but Dylon was granted enough time to shake off the other two henchmen.

Fists flew in all directions while Dylon battled the overwhelming odds on a leg that twice threatened to buckle beneath him. Although he had landed several punishing blows, Gilbert and Figgins clutched at him so

Donnely could turn his opponent into a human punching bag.

Blow after devastating blow jarred bone and flesh. Dylon struggled against the numbing pain that engulfed him. Simon had surrounded himself with a three-man army which tipped the odds heavily in his favor. But Dylon refused to accept defeat, even as the world slid out from under him. When Dylon slumped backward, Donnely raised an arm to deliver the last formidable blow. Simon caught his arm, restraining him.

After wiping the trickle of blood from his lips, Simon snatched up his discarded weapon. With a vicious sneer, he pistol-whipped Dylon until he had drawn blood. When Dylon collapsed, Simon chuckled in fiendish pleasure.

"Take his carcass outside and dump it in the swamp," he ordered his henchmen. "If he drowns, 'tis all the better. And if he does survive, he won't be foolish enough to come around pestering us again."

While the men carried Dylon away and loaded him in the bed of a wagon, Simon inspected his bruised jaw and bleeding lip. "I'll make that saucy bitch pay for all the trouble she's caused me," he vowed spitefully. "She and her knights in shining armor! And Dylon Lockhart can rot in hell for all I care. Nothing pleases me more than taking the woman he wanted for his bride. My satisfaction comes in knowing his torment. For once, he can lust after what I possess!"

"I think perhaps a drink is in order," Luther mumbled out the side of his mouth Dylon hadn't punched. "'Tis time to celebrate our success."

Simon stared speculatively at the steps, eager to saunter into Liberty's room to enjoy the ultimate victory over her and Dylon Lockhart. But perhaps he did need a few drinks to soothe his temper. After all, what was the rush? It was for certain that his new bride wasn't going anywhere. She was still battling the aftereffects of the drugging potion he'd given her before he dragged her to the wedding ceremony. Liberty would be too sluggish to resist his amorous advances, but he wanted to ensure she was awake enough to remember he had taken his pleasure with her.

"Perhaps we do need a drink," Simon responded belatedly.

"I'll fetch the decanter of brandy while you retrieve a cloth to wipe your face," Luther volunteered.

Nodding agreeably, Simon ambled off to make himself presentable. When he returned to the parlor, Luther thrust a glass into his hand.

"To wealth and success," Luther toasted. "All my gambling debts to you have been repaid. As we agreed, I shall retain control of Triple Oak and you will have charge of Liberty's business interests in the Indies."

Simon took a long sip of brandy and slouched in his chair. His gaze narrowed on his associate. "I hope you don't expect any other benefits from our agreement. For if you do, you will meet with the same punishment my henchmen doled out to Lockhart," he warned.

Luther stared at the far wall. "Why should I complain? I now have complete control of the plantation and you are left to deal with that feisty niece of mine. As I see it, I have the better end of this bargain."

Simon smiled like a Cheshire cat. "Not quite, Luther. I have the satisfaction of pleasuring myself with that sassy firebrand whenever it meets my whim. And if Liberty learns her place and I don't tire of that curvaceous body of hers, I might even allow her to live. She is, after all, incredibly more desirable than my first two wives."

"Shall we drink to your honeymoon?" Luther scooped up Simon's empty glass and refilled it. "But I suggest you keep that drugging potion handy. It may be wise to force it down her throat until she realizes 'tis useless to fight you."

Simon tapped the vial that was tucked in his pocket. "An excellent suggestion." He chuckled before downing his brandy in one swallow. Setting his glass aside, he rose to his feet and wobbled unsteadily.

"Dylon's blow and the brandy had a stronger effect than I thought," he mumbled sluggishly.

"I'm sure you won't be the least bit impaired when you approach your bride," Luther consoled him. "Enjoy your wedding night. I'll make certain you aren't disturbed."

Nodding mutely, Simon weaved into the vestibule. His lusty thoughts centered on the vision of blond hair, violet eyes and a voluptuous body that would soon be intimately pinned beneath his. By sunrise, Liberty would have succumbed to him as many times as he desired.

That arousing thought cut through the haze that had begun to cloud Simon's brain, putting a devilish smile on his lips. Eagerly, he propelled himself toward Liberty's room. His extensive and exhausting search to retrieve that spitfire had been worth the wait. He was now in control of Liberty's vast inheritance and the master of her delicious body.

Mulling over that lusty thought, Simon staggered down the hall to let himself into Liberty's room. . . .

Chapter 24

After Donnely, Figgins and Gilbert halted the wagon, they hauled the limp carcass toward the swamp. With a heave-ho, the three men hurled Dylon into the bog.

The splash of water and cold darkness served to jolt Dylon to his senses. With an agonized groan Dylon floated back to the surface. He clawed at the slimy reeds and moss that clung to him, leaving him feeling like a rotting mummy.

Lord, he hurt in places he didn't even know he had! The pain in his leg was now compounded by a throb in his belly and a pulsating sting caused by the repetitive blows to his face. Dylon's preservation instincts were hard at work and raw fury pounded through his bloodstream. His ordeal with Simon and his backwoods ruffians was starkly reminiscent of those days of hell he had endured during the war on the outposts of civilization.

Liberty . . . Dylon's groggy brain shifted gears when Simon's taunting words rang in his ears. Frantic, Dylon thrashed through the swamp and crawled toward solid ground. He had not one minute to spare! Liberty faced impending doom. The repulsive thought of Simon forcing himself on Liberty while she was incapable of defending herself turned him wrongside out. He had to return to Simon's plantation to retrieve Liberty. He *had* to . . .

The clomp of hooves in the distance pierced Dylon's tormented thoughts. On a leg that had become stiff and even more tender, Dylon gritted his teeth and hacked his way through the dense tangle of vines and brush to reach the road.

A startled squawk erupted from Phillipe's lips when an unidentified form plunged through the thick foliage to jerk him out of the saddle. Instinctively, Griffin clutched at his pistol to protect Phillipe from attack. His hand stalled in midair when the silvery moonlight sprayed over the puffy face and bedraggled body of the man who had sent Phillipe sprawling facedown on the ground.

"Dylon? Good Lord, is that you?" Griffin chirped as he gaped at what was left of his brother. "What the hell happened?"

Dylon had no time for lengthy explanation. Liberty was in grave danger of being molested and murdered by her new husband—merciless bastard that he was. Gouging the steed, Dylon shot off like a discharging cannonball, leaving Griffin to peer bemusedly after him while Phillipe scraped himself off the ground.

"What the devil is going on here?" Phillipe crowed. "I have come to lend assistance and I am treated like a criminal. I shall have to call that scoundrel out to duel if he doesn't cease—"

"Do shut up and climb on behind me," Griffin demanded impatiently. He extended his hand to assist Phillipe onto the horse. "Obviously Dylon ran headlong into trouble and had no time to spare."

"Well, I should think he could at least have had the courtesy to—"

A shocked yelp erupted from Phillipe's lips when Griffin jabbed the steed in the flanks, sending him clattering down the path at full gallop. Phillipe had no time to complete his indignant remark. He had to cling to Griffin's shoulders for dear life. Griffin had every intention of chasing his brother down to lend assistance and there was little time for Phillipe's long-winded soliloquies on honor, nobility, chivalry and propriety!

Hot on Dylon's heels, the twosome galloped down the path that led to Simon's plantation, unaware of the reception which awaited them. It was a shame Dylon hadn't spared the time to warn his brother about Donnely, Figgins and Gilbert. Unfortunately, Phillipe and Griffin were about to make their acquaintance without introduction. . . .

As if she had been awakened after a couple of centuries had passed, Liberty sluggishly responded to the voice that called to her from her trancelike dream. Although her companion tried to shake her awake, Liberty felt as if she were drifting on the perimeters of a fuzzy world that was clogged with cobwebs. Bleary-eyed, she peered up at the hazy image that floated above her. A relieved smile trickled across her lips as she reached up with a limp hand to limn the face of the man who had materialized from her whimsical dream.

"Dylon . . ." she sighed contentedly.

A murderous growl exploded from Simon's lips. He was incensed to hear his bride breathe Lockhart's name. He backhanded Liberty to bring her to her senses.

"Nay, little bitch. 'Tis I, your husband, and you will perform for me. Never for him!" Simon snarled as he braced his arms on either side of her shoulders.

The ominous tone of Simon's voice and his menacing words brought Liberty to another level of consciousness. When she felt Simon's hands clumsily groping at the bodice of her gown, she struggled in earnest. The rending of cloth struck fear, the likes Liberty had never known. Groggy though she was, and unable to make out Simon's puckered features, she struck at the blurred shadow and clutching hands.

When Liberty's flailing arm collided with Simon's

tender jaw, he sneered several colorful curses and shook his head to clear his own dazed senses. The drinks he'd consumed before ascending the stairs had left him dizzy and slightly nauseated. But he was determined to share this vixen's bed, to prove his supremacy over her, once and for all.

An outraged screech spewed from Liberty's lips when she felt Simon's knee wedging itself between her legs. Like a cornered cat, Liberty bit and clawed to prevent being violated by this brutish man who had roughly assaulted her.

Again Dylon's name filled the air, this time in a frantic plea for help, no matter how useless it was. Again, Simon swore vehemently. Clutching Liberty's hair, Simon forced back her head and glowered into her waxen features.

"Damn you, woman." His face was set in a hideous sneer that made Satan look like a saint. "I want it to be my face you see when I take possession of this luscious body of yours, not that arrogant bastard's. Mine, damn you, mine!" he snarled savagely.

Although Liberty's vision left her seeing blurred doubles of everything, her brain had begun to function normally. And even though her body was still sluggish from the effects of the drugging potion, she writhed and bucked to unseat Simon. When she gouged him in the private part of his anatomy he let out a howl that could have raised the dead.

While Simon sucked air and gulped down the wave of nausea, Liberty dug the heels of her hands into his heaving chest and sent him rolling across the floor.

Cursing the hindering garments of the gown, Liberty scrambled off the bed and blindly groped across the fuzzy room to locate the door. The room was unfamiliar to her and the gray haze severely impaired her vision. Furniture kept popping up in places she least expected them as she made her frantic escape.

"Come back here, bitch!" Simon bellowed, swallowing

down his churning stomach.

A pained hiss tripped from Liberty's lips when she stumbled against another chair that blocked her path. Flinging the object aside, Liberty felt her way along the wall until she grasped the door latch. The cool air that filled her nostrils indicated she had escaped via the terrace rather than through the hall. Behind her she heard Simon cursing the chair that had tripped him up.

Half blinded and choked with panic, Liberty felt her way along the terrace. Just as she swung her leg over the railing, Simon charged forward to jerk her into his arms. His mouth came down on hers in a bruising kiss. His fingers dug into her ribs, holding her intimately against him. Liberty could taste the whiskey on his breath, feel his lean body mashing suggestively into hers. Repulsion shot through her when Simon's slobbery kisses tracked along her neck to the swells of her breasts.

Wildly, Liberty doubled her fist and pummeled the man who held her chained in his arms. His snarls mingled with her outraged shrieks as they battled each other beside the wrought-iron terrace railing.

Dylon died a thousand agonizing deaths as he rushed toward the back staircase that led to the second-story balcony. He could see the two shadowed forms above him, hear Liberty's screeching protests and Simon's mutinous growls. Despite his injured leg and bruised ribs, Dylon raced up the steps two at a time. His heart pounded ninety miles a minute as he watched the shadowed silhouettes swaying precariously toward the railing. Liberty lacked her usual agility and coordination, as did Simon, who staggered more than he stood.

Favoring his wounded leg, Dylon pulled himself up the last step and hobbled across the terrace. His heart stalled in his chest when Simon teetered unsteadily, causing Liberty to arch backward over the railing. Her feet flew off the tiled balcony, leaving her balancing on the railing on her back. And then suddenly she was flying fists and feet, pelting Simon in every fashion imaginable.

Another furious roar filled the night air as Simon doubled over the railing to clamp his hands around Liberty's throat. But for some reason, which Dylon was unable to determine in the darkness, Simon lost his balance. When he floundered on top of Liberty, she squirmed and twisted to prevent being pushed to her death.

By the time Dylon crossed the terrace to pry the warring combatants apart, Liberty had shoved at Simon with every ounce of strength she could muster. As she twisted in midair Simon completely lost his balance. They were like two drowning victims clawing at each other to remain afloat.

When Liberty gave her captor a final shove in an attempt to upright herself, a terrified howl gurgled in Simon's throat. He hung upside down on the railing, struggling to brace himself before he fell to his death on the stone path below.

Dylon lunged forward to push Liberty away before she slipped over the railing. She went rolling across the terrace like an overturned keg. Dylon's right hand knotted in the nape of Simon's jacket, attempting to lend support.

A gurgling growl echoed across the terrace as Simon's body shuddered and thrashed in midair. He clutched at Dylon's arm and glowered into the puffy, battered face of his archrival.

The sound of barking pistols blared against the night and bullets zinged through the air. Shouts and snarls seemed to come from all directions at once. There was a scuffling sound on the rock path below, but Dylon was too preoccupied to determine what was going on. Nor could he see Griffin and Phillipe battling the guard dragons who had pounced on them.

Dylon braced himself when Simon thrashed his legs and attempted to pull himself to safety. And suddenly,

Simon's eyes rolled back in his head and his grasp on Dylon's arm slackened.

Two more shots rang in the darkness.

A pained groan tumbled from Dylon's lips when he found himself supporting Simon's bulky weight with only one arm. His wounded leg buckled beneath him. The loss of blood and physical exertion had caught up with him. While Simon hung in the air like a feed sack, Dylon clenched his teeth and tightened his grasp. But Simon seemed to exert not one iota of energy to clutch at Dylon's trembling arm and save himself from certain death.

Her vision still blurred, Liberty crawled onto her hands and knees and then staggered to her feet. Through the indistinguishable gray haze, Liberty leaped on the hunkered form of the man beside the railing. Unaware that it was Dylon instead of Simon she was attacking, she struck out with both fists.

Dylon's bruised ribs and hip slammed against the iron railing when Liberty launched herself at him. His leg completely folded beneath him. With the dead weight of Simon's body clutched in one hand and the force of Liberty's momentum scraping him against the unyielding rail, Dylon lost his grip on Simon. Through no fault of his own, or Liberty's, who was blindly waging war against the wrong man, Dylon felt Simon slip into the expanse of nothingness.

Not one sound erupted from Simon's throat as he plunged toward the stone path. A dull thud wafted its way back to the terrace before the thrashing in the shrubs and the scuffling of boots muffled the sound of Simon's fatal fall. Voices flared in the nigiht and footsteps clattered on the steps. But Dylon was more concerned about the painful blows being leveled on his already bruised face and tender ribs.

"Godamercy, Liberty, stop that!" Dylon snapped as he raised his forearm to shield himself against her incessant blows.

Liberty blinked and strained to make out the image that towered over her. "Dylon? Is that really you?" she bleated in disbelief. Her trembling hand limned his battered features and she cursed the fuzzy haze that swam before her eyes. But even as her fingertips trailed over his swollen features, Liberty swore it was not Dylon. It didn't *feel* like Dylon and she still couldn't *see* if it was Dylon and not Simon Gridley.

Before Liberty could determine if Simon was trying to play some cruel trick on her, Phillipe raced across the balcony to scoop her up in his arms and shower her with kisses.

"Liberty, my beloved! I failed you while I was forced to rescue Cayla from the swamp. Forgive me for not finding you in time." He glanced down at the darkened path where Simon lay motionless. "But I took aim on that vicious fiend and brought him to his miserable end."

"*You* shot him?" Griffin snorted caustically. "Nay, 'twas I. I'm not sure you could hit the side of a barn."

Phillipe set Liberty to her feet and glared at Griffin. "I assure you, monsieur, that it was *my* bullet that launched that loathsome lout into hell. I"—he tapped his inflated chest to emphasize his point—"happen to be a marksman extraordinaire!"

"If you shoot as poorly as you draw down a bow, I would expect to find your buckshot lodged in yonder tree," Griffin scoffed.

The debate over whose bullet had plugged Simon while he hung in Dylon's grasp was interrupted by an agonized groan. Weakly, Dylon clutched the rail to pull himself up on his injured leg.

"Dylon, Lord, you look worse than I first thought!" Griffin croaked when the lantern light from the bedroom slanted across the disfigured face. "What the sweet loving hell happened?"

"Dylon? Where are you?" Liberty demanded as she felt her way around the bodies that blocked her path.

When Dylon snaked out an arm to draw her to his side, she half collapsed in relief, which wasn't a good thing since Dylon was having enough trouble keeping himself upright. Staggering, Dylon propped himself against the rail to cuddle Liberty against him.

The ordeal that had awakened Liberty from a drugged sleep hit her full force as she nuzzled against Dylon's foul-smelling jacket. She had never been a crier, but if ever there was a time to cry one's heart out, now was the time. Tears boiled down her cheeks as the bottled-up emotions came flooding out, leaving her body wracked with convulsive shudders. Her hands entwined around Dylon's neck, clinging to him as if he were the only stable force in a hazy universe of unrecognizable images.

"Sh . . . sh . . . It's all right now," Dylon murmured through bruised lips. "It's over. Simon will never hurt you again."

Comforting though his words were, Liberty couldn't dam up the river of tears that trickled down her cheeks. Her body was a mass of spasmodic shudders and soul-wrenching sobs. She wasn't sure if it was the aftereffects of stark fear or the drugging potion that caused her to blubber in huge hiccuping gulps. But she seemed to have no control whatsoever over her emotions. The harder she tried to restrain herself the more she cried. She had saturated Dylon's grimy shirt with tears but he didn't mock her. He simply held her until she had bled the full river of emotion.

Phillipe gaped at the bundle of white silk that clung to Dylon like a vine. "Liberty, my love. I have never seen you fall apart. I didn't know you had so much water in you!"

That set her off again and she wept like an abandoned baby.

"Phillipe, why don't you go make yourself useful by rounding up some horses," Dylon suggested.

Phillipe snapped to attention, marched across the

balcony and scurried down the steps to disappear into the darkness. When he was out of earshot, Griffin sighed heavily.

"Lord, we had a royal battle on our hands when we reached the house. If you met up with the same three guard dragons we encountered, I can see why you look the way you do." Griff peered sympathetically at his brother. Dylon's features were so swollen and discolored that it was difficult for Griffin to recognize his own flesh and blood.

Dylon merely shrugged. His attention was fixed on the teary-eyed blonde who was cradled protectively in his arms. He had no need to spout his heroic attempt to battle his way through Simon's three-man army while Simon and Luther held him at gunpoint. All that mattered was that Liberty was safe and sound and that Simon was no longer a threat to her.

And it wasn't Griffin's or Phillipe's pistol shot that had ultimately caused Simon's death. Dylon was the one who had dropped Simon after Liberty shoved him away in self-defense. Simon may have been wounded but it was the fall that actually killed him—the one Dylon caused him to take because he couldn't hold on when Liberty slammed into him.

While Dylon stood there mulling over the rapid sequence of events that led to Simon's death, only one thought rang clear in his mind. He loved this daring she-male with spun-gold hair and amethyst eyes. He didn't give a damn if she had been Simon's wife or that Phillipe anxiously awaited to make her his bride. He didn't care that his own brother was hopelessly entranced with Liberty. And Dylon didn't give a flying fig that Brewster had promised him to Nora Flannery. Dylon wanted Liberty, not the kind of *liberty* that allowed him to flit from one shallow, meaningless affair to another. That sort of freedom was dim in comparison to keeping Liberty by his side in the years to come. She alone had made him long for something he'd never had. He wanted security, to call her his own, to dream of a promising future. Liberty was a rare breed of woman who lived every moment to its fullest, a woman teeming with adventurous spirit. When she was underfoot things naturally happened. Dylon yearned to be a part of her life, even if she had her heart set on sailing off to the islands with Phillipe. Even now, he couldn't bear the thought of letting her out of his arms when he had come within a hairbreadth of losing her, first in marriage and then to death itself!

"Here, let me assist Liberty down the steps," Griffin volunteered as he pried the sobbing blonde away from his brother. "You'll have enough difficulty navigating on your own."

"Nay, we'll manage," Dylon insisted, clutching Liberty protectively against him.

"Dylon, for crying out loud, look at you," Griffin muttered. "You're covered with swamp slime. You can't walk without limping. One eye is practically swollen shut and your face is as puffy as a pumpkin."

"It is?" Liberty tilted her face upward, annoyed that Dylon was still only a blur to her. Tenderly, she traced his swollen lips, ones that had been split by Donnely's meaty fist. "I'm so sorry . . ." Another mist of tears welled up in the back of her eyes. "I never meant for you to become involved in my conflict with Simon and Luther. I lo . . ."

Dylon pressed his forefinger to her quivering lips to shush her. "'Tis over and done, remember? All I want is a warm, relaxing bath. As Griff has so candidly reminded me, I look like hell . . ." He grimaced when his gaze dropped to the torn bodice of Liberty's wedding gown. Even in the dim light he could see the red streaks on her breasts, caused by Simon's clawing attempt to molest her.

Although Dylon clung protectively to Liberty, Griffin whisked her away. Alone, Dylon hobbled to the bottom of the steps. Phillipe had retrieved the horses and had returned to sweep Liberty away from Griffin. Rattling in a mixture of French and English, Phillipe apologized all over himself for getting lost and detained while Liberty desperately needed him.

Although it was Dylon's want to keep Liberty beside him, he found his brother and Phillipe fussing over the shapely blonde who had been wed and widowed in the course of one night. Exhausted, Dylon rode behind the threesome, wondering if he would ever be granted enough privacy to tell Liberty how he felt.

Dylon sighed heavily. Since the moment he'd laid eyes on this captivating sprite he had attempted to project an air of casual indifference, refusing to let her know how deeply she had burrowed into his heart. Liberty hadn't appeared all that thrilled with the prospect of marriage when Brewster made his announcement, Dylon reminded himself glumly. Ah, wouldn't it be an ironic twist of fate if he had fallen in love a second time, only to be rejected again? Damnation, sometimes he swore love was more of a curse than a blessing!

Grappling with dismal speculations, Dylon trotted back to Lockhart Hall. He supposed he should be content that he had rescued Liberty from certain death, even if he couldn't claim her forevermore. But it wasn't enough and he doubted if he could adjust to the idea of letting Liberty walk out of his life, even if that was her wont. Damnit, why was it that the women he loved never loved him back? Dylon was on the verge of believing that, when it came to love, he simply had no luck at all. . . .

Chapter 25

The instant the foursome returned to Lockhart Hall, a flood of humanity poured out the front door. Brewster raged at Dylon for thundering off on his wounded leg. Edgar Flánnery demanded to know when the wedding between Dylon and Nora would take place. Phillipe was scampering around, simultaneously fawning over Liberty and Cayla who was nursing the bite on her ankle. Griffin was constantly wedging himself between Liberty and whichever man was hovering around her at the moment. The guests, whose curiosity had kept them at the plantation after the others had departed, were whizzing hither and yon to ascertain the details of the incident that had left Simon Gridley dead.

Finally, Dylon had enough! The chatter of family and guests contributed to the horrendous headache that hammered at his skull. All he wanted was to sink into the spacious stone tub and soak away all his aches and pains. He would have preferred to take Liberty with him to enjoy a few moments of peace and quiet. But hell! The placed was crawling with people who had swarmed around Liberty to such extremes that he couldn't even determine where she was!

"Percy, fetch me a fresh set of clothes and towels for a bath in the pavilion," Dylon requested tiredly.

Percy stared at his battered, bedraggled master in

concern. "Sir, don't you think you have been wet enough for one night? I fear a bath would only aggravate your condition and contribute to ailments which will plague you for the rest of your life. It would be healthier to simply sponge off in your room."

Dylon was completely out of sorts and as exhausted as one man could get. Unlike his usual good-natured self, Dylon very nearly bit Percy's head off for standing there arguing instead of scurrying off to comply with the order.

Unaccustomed to enduring Dylon's harsh tone, Percy jerked his head up to stare into Dylon's barely recognizable face. "Sir, I was only concerned about your welfare," he defended self-righteously. "And I think this would be a most beneficial time for you to begin carrying a potato on your person to ward off rheumatism. Now that you've injured your leg and exerted yourself to such extremes, painful afflictions are apt to set in and—"

"Forget the damned potato and fetch towels and soap!" Dylon roared, bringing quick death to every conversation (Percy's included, thank the Lord) that was taking place on his front lawn. "All I want is a bath, not a lecture on rheumatism. Good God, can't a man take a bath around here without a long-winded dissertation from a self-acclaimed physician?"

The blistering remark caused Percy to slam his mouth shut like a drawer. After executing an exaggerated bow, he pivoted on his heels and stamped off to do as he'd been told.

Scowling at his own irascible disposition, Dylon limped around the side of the house and hobbled toward the vine-covered pavilion that sat beside the target range. Once inside, Dylon pulled off his soiled garments and slid into the cool bath. For several minutes he simply submerged and resurfaced, relishing the soothing effect of the tepid water on his multiple wounds and abrasions. Geezus, he felt like a human punching bag! He'd been hit, kicked, shot and beaten until even his eyelashes ached!

The sizzle of heated stones which Percy plunked in the

tub raised the temperature of the water several quick degrees. While the pinch-mouthed valet scuttled around the circular tub, dropping stones at regular intervals, Dylon expelled a long sigh.

"I'm sorry I growled at you, Percy," Dylon murmured as he dragged the wet sponge over his tender ribs and shoulders. "Just because I'm miserable is no reason to take my frustrations out on you, and in front of an audience."

"All is forgiven, sir," Percy responded, dutifully attending his tasks. "If someone beat me black and blue, I suspect it would even spoil my unflappable disposition."

Dylon breathed a thankful sigh when Percy poured fragrant soap into the now-warm bath. "I trust Liberty is resting comfortably after her ordeal."

Percy shrugged enigmatically. "She was escorted to her room by Brewster, Griffin and Phillipe. Her maid, a shrew of a woman with a foul temper and dagger tongue, was sent up to help her out of her wedding gown. Her *second* wedding gown," he clarified.

After casting Dylon a discreet glance Percy inconspicuously tucked a potato into the pocket of his master's fresh clothes (for Dylon's own good, of course). "I was most distressed to hear that the despicable Simon Gridley had drugged Liberty and dragged her through a wedding ceremony she can barely remember. I'm sure she is relieved to have been rescued and returned to Lockhart Hall. With so many men chasing after her for a various sundry of reasons, 'tis a wonder she hasn't sworn off men for the rest of her life."

"No doubt she has, and with excellent reason," Dylon grumbled. "I expect she will be packed and eager to race back to Charles Town to catch the first schooner bound for the Indies."

Ponderously, Percy glanced at Dylon. "But, of course, it will be of no consequence to you since Nora is already scrawling addresses on invitations and making a big to-do of announcing your upcoming marriage."

"That chit didn't waste a minute, did she?" Dylon scowled.

"Indeed not!" Percy declared. "She demanded that I hand over the extra invitations I had left from your engagement party. The last time I looked over her shoulder on my way through your office (which she has taken over as if it were her own), she was crossing out Liberty's name and printing her own!"

"When Nora nestles into bed tonight, burn the invitations," Dylon requested before squeezing the sponge over his head. "Edgar Flannery can raise all the hell he wants but I'm not marrying that devious little tart. I'd rather have both legs shot out from under me than become her husband."

Percy stifled a pleased grin. "If you will excuse me, sir, I will see to that matter immediately."

As Percy's buckled shoes clicked across the stone floor, Dylon sank to the bottom of the pool. He sat there until his lungs very nearly burst. The watery silence was welcomed solitude. Dylon was lost to the enchanting vision that floated in his mind.

Liberty . . . He could see her swinging through his magnolia tree like poetry in motion. He could see her golden hair undulating behind her like a flag as she raced across the meadow on a swift steed. He could still visualize her on the moon-dappled terrace, battling for her life when Simon attacked her. But the vision that warmed his blood and ironed the wrinkles from his troubled soul was that of her luscious body lying beside his on the grass-carpeted creek bank.

Even now, he could picture her bewitching face below his, see the radiant smile, the unmistakable spark of passion in her eyes—the sparkle that he had put there with his intimate caresses and worshipping kisses.

Good God, the thought of never again making love to that beguiling siren was killing him, bit by agonizing bit. He'd even consent to allowing Donnely and those other two surly goons stake him out and beat him to a pulp if he could share a lifetime of glorious passion with that saucy sprite! No other woman, not even Patricia, stirred Dylon the way Liberty had been able to do. She had given his life new meaning. She had put the *love* in lovemaking.

When Dylon drifted back to the surface to gasp for air, he blinked in surprise. (At least his left eye blinked. The right one was still partially swollen shut.) To his disbelief, Liberty sat on the wooden bench with her legs tucked beneath her chin, staring sympathetically at him. He could tell by the look on her enchanting features that her vision had finally cleared and she could see the bruises and welts that marred his face.

"It looks as if you ran into Donnely, Gilbert and Figgins," she speculated. "It seems I was the lucky one. They only wrenched my arms and attempted to pinch me in two when I tried to escape them. But they obviously had a field day with you."

His shoulder lifted in a careless shrug. "I've endured worse battles in the past," he replied. "The wounds will heal and the bruises will fade."

"Oh, Dylon, I'm so sorry!" Liberty wailed and then caught herself before she broke into another round of infuriating tears that kept gurgling up from out of nowhere.

A tender smile traced his swollen lips. Stiffly, he eased toward the rim of the tub and extended his hand. "Come here and kiss me where it hurts. That will be apology enough."

Muffling a sniff, Liberty eased down from the bench to press a cautious kiss to his puffy lips—carefully avoiding the noticeable split of skin on the right corner of his mouth.

"And here—" He tapped his index finger against the purple bruise that surrounded his right eye.

Gently, Liberty complied.

"And here—" Dylon directed her attention to the reddish welt on his jaw. The feel of her warm lips whispering over his flesh provoked a quiet sigh to tumble off his tone. "Mmmm . . . I feel better already. . . ."

Liberty drew back. Her gaze focused on the air above his wet raven head. "You will feel ten times better when I inform you that Stella and I plan to leave for Charles Town at the crack of dawn. Nora informed me of your upcoming wedding and she, of course, thought it best if I took my leave. As she said, former fiancées do not make pleasant company for future wives."

"And, of course, you cannot wait to flit away from Lockhart Hall," Dylon grumbled bitterly. "I suppose Phillipe has been rattling incessantly about how he will protect you from harm once you've sailed back to the islands."

It was Liberty's turn to shrug evasively. "Phillipe is Phillipe. I'm afraid he was born a few centuries too late. Chivalry and martyrdom are tremendously important to him. He envisions himself as my guardian and protector, especially after Papa's death."

"But do you love him?" Dylon questioned point-blank.

Liberty forced herself to meet Dylon's solemn gaze. She cringed at the disfigured face of the man she truly loved. Even though he looked like hammered hell, she still adored him. Even if his right eye forever remained at half-mast, even if his flesh was permanently discolored with red, blue and deep purple bruises, he would still be the man who had taken possession of her heart. But because of her, he had been shot with an arrow and beaten within an inch of his life. Yet, it wasn't pity that provoked the sentimental stirring of emotions inside her. It was selfless love, a love so fierce and wild that nothing could contain it.

Even though she was a widowed bride and Dylon's latest fiancée was upstairs making preparations for her wedding, Liberty was compelled to express her love for the only man who really mattered to her. It was shameless and unethical, she knew. But just once more before she sailed away, she wanted to brush her fingertips over his hair-roughened flesh, to caress away all the aches and pains she had inadvertently caused him, to communicate her affection in erotic ways that required no words.

Dylon blinked his good eye when Liberty's hands nimbly flew over the buttons of her muslin gown, revealing the luscious swells of her breasts beneath the soft fabric. As the garment drifted to her waist, Dylon swallowed air. When she eased off the stone tile just far enough to slide the gown from her curvaceous hips, Dylon's brain malfunctioned. He was all eyes and strangled breath.

Liberty could not begin to define the tumultuous pleasure that rippled through her when Dylon's hungry gaze flooded over her as if she were a masterpiece he was admiring. He would never love her the way she loved him, but he still desired her. For tonight, it would have to be enough. Tonight was all she had.

She wanted to create a sweet lingering memory to sustain her throughout all the long lonely years to come. She wouldn't say the words that stampeded to the tip of her tongue, but she would physically display the deep-felt emotion she had for Dylon. And if he couldn't hear the love beating in her heart, then he wasn't listening because it was there—just a pulsating touch away.

She eased down in front of him in the warm pool. Her body glided against his virile torso in a suggestive caress. "Now, where did you say you hurt?" she murmured provocatively.

Dylon's heart slammed against his bruised ribs and threatened to stick there. "God, I ache all over," he groaned as he curled his arm around her trim waist, yearning to mold her satiny flesh intimately to his.

Dylon decided, there and then, that Liberty could have made a living as a masseuse if it had been her wont. Her tender touch worked magic on his battered flesh. Her gentle hands wandered to and fro, soothing him, teasing him, arousing him until he swore the pool of water had evaporated into a puff of steam. Over and over again, with concentrated patience, Liberty mapped his steel-honed body and sent scintillating pleasure leapfrogging through every fiber of his being.

An hour earlier, Dylon swore he hadn't the strength to stir another step without collapsing. But Liberty's evocative caresses and steamy kisses rejuvenated his energy and inflamed him with desire. Her hands and lips were never still for a moment, leaving him adrift in a sea of indescribable rapture.

"To hell with Phillipe and Nora," Dylon growled. "If they're in such an all-fired rush to marry, they can wed each other. As for me, all I want is you for as long as I can have you. . . ."

His mouth came down on hers in a hot, explosive kiss. The drugging potion Simon had forced down Liberty's throat that afternoon was nowhere near as potent as Dylon's intoxicating embrace. He set her ablaze with fiery passion and wove a tapestry of exotic fantasies that far exceeded the hallucinations she had experienced under the influence of the potion.

This was real! These sublime sensations could never be imitated or duplicated. What she experienced while she was engulfed in Dylon's sinewy arms defied description. He'd always had the most remarkable knack of sending her spiraling into wondrous dimensions of passion. He touched her and she lived only for his masterful kisses and arousing caresses. He could weave a lifetime of glorious ecstasy into the span of a few minutes. He could send her skyrocketing beyond the stars without ever leaving the mystical circle of his arms. He was her one and only love, the one man who had taught her the meaning of ecstasy. She lived for his lackadaisical smiles, for the bright ringing peal of his laughter. He was her reason for being. . . .

Her thoughts became hopelessly entwined when his practiced hands swirled over the throbbing tips of her breasts and then scaled her ribs. As his hands splayed over her abdomen to trace the curve of her inner thigh, Liberty gasped for air. And Dylon was there to breathe new life into her with his fiery kiss.

With one arm, he held her suspended on the bubbly surface. His free hand and moist lips teased the rose-tipped peaks, leaving her to burn on a white-hot flame. As he mapped the slender contours of her quaking flesh with tender loving care, Liberty swore she'd die long before he got around to satisfying the maddening needs he had evoked from her. Her body was like putty in a sculptor's hands, molded to fit his intimate caresses. She could feel the impression of his warm lips on her flesh and she craved more, begged for all he could offer.

Repeatedly, he dragged her to the edge of total abandon and then pulled her back, leaving her aching and shuddering in his arms. And just when Liberty resigned herself to death by tantalizing torment, he came to her, filling her with the pulsating flames of ungovernable passion.

Liberty was wild and breathless with the want of him. Her feminine body cried out to his. She met each hard impatient thrust with an eagerness that left Dylon reveling in unparalleled pleasure. They were like two famished creatures who could not get enough of each other, could not bear for the splendorous moment to end and yet frantic to appease the tormenting needs that consumed them.

On and on they soared from one deliriously sensuous plateau to another, scaling snow-capped mountains to orbit the galaxy of glittering stars. And when passion burst between them, they were flung through the diamond-studded universe, clinging to one another as if the world had come to an end. . . .

And for all practical purposes it had. Dylon, whose vision was already impaired by his swollen right eye, could see nothing but a hazy blur of rapture. He was so numb with pleasure that he felt no pain whatsoever. His left leg could have dropped off at the hip joint and he wouldn't have noticed or even cared. Passion this wild and free could only be experienced when Liberty was in his arms. She was his willing partner in passion, his equal and perfect match in any arena. Together they made sparks fly. Together they created a holocaust of fire that brought the walls of the world tumbling down into crackling flames.

"God, woman, I cannot begin to describe what you do to me," Dylon rasped as his body shuddered against hers. "When we make love, my mind goes blank and words fail me."

Liberty pressed a light kiss to his swollen lips and sighed in absolute contentment. Leisurely, she swam to the edge of the tub, pulled herself up and draped the towel around her. Curling her arms around her bare legs, she rested her chin on her knees and stared at Dylon with blatant appreciation. "Do you know, Dylon, you are the handsomest, most delightfully fascinating man I've ever met, despite your failing graces."

A ripple of laughter echoed through the pavilion. "Handsome?" Dylon regarded her skeptically. "Your eyesight must still be faulty. I'm pitifully disfigured and I can't walk without limping. I do not qualify as handsome, not by any stretch of the imagination."

"All the same, you possess the kind of charm that delves beneath the flesh. I shall always remember that about you."

The remorse in her voice caused Dylon's heart to twist in his chest. Damn her! She had come to him, engulfing him in a passion that defied rhyme and reason and then she announced she was going away forever. She spoke of the splendor they'd shared as if it were already a fading memory. Blast it, Dylon couldn't tolerate the thought!

With long graceful strokes, he crossed the pool and eased onto the tiled floor, oblivious to his nudity. He reached out to draw Liberty into his arms and beg her to stay. Aye, *beg* her (the get-down-on-your-knees kind of begging, if that's what it took!). If she left him, he'd never be the same again. She'd take his heart with him when she sailed away and he would be only the shell of a man. Then where would he be? What use would he be to anyone, especially to himself? *None at all,* the way Dylon had it figured.

Before Dylon could speak one word, footsteps clattered along the stone path that led to the bathing pavilion. With a frantic gasp, Liberty clutched the towel more tightly around her and stood up. Dylon, clumsy though his lame leg made him, bounded to his feet to clutch the nearest garment—Liberty's discarded gown. Hugging the dress to his chest, Dylon waited with sickening dread, wondering who was about to burst in to find them in a most embarrassing predicament.

"Sir, I thought you would want to know that Liberty has disappeared," Percy announced as he rushed into the pavilion.

When he spied the barely clad blonde behind Dylon who clutched the pink muslin gown to his chest, Percy froze in his tracks. His abrupt halt set off a chain reaction. Brewster slammed into Percy's backside. Edgar Flannery collided with the patriarch, causing him to expel a pained grunt. Nora rammed into her father's stiffened back. All three men stared frog-eyed at Dylon, who looked visibly distressed and utterly ridiculous clinging to the pink gown which extended to midcalf. The men stood there looking politely incredulous, but it was Nora Flannery who broke the stilted silence with a loud wail and a burst of furious indignation.

While Nora cried her eyes out, Edgar stomped forward to brandish his fist in Dylon's battered face. "You have a previous obligation to my daughter, you . . . you . . . philistine!" he spewed like a geyser. "This female is a recently widowed bride and the supposed fiancée of that zany Frenchman who is presently turning the house upside down to locate her!"

While Edgar Flannery raged on in his loud booming voice that shook the pavilion like a clanging gong, Liberty shifted uncomfortably from one foot to the other and turned every color under the sun.

Two minutes later, when Edgar paused from his tirade of fury, Dylon expelled an annoyed sigh. "If you're finished, I would like to dress."

"Not in that frilly pink gown, I hope." Brewster snickered, amused by the predicament Dylon had managed to get himself into this time. "That shade of pink clashes with the red welts on your face."

Edgar lurched around to glower at the gray-haired man who found amusement where there should have been none. It was obvious where Dylon Lockhart acquired his unshakable sense of humor—from his cussed grandfather!

"'Tis not one bit funny," Edgar snapped crankily. "Your indiscriminate grandson has proved himself to be a rake and a rounder. I hardly think you should shrug off his unpardonable sins and make light of this situation! The sooner that rascal marries Nora and settles down the better off we all will be. He's ruining the reputation of every respectable young lady in the colony!"

"Your point is well taken, Edgar." Brewster managed to smother his laughter behind an artificial cough. With tremendous effort, he masked his amusement behind a somber stare, even though he was inwardly chuckling at Dylon and Liberty's obvious inability to keep their hands off each other. "However, I don't think this is the time or place to discuss Nora's wedding arrangements. We will wait until Dylon has the opportunity to make himself presentable." With a quick flick of his wrists, Brewster silently ordered the search party to return to the house.

When the coast was clear, Dylon handed Liberty her gown and hobbled over to fetch his fresh set of clothes. Muttering at the untimely interruption, Dylon rammed his arms and legs into his garments.

"I'm sorry," Liberty apologized. "It seems all I do is make trouble for you. But after tomorrow you won't have me around to jinx your life."

"Damnation, come back here!" Dylon muttered when Liberty shot off into the darkness. With a scowl and a curse, he snatched up the potato Percy had stuffed in his pocket and hurled it against the wall. Why should he fret over contracting rheumatism when his main concern was keeping his sanity? Dammit to hell, he and Liberty needed to sort out their feelings for each other, but the plantation was crawling with too many people who caused too damned many unexpected interruptions. What he and Liberty needed was to be marooned on an uncharted island until they had the chance to talk privately and candidly.

Still growling in disgust, Dylon hobbled back to the house. But he only *thought* he had trouble before he set foot in the back door. Suddenly the mansion was buzzing like a beehive. Bodies were scurrying everywhere and the drone of whispers filled the air. Each individual he passed glanced sympathetically at him because of his disfigured face and then leaned close to a nearby ear to convey some confidential tidbit of gossip.

"Now what the hell is going on?" Dylon demanded gruffly.

Percy vaporized from the fog of guests and nervously wrung his hands in front of him—a gesture that indicated the internal twist of turmoil he was experiencing. "Brewster did all he could to dissuade the authorities, but they had an arrest warrant and there was nothing to be done except—"

"What authorities?" Dylon quizzed his valet. "Arrest whom for what?"

Hurriedly, Percy composed his thoughts. "Constable Grayson and his deputies from the village arrived with a warrant to arrest Liberty for killing her new husband."

"What!" Dylon hooted in disbelief. "Who would dare to accuse her of that?"

Percy shrugged helplessly. "I cannot say, sir. All I know is that, despite Brewster's pleas and Phillipe's loud protests, Liberty was put in shackles and hauled away."

Spouting the most colorful expletives in his vocabulary, Dylon cut his way through the guests like a shark through water. In quick, limping strides, he stalked toward the front door, barking orders as he went. By the time he hobbled outside, a saddled mount awaited him.

In fiend-ridden haste, Dylon thundered down the winding path that led to the village. Godamighty, how could one mere wisp of a woman manage to embroil herself in so many simultaneous tangles? Dylon asked himself incredulously. And what idiot had demanded her arrest?

Luther, Dylon speculated with a contemptuous snort. That worthless uncle of Liberty's had made her life miserable since the instant she set foot on Carolina soil. Damn the man! When Dylon got his hands on that devious weasel he'd . . .

A low growl erupted from his lips. Ah, he'd like to have ten minutes alone with that conniving little rodent! Luther Norris would be in no condition to accuse anybody of anything ever again!

Chapter 26

Tiredly, Dylon swung from the saddle. After his high-speed ride cross-country, his wounded leg was as stiff as a fence post. Grimacing at the recurring pain, Dylon hobbled into the constable's office. To his fury, Donnely, Gilbert and Figgins leaned negligently against the wall, smiling in smug satisfaction. It seemed these three backwoods ruffians were the ones who had brought charges against Liberty for the death of their employer rather than Luther, as Dylon had suspected.

The tables suddenly turned when Constable Grayson inquired about Dylon's noticeable bruises and wounded leg. Dylon explained that he had been brutally assaulted, tossed in the swamp and left for dead by these very men. Then he filed a formal complaint of attempted murder. Despite the three henchmen's contradicting stories, Dylon carried more clout. The surly ruffians were led into the stockade at gunpoint.

It was Liberty who smiled in triumph when she was allowed to vacate her cell. The henchmen, who had stood guard around her room the night she had attempted to escape on the eve of her wedding, were locked behind bars where they belonged. Justice had been served a mite late, but Liberty reckoned that was better than never.

Heaving a disconcerted sigh, Constable Grayson plunked down in his chair and stared bewilderedly into

Dylon's disfigured face. "You have sufficiently explained the incident with those three ruffians but there is still Simon Gridley's death to be resolved. According to those three baboons, they saw this young lady shove her husband over the railing."

"Shoved him in self-defense," Dylon clarified. "And none of those three miscreants were eyewitnesses to the incident. I had a far better view of what transpired. Simon tried to strangle Liberty in a fit of rage." He reached over to unbutton the top two buttons on Liberty's gown and indicated the claw marks on her neck.

Thaddeus Grayson gasped in dismay and then frowned in confusion. "But how could you know what happened, Dylon? I thought you said you were wading out of the swamp at the time. And how do you explain the bullet hole in Simon's shoulder?" He raked his fingers through his thin brown hair and sighed in exasperation. "This doesn't make much sense."

While Liberty offered her rendition of the events, beginning with the duel, her kidnapping and unwilling marriage, Dylon frowned ponderously. Something still didn't ring true here. Over and over again, he rehashed those frantic few minutes of struggle on the terrace. It occurred to him that it had been highly unlikely that Liberty, dazed by the drugging potion, and her vision seriously impaired, could have managed to shove Simon over the rail . . . unless he had been stumbling-down drunk.

"Had Simon been drinking heavily?" Dylon questioned out of the blue.

Liberty sorted through the fuzzy, incoherent memories and then nodded affirmatively. "Aye, I believe he had. I could smell the liquor on his breath when he tried to assault me. I was staggering about because of the potion he'd forced me to drink, but he seemed as clumsy as I was."

Thaddeus Grayson reached over to rip up the

complaint which had been filed against Liberty. "I have heard enough. It seems to me that if you actually did shove Simon over the railing that you had sufficient grounds to attempt to preserve your own life after what he did. As far as I'm concerned the matter should be dropped."

That suited Dylon just fine. He had no desire to go into detail about his subsequent involvement and the shot which had been fired by either Griffin or Phillipe and only God knew which one.

But even as Dylon and Liberty rode quietly through the night, he had the uneasy feeling that in his frantic state, he had missed something of vital importance in the incident. The sight of Simon glowering up at him with that glazed look in his eyes kept flashing in Dylon's mind. Simon had clutched at Dylon's arm to pull himself back to the terrace. Then the shots had barked in the darkness. And yet . . . wasn't it a second earlier that Simon had slumped and loosened his grasp on Dylon's arm . . . ?

"You're terribly quiet," Liberty observed as she peered at the bruised face that was shaded with moonshadows.

"I'm incredibly tired," Dylon confessed. "And my leg hurts like hell, if you want to know." He tossed his troubled thoughts aside and flashed Liberty a suggestive smile. "I could do with another of your massages."

Liberty stared into the distance, squelching the warm tingles caused by the titillating memory of the last massage she'd offered him. "I doubt Nora would approve. She is already hysterical after she caught us sharing the same bathtub."

When Dylon extended his arm to grasp her steed's reins, Liberty's thick lashes swept up. Her gaze locked with those sparkling pools of blue that could so easily entrance her. Aching needs bombarded her like bullets. She couldn't resist reaching out to trace her fingers over his sensuous lips.

Dylon kissed her fingertips. "I want you in my bed, tonight and every other night. Please don't leave me. . . ."

Liberty decided that was probably as close as Dylon would ever come to a commitment. But it wasn't enough. There was a vast difference between wanting and loving. He hadn't offered his love and she couldn't settle for anything less, not when she loved him beyond reason.

Shaking off the hypnotic spell, she nudged her steed down the moonlit path that cut through the canopy of trees and tangled vines.

"Confound it, woman, you love me and we both know it. Why else would you have run from every other man except one?" Dylon called after her.

Whether she loved him or not was debatable. But the remark served its primary purpose—to stop her dead in her tracks. It also ignited her flammable temper. Liberty wheeled her horse around and glared at him. Even the darkness couldn't camouflage the sparks in her snapping amethyst eyes.

"Love you?" Liberty flung back at him. Aye, she loved him to distraction but she would be damned if she admitted it. Her stubborn pride refused to let her. "I cannot think of one good reason why I should! Every time I come near you I find myself wading neck-deep in trouble!"

"You? Wading in trouble?" Dylon hooted as he eased his steed up beside hers. "You court disaster and flirt with catastrophe without anybody's assistance. I got myself shot and pounded flat trying to rescue you from calamity. And if not for me, you'd be spending the next few weeks in the stockade awaiting trial. The very least you could do is thank me."

"Thank you," Liberty begrudgingly muttered. "And you can thank me bright and early in the morning when I ride off, never to interfere with your life again. I hope you and Nora Flannery will be deliriously happy in wedlock."

"Nay, you don't." Dylon chuckled as he urged his steed down the path. "You know I'm as eager to marry Nora as you are to wed that flamboyant Frenchman. True, he would be a constant source of entertainment. Phillipe is teeming with dramatic talent and is most amusing with his theatrical antics. But you'll never love him."

"Dylon Lockhart, you are the most arrogant, insufferable man I have ever met!" Liberty spumed in frustration.

"I thought you said I was handsome and intriguing," he teased her unmercifully.

"I changed my mind." Liberty tossed her golden head of hair and looked the other way.

"I haven't changed *my* mind." His voice dropped to a husky pitch that sent a skein of goose bumps flying across her skin. "I love you and I doubt that those feelings are ever going to change. I cannot imagine why they would."

Liberty gasped at him as if he'd sprouted antlers. "What did you say?" she squeaked when she gained control of her vocal apparatus.

"I said I can't imagine why it would," he repeated with a faint smile, trying to decipher her reaction to his declaration and unable to do so.

"Nay, before that," she insisted impatiently.

"I said I wouldn't change my mind." Dylon shifted awkwardly in the saddle. The words hadn't come easily to begin with and Liberty was tormenting him to death.

"Curse it, repeat the first part, you imbecile!" Liberty spouted irritably. "Do you truly love me or don't you? For once, be serious!"

Well, it was all or nothing, Dylon decided. Gritting his teeth, he swung down on his tender leg and contorted his body into a position—one into which he had never forced himself in all his thirty-one years. On bended knee (and one stiff leg stretched uncomfortably out beside him) Dylon knelt before Liberty and her steed.

"I love you, little wildflower," he confessed with

genuine sincerity. "I don't know when the *liking* trailed off and the loving actually began. But I know what I feel and what I desire most in life. I want you and I need you with me all the rest of my days. I've been to hell and back and I even fancied myself in love once before. I had promised myself to live only for the moment, taking pleasure where it came. But that isn't enough anymore, not after I found you. The thought of another man touching you cuts me to the quick. I want you as my own."

Dylon peered up into her startled expression, noting that her jaw had dropped off its hinges. "I want you to marry me and share my life and my dreams, Liberty."

Dylon loved her? He honestly and truly loved her? He wanted to marry her? Liberty could scarcely believe it. Dylon had always been a master at hiding his emotions behind laughter and nonchalant smiles. She had never been certain if she were merely a temporary amusement or . . .

"Well?" Dylon prompted when she sat atop her horse, gaping at him as if he were some prehistoric monster, come to gobble her up. "Will you marry me? I will be very tolerant of your unconventional behavior. You will have very few restrictions. However, I would prefer that you don't go tromping through snake-infested rice paddies or get yourself toted off to jail. Other than that, you can run with a free rein. I won't even expect you to love me back if you cannot. But I want you in my life, for now and always."

"Not love you?" Liberty erupted. "You know perfectly well that I do."

"You do? Truly?" Dylon blinked (at least his left eye did. The right one still wasn't functioning properly).

Liberty couldn't recall seeing this raven-haired rake look quite so surprised and relieved, all in the same moment. It occurred to her, just then, that he had been bluffing. He had been as unsure of her feelings for him as she had been about his affection for her.

Her heart was in her eyes as she gazed down at him. "Truly, I love you," she assured him softly. "And if you would kindly stand up, I'll show you exactly how much you mean to me."

Dylon would have eagerly leaped at the invitation, *would* have, if only he could have. His bum leg had stiffened up to such extremes that it would no longer bend in the middle. "I don't think I can get up," he groaned as he levered all two hundred pounds on his good leg. The rest of his body was so achy and sore from his fisticuffs with the backwoods baboons that he couldn't even push himself upright.

With an amused giggle Liberty bounded from the saddle to assist Dylon to his feet and onto his own steed. "Perhaps I should wait until we get back to the plantation before I express my love," she murmured provocatively. "Then I won't care if you're flat on your back and can't get up."

Dylon grinned rakishly as he settled himself in a somewhat comfortable position in the saddle. "I won't care if I get up either."

Wearing a contented smile, Liberty glided her hand into his as they rode side-by-side, staring at the silhouette of Lockhart Hall in the distance. She didn't want to dwell on the fact that she still had to contend with Phillipe and Dylon had Nora and Edgar Flannery breathing down his neck. But somehow or another, she and Dylon would make a life together, despite the external influences that sought to keep them apart.

Lovingly, her gaze focused on the battered man who rode beside her. Dylon had come to mean so much to her, so much that it was always frightening. He was not only her secret lover, but her companion and friend. Although he was dedicated to his position in the Assembly and to making the plantation prosper, he had a positive, refreshing outlook on life. He was the pulse of every party he'd ever attended, the driving force on the plantation. He had a remarkable knack of making every individual he confronted feel special and welcome. He possessed that unique brand of charm, confidence and sense of humor that naturally attracted people to him. The only enemies he had confronted these past few years were the ones Liberty had made for him—except for their mutual foe—Simon Gridley. Dylon was competent, resourceful, dependable and efficient and Liberty adored him for a million excellent reasons!

And if Nora Flannery thought to entrap Dylon into a marriage he didn't want with her wailing sobs and tantrums that was just too damned bad! Liberty intended to fight for what she wanted in life. She wasn't running away again. She was remaining in the colonies because that was where her heart would always be—with this blue-eyed, midnight-haired rake who had taught her soul to sing!

By the time Liberty and Dylon ambled up the front steps of the mansion, Brewster and Percy were the only ones who hadn't retired for the night. With Percy's assistance, Dylon scaled the steps and hobbled toward his bedchamber. He was so stiff and exhausted that he could barely move without gritting his teeth in pain. And ironically, he'd never been quite so content.

When Brewster opened his mouth to convey Edgar Flannery's latest threat, Dylon forestalled him. "I'm dealing with no more crises tonight," Dylon announced with finality. "Edgar can wait."

"But—" Brewster tried to protest but Dylon closed the bedroom door in his face.

Muttering at the turmoil he had been forced to endure the past few days, Brewster stamped off to bed. Behind him, he heard Percy clearing his throat. Brewster spun about to peer at the valet who lingered in the dark reaches of the shadowed hall.

"He's like an agile cat, you know," Percy murmured in consolation. "No matter which way you throw that grandson of yours, he always manages to land on his feet." Percy emerged from the shadows to peer into Brewster's strained features. "I've fussed over that carefree rake for years. But it has begun to dawn on me that Dylon needs very little advice or assistance. He will find his own way to handle Edgar Flannery. I wouldn't fret."

Brewster let out his breath in a rush. "Percy, I fear Dylon's nonchalant attitude has begun to rub off on you. I wouldn't have thought it."

Percy broke into a sly smile. "Forgive me for saying so, sir, but I think perhaps your vision has failed you. Perhaps you missed those stolen glances Liberty and Dylon flung at each other before they parted company. What I saw was the look of a man who knows what he wants, a capable, resourceful man who will ensure that he gets it. Unless I have totally misread the situation, springing Liberty Jordon from jail wasn't the only obstacle your grandson overtook tonight."

Brewster perked up immediately. "Are you saying what I think you're saying?" he asked hopefully.

Percy nodded in absolute assurance. "Simon Gridley wasn't the only one hereabout who has been shooting arrows. Dylon caught Simon's in the thigh, but I do believe he caught Cupid's in the heart."

"And Liberty?" Brewster anxiously questioned.

"Another of Cupid's victims," Percy confirmed. "Only a woman in love would risk sneaking to the bath pavilion when immersing oneself in water at frequent intervals is known to be hazardous to one's health. If that isn't love, I don't know what is."

Brewster burst out laughing at Percy's warped logic. He had never thought to compare the depth of love to the frequency of bathing. "I hope you're right, Percy," he said, smothering a snicker. "I tried my hand at matchmaking without success and I have promised to mind my own business, difficult though it is. But as for myself, I can't imagine Dylon settling down with any other woman besides that high-spirited sprite. They belong together."

Percy frowned as he turned away. "I only hope Griffin and Phillipe come to realize that."

Brewster hoped so too. There were enough complications without pitting brother against brother and that duel-happy Frenchman against both brothers. Blast it, Brewster wished Phillipe would pack up and go back where he belonged as fast as he could get there!

Dylon swore there wasn't enough air on the planet to fill a bucket, let alone his lungs when a vision of pure loveliness appeared at the terrace door. From the skipping moonlight and swaying shadows of the night, a shapely goddess emerged, drawing nearer to his bed. A shimmering cape of gold cascaded over Liberty's shoulders as she moved silently toward him. She spoke not a word as she shrugged off the gossamer gown, letting it ripple into a pool at her feet.

Wearing nothing but a seductive smile, Liberty eased beneath the sheet to cuddle up against Dylon's hair-matted chest. There was no question why she'd come—to give the massage she'd promised, to offer the love that was his for the taking. There was something different, almost reverent about the way her hands whispered over his bruised flesh. Dylon swore he'd sunk into his feather mattress when Liberty breathed love words on his skin and treated him to the most languid caresses imaginable.

Earlier that evening they had made wild, passionate love and sailed away on the most intimate of journeys beyond the stars. But now she made no demands. She was offering gentle compassion and tantalizing comfort. The love they'd created transcended the physical bounds. Many times before they had expressed their hungry needs for each other, but now . . . Now, her caresses were more therapeutic than sensual. Liberty wanted no more than to comfort him and to sleep by his side, allowing him time to recuperate from his exhausting ordeals. She had placed his needs above her own insatiable desire to share that rare brand of passion she had found with him.

This delightful imp had only meant to caress him until his aching muscles melted into butter and his bruised bones dissolved into jelly. Then she intended to call it a night, Dylon realized. Touched by her sensitivity for his condition, Dylon pressed a fleeting kiss to the tip of her dainty nose and grinned.

"It seems I've found myself a most understanding and undemanding fiancée," he chortled softly.

Liberty laid her head against his sturdy shoulder and absently trailed her hand over the thick carpet of hair that trickled down his chest. "Tonight, I won't be demanding. Only because you need your rest. But don't expect me to be so lenient with you in the future."

One thick black brow jackknifed in response to her provocative threat. "Good God! Am I to understand that every other night when I come to bed I will be expected to perform for your unquenchable feminine pleasures?" The idea had tremendous appeal!

"At least once a night," Liberty assured him as her hand brazenly migrated over the washboard terrain of his belly to investigate the lean curve of his hip.

A delighted peal of laughter reverberated in his chest when her knee glided between his thighs. "You won't hear one complaint from me, love." His lips feathered over her petal-soft lips. "Since your tender massage has turned the trick, I have no need to wait until tomorrow to show you how much I love you. . . ."

Despite the shock waves of pleasure that undulated through her when his masculine body slid familiarly over hers, Liberty stared curiously at him. "All teasing aside, Dylon. Are you sure you are up to this?"

The feel of her curvaceous body molded to his ignited that eternal spark of desire that kindled inside him. Dylon hurt all right, but in an entirely different place. The ache had localized in his loins. Bruised and battered though he was, weary though he had become after a full rich day of battling difficult odds to get Liberty back in his arms, he still yearned for this bewitching sprite in the most arousing way imaginable.

"All teasing aside"—Dylon whispered, his voice growing more ragged with each syllable—"I don't think there's any possible way to lie beside you without making love to you . . . even if I do look like Beauty's Beast."

Never that! Liberty thought as her body instinctively surrendered to Dylon's mystical touch. He may have looked the worse for wear with all his battle scars. But she had learned the true meaning of "beast" when Simon clawed at her like a brutish heathen. Dylon's touch had always been embroidered with tenderness. He didn't take; he gave. He accepted only what she offered and in her eagerness to share the wild splendor, Liberty always found herself giving all within her power to give—the breathless passion, the unconditional love.

As she returned each tantalizing kiss and caress, their hearts and bodies beat as one vital essence. And somewhere in the night, Liberty realized that Dylon's wounds and bruises hadn't inconvenienced him in the least. It was a passion tempered with love that provided unfailing strength. Although Dylon usually passed himself off as an easy-going Southern gentleman, there was far more to this magnificent man than met the eye.

It touched her deeply that he never flaunted his formidable strength and skills, that he made no excuses when he lost his battle against Simon's three grizzly gorillas. He had never tried to impress her or put on airs the way Phillipe had. Nor had he browbeaten her the way

Simon had done. Dylon demanded only a few reasonable restrictions. And most importantly, he freely offered his love. Liberty wondered how any woman could want for more. She could only hope Edgar and Nora Flannery would graciously bow out. But considering Edgar's persistence and the extremes to which Nora had gone to entrap Dylon, Liberty wondered if another battle didn't await them in the near future.

Well, I'll stew over that possibility later, she procrastinated as she nestled in Dylon's possessive embrace. Tonight she was going to revel in the sublime fulfillment that flooded over her. Tomorrow they would deal with the obstacles that sought to trip them up . . . But definitely not tonight . . . !

Chapter 27

Wistfully, Liberty stared into the mirror and fiddled with her coiffure. Although Stella bustled around the room, grumbling at the thought of remaining in the colony while a perfectly good estate in the West Indies was going to waste, Liberty wasn't listening. Her mind was on the splendorous memories of the previous night, of the man who had fulfilled her every fantasy. Liberty could never have imagined that she could fall so hopelessly in love that she wandered around in a hypnotic trance. But that was exactly what she was doing.

"Curse it, child. I swear you haven't heard one word I've said," Stella groused as she refolded Liberty's gowns and transferred them from one drawer to another for lack of anything better to do while she steamed and stewed. "I simply don't understand what's gotten into you. Agreed, Dylon Lockhart is handsome and wealthy and personable. But for heaven sake! There is another woman in this house who has been scribbling invitations to her wedding with Dylon. And you have a long-standing obligation to Phillipe. If you ask me, we should shake the dust of South Carolina off our heels and sail home as soon as possible."

"I happen to be in love with Dylon and he loves me," Liberty said, as if that solved everything.

Liberty was walking around with stars in her eyes and a disgustingly lovesick smile plastered on her face. In Stella's opinion, her mistress had fallen off the deep end.

"And Phillipe has loved you for more than two years," Stella reminded her tartly. "And just where has it gotten him?"

Before Liberty could reply, the rap at the door resounded around the room.

"What now?" Stella grumbled. "No doubt, 'tis that pesky Nora, handing out invitations and wondering when we're leaving."

Stella whipped open the door to find Percy standing stoically before her. Without changing expression, he extended the message to Liberty's maid.

"This letter was slipped under the door, along with the request that it be placed in Liberty's hands as soon as possible." Percy glanced past the frowning maid to survey the radiant smile that hovered on Liberty's lips. That was the look of love, Percy surmised. It was just as he thought. . . .

"Was there something else or do you have nothing better to do than linger in the hall, peeking into ladies' boudoirs?" Stella mocked sarcastically.

Percy jerked to attention. His critical gaze leaped back to Stella. "Aye, madam, I do have other matters to attend," he replied with elaborate politeness. "But at least I have the courtesy not to jump down the throat of every person I encounter along the way."

"Then why don't you go attend your duties, Percival," Stella shot back. "I also have tasks to tend and you have bent my ear long enough with your long-winded prattle."

Percy doubled over in a greatly exaggerated bow. "As you wish, my lady. 'Tis plain to see why you haven't married. Your foul disposition and razor-sharp tongue are chaperones no man could overcome."

Having delivered his parting shot, Percy dusted an imaginary piece of lint from his sleeve, flung his nose in the air and marched off.

Muttering, Stella slammed the door, causing dust to trickle from the woodwork. "The nerve of that pompous ass! I'd like to take the starch out of his collar and give him a good piece of my mind! The stuffy lout!"

Liberty bit back an amused grin and retrieved the letter Stella had clenched in her fist. Somehow or another Stella and Percy had gotten crosswise of each other and Liberty couldn't fathom how. They had struck an instant and mutual dislike. Probably because of their diametrical differences and agitating similarities, Liberty speculated. At each encounter, she had heard Stella fling insults which Percy countered with his own dry sarcasm before each one retreated to engage in battle on the next field of confrontation.

Her thoughts scattered when she scanned the letter. Frowning fretfully, Liberty buzzed toward the door.

"Now where are you going?" Stella insisted on knowing.

"I also have an important matter to attend," Liberty murmured as she sailed down the hall like a flying carpet.

Stella threw up her hands and muttered under her breath. Having been left with little else to do, Stella ambled down the hall to antagonize Percy. It had become her only pleasure of late. For some unexplainable reason, she delighted in badgering that stuffed shirt. He just seemed to invite her ridicule.

The demanding rattle on the door brought Dylon awake with a start. Since Liberty had left him at dawn, he had lounged in bed, drifting back and forth between dreams and reality.

Another impatient knock echoed around the room and Dylon scowled. He had just levered himself up on his elbow when Edgar burst into the room without invitation, followed by his determined daughter.

"Now that things have simmered down, I demand to know when your marriage ceremony is to take place."

Edgar cut right to the heart of the matter, which wasn't so surprising, being a surgeon and all. "I think midday this afternoon will give you ample time to prepare for the wedding."

Never in his life had Dylon allowed anyone to maneuver him and he certainly wasn't about to start at this late date. Wearing his customary smile, Dylon stared at his unwanted bride and his would-be father-in-law.

"There will be a wedding," he declared. "But it will be between Liberty and me. You and Nora are welcome to attend if you are so inclined."

Having dropped the bomb Dylon waited for the Flannerys to explode. Sure enough, they did.

"You promised to wed my daughter," Edgar growled while Nora burst into eardrum-shattering wails of despair.

"I made no such agreement," Dylon clarified. "My grandfather did. But no one speaks *for* or dictates *to* me."

The veins on Edgar's face popped. He lurched around and stormed toward the door. "We'll just see about that! Brewster!" he bellowed like a tattling child on his way to summon a higher authority.

Within seconds, the elderly patriarch appeared in the doorway. "What is the problem, Edgar?" As if he couldn't guess.

"This grandson of yours refused to comply with your agreement to marry my daughter," Edgar roared over Nora's howling sobs.

Brewster glanced past the raging physician to scrutinize his bare-chested grandson. Despite the incorrigible smile that quirked Dylon's lips, Brewster could detect the determined glint in those sky-blue eyes. Dylon wasn't budging an inch. Good for him. It seemed Percy was right. At long last, Dylon knew what he wanted and *no one* was going to prevent him from having it. . . .

"Well, don't just stand there," Edgar spouted impatiently. "Tell this rapscallion that he is honor bound to fulfill his obligation to Nora and to comply with the agreement we made."

Brewster half turned to meet Edgar's furious glare. "As I recall, I did declare that my grandson would wed. However, I don't recall that I specified *whom* he was going to marry."

Edgar's face turned a remarkable shade of purple and his heaving chest swelled up as if it were about to burst. "Damn you, Brewster! You tried to trick me and you are trying to weasel out on a technicality. Well, I won't stand for it. My daughter's virtues have been compromised and I will not have her shouldering her humiliation alone."

Before Dylon could interject a comment, Percy appeared at the door. "Forgive me for the intrusion, sir." He darted the fuming physician a hasty glance and then fastened his concerned gaze on Dylon. "This morning, a message arrived for Liberty."

"From whom?" Dylon frowned curiously.

Percy's shoulders lifted in a shrug. "I do not know, sir. But I just saw her thundering off on horseback, cutting across the meadow to the north. Considering her past track record, I thought I should report to you before she gets herself into trouble . . . again."

"Damn," Dylon growled. It frustrated him beyond words that Liberty hadn't confided in him and it irritated him to the extreme that he was lying abed—start-bone naked—with an audience.

Taking advantage of Dylon's awkward situation, Nora squirted through the wall of men to glare at the bed-bound rake she was determined to marry. "None of us are leaving this room so you can go chasing after that blond-haired harlot of yours," Nora spewed.

It was amazing how quickly Nora's heart-wrenching tears dried when she insisted on speaking her piece. It was obvious to everyone in the room, Edgar included, that Nora was an accomplished actress who could turn her emotions off and on at the drop of a hat. Edgar gaped at his daughter in astonishment, seeing her in an entirely different light.

"You are going to marry me, Dylon Lockhart, and that is that!" she all but yelled at him. "I will not be cast aside as one of your forgotten conquests so you can marry that slut!"

By the time Nora finished slandering Liberty's name Dylon was good and mad! And he was growing more impatient by the second. While he tarried, Liberty was thundering off to only God knew where. With a wordless scowl, Dylon wrapped the sheet around his hips and stood up. But Nora was in a full-fledged snit and she shot forward to block Dylon's path.

"You will agree to *our* marriage or I will . . ." Her voice trailed off and she retreated a step when Dylon expelled a thunderous growl. She had never seen this even-tempered rake explode. Nora was no longer staring at the nonchalant gentleman she had sought to entrap. The civilized veneer had peeled off and there was a dangerous sparkle in Dylon's eyes, a foreboding snarl on his lips. The fact that his face was a mass of blue and purple bruises made him appear even more threatening.

"I've allowed you to carry this ridiculous idea of marriage far enough without spoiling your father's idealistic impression of you," Dylon said in a whiplash voice. "But enough is enough. Because of your deceptiveness, you have forced me to abandon courtesy and tact."

His steely glare focused on Edgar. "It was not I who sought to seduce your daughter," he told her father candidly. "'Twas the other way around and for the express purpose of coercing me into marriage. Until now, I have been generously tolerant because my grandfather taught me that rudeness was the mark of bad breeding. But I will not be blamed for what I have not done. I hardly consider myself a qualified physician, but I do know when a woman is lying about her untainted virtues. If you demand that she marry the first man who touched her you will have to sort through a long list of candidates to determine who truly was the first."

When Edgar gasped and turned burgundy red, Dylon muttered sourly. He hadn't wanted to be cruel and insulting, but he was not tolerating another second of Nora's deceitful lies. She deserved this embarrassment, even if her father didn't.

Dylon's muscular arm shot toward the door. "Now kindly take your leave and take this lying little snip with you!"

Then Nora did cry in earnest. In a burst of mortified fury she launched herself toward Dylon to pummel his chest with her fists. "Curse you, Dylon Lockhart," she railed hysterically. "I shall see you pay and pay dearly for this. I will find a way to make you suffer for humiliating me!"

"Nora! That is enough!" Edgar snapped, annoyed and embarrassed to no end.

After voicing her threat Nora darted out the door. Tucking his tail between his legs and folding his injured pride in his pocket, Edgar slinked out of the room without a backward glance.

"That was a most unpleasant scene," Brewster grumbled. "You don't suppose the message which arrived for Liberty was actually sent by Nora, do you? Maybe she was trying to clear the area of competition by conjuring up another of her convenient lies."

While Dylon was contemplating that possibility (and he wouldn't have put anything past Nora, by the way) Griffin strode into the room, wearing a perplexed frown. "What the devil was all the yelling and crying about?" he wanted to know. He counted noses and then frowned again. "And where the blazes is Phillipe? I walked past his room and all his belongings are stacked up as if he were planning to leave."

Dylon digested the information with a muffled curse. "Damn that Frenchman. He was probably the one who left the message for Liberty to meet him somewhere. Maybe he's trying to persuade Liberty to sail off with him."

"Or maybe Nora conspired with Phillipe to have Liberty conveniently out of the way while she finalized her wedding arrangements," Brewster speculated.

Scowling colorful profanities, Dylon scooped up his clothes and limped behind the dressing screen. In less than a minute, he reappeared. His white linen shirt hung open and he fastened his breeches as he hobbled toward the door.

Hurriedly, Percy scuttled over to retrieve Dylon's stockings and boots. "I expect you will need these items as well, sir."

Mumbling his thanks, Dylon plunked down on the nearest chair to yank on his stockings and pull on his boots. Although his left leg complained about bending at the knee, Dylon gritted his teeth and completed the task. As he surged off the chair and out the door, the other occupants in the room followed in his wake.

Brewster clambered into his carriage, which Percy volunteered to drive, while Dylon and Griffin swung into the saddle and shot off in the direction Liberty had taken. Over and over again, Dylon cursed the vision of blond hair and violet eyes that hovered over him. The previous night he had found all his dreams coming true. But by the light of day, his nightmares were recurring. It infuriated him that Liberty had galloped off without divulging her purpose or destination. Although it had been her independent nature and undaunted spirit that attracted him to her in the first place, there were times when he condemned those very characteristics that he adored about her. This was one of those times.

Damnit, she should have confided in him first! She could find herself in a trap or whisked away by that idiotic French Casanova who had enough trouble taking care of himself!

With each passing moment, Dylon's aggravation multiplied. He kept envisioning Liberty in the same terrifying predicaments she'd encountered the past few days. God, he hoped he was worrying for naught! And if he was, he was going to chew that daring female up one side and down the other for scaring the living daylights out of him. Blast it, a man needed an anchor and ropes to ensure that gorgeous sprite stayed put!

Liberty ducked beneath the low-hanging branches of the trees and paused on the slope which overlooked the wharf of her family plantation of Triple Oak. Cautiously, she glanced around her before making her way toward the stone warehouse that stood on the shore of the river.

The curious note from Luther had prompted her to leave Lockhart Hall posthaste. But now she was leery of approaching her uncle without reinforcements. It was probably a foolish thing to do, she thought in retrospect, but Luther had requested a private conference with her.

Apprehensive of walking into another trap, Liberty chose to inch toward the meeting place and scan the surroundings before stumbling ignorantly inside. There was no telling what Luther had planned for her. Liberty had taken a chance by coming in the first place. To invite more trouble, such as an unexpected attack, was foolhardy indeed.

With the silence of a stalking cat, Liberty crouched beneath the window and peered inside. To her surprise, Luther was lounging at the small oak desk, patiently awaiting her arrival. As far as she could tell, there was no one else lurking about to pounce on her. Assured of her personal safety, Liberty circled toward the door and sailed inside without knocking.

The creak of the rusty hinges brought Luther out of his chair and onto his feet. When he was certain Liberty had come alone, he gestured for her to plant herself in the chair across from him.

When Luther simply peered at her, Liberty sighed impatiently. "Now what is all this supposed mysteriousness about Simon's death? As far as I know, there was only—"

Luther flung up his hand to demand silence. "As far as you know, which could not have been much, considering Simon forced that potion down your throat—"

"Get to the point," Liberty demanded.

Luther grumbled at Liberty's refusal to allow him to proceed as he had rehearsed. "In the first place, I want you to know I had no choice in this entire matter with Simon," he declared. "I would not have conspired against you if Simon hadn't demanded that I assist him. He was a shrewd, calculating man who had evil ways of maneuvering people into doing as he commanded. I was as much the victim as you were, I assure you."

Of course he was, the sniveling bat. Liberty clamped her mouth shut and listened. Why? She had no idea. Luther deserved no consideration whatsoever.

"Six months ago, I had the misfortune of entering into a card game at one of Charles Town's gaming halls with Simon and several other men," Luther explained. "'Tis true that I imbibe too heavily in liquor from time to time. Simon took full advantage of my dull-witted condition and ensured my mug was refilled each time it went dry. When I incurred heavy losses for which I did not have ready cash, he insisted that I sign for the debt. It was not until the following day that I was able to read the note that bore my signature. Simon had deviously manipulated me into turning the title of Triple Oak over to him to compensate the losses."

"What?" Liberty croaked in disbelief. "But you couldn't possibly have deeded over the land which wasn't yours to give."

"I debated that point with Simon," Luther continued. "He had falsely assumed that I owned the land he had cast his greedy eyes on for expansion. And come to find out, he had doctored my drinks with the same stupefying potion he forced you to drink. When he realized his error he was outraged with me. He threatened to send me to debtor's prison if I didn't help him acquire the deed to the property that lay beside his land."

"The land *he* inherited from his departed wives," Liberty surmised with a disdainful sniff.

"Exactly." Luther inhaled a deep breath and plunged on. "I am not the scheming man you have assumed me to be. I am, however, a coward when it comes to threats against my life," he admitted. "Simon swore to turn his henchmen loose on me if I didn't help him lure you into a wedding."

"But he didn't even know me!" Liberty interjected.

"That hardly mattered to Simon. You were the key that unlocked Triple Oak to him. 'Tis one of the most fertile plantations in the area. Simon had exhausted his land by overplanting crops. He had also made several bad investments in land speculation in the area Parliament has now restricted to the Cherokees rather than colonial settlement. He needed ready cash to continue his operation.

"When I received word of your father's death, Simon demanded that I derive an excuse to send for you," Luther informed her.

Liberty was only beginning to realize how ruthless and greedy Simon Gridley was. Upon their first meeting he had tried to pass himself off as a noble gentleman. But feminine intuition had refused to allow her to trust him. And time had proved her correct. Simon was a vicious scoundrel.

"Simon promised to keep me out of debtor's prison *and* the grave if I contracted your marriage. I was to manage Triple Oak as I had been doing the past decade, if I agreed to his scheme."

"And you expect me to forgive you and take pity on you because you were browbeaten into submission?" Liberty scoffed resentfully. "I hardly think I owe you the slightest consideration."

Luther gnashed his teeth. Dealing with this feisty hellion had never been easy. She had a low tolerance for those who were not as bold and courageous as she had proved herself to be.

"I had hoped for your understanding of my situation and your compassion," Luther replied, struggling to maintain his temper.

"You expect more than I can give. As far as I'm concerned—"

Luther waved her to silence. "I'm not finished yet," he snapped. "You may find yourself more willing to bargain with me when I reveal the truth about Simon's death."

Begrudgingly, Liberty settled back in her chair, doubting anything Luther had to say would convince her to like this lout.

"Since you were heavily drugged and too bleary-eyed to know exactly what transpired, I will tell you," Luther insisted. "While you were upstairs sleeping off the potion, Dylon managed to subdue the two guards posted outside and barged in to confront Simon. When Dylon learned the marriage had taken place, he was furious and vowed to kill Simon. There has been bad blood between the two men for years. It was Dylon who had cast the shadows of suspicion on Simon after his second wife's death. And when Simon challenged Dylon's elected position in the Assembly, rumors about his checkered past began buzzing."

"Simon blamed Dylon for losing his quest for a seat in the Assembly?" Liberty mused aloud.

Luther nodded positively. "That and his dishonorable discharge from the army of regulars. Simon took devilish delight in marrying you—the woman Dylon apparently wanted. When Simon sicced all three of his henchmen on Dylon, he thought he'd seen the last of his archenemy. They hauled Dylon's unconscious body to the swamp to dispose of him. But by some miracle, Dylon survived and returned with a fiendish vengeance."

Luther leaned forward, bracing his spindly arms on the top of his desk like a bat outstretching its black wings. His dark, beady eyes drilled into Liberty. "It was murder Dylon Lockhart had in mind when he attacked Simon on the balcony."

"'Twas not!" Liberty bolted out of her chair to glower across the desk at her uncle. "He was trying to save me from certain death!"

"I was in the adjoining room watching!" Luther growled at her. "I saw the entire incident—from start to finish—through the terrace door. I know for a fact that you couldn't determine who you were battling, much less see clearly enough whom to attack. You even clubbed Dylon, thinking he was Simon. But when you pushed Simon away, Dylon shoved you aside and tried to heave Simon over the railing. Simon tried to crawl back to safety but Dylon let him drop to his death."

Now, there were some females who foolishly took the word of less dependable sources rather than the men they loved. But Liberty wasn't one of them. She had always been a reasonably good judge of character and she knew damned well who was teeming with reputable character and who was without it. Luther was definitely without!

"Dylon did not kill Simon!" Liberty spewed furiously. "You are twisting the truth to suit your own purpose."

"That would hardly be necessary." Luther smirked as he plunked back into his chair. "Dylon had already vowed to see Simon dead. Your struggle with Simon provided the perfect opportunity for Dylon to dispose of the man who stood between him and the woman he wanted, the woman he had claimed to all the world as his fiancée at the engagement party. I may be a coward but Dylon Lockhart is a ruthless murderer. He allowed you to take the blame for Simon's death by insisting you acted in self-defense. And, of course, in your dazed state, you could hardly dispute him."

"That's preposterous! Dylon is not the kind of man who would let a man drop to his death when—"

"Nay?" Luther chuckled sardonically at her defensiveness. "What good would it have done to have Simon stashed in prison? He still would have been your lawful husband. Dylon knew that. Only Simon's death would set you free. And no doubt, Dylon proposed again, despite your husband's recent death." He dared her to contradict him. "Lockhart is hardly a fool, Liberty. You are an heiress with a pedigree as long as a man's arm. But Dylon will be the one rotting in jail when *I* go to the constable to explain the entire episode and the fatal incident that took Simon's life. Dylon committed cold-blooded murder and let you take the blame."

When Liberty sank limply into her chair, Luther smiled triumphantly. "Now, it seems I am faced with a dilemma. Should I go forward as the only true eyewitness and divulge the ghastly truth about one of our colony's leading citizens? Dylon's reputation will be ruined, he will besmirch the family name, and he will be marched off to prison. Even if Dylon bribes the judges and gains his freedom, the accusations and scandal will destroy him politically." He touched his chin, as if pondering his options. "Or, to protect the man you seem to have chosen for your husband, should I hold my tongue and forget what I saw?"

Liberty had the inescapable feeling Luther was leading up to a proposal of blackmail. That wasn't surprising, considering Liberty had all but announced Luther was no longer welcome at Triple Oak and he would be ousted without a penny.

"What do you want from me, Luther?" Liberty hissed in question.

"Security, of course," he replied with a goading smile. "I intend to ensure that I live out my life in the fashion to which I have grown accustomed. I should think a percentage of your father's shipping business and control of his residence in the West Indies would be sufficient enough to ensure my silence."

Liberty's fingers curled, itching to grab Luther by the throat and choke the life out of him. "What percentage?" she muttered.

"Forty percent of the profits and an equal share in the shipping business," he demanded.

"Nay! You will have nothing for that is exactly what

you deserve after you conspired to have me married and quickly buried!" Liberty screeched in outrage. "I'll make no deals with you, Luther. You have concocted a crock of lies to extort money from me. My father tolerated you because you are my mother's stepbrother, worthless though you are. But I have no sentimental attachment for weasels like you. . . ."

Liberty flinched when Luther reached into the desk drawer to snatch up two pistols. A menacing sneer swallowed his rodentlike features. "I was prepared to be lenient with you and spare your life. But since you have been so difficult, you leave me no other choice."

When Liberty dared to make a dash toward the door, Luther fired at the latch before her hand could fold around it. In disbelief, Liberty plastered herself against the wall and stared down the barrel of the loaded flintlock.

"I'm afraid you will have to suffer a nasty accident since you refused to cooperate," Luther growled at his defiant niece. "And when your body washes ashore somewhere downriver, I will be the only living heir to claim title to your inheritance, as well as the lands owned by your poor departed husband." A diabolical smile stretched across his thin lips. "You see, little bitch, I was being generous by offering blackmail. Now I will take it all and you won't need one shilling where you're going."

"I've changed my mind," Liberty chirped, buying precious time. "Blackmail does have an appealing ring to it."

Luther shook his head and grinned benevolently. "I only planned to ask you once. Since you vehemently declined, you will face the consequences."

Liberty stared at her uncle and then at the loaded pistol. She would be damned if she allowed Luther to enjoy the ultimate victory. If she was going out of this world, she would go out in a blaze of glory and with a bullet in the back. There would be nothing accidental about her death! Let Luther explain how his niece had died accidentally with a bullet hole in the whalebone stays of her gown! She may be launched into eternity, but Luther Norris would be lynched for her murder, just see if he wasn't! Dylon would realize what had happened and he would ensure Luther paid with his life.

With that grim consolation beating in her palpitating chest, Liberty pounced toward the door, expecting to hear the bark of Luther's flintlock. But Luther proved himself to be extremely adaptable. When Liberty made her valiant escape attempt, daring him to shoot her in the back, he flipped the pistol in his hand and lunged at her.

Liberty had only swung open the door and taken one step when she felt the butt of the flintlock crash against her skull. What was it about her, she wondered as the world faded into nothingness, that provoked so many men to pound her over the head every chance they got . . . ?

Like a delicate flower wilting beneath the blistering summer sun she pitched forward in the grass and lay there like a slug.

Chapter 28

Dylon's face locked in fury when he spied two bodies entangled in the sun-dappled shadows beneath a grove of trees. It only took an instant to recognize Phillipe LaGere and his helmet of blond hair gleaming in the light. Dylon's tormented mind leaped to the most distasteful conclusion imaginable. He was certain that the woman trapped beneath Phillipe was none other than Liberty Jordon. Damn that overzealous Frenchman! He had forced his attention on Liberty in his eagerness to convince her to sail away with him.

Phillipe had damned well better be *forcing* himself on Liberty, Dylon silently fumed. If she was a willing participant in this romantic tête-à-tête he'd strangle her! She had vowed her love to him just last night and he had believed her. But then, he'd foolishly fallen for Patricia's pretended affection years earlier, Dylon reminded himself sourly. The last woman he'd loved had sailed off with a titled Englishman. Now Liberty was making plans to flit off with this flamboyant Frenchman.

Damn her! She had betrayed him! Dylon swore fluently as he nudged his steed forward. So this was why Liberty hadn't divulged her destination to him. She had sneaked off to tumble in the grass with Phillipe and to plan her escape. She had only pretended to love Dylon while she devilishly seduced Phillipe.

Curse that witch and curse all women everywhere! Dylon's logic was being twisted by such torment that a winged stallion couldn't have flown him to the scene of betrayal fast enough to suit him. He kept remembering all the quietly uttered confessions he'd whispered to Liberty in the darkness. She had probably laughed at him all the while, curse her. And if she'd felt anything at all for him, it was no more than sympathy. Dylon had been wounded, battered and bruised and Liberty had taken pity on him. She had seduced him the night before she planned to spirit away with that blockheaded Casanova.

By the time Dylon skidded his steed to a halt he was good and mad! Phillipe vaulted to his feet and both men gaped at each other. While Phillipe's refined features burst with color, Dylon's murderous gaze dropped to the young woman whose red hair was a mass of leaves and tangles.

"Cayla?" Dylon croaked, frog-eyed. He was relieved that Liberty hadn't betrayed him and shocked to find the comely redhead in Phillipe's arms. This Don Juan had been spouting his affection for Liberty since the instant he arrived. Obviously Phillipe was one of those fair-weather fiancés whose romantic affections changed with the wind.

"What on earth . . . ?" Griffin chirped when he spied Cayla sprawled in the grass, her lips swollen from Phillipe's passionate kisses.

With cavalier gallantry, Phillipe thrust himself between Cayla and the Lockharts' incredulous stares. "The lady is not responsible," he nobly declared. "It is I who have caused her this embarrassment."

"Upon my word, you are a most difficult man to understand. I thought you were madly in love with Liberty," Brewster snorted as he stepped down from his carriage. "If you are, young man, you have a most peculiar way of showing it." His eyes flashed like hot blue flames. "You had better explain yourself at once. I'm beginning to think that you, like Simon Gridley, are ultimately after Liberty's inheritance."

Phillipe drew himself up after being soundly slapped with the insult. "I resent that, monsieur! I was prepared to love Liberty long and well, to fulfill my promises to her father. But Liberty has made a point of avoiding me every chance she gets. But even so, I was prepared to die for her honor."

His blond head swiveled on his shoulders to stare longingly at the flush-faced Cayla. "But while this enchanting goddess and I were lost in the swamp, we realized that Fate had intervened and that there was far more between us than our mutual desire to rescue Liberty from catastrophe." He extended his hand to hoist Cayla to her feet and pulled her protectively against him. "It is Cayla whom I love and she loves me. She has agreed to sail back to the West Indies with me."

Phillipe's gaze lifted to Griffin who had arrogantly assumed Cayla had a crush on him while he secretly longed to exchange places with his older brother.

"I regret, monsieur, that I have stolen your lady away from you. But being the noble gentleman you are, I know you would not stand in the way of true love," Phillipe declared philosophically.

True love or not, Griffin voiced no complaint. He had grown to like Cayla Styles after Liberty had freed her oppressed sister from her restrictive upbringing. But *liking* Cayla was a far cry from *loving* her, which Griffin didn't. It was Liberty who aroused deep affection within him.

"I bear no grudge," Griffin assured the Frenchman. "As you said, who would dare to stand in the way of true love?"

"If you sneaked away with Cayla then where in the hell is Liberty?" Dylon growled in question.

Cayla and Phillipe blinked, baffled.

"Maybe it really *was* Nora who sent Liberty that

mysterious message which prompted her to race off without a word," Brewster interjected.

"Oh my God!" Cayla's hand flew to her lips. A flash of memory leaped to the center stage of her mind.

In her eagerness to sneak away with Phillipe to take target practice with bows and arrows, Cayla had forgotten about the unexpected visitor she had seen jogging up the walkway. When Phillipe helped her dismount in this secluded grove of trees, Cayla had been swept off her feet. She'd forgotten all about wielding a bow and the unlikely houseguest!

"I saw Luther Norris scurrying up to the door with an envelope in hand this morning while I was making my way to the stables," she gasped in dismay.

"Sweet merciful heavens, not Luther!" Percy piped up and then half collapsed on his perch atop the carriage.

Dylon would have kicked himself if he had been physically able, but his bum leg wouldn't permit it. "Luther . . ." He scowled the man's name like a curse, furious at himself. Simon had overshadowed his accomplice to such extremes that Dylon had almost forgotten about that little rodent. Dylon had been so frustrated by Liberty's mysterious disappearance, fear of betrayal and his unpleasant confrontation with the Flannerys that he had failed to consider the obvious! And what with Brewster spouting his assumptions about Nora's involvement in some devious scheme to put Liberty to flight, Dylon had overlooked the fact that Luther was still lurking about, his plans foiled by Simon's death.

Curse that man to hell and back! If Luther harmed one hair on Liberty's head, Dylon swore he'd tear that scoundrel limb from limb. Luther was undoubtedly making some grandstand play for his personal gain. Had he lured Liberty into a trap? Would another message arrive at Lockhart Hall, demanding a ransom for Liberty's safe return?

Safe return? Dylon cringed at the unnerving thought

that skittered through his mind. Considering all Luther had to gain, Dylon wondered if that bastard cared whether Liberty wound up dead or alive. *Dead* would probably suit Luther better!

In fiend-ridden haste, Dylon sent his steed plunging through the thicket, taking the shortcut to Triple Oak that lay several miles upriver. While Percy, Brewster, and Griffin followed in Dylon's wake, Phillipe and Cayla gathered their horses which were laden with the bows and arrows they'd brought for target practice. The bows, however, had never seen any action because of the impulsive lovers' unquenchable needs for each other.

And so the Lockhart-and-friends rescue brigade sped cross-country. Dylon cursed himself at regular intervals for allowing the cynic in him to think Liberty had betrayed him. She had never given him cause to doubt her sincerity, only cause to curse her for her independent nature. She was the kind of woman who would confront Luther alone, leaving Dylon to recover from his wound. Her consideration, though commendable, was infuriating! Being considerate wouldn't do her or Dylon one bit of good if she wound up dead. And she'd better not, Dylon mused furiously. He wanted her alive so he could kill her for scaring twenty years off his life!

Dylon rode hell-for-leather, wavering back and forth between his desire to have Liberty back in the protective circle of his arms and the frustrated need to choke her for refusing to consult him. If Luther had disposed of that daring imp, Dylon vowed to show that bastard no mercy. And that was one promise Dylon intended to keep!

Luther maneuvered Liberty's unconscious body over his thin-bladed shoulder into a jackknifed position that left her blond hair trailing down his hip. He scurried along the wharf that extended over the depths of the river. It had been his intention to submerge his pesky niece while she was in no condition to fight him. But the jostle of being carried upside down at a frenzied pace jarred Liberty awake. When she moaned groggily, Luther cursed fluently.

Panting for breath, Luther struggled to lay Liberty on the wooden planks. Before she was fully conscious, Luther grabbed a rope to bind her ankles. That done, he tossed the loose end of the rope over the pulley that was usually utilized to load heavy cargo onto a waiting schooner which took farm produce to Charles Town. But today the pulley would be employed to leave Liberty dangling upside down in the river like a carcass of beef.

When Luther tugged on the rope, yanking Liberty's feet upward, blood rushed to her head, bringing her fully awake. Her furious squawk erupted in the muggy air when Luther swung her out over the river. Liberty glanced down to see the lapping water inch steadily toward her. She screamed bloody murder.

Luther hadn't counted on the fact that Liberty's full skirts would form a pocket of air around her head as he lowered her to her death and held her there indefinitely. But that was exactly what happened. As he plunged her into the river, Liberty curled her body upward to inhale much needed air, prolonging destiny.

Luther snatched up a barrel with his free hand and flung it toward his niece, hoping to saturate her skirts and deplete the supply of air that was trapped in her garments. But that tactic didn't turn out as he anticipated either. Damn that woman, she seemed to have as many lives as a cat! Liberty clutched the barrel to her chest and it became her buoy. No matter how roughly Luther jerked up on the rope that held her feet suspended and then plunged her downward, the barrel prevented her from drowning in the river. . . .

The sound of thundering hooves drew Luther's frantic gaze. He lurched about, still clinging to the rope. In shock and fear, Luther saw the cavalcade, led by Dylon Lockhart, galloping across the meadow toward the wharf. Hastily, Luther secured the rope, leaving Liberty hanging upside down. He scrambled toward a nearby skiff and leaped into it. His mind raced, searching for an alternate plan of action. Since Liberty had refused to be blackmailed and her "accidental" death was now out of the question, Luther decided to ransom his niece. If he could escape Dylon, he could demand cash to return this indestructible imp before he sailed away to safety.

Still monitoring Dylon's rapid approach, Luther rowed the skiff beneath his upended niece. Balancing himself, Luther stood up in the boat to cut the rope. With a thud and a groan, Liberty dropped into an untidy heap. Before she could rake the long tendrils from her face and claw Luther to shreds, he bound her wrists with the free end of the rope.

Casting an apprehensive glance over his shoulder, Luther hurriedly paddled into midstream, allowing the current to whisk him downriver. A triumphant smile pursed his lips while he listened to Liberty curse him up one side and down the other and Dylon roar at him like an enraged lion.

The self-satisfied smile that hovered on Luther's lips evaporated when he saw Dylon clatter down the planked wharf atop his wild-eyed steed. When Dylon reached the end of the dock, he jabbed his mount in the flanks, sending him plunging into the water in determined pursuit.

Muttering, Luther paddled as fast as his aching arms would permit, hoping to outrace the dark-haired demon who cut through the water like a barracuda.

"Get downstream!" Brewster bellowed, indicating the bend in the river that would slow Luther's pace. The rescue brigade, which had been left behind on the riverbank, circled around to gallop along the water's edge.

While Dylon swam his steed toward the skiff, the rest

of the rescue posse tried to cut Luther off at the bend in the river. Dismounting, Griffin whipped out his pistol to take aim at Luther. Not to be outdone, Phillipe grabbed his bow and arrows to take aim at the fiendish villain who had abducted his former fiancée.

Swearing furious oaths, Luther sprawled atop Liberty when the pistol barked and arrows swished past him. But Griffin's bullet, though it had missed the target of Luther's shoulder, had hit the skiff, leaving a sizable hole in the stern.

Water poured into the boat and Luther was forced to abort his third plan in an attempt to save himself while he could. Avoiding the hissing arrows, Luther rolled over the edge of the skiff and swam toward the opposite bank.

While Luther dog-paddled for his life, the sinking skiff drifted toward the reeds that clogged the bend in the river. Gasping for breath, Liberty struggled to upright herself. But Luther had strapped the rope, which held her wrists, around the planked bench in the skiff. As the boat sank deeper in the river, Liberty reared back, struggling to keep her head afloat. But there was as much water in the boat as there was in the river.

Although Griffin and Phillipe were wading toward her, thrashing their way through the entangled weeds, they weren't able to reach her before the water level rose over her head. Refusing to waste another ounce of energy, Liberty slumped against the bottom of the skiff where she had been anchored. There was nothing for her to do but save her breath and pray that Griffin and Phillipe could reach her before she drowned.

They had damned well better hurry! thought Liberty when her lungs began to ache and threatened to burst. She was savoring her last ounce of breath. . . .

Just when Liberty swore her lungs would explode, she felt frantic hands clawing at her. She wasn't sure she had enough air left to sustain her while Griffin freed the rope that held her down. But in the nick of time the rope slackened and he jerked her into his arms.

A muted scowl erupted from Dylon's lips when he realized how close Liberty had come to another disaster. Assured that she was still alive, he focused absolute attention on the scoundrel who was frantically swimming toward shore. Rage boiled inside Dylon. Oh, how he itched to tear Luther to shreds for threatening Liberty's life. Simon and Luther were both cut from the same scrap of rotten wood, Dylon decided.

Luther strangled on his breath when he glanced back to see Dylon coming toward him with blood in his eyes and a vicious snarl on his lips. Panicky, Luther thrashed through the reeds to reach solid ground. Before he could pull himself ashore, Dylon launched himself off his horse and sent Luther plunging headfirst into the slime.

Clenching his fist in the nape of Luther's cape, Dylon held his foe's head under water, satisfying his need for revenge. He allowed Luther a scant breath before shoving him down again, letting the bastard experience the same desperation Liberty had suffered while she hung upside down on the pulley and lay anchored in a sinking skiff.

When Luther went limp, Dylon jerked him back toward his mount. Towing Luther behind him, Dylon crossed the river on horseback. The instant Dylon reached the shore, Griffin and Percy grabbed hold of Luther and marched him toward a tree, binding him with the rope he'd used on Liberty. With Luther secured, they scuttled back to where Liberty lay gasping for breath and cursing in a most unladylike manner.

Despite the catastrophe that had befallen her, Liberty wasn't the least bit subdued. In fact, she was madder than a wet hen! Although her self-appointed nurses refused to let her stand up until they were certain she hadn't swallowed half the water in the river, Liberty vaulted to her feet.

Dylon stamped toward her, wearing a thunderous scowl. If she expected sympathy, she was painfully disappointed. Dylon was positively livid! He was glaring at her as if *she* had committed an unpardonable crime instead of Luther. Her amethyst eyes widened in disbelief when Dylon clenched his fist in the bodice of her soggy gown and yanked her to him.

He shoved his face into hers and yelled at her. "You muleheaded moron! Don't you ever again prance off without my permission, without telling me your destination. You almost got yourself killed, damn you. And if anybody deserves to be the one to dispose of you, it should be me!"

That was definitely not the sort of reception Liberty expected or needed after her near brush with disaster. For all his redeeming qualities, Dylon seemed to possess all the sensitivity of a rock! If he loved her as much as he said he did, he should have been showering her with kisses instead of growling insults.

His unexpected display of anger set fuse to her temper. "Without *your* permission?" she yelled right back into his menacing sneer that did his handsome features no justice whatsoever. "I do not need *your* permission. I am my own woman and I will thank you to remember that!"

"The only kind of woman you're going to be if you insist on behaving like a fool is a dead one!" Dylon blared.

Liberty was positively certain Dylon had a full set of pearly white teeth when he opened his mouth and bit her head off with another insult. Before she could fling a suitably nasty rejoinder, Brewster thrust himself between them.

"Emotions are running high and with good reason," he snapped as his gaze bounced back and forth between the two glowering faces. "And before you both say something you'll live to regret, I suggest—"

Liberty flung herself away before she did spout

another insulting remark. Hissing furiously, she glared at her uncle who had been strapped to a tree. Now here was the true source of her irritation—the man who'd made her life a veritable hell since she set foot in the colonies. Glancing around, Liberty spied Phillipe's discarded bow and arrows.

Muttering a curse to Luther's name with every agitated breath she took, Liberty snatched up the bow and drew down on her uncle. Luther's eyes widened in terror when he realized he had become the target of Liberty's fury.

"This is for all the torment you've put me through, Luther," she spumed as she squinted down the arrow. Liberty released the taut string. The arrow whistled through the air and stabbed into the bark, a scant two inches from Luther's left ear. "And this is for clubbing me over the head with your pistol." Liberty let another arrow fly. It notched an inch from Luther's right ear and he turned a squeamish shade of white. "And this is for—"

"Gimme that," Dylon growled as he lunged toward the bow. Quick as he was, he was way too slow to grab the weapon before Liberty fired. The misdirected arrow hissed through the air, causing the amused onlookers to dive to the ground before they were accidentally struck. The arrow stuck in the side of Brewster's elegant black coach, directly above the five bodies that had wisely chosen to sprawl in the grass.

Dylon ensured his family and friends were still alive, though visibly shaken. Then, wearing a most intimidating scowl, he fixed snapping blue eyes on Liberty. "If you kill that worthless scoundrel, it can hardly be deemed self-defense. That plea worked with Simon, but it won't work with Luther, especially with these witnesses who will be honor bound to testify that you were only satisfying your vengeance."

Liberty yanked the bow from his grasp and put out her chin. "You might be taking pot shots at Luther yourself if you knew that he claimed *you* were the one who really murdered Simon and let me take the blame," she flung at him.

"What?" Dylon blinked, incredulous.

Liberty nodded affirmatively. "Luther first tried to bribe me into giving him half my inheritance for his silence. He told me all about your previous confrontations with Simon. He also declared that you saw your chance to dispose of my husband so you could marry me and acquire even more wealth than the Lockharts already possess, greedy rascal that you are!"

"That's a damned lie!" Dylon wheeled to glare at Luther who was dripping wet and scared stiff.

Cursing, Dylon stamped over to retrieve Cayla's bow and quiver of arrows from the saddle. Suddenly he had no qualms about scaring the living daylights out of Luther by using him for target practice.

Poised, Dylon drew back the string and glared at his peaked target. "Tell her the truth, Luther, or you're going to become a human pincushion." The arrow sailed through the air and stuck in the bark that lay an inch away from the pulsating veins in Luther's neck.

"All I know is that you saw your chance to take possession of Simon's property and have him out of your way forever!" Luther bleated like a sick lamb. He was living on the hope that Dylon's family would intervene before he was shot down in cold blood. But he wasn't sure anyone could stop Liberty Jordon. She seemed hell-bent on torturing him before she murdered him.

"Now that I know what makes you tick, I wouldn't be surprised if you had managed to kill Simon so *you* could acquire a fortune after you disposed of me," Liberty accused before she launched another arrow.

Luther flinched when the arrow lodged between his legs. Two inches higher and she would have castrated him in a most agonizing manner.

Dylon frowned pensively when Liberty's impulsive

remark echoed in his ears. Flashbacks of that fateful night sparked in his mind. Over and over again, he kept seeing Simon glaring up at him while he dangled over the balcony railing. Dylon vividly remembered being baffled when Simon ceased his struggling attempt to pull himself to safety. The vicious sneer had faded from Simon's puckered features and he had slumped before the pistol blasts could have put an end to him.

Something still didn't ring true about that incident. Simon should have collapsed soon after the shot, if it had been fatal, which it wasn't, unless . . .

Dylon growled under his breath and steadied his bow. "It was you who planned Simon's death, you who let Liberty and me take the blame," he harshly accused.

"I did no such thing!" Luther squawked in protest. "You were the one who let Simon drop to his death instead of dragging him back to the balcony . . ." His voice trailed off into a terrified shriek when Liberty's arrow stabbed into the fabric of his cloak, just beneath his left arm.

Dylon drew down his bow and stared at Luther who was oddly reminiscent of a turkey with its feathery quills protruding from the sides of his body. "I didn't have the chance to kill Simon, even if I'd wanted to," he muttered. The dawn of recognition hit him full force and he swore under his breath. "Simon died while he hung weightlessly in my grasp."

Everyone except Luther and Dylon were baffled by the remark. Frowning, Liberty peered into Dylon's ominous expression.

"What do you mean Simon was already dead before he hit the ground?" she wanted to know.

Dylon's gaze never wavered from Luther's blanched face. "Tell her," he demanded gruffly.

When Luther slammed his mouth shut and tilted a defiant chin, Dylon put his arrow to flight. The missile quivered into the tree, pinning the crotch of Luther's breeches to the bark.

"There is nothing to tell," Luther chirped when he recovered control of his vocal chords. "You are trying to terrorize me into accepting the blame for your crime!"

"What is it you're suggesting?" Liberty questioned bemusedly.

"Unless I miss my guess, Simon was drugged or poisoned before he stalked upstairs that night," Dylon explained. "I knew he'd been drinking by the way he was staggering about. I suspect Luther poisoned him in hopes that both of you would meet with your death. He would have been the only living heir to your fortune, as well as your husband's."

"I did nothing of the kind and you can't prove it!" Luther screeched furiously. "Release me at once. I intend to have you arrested for murder before you can conspire against me!"

"So that's why it wasn't too difficult for me to escape Simon when he tried to attack me," Liberty pondered aloud.

She, too, had sensed that Simon had been drinking heavily. Even in her dazed condition, she had been able to push Simon aside and stumble out to the gallery. And if what Dylon speculated were true, Simon would have collapsed during their tussle, sending both himself and Liberty plunging to their deaths. But Dylon had arrived to complicate Luther's devious scheme. So naturally that conniving little bastard had set about to devise another plan of parting Liberty from her inheritance.

"Why that miserable, lowdown, good-for-nothing . . ."

Dylon shoved Liberty's bow downward before she completely lost control of her inflammable temper. A wry smile pursed his lips as he glanced speculatively at Phillipe LaGere.

"Luther knows neither of us will kill him, though he richly deserves it," Dylon contended. "We have displayed our skills a trifle too well in the past." A devilish grin quirked Dylon's lips as he glanced from Liberty to her uncle. "Perhaps we should allow Phillipe to take target practice on Luther in hopes of wresting the information from him. And if Phillipe happens to plunge an arrow through Luther's heart, it would be quite by accident, considering he is just a novice at the sport."

When Luther turned a fascinating shade of green, Dylon chuckled wryly. "And we all know how fond Luther has become of *accidents*, since he has planned at least two of them himself."

Liberty returned Dylon's wicked grin. "'Tis a grand idea. Phillipe could use the practice for future duels on the field of honor. And if by chance he strikes Luther instead of the tree, none of us will hold a novice at fault. And Luther can't complain because he'll be dead." Another impish grin pursed her lips as she ambled over to return Phillipe's bow. "Shall we re-enact the adventures of William Tell? If Phillipe manages to shoot an object atop Luther's head, we shall applaud his skills. And if he misses . . ." Liberty sighed and shrugged carelessly. "Ah well, it will be no great loss to the world if Luther takes an arrow in his hard heart."

Luther's chin jutted out in stubborn defiance . . . until he watched the flamboyant Frenchman fumble with his bow. It only took an instant for Luther to realize he was no longer dealing with skilled marksmen. Phillipe hadn't improved one whit since that day on the dueling field with Simon.

When Phillipe made a superb display of positioning himself to shoot, he accidentally released the string. Luther squealed like a stuck pig when the arrow wobbled through the air, nose-dived, and struck the buckle of Luther's shoe.

"Aim higher, Phillipe," Liberty instructed with a mischievous grin.

When Phillipe fumbled with the bow and arrow a second time, Luther screeched at the top of his lungs, ordering the unskilled archer to stop!

"All right, I admit it," Luther choked out. "I poisoned Simon's drink when we toasted our success in seeing Liberty wed and in beating Dylon to a pulp. I knew Liberty's drugging potion would wear off well enough for her to resist Simon's advances. Since he was not in full control of his senses after the fatal dose of hemlock, he would cause Liberty's death when she tried to escape. I even locked the door to the hall so there would be only one way for her to run."

"How dare you threaten Liberty's life, you insufferable cad!" Phillipe jeered with his customary flair for the dramatic. "You do indeed deserve to die and I shall cut you down like the loathsome villain you are!"

Hurriedly, Phillipe jerked up the bow and took aim. When Dylon knocked the bow aside, the arrow went astray again. Brewster, Cayla, Griffin and Percy hit the ground the split-second before the projectile zinged between the spokes of the carriage wheel and stuck in the grass.

"Confound it, take that bow away from that maniac before he kills us all!" Brewster roared as he climbed onto his hands and knees. "You have your confession, Dylon. And I'm going to suffer heart seizure if the three of you don't stop this nonsense!"

Having accomplished his purpose, Dylon snatched Phillipe's bow away and tossed it to Griffin. "Take Luther to the constable's office," he instructed his brother. "He can mildew in jail, along with Simon's three henchmen."

"With pleasure," Griffin enthused as he strode over to fetch the horses.

In a matter of minutes, Luther was bound to the saddle and led away. Without a word, Cayla and Phillipe melted into the grove of trees that skirted the river. Percy and Brewster whizzed off in the carriage, leaving Dylon staring pensively at the disheveled beauty with vivid lavender eyes and a tangle of windblown blond hair.

"I hope you are not planning to read me the riot act again," Liberty grumbled as she stamped toward her steed. "After being clanked over the head with the butt of a pistol and narrowly escaping drowning twice, I'm in no mood for your lectures."

"Not even if you deserve it?" Dylon queried as he ambled behind her, still favoring his tender leg.

"I don't deserve it," Liberty declared with absolute certainty. "Just because I love you doesn't give you the right to demand to know what I'm doing during every single second of every single day." Massaging her throbbing temples, Liberty exhaled an exhausted sigh. "Sometimes I think Stella is right. I've been out of my element since the day I left the islands. Perhaps I should sail back with Phillipe."

Her subtle tactic of drawing a confirmation of affection from Dylon after he'd raked her over the coals didn't work as she'd hoped. Liberty hadn't taken kindly to his terse scolding, especially one delivered in front of an audience. What she needed was to hear Dylon say that he still loved her, despite her stubborn, independent nature, despite her explosive temper.

Instead of reassuring her, Dylon only lifted a broad shoulder in a shrug. "You can sail off to the Indies if that is your wont, but Phillipe has had a change of heart." He nudged his steed into a faster clip as they zigzagged along the river which flowed like black glass beside the cypress, cedars and briars. "It seems Fate threw Phillipe and Cayla together once too often. He plans to marry her and take her back to the islands with him."

Liberty gaped at him in disbelief. "Phillipe and Cayla?"

"Aye," Dylon confirmed with a wry smile. "And now that Nora has displayed her scheming nature in front of her father, Edgar has abandoned his crusade of seeing me unhappily wed. Now, it seems neither of us have to marry anyone unless it suits us."

Liberty was growing more agitated by Dylon's cool detachment by the second. They had done more living the past few weeks than some folks could squeeze into an entire year. They had experienced the full spectrum of human emotions and had risked their lives for each other. And now, after all they'd been through together, Dylon was so blasé Liberty could have cheerfully choked him! How dare he shrug off the quiet confessions of love he'd whispered to her the previous night! How dare he pretend there was nothing more than wild adventure between them!

"Is that what you want? For me to pack up and leave? What was I? The lesser of two evils when it came to choosing between me and Nora Flannery?" she spumed.

"I did not say I wanted you to leave," Dylon clarified in a much calmer tone than Liberty had employed. Ah, he delighted watching her hiss and spit like an enraged cat. He adored that fiery, undaunted spirit of hers.

"Well, you certainly didn't say you wanted me to *stay*," she pointed out, growing more exasperated by the minute.

"Of course I do," Dylon assured her, though his tone was nowhere near enthusiastic.

"Well, you certainly don't sound all that thrilled about it," Liberty retorted sarcastically.

"It has occurred to me that each time a man actively courts you and begs for your hand in marriage that you have the instinctive need to take flight. Why should I shower you with loving affection and undivided attention when you don't seem to want it?"

"It depends on who's giving it," Liberty qualified.

Dylon halted his steed to stare at the bedraggled beauty. "Being a woman of independent nature and strong-willed spirit, it seems the only way a marriage will work, when you are involved in it, is for *you* to do the proposing. When I got down on bended knee and begged for your hand, you went tearing off to meet your uncle without consulting me first. You very nearly got yourself killed and you gave no consideration whatsoever as to how the report of your death would have affected me. I've begun to think that you see me only as an object for your feminine pleasures. I am neither your confidant, your knight in shining armor *or* your trusted friend. All you want is me in your bed when you wish for me to be there!"

"That is the most preposterous thing I've ever heard!" Liberty exploded like a keg of blasting powder.

"You are entitled to your opinion and I'm entitled to mine," Dylon allowed. "But all the same, I'm not proposing to you again, even under penalty of death. When you come to me, *offering* to be my wife, then and only then will I know where you truly want to be."

When Dylon gouged his steed and bolted off, Liberty glared at his departing back. The nerve of that man! *Me? Propose to him? Why should I?*

Because, you imbecile, you love him and you damned well know it, came the annoyed voice from deep inside her. Liberty was sorry to report that she was stubborn to the core. When men pressured her, she did take flight. She had been running away from a commitment for years. She hadn't wanted a man to dominate her life after her father had permitted her to grow up wild and free and unrestrained. And still she refused to be oppressed and dictated to. All she had ever wanted was to be loved for herself, to be allowed her own space without being stifled the way Cayla Styles had been.

"He demands a proposal, does he? Indeed!" Liberty muttered aloud. "Hell will sooner freeze over!"

Will it, Liberty? came the mocking reply of her conscience. *Would you sacrifice your love for that dynamic, magnificent man, just to appease your colossal pride?*

While Liberty rode back to Lockhart Hall at a slow

pace, she spread out her emotions and analyzed them one by one. Why had she fallen in love with Dylon in the first place? Because he wasn't as comically flamboyant and dramatic as Phillipe. Because Dylon had a delightful sense of humor and he wasn't as greedy and devious as Simon. Because he lived every moment without taking himself so seriously. Those were certainly points in his favor. He was charming and kind and gentle and he didn't consider himself better than other men, even though he truly was in a class all his own. He had allowed Liberty to live by her own unconventional standards until her spirit of independence nearly got her killed. Was it so unreasonable for Dylon to be concerned about her welfare? Would she have loved him if he hadn't worried about her? After all, she had been overwrought when Simon shot Dylon in the leg and sicced those three burly gorillas on him! That was what caring was all about, wasn't it?

So why am I putting up such a fuss? Liberty asked herself rationally. Dylon was allowing her the chance to plan her own future. Phillipe had *assumed* she wanted to wed him. Simon had *forced* her to marry him. Dylon neither forced nor assumed what she felt. He was simply offering her a choice, allowing her to make her own decisions. Now what woman in this day and age could ask for more? How many other women were given the choice about anything that truly mattered? Damn few, Liberty realized sadly.

What this whirlwind affair boiled down to was that Liberty did love Dylon madly, completely. Now, she could sail off to the islands or she could swallow a little of that Jordon pride and spend the rest of her life with the only man she'd ever loved.

A slow smile worked its way onto the corner of her mouth and spread across her lips. Very well then, if Dylon wanted a proposal, he would have it. Of course, it wouldn't be the demanding, insistent type that she despised. Two could play his game. She would nonchalant him to death! This marriage would be one of mutual consent and agreement—no pressure from either the prospective bride or groom.

Snickering at the impish idea that had hatched in her mind, Liberty trotted along the path beside the river. She was not going to be outdone by that imperturbable rapscallion. Just wait until he received her proposal of marriage and see how he liked it! She was going to give him exactly what he asked for and nothing more. . . .

Chapter 29

Dylon paced across his room, trying to walk without a limp, even though it pained him considerably. Since he had issued his challenge to Liberty and thundered off, he had seen hide nor hair of that minx. That worried Dylon. He kept wondering if he had pushed that sassy sprite too far, giving her every reason to abandon him. Twice he had been compelled to hunt her down and twice he had forcefully restrained himself. He had vowed not to pressure her, to allow her to make her own decision. And damnit, he would abide by that promise, even if it killed him . . . which it probably would if she chose to sail back to the islands.

First Patricia had betrayed him for a titled Englishman and now that wild-haired hellion was trampling on his heart and he was letting her! But Dylon had learned, through an anguishing experience, that if a man and woman didn't love each other to the same degree, it wouldn't work. . . .

The rap at the door brought Dylon's head up with an anxious jerk. Liberty . . . He strode across the carpet to whip open the door. To his chagrin it was Percy rather than Liberty who greeted him.

Poised in his courtly fashion, not a hair on his Bag wig out of place, not a speck of lint on his jacket, Percy extended the message that was rolled in his hand.

Dylon stared at the parchment as if his valet was trying to foist a three-day-old dead fish on him. "More bad news?" Dylon questioned apprehensively.

"That depends on one's viewpoint, sir," Percy responded, poker-faced. "You will have to read the note and decide for yourself."

Obviously, the snoopy valet had taken the liberty of scanning the message before he delivered it. Dylon glared reproachfully at Percy, who didn't look the least bit repentant about what he'd done.

Warily, Dylon unrolled the parchment, glanced at the signature at the bottom and read the contents.

To: Dylon Lockhart, esquire,

A distasteful sniff broke the silence. Liberty was certainly being formal, thought Dylon. She had spent too much time with Percy. Her formality spelled disappointment. Reluctantly, Dylon read on:

At five o'clock this afternoon, a wedding will be held at the stone chapel near the village. If you are so inclined, I invite you to participate in the ceremony. If you choose to decline, please notify me at your earliest convenience.

Thank you,
Liberty Jordon

Dylon scowled wordlessly. How much more detached and indifferent could one woman sound? Damn her, he had wanted a total commitment, not an impassive invitation!

"I was told to wait for a reply," Percy prompted jolting Dylon from his resentful thoughts.

"I'm not certain if I'm being invited as a guest or the groom," he grumbled grouchily.

"It appears the choice is yours, sir," Percy remarked, stifling an amused grin. "Knowing how quickly Miss Jordon attracts eager fiancés, I would not tarry too long in making a decision. I would imagine Griffin would—"

He was cut off by Dylon's disgusted snort. "I'm perfectly aware that my own brother would snatch up this invitation in a second," Dylon muttered as he stalked over to grab a quill and scribble a hasty acceptance. Irritably, he thrust the note at Percy.

"Knowing how efficient you and my grandfather are, I suppose you posted the banns when you planned the surprise engagement party."

Percy nodded affirmatively. "Brewster has had the papers in hand since he arrived here. There will be no problem with the legality of this wedding."

Dylon let out his breath in a rush. "Then the wheels are already in motion. I only hope my intended bride doesn't have a change of heart and leave me standing at the altar like—"

"Patricia?" Percy finished for him. "If I have learned one thing the past few weeks, sir, 'tis that Liberty is absolutely nothing like Patricia. If she says she will be at her wedding, then I believe she shall be."

When Percy took himself off, Dylon glared at the frustrating and very bewitching image that floated above him. "Ornery little imp," he grumbled at the room at large.

Stella stepped back to admire the gown she had altered for this monumental occasion. It was a combination of the two wedding gowns Liberty had been forced to don during her unfortunate encounters with Simon Gridley. But by snipping off a bow here and there and stitching lace there and here, Stella was satisfied with the results.

"'Tis a grand gown," Stella declared. "I only hope this wedding turns out far better than the . . ." Her voice evaporated when Cayla Styles poked her head inside the small room that was attached to the quaint chapel in the wildwoods.

Sporting a radiant smile, Cayla breezed into the room to offer Liberty the elaborately crocheted veil she had created from her trousseau of doilies and tablecloths. "I made this for you," she announced. "I hope you bear me no ill feelings because of Phillipe. Quite honestly, I don't know how you ever resisted him. He is so suave and debonair."

That, Liberty mused, was a matter of opinion. With a smile, she accepted the veil. "I'm sincerely happy for both you and Phillipe. I will return this lovely creation after I use it so you can wear it in your own wedding."

Cayla expelled a relieved sigh. "I'm glad you aren't upset with me. I could not bear that, Liberty. You are the one who gave me my freedom to live my life as I pleased and Phillipe pleases me very much."

"Have you informed your family of your engagement?" Liberty queried as she set the veil in place.

Cayla grimaced. "Nay, not yet. I'm sure it will come as another shock to my parents when they learn I have not only burst loose from the rigid confines of womanhood but that I am marrying a man I have only known for a week."

"You have indeed burst loose, but you will bloom in the islands where the social structure is not quite so rigid," Liberty guaranteed with an impish grin. "I hope you and Phillipe will consent to take up residence at the Jordon estate. I need someone capable and dependable to ensure that it doesn't fall into ruin."

Cayla fairly beamed with pleasure and gratitude. "We would be delighted!" Composing herself, she pivoted to grab Stella's arm. "Stella and I will see you at the altar. 'Tis almost time for the ceremony to begin."

When Liberty was left alone to contemplate the giant step she was about to take, an unexpected rattle resounded on the back door. Lifting her skirts, she swept across the room to answer the knock. The last person Liberty expected or wanted to see charged toward her with a makeshift club in hand. Before Liberty could protect herself from the oncoming blow, the improvised weapon clanked against her skull. The world turned black and Liberty pitched forward on the floor in an unconscious heap.

A triumphant grin pursed Nora Flannery's lips as she sank down to unfasten the whalebone stays and remove Liberty's wedding gown. She intended to enjoy her revenge on Dylon and Liberty for humiliating her. Thanks to this blond-haired virago's interference and Dylon's blunt remarks, Edgar Flannery had refused to speak to his daughter and he had stormed off without her. When Nora heard the excited whispers of the servants who were preparing for the wedding reception, she had formed her ingenious plan. Only too late would Dylon realize he had married the wrong woman. (Or rather the right woman in Nora's opinion.)

Grinning wickedly, Nora wormed into the elegant gown, pulled up the white gloves that extended past her elbows, and stuffed her dark hair beneath the concealing veil. With Liberty bound and gagged and dragged into the corner, Nora swept toward the front door to await Brewster's arrival.

In a matter of two minutes, Brewster eased open the door to lead the bride down the aisle. A pleased smile pursed his lips as he peered at the camouflaged face behind the thick veil.

"You look lovely, Liberty," he complimented as he offered her his arm. "I am pleased that, very soon, you will be my granddaughter."

Unaware that a switch had been made, Brewster escorted the bride through the vestibule which led into the chapel. A small gathering of family, friends and servants had congregated to witness this long-awaited ceremony.

A sly smile formed on Nora's lips as Brewster escorted

her toward Dylon who stood at the altar. She could hardly wait to see the shocked expression on his face when he raised the veil at the end of the ceremony to kiss his bride! Ah, how sweet was the taste of revenge!

Dylon half turned as his grandfather led his bride down the aisle. He couldn't see her enchanting face because of the concealing veil, but he imagined Liberty was smiling impishly at him. He had requested a proposal of marriage and instead he had received a formal invitation he didn't dare refuse, not with Griffin chomping at the bit! Griff would have snatched Liberty up in a second and Dylon knew that as well as he knew his own name.

Brewster bowed out, leaving Dylon to curl his arm around his intended bride. A satisfied smile hovered on the patriarch's lips and his eyelid dropped into a wink. "'Tis a fine match," he murmured to Dylon. "Be as happy as Lucinda and I were all the years we spent together."

Dylon glanced down at his bride and then focused absolute attention on the clergyman who stood before them. It *would* be a fine match, Dylon mused while the preacher murmured the words that would join him and his lovely bride together forevermore. He only wondered what his feisty wife was going to say when the clergyman asked her if she would love, honor and obey her husband. Knowing this sassy sprite, she would demand some stipulations when they got to the part about *obeying*. Liberty, Dylon was sorry to say, didn't have a submissive bone in that curvaceous body of hers!

An agonized groan rumbled in Liberty's throat when she slowly returned to her senses. The headache that hammered against her skull left disjointed fragments of memory tumbling around in her brain. When the realization of what Nora intended dawned on her, Liberty rolled to her knees and frantically worked at the strands of fabric that bound her wrists and ankles. Blast it, if one more person clubbed her over the head and tied her up again she was going to . . .

Liberty flung the wasteful thought aside. "Curse that witch," she muttered into the gag that left her mouth as dry as cotton.

Despite the nausea caused by the forceful blow to her head, Liberty shoved her shoulder against the wall and pushed herself into an upright position. Swallowing down her stomach, she glanced down her torso at the chemise which now was the only garment of clothing she had left! Damn that Nora Flannery. She had stripped Liberty from her wedding gown and was in the process of marrying the man she had schemed to wed!

In the process of . . . Liberty shook her head to clear her groggy senses. Godamercy, what if Nora and Dylon had already spoken the vows to bind them together? At this very moment, Dylon could be standing at the altar in stupefied disbelief, staring at his new bride.

Muttering several unprintable curses into the gag, Liberty leaped across the room like a kangaroo. Although her wrists remained tied behind her, Liberty pivoted to inch toward the door latch. When the portal swung open, Liberty maneuvered around to hop down the hall toward the chapel. Totally disregarding modesty, Liberty jumped into the church.

"I now pronounce you man and—"

Liberty's muffled howl interrupted the preacher. Every head in the chapel turned in synchronized rhythm to gape frog-eyed at the indecently clad female who was bound, gagged, and jumping around like a crazed grasshopper.

Thunderstruck, Dylon stared at Liberty before his gaze swung back to the woman who was disguised in the thick, crocheted veil. With a rough jerk, Dylon yanked up the veil to see Nora's pinched features and her furious sneer. Dylon had never struck a woman but, at that moment, he came as close as he ever wanted to come.

"You are *my* husband," she hissed at him. "Mine! Do you hear me!"

Who couldn't? Her voice reverberated around the chapel like a clanging cymbal.

Dylon's lips tightened in a poisonous scowl and his lean fingers curled, itching to put a stranglehold on Nora's skinny white neck. With a terrified shriek, Nora took a precautionary step in retreat before Dylon did what he looked as if he wanted to do—choke her to death. In her haste to remove herself from harm's way, Nora tripped over the hem of the gown, one which had been a trifle too long for her in the first place. With a loud squawk, Nora tumbled backward and Dylon pounced on her like an enraged tiger.

To her relief, he didn't shake her until he broke her neck. He merely jerked her to her feet so quickly that it made her head spin. Dylon cursed her soundly and then hastily threw an apology to the clergyman. Without delay, he bustled Nora toward Liberty who had been surrounded by a cloud of startled guests.

Cayla thrust herself in front of Liberty like a dressing screen, protecting the intended bride from the stares she had been receiving. But Cayla was elbowed out of the way when Dylon shouldered his way through the congregation. Without breaking stride, Dylon hooked his arm around Liberty's waist and hoisted her off the floor. With Liberty draped under one muscular arm and Nora clamped in the other, Dylon stamped toward the small chamber which sat beside the chapel.

Still holding onto both women, Dylon kicked the door shut and emitted a growl that would have sent a lion cowering in its den. "I wouldn't marry you if you were the last female on this planet!" Dylon shouted at Nora

"You already have," she spat spitefully. "'Tis done. We are man and *wife!*"

Dylon spun Liberty around to untie her hands and then knelt to free her feet. And all the while he was hurling daggers at the gloating Nora. "The clergyman didn't pronounce us husband and wife," he qualified. "We are not married and we never will be."

His voice boomed like a cannon but Nora's temper was in full bloom. She all but yelled at him to vent her own frustration. "Aye, we are wed. We spoke the vows to each other."

A shocked yelp bubbled from Nora's throat when Dylon spun her around to unfasten the stays to the gown. Despite her struggles, Dylon forcefully jerked her from the stolen dress and left her standing in her chemise.

"Put this on and be quick about it," Dylon ordered as he thrust the garment at Liberty.

Liberty peered somberly at him as he yanked the veil from Nora's head. "Are you absolutely certain this is what you want, Dylon?" she wanted to know.

The anger and hostility drained out of him as he peered into Liberty's beguiling violet eyes and delicately carved features. Despite the fact that Nora was in the room, he scooped Liberty into his arms to brush his lips over her petal-soft mouth.

"The truth is I have never wanted anything so much in all my life," he whispered with genuine emotion. "No other man has been able to make you his bride. I just wonder what it's going to take to get you married to me, once and for all. The way my luck has been running, I wouldn't be surprised if a lightning bolt sizzled through the roof to prevent us from speaking the vows."

"Perhaps all the trouble we've had is an omen," Liberty murmured, tracing the battered lines of his face.

Dylon gave his raven head a negative shake and broke into a smile. "Every obstacle we've encountered only served to test the bonds of our affection and devotion. I love you, Liberty, more than life itself. If I can't have you, I want no one at all. . . ."

The words were barely out of his mouth before Griffin burst through the door. Drawing himself up to full stature, he stared at Liberty with his heart in his eyes—eyes the same intriguing shade of blue as Dylon's and Brewster's.

"I have tried to do the honorable thing and hold my tongue," Griffin burst out. "But I cannot let you walk down that aisle without declaring that I love you. I detest speaking out against my own brother, but family obligation and nobility be damned! Will you marry me, Liberty?"

Dylon clenched his teeth and glared at his brother. "Griff . . ." The quiet threat didn't faze Griffin one tittle.

"I thought I could permit this wedding to take place without interfering," he said with a long-suffering sigh. "But after this interruption, it seemed Fate is demanding that I speak my piece."

While Liberty stepped into her gown and Dylon fastened her into it, Griffin pleaded his case. "You have your choice, Liberty. But do not think you will be pressured into this wedding with Dylon if 'tis not your want. Brewster will understand if you choose me instead of my brother."

Liberty felt terribly awkward standing between both handsome men while Nora kept insisting that Dylon was her lawful husband. Finally, Liberty muttered under her breath, grabbed Nora by the back of her chemise and shoved her out the back door. That done, she peered beseechingly at Dylon.

"Please leave us alone for a moment," she requested.

"I'm afraid to," Dylon grumbled. "Considering everything that has happened, you probably won't be here when I get back."

When Liberty cast him another pleading glance, he expelled his breath and stalked out the door.

When they were alone, Liberty peered levelly at Griffin. "I'm fond of you, Griffin. I find you delightful company, but—"

When Liberty faltered and stared at the air above his head, Griffin's shoulders slumped defeatedly. "But you don't love me," he finished for her.

"Nay," she admitted softly. "Not the way a wife should love her husband."

Griffin frowned. "And what do you feel for Dylon? Is it special or is it that you have simply grown tired of being chased and you view marriage to him as salvation against your suitors?"

Liberty slipped her hand around his, giving it a fond squeeze. Her thick lashes fluttered up to meet his somber stare. "I have never felt this way about another man. Dylon gave me the choice of staying or going. I'm not marrying him out of desperation or for security and protection. I'm not marrying him because Brewster played the wily matchmaker. 'Tis because I love him, Griffin. And that makes all the difference."

A disappointed sigh tumbled from Griffin's turned-down mouth. "Then I suppose it would be best for me to accept Brewster's invitation to sail to Newport, Rhode Island, with him for the summer." Bitter laughter tripped from his lips. "They call it the 'Carolina hospital' because so many Southerners migrate there to escape the heat."

"So I have heard," Liberty murmured.

"Let's hope the climate can also cure broken hearts." Tenderly, he trailed his forefinger over her soft lips. "Perhaps by the time I return, I'll be able to adjust to the idea of having you as a sister-in-law rather than a wife."

Liberty grinned affectionately. "Somewhere, there is a woman who can love you the way you deserve to be loved. And perhaps the truth is you only proposed because you wanted what you thought Dylon had. Brotherly rivalry, perhaps?"

Griffin scoffed at her analysis. "You do not give yourself full credit, little imp. 'Tis not envy so much as affection. I'm certainly old enough and worldly enough to know the difference."

Without warning, Griffin pulled Liberty into his arms, bent her over backward and kissed the breath out of her. And it was then that Liberty knew beyond all shadow of a doubt that she was marrying the right man for all the right reasons. As skillful and seductive as Griffin was, his kiss did not set sparks in her blood the way Dylon's did. Only one man could ignite forbidden flames that scorched every fiber of her being.

Dylon picked the worst of all possible times to burst through the door. The unnerving scene put a growl on his curled lips and a scowl on his bruised face.

Undaunted and uncaring that he had been caught in the clutch, Griffin took his own sweet time about uprighting Liberty. "Now you know how I've felt the past few weeks," he remarked as he ambled past his brooding brother. "Of course, it did no good whatsoever, you understand. Not even a wizard could kiss away the love she feels for you. It seems some have the luck of the Irish, Dylon."

As the door eased shut behind Griffin, Dylon glared at the blond-haired beauty who was far too lovely and spirited for her own good.

"Well?"

"Well what?" Liberty questioned his question.

"Are you going to marry me or not?" he wanted to know that very second.

"The question is—Do you still want to marry *me?*" Liberty asked with a mischievous smile. "After all, I am the one who invited you to my wedding. But rake that you are, you tried to marry someone else in my stead."

"I?" Dylon hooted, running terribly short on patience. "I certainly didn't ask Nora to exchange places with you. As ornery as you are, I wonder if you put her up to this so you could flash Griff one of your come-hither glances and leave him groveling at your feet!"

"I did nothing of the kind!" Liberty snapped defensively.

Before their playful banter landed them in the middle of an argument, Dylon grabbed her hand and towed her toward the door. "We are not continuing this discussion until we have a legal license to fight," he declared. "And don't you dare argue with the preacher when he spouts the part about *obeying* your husband 'til death do you part either. We can negotiate the terms later."

But sure enough, Liberty *did* question the fact that the vows included obedience. Dylon really hadn't expected that saucy imp to let it pass. In his haste to make Liberty his wife before another unforeseeable disaster struck, Dylon requested the clergyman strike out the *obey* since he was perfectly willing to settle for being loved and honored.

With the wedding party following in their wake, the newlyweds returned to Lockhart Hall for the reception. Dylon allowed the festivities to drag on for two hours (which was an hour and a half longer than he preferred to begin with). Casting tact and diplomacy to the wind, Dylon announced that he and his bride were retiring to their chambers and that anyone who dared to interrupt them would be shot.

"My, what has become of the tolerant, good-natured man I thought I married?" Liberty teased as Dylon whisked her along in impatient strides.

Dylon didn't respond. He merely ushered his bride into his room and locked the door. Then he searched every nook and cranny for fear someone or something would leap out to interrupt their honeymoon.

Assured they were alone at last, Dylon wheeled around to face his bewitching bride. "Come here, madam," he commanded. "'Tis time you concentrated on your wifely duties."

Spouting orders at Liberty Jordon Lockhart was a definite mistake. Dylon realized that a mite too late (the half second after the reckless remark stampeded off his tongue, as a matter of fact).

Liberty did not come like an obedient puppy or devoted servant. She stood rooted to the spot as if she had been planted there.

An exasperated sigh passed Dylon's lips as Liberty stared at him like defiance personified. Whoever it was who declared a man's wedding day was the happiest day of his life had played a cruel joke on those of the male persuasion, Dylon decided. Surely it must have been an ornery female who dreamed up that idealistic phrase. Dylon Lockhart had enjoyed better days, believe you him. And *this* had not been one of them!

He had endured nine kinds of hell when Luther tried to drown Liberty. He had suffered all the torments of the damned when he raised the veil to find Nora staring smugly up at him. And after all the anguish he'd been through, Dylon had carelessly blurted out a command—the kind a man might give his mistress whose duty it was in life to provide him with sexual diversion at his convenience. For a man who usually knew the right thing to say in any given situation, Dylon had royally botched up! Damn, this day wasn't getting better. It was getting worse!

"Liberty?"

Liberty said nothing. She simply stood on the far side of the room, assessing the raven-haired rake who was now her husband—the one who had arrogantly ordered her to come to him to perform her "wifely duties."

"Good God," Dylon muttered sourly. "Are we going to have a fight on our wedding night? If you are girding up for battle, at least have the courtesy to tell me so I can fetch my sword and shield."

Still, his bride said nothing. She stood motionless, staring at him with an undecipherable expression that left Dylon frustrated to no end! Damnation, how he wished she would say something . . . anything! It had to be better than this tormenting silence.

Had his thoughtless comment set her off to such a degree that she was contemplating turning on her heels and storming off? Dylon wouldn't have been the least bit surprised, hot-tempered as she was. That would be the crowning glory on the helllish day he'd had!

Chapter 30

Liberty's amethyst eyes remained fixed on her new husband. When Dylon had blurted out his demand, her temper had risen to a quick boil. She had no intention of being taken for granted ever again! But before impulse prompted her to jump down his throat for the carelessly worded command, she saw regret flash in his eyes—eyes the color of forget-me-nots. And forget him, she never would. He was the stuff dreams were made of, the one man who touched every emotion deep inside her.

Dylon hadn't apologized because he was every bit as stubborn and proud as she was. But he was aware of his mistake and that was enough to appease Liberty's temper. However, she wasn't above letting him squirm a bit, wondering about her reaction. She intended to set a precedent, to make her feelings understood, now and forevermore.

For several moments Liberty allowed herself to take inventory of this raven-haired rake. He was as bold as a badger and he possessed the courage of a lion. Yet, his dynamic strength of character was tempered with astonishing charm and remarkable tenderness.

Aye, she would have preferred to be *asked* rather than *told* to fling herself into his arms. But did it matter so much how she got there, only that she was where she wanted to be? Liberty didn't think so. After all the obstacles that had torn them apart, it seemed silly to quibble over ill-chosen words on their wedding night.

To Dylon's surprise, the pensive frown that knitted her brow disappeared. He half collapsed in relief when she flashed him a provocative smile. His gaze flooded over every inch of exposed flesh as she loosened her gown and let it cascade into a pool at her feet. His breath stuck in his throat when Liberty slid the straps of her chemise down her shoulders. In the most seductive manner imaginable, she wiggled from the garment, letting it flutter down to join her discarded gown.

Wearing nothing but a suggestive smile that made her eyes shine like polished jewels, Liberty sashayed toward him, holding him spellbound and arousing him to the very limits of his sanity.

When her silky arms glided over his shoulders and she molded herself into his masculine contours, Dylon's hungry mouth came down on hers. He savored and devoured her for a long breathless moment before he pried his lips away to nibble at the corner of her mouth.

"If I make offensive demands on you, 'tis only because I love you," he assured her huskily. "I want you beyond reason and tact escapes me when my passion for you consumes me."

It wasn't an apology but it was an explanation and a compliment Liberty could accept. She tipped her head back and peeked up at him from beneath a fan of long curly lashes. "I don't think you'll find the need to fetch your sword and shield this evening," she murmured in a throaty voice that sent a battalion of goose bumps parading over his skin. "Engaging in a senseless battle is the very last thing on my mind."

Dylon returned her seductive smile. "Then how would you like to spend the evening, my lady? A game of cards perhaps?"

"Nay, I think not," Liberty whispered as she nimbly worked the buttons of his shirt to caress the whipcord muscles of his chest.

"Maybe you would like to read a good book," he suggested in a voice that was raspy with unfulfilled desire.

Liberty rejected the suggestion. Her hands drifted down his lean belly to loosen the buttons on his breeches.

The feel of her caresses roaming over his sensitized flesh caused his heart to cartwheel around his chest like an acrobat. His chest caved in when her adventurous caresses dipped lower. Desire pulsated through his loins and his hands began to wander over her satiny flesh, returning touch for arousing touch. It took incredible self-control to prevent pouncing on her like a starved tiger. Lord, he burned with a fever only this one woman could cure. He had come so close to losing Liberty so many times the past few days that every moment he held her in his arms was as priceless as twenty-four-karat gold.

With a growl and a groan, Dylon swept Liberty into his arms and strode toward the bed. He tumbled her onto the sheets and then levered up on his elbow to peer into her enchanting features.

It dawned on him just then that, after urging this lively imp to stay "a few more days," she was now his forever. And, for a man who'd religiously avoided marriage the past few years, he'd been in a great rush to wed this saucy little sprite before someone else stole her away from him. But now he had no need to rush this moment. Liberty was here; she was his; and here she would stay. . . .

"Dylon? Is something amiss?" Liberty stared into his battered face, wondering at the myriad of emotions that chased each other across his rugged features. "Dylon?"

A tender smile grazed his lips. Adoringly, his forefinger trekked across her high cheekbones and drifted down the delicate curve of her jaw. "For once, nothing is wrong and everything is right," he murmured. "And I'm going to love you the way I've never loved you before. . . ."

Liberty stared dubiously at him. *She* was the one who had been clubbed over the head twice in one day and *he* was the one who was behaving in a most peculiar manner and saying the oddest things. "Whatever is that supposed to mean?" she wanted to know and didn't hesitate to ask.

A rakish smile settled on his bruised face, making his eyes twinkle with seductive magic. "You're about to find out, little wildflower," he whispered before his lips slanted over hers.

When her straying hand drifted over his hip, heading for more intimate places, Dylon clasped her wrist and drew both her arms over her head.

"Dylon, what are you doing . . . ?"

The question caught in her throat when his worshipping kisses trailed over her shoulder to swirl around the taut peaks of her breasts. Spreading a path of fire, his lips skimmed over her belly to the sensitive flesh of her thighs.

"I'm loving you, totally, completely . . ." he assured her huskily.

A tiny moan tumbled from her lips as his scintillating kisses fanned the flames into a raging holocaust of desire. In a few breathless seconds Liberty understood what Dylon meant about never loving her the way he was loving her tonight. He introduced her to the most evocative, erotic kisses and caresses she'd ever experienced. And here she thought Dylon had taught her all there was to know about passion! It seemed this seductive wizard had a dozen more arousing techniques at his disposal. And where he'd learned to do what he was doing to her, Liberty couldn't imagine! He introduced her to a wildly sensual dimension of lovemaking and Liberty swore she'd die long before he took absolute possession with his body.

His hands and lips sought out every ultrasensitive point on her skin, leaving her shuddering with the fervent want of him. Her pleas to end the sweet maddening torment were met with quiet, provocative laughter and the tantalizing promise that she had even more to learn about the sublime pleasures of lovemaking.

Over and over again, he assaulted her trembling body with nerve-shattering caresses and heart-stopping kisses, leaving not one inch of her flesh untouched by his potent magic. Liberty was positively certain she'd died a half-dozen times before he revived her. He drew her back from the tumultuous edge of ecstasy and proceeded to torture her with exquisite pleasure all over again. The turgid sensations burst, subsided and burgeoned repeatedly until Liberty feared she couldn't endure another moment of this wild, spasmodic torment.

"Come here, Liberty . . ." Dylon demanded as he eased onto the side of the bed.

"Ornery rake," Liberty groaned, her body shuddering convulsively. But she eagerly came to him, just as he knew she would. "You did that a-purpose. You seduced me until you gave a command you knew I couldn't resist without going mad with the want of you."

Her aching body settled exactly upon his, letting him guide her hips intimately to him, longing to end the wild torment caused by his incredibly arousing kisses and caresses.

"'Tis the only command I'll ever give," he murmured huskily. "When the heart commands, love must obey. And you come because you know how very much I love you, need you . . ."

Tears sprang to her eyes when he became the pulsating flame inside her. They were flesh to flesh and heart to heart, moving as one beating, breathing essence. Their bodies communicated the fierce, eternal love that blazed between them, forging mind, body and spirit. Liberty clung to Dylon, engulfed by heat that burned like a thousand suns, feeling each wondrous sensation flare like sparks flying up from a fallen log in a blazing hearth. She could feel the hindering garments of the flesh peel away as her soul soared upward. On pinioned wings, she dipped and dived like a graceful eagle in flight, skimming over rainbows and soaring past the far-flung stars.

In this one magnificent man's embrace she experienced the paradox of ecstasy. She could sail to paradise without ever leaving the magical circle of his loving arms. For within those boundless confines was a love that pursued the speed of light and captured eternity. . . .

When Dylon's muscular body shuddered beneath hers, Liberty found ultimate satisfaction, shared the climactic rapture that only their unique brand of passion could offer. And as the haze of sublime pleasure lifted, leaving her hovering on the perimeters of reality, Liberty knew beyond all doubt that she had discovered the kind of love Dylon had teased her about the first day they'd met.

Ah, that Romeo and Juliet could have been so lucky to experience the joy of being so cherished and adored! Now *this* was the kind of love to write books about! And yet, Liberty doubted there were words to accurately describe what she and Dylon shared. Theirs was an untold love story that simply had to be experienced to be fully understood. This incredible depth of emotion didn't come around even once in a lifetime for some unfortunate souls.

In the aftermath of love, Liberty eased away. She heard Dylon's methodic breathing, aware that he had drifted into lazy dreams. Tempted though she was to wake him and treat him to the same incomparable techniques of passion that he'd employed—ones which left her a quivering mass of monstrous cravings—she didn't disturb his much-needed sleep. She knew Dylon's thigh was still tender and the devastating blows of battle still pained him. He had foregone rest to rescue her from one disaster after another.

Liberty plucked up his discarded linen shirt and shrugged it on. Tossing Dylon a dreamy glance, she tiptoed onto the terrace. With a contented sigh, she stared up at the timeless sentinels of the night that she'd touched while she and Dylon had taken their star-spangled voyage across love's limitless horizon. . . .

Muffled laughter interrupted her pensive reflections.

Liberty sought out the source of the sound to see her maid (of all people) lingering in the moonlight that glowed in the garden below.

"Stella?" Liberty squinted into the shadows, trying to identify the man who held Stella in his arms.

"What is it that you find so intriguing out here, that I cannot possibly offer you in *there?*" Dylon's quiet voice lightly admonished her for leaving him. He had awakened with a jolt, wondering who had stolen this elusive beauty from him *this* time.

"Who the blazes is that with Stella?" Liberty directed Dylon's attention to the two silhouettes who looked like Siamese twins, joined at the mouth.

"Good God!" Dylon gasped. "That looks like Percy without his wig!"

Both Liberty and Dylon stared owl-eyed as the two heads moved together to share another steamy kiss.

"All this time Stella has been telling me she had little use for that pompous stuffed shirt you call a valet," Liberty giggled impishly.

A deep skirl of laughter vibrated in Dylon's chest as he glided his arms around Liberty, cushioning her curvaceous body against his. "Now *that's* true justice. All this time Percy has insisted that your maid was an ill-tempered shrew. But whatever is going on between them must be rather serious. Percy doesn't remove his wig for just *anybody*, you know."

A naughty grin pursed Liberty's lips as she watched Stella and Percy fling their arms around each other to kiss each other blind and breathless. "I don't think carrying a potato in his pocket is going to cure Percy of what ails him," Liberty speculated. "My, hasn't Cupid been working overtime in these parts. First Phillipe and Cayla, and now Percy and Stella."

"Haven't you overlooked someone?" Dylon teased as he turned Liberty in his arms.

"Have I?" Liberty blessed him with a mock innocent smile and looped her arms over his bare shoulders. "I cannot imagine who."

"You and me," he said with low, caressing huskiness. "Since the moment you came into my life—" Dylon frowned suddenly, curiously. "And by the way, little minx, just how *did* you get into my life in the first place? I never did puzzle that out."

"Fate brought me," Liberty teased playfully.

"Be serious," Dylon demanded.

"*You* want *me* to be serious?" Liberty taunted him, loving every minute of it.

A devilish grin quirked his sensuous lips as his masterful hands tunneled beneath the oversized shirt to map the sumptuous curves and luscious swells of her body. "I have my ways, sweet nymph, of making you beg to do exactly as I command. Need I remind you of how eagerly you obeyed me awhile ago?"

His skillful touch jarred the erotic memories and sent tingles of anticipation skittering down her spine. "I remember with vivid clarity how you can make a woman your willing slave, Master Dylon," she murmured, her voice nowhere near as steady as it had been the moment before. "And after I do what you did to me, I'll tell you everything you want to know."

"I hardly think that's possible, considering you're a woman and I'm a man," Dylon replied with a rakish grin.

Liberty slipped her small hand in his and led him back to the bedroom, leaving Percy and Stella to do whatever it was they were planning on doing. As if she couldn't guess. "I should think, that with a few alterations in technique, I can . . . *improvise* on your seductive magic."

Dylon was rather skeptical of her ability to seduce him in the same intimate manner he'd utilized earlier to express the full extent of his love for her. But she proved him wrong when she pressed him to the bed to weave her delightful spell of ecstasy around him. Liberty was remarkably imaginative and inventive, even more than he'd given her credit for being! Ah, what an incredible seductress she had become. And ah, the things she did to him with her hands, lips, teeth and silky body. . . . Suddenly Dylon couldn't formulate a sane thought to save his soul.

"Come here, Dylon," Liberty commanded a good while later.

'Twas a wonder Dylon even heard her, considering how his heart and pulse were pounding in his ears and passion was gobbling him alive. But come he did, fulfilling every wild, breathless fantasy, whispering his love for Liberty with every urgent, demanding thrust of his body. Their union was the sublime physical expression of the words of love that echoed in their hearts. Ecstasy burst between them like a spectacular kaleidoscope. The glorious colors of passion exploded and shattered in rapturous oblivion.

And it was another good while later before the numbing pleasure wore off and Dylon could think to question Liberty about her mysterious appearance on his plantation. When he did pose the question, he was met with Liberty's mischievous smile.

"I'll never tell." She giggled as Dylon crouched over her like a sleek, muscular panther whose eyes sparkled with challenge and intimate promise.

"We shall see about that, sweet Liberty," Dylon growled before his lips captured hers in a devouring kiss.

And sure enough, she told him everything he wanted to know after they had scaled passion's peak to count the glittering stars.

"In the baggage compartment of my carriage?" Dylon croaked in disbelief.

"It wasn't all that uncomfortable, Dylon *dahling*," Liberty purred like a contented feline. "And now I am here to stay. I'd fold myself up in the back of a hundred carriages if you were waiting at the journey's end." Her lips feathered over his in the lightest breath of a kiss. "I love you with every fiber of my being, Dylon. You are my only love. . . ."

And for the first time in a very long time, Dylon took

women seriously—this woman, at least. How could he not? When Liberty got down to the very serious business of communicating her heart-felt affection with highly skilled techniques and whispered words of love, Dylon knew he had found his soulmate, the enchantress who could share his dreams and fulfill his fantasies from now until the end of eternity. . . .